RAVE REVIEWS F

"His books combine the sc... Stephen King with the roller-coaster plots of Dean Koontz and an imagination that defies comparison."

—Starburst

"*Darkfall* has all the style and graphic detail of any Stephen King book."

—Brecon and Radnor Express

"Laws is a master craftsman."

—Shivers

"Stephen Laws presents a fresh, chilling voice among the multitude of authors feverishly clawing to imitate Stephen King or Peter Straub. Laws is no imitator!"

—Seattle Post Intelligencer

"Laws's work typifies a new generation of horror writing: [It] inhabits the world as we know it, and is all the scarier for it."

—Maxim

"Nobody sleeps when Stephen Laws writes."
—Time Out (London)

"Makes the reader distinctly uneasy about touching any walls or doors when the thunder rumbles."

—Penthouse

"Laws is unquestionably our most promising genre writer."
—Samhain

"Stephen Laws, the real thing. For me, he's *the* classic horror writer."

—Dark Asylum

INTO THIN AIR

Alec burst into the office.

It was empty.

"Come *on!*" he shouted. "Where the hell is everyone?"

He stamped back out of the corridor, any threat of imminent danger pushed firmly to the back of his mind now as he caught sight of the elevators. One was still on Floor 7 . . . but the other was somehow sitting on Floor 1, waiting for him. He pushed inside and stabbed the button for Floor 2. The hell with it!

McEwan's Loans and Investments and Holsten Computer Inc. occupied the bulk of the offices on Floor 2. Parties had been taking place in both of them . . . but both offices were empty.

Alec tried all the floors until he had reached the top.

There was no trace of a single soul on any of the floors.

No one in the offices.

No one in the cupboards.

No one in the toilets.

No one.

But on the fourteenth floor, Alec found something lying on the carpet that sent him staggering in panic back to the elevators.

"Oh my *God* . . ."

DARKFALL
STEPHEN LAWS

LEISURE BOOKS NEW YORK CITY

To Mel, with Deepest Love

A LEISURE BOOK®

June 2003

Published by

Dorchester Publishing Co., Inc.
276 Fifth Avenue
New York, NY   10001

ISBN: 0-8439-5218-0

Visit us on the web at www.dorchesterpub.com.

Acknowledgments

I'd like to say a Big Thank-You to George Jackson and his colleagues at Northumbria Police for their invaluable assistance on operational detail and police procedure.

The aberrant behaviour of some of the characters in DARKFALL and their flouting of police rules and regulations are all inventions of the author and no resemblance to persons living, dead or undead is intended.

DARKFALL

PROLOGUE

A Storm was coming.

It was 3.00 p.m. on Christmas Eve. There was no snow, but the weather had been bad all day in the north-east of England. Winter had not yet vented its full fury on the city. Thin, miserable rain had been drizzling down since early morning without surcease, and the air contained a dank chill that was much worse than the clean, icy blast of a true winter's wind. The rain seemed to have first been drawn from the thin and vapid miseries of the industrial towns below by the roiling, darkening clouds above. Unable to contain this misery any longer, the sky was giving it back.

The Storm began gradually, as it always did, bringing with it a myriad of symptoms to those living below. Headaches, nausea, neck pain, migraine, disorientation and a draining of energy. Parents became irritable, blaming Christmas and all its paraphernalia for their loss of temper with the kids, never dreaming that the onset of a storm always brought about such symptoms, not realising that sixty per cent of the population suffered at least one or more of these symptoms as the prelude to a thunderstorm.

Dogs scratched at doors and were let outside to do their business, where they vomited; another symptom of an oncoming storm. Cats fussed, could not settle, and would not be stroked. Cattle that had not yet been led to shelter lay down and would not move until coaxed.

Between pylons, the overhead power cables carrying five hundred kilovolts reacted to the gathering of the Storm. The electrical field around them began to swell, causing

3

temporary power surges and black-outs throughout the region. Dozens of people living within close proximity to these pylons felt a prickling of anxiety, and discovered with only mild curiosity that the hairs on their arms were standing up, another not-unusual phenomenon.

The Storm gathered and moved over the city. Already, its thunderclouds were charged with electricity as it passed over the urban sprawl below. When the insulating properties of the air broke down, the clouds would be discharged with a momentary electric current . . . and the first lightning flash would occur. The chances of a lightning strike on a house or person are four per cent of one in twenty-five.

But this storm was different.

The office block stood fourteen storeys high on the edge of the city. In one of the walls of its Reception area was a brass plaque, revealing that the block had been christened 'Fernley House' on its opening by a civic dignitary ten years ago; the name deriving from the suburb of Newcastle upon Tyne in which it had been built. A great, granite-grey monolith, it occupied a sizeable wedge of 'prime development site' in the vee-shaped wedge between the two motorways that fed into the city. Streams of glittering traffic gushed down those concrete arteries, feeding the city with feverish and neurotic lifeblood. At the base of the office block, there was a forecourt and private car park for the use of the staff employed by the twelve companies that occupied its fourteen floors. The Ground Floor contained the main Reception area and elevators. Above that, a shipping firm, two administrative headquarters for national building societies, two firms of chartered accountants, an architect, three loan and investment firms, one computer wholesaler, one secretarial agency and a sex-telephone operation.

From the third floor and above, it was possible on a clear night to see a Polytechnic college on the other side of one of the motorways. It was deserted now at the end of term. On the far side of the other motorway, it was also possible to see the first office blocks, factories and buildings of the

4

city centre. But it was not a clear night tonight, and conditions were getting worse. The rain was harsher now and growing more intense by the minute.

Christmas parties were ongoing in the offices of five of the twelve companies. Alcohol flowed, temporary trysts were made and for the most part, the occupants of the office block were unconcerned that the weather conditions were harshening and might make it difficult for their respective journeys home. The concrete arteries on either side of the block were crowded with late Christmas shoppers battling through the slush and the wind into the city, while the denizens of the city centre were battling outwards. But inside Fernley House, on this eve of a celebration of peace and goodwill, the occupants were allowing themselves the indulgence of believing that everything would change; that the world would be a new and better place, that they would become new and better people. There was a change coming, but no one could guess in their wildest dreams what the nature of that change might be. Because it was also the Eve . . . of something else.

The Storm had ceased to move.

Its nucleus was here, in Fernley, and would stay here while it continued to build strength. The roiling clouds darkened from grey to black, and the first grumblings of thunder resounded within them.

It had begun.

PART ONE

RIDERS ON THE STORM

"This way for the sorrowful city
This way for eternal suffering
This way to join the lost people . . .
All hope abandon, ye who enter here!"

Inscription at the entrance to Hell: Dante

ONE

"Bastards," grumbled Alec Beaton.

The boiler room beneath Fernley House was badly lit, and he had barked his shin on the staircase as he'd made his way down. Despite the winter chill outside, the temperature down below amidst these hissing, throbbing canisters was sub-tropical. Alec liked the warm air down here; it reminded him of older and better days when he was in the Navy. The boiler room was like a ship's engine room, and the temperature also reminded him of some of the places he had visited in his youth before settling down in the bloody-freezing-cold north-east of England. They were days when he had commanded more respect than now . . . as janitor/caretaker of a bloody office block.

"Bastards," he said again as he rubbed his shin and hobbled over to the far side of the boiler room. He was not in a good mood.

The only windows down here were set high up next to the ceiling, on the far wall. Although almost at ceiling-height in here, the windows were actually at pavement-level outside; half a dozen three-by-six rectangles of glass installed to give the boiler room some natural light. But there was no natural light tonight; just a rain-streaked blackness which further enhanced the fantasy which Alec often retreated into. He could not really see the bad weather beyond, could not see the glittering traffic on the highway. There were also no bloody Christmas decorations down here. In other words, nothing to remind him that the Spirit of Bloody Goodwill had descended. There were three rolls of disintegrating carpet in the far corner. He moved

9

over to them and, bones creaking, he knelt down, rubbed his sore shin again and began to turn them over. Earlier, he had "done his rounds" of the offices upstairs . . . and it had been made plain by all of the snotty buggers up there that there would be no chance of a Christmas drink, or a tip. It was plain that they had no time for him. He'd tried his luck on four different floors – the ones he thought might bear fruit – but his luck was out. Apparently, the Season of Goodwill did not extend to him. Didn't they appreciate how much he did for them all during the year? He was the one who supervised the cleaners, he was the one who cleared up their bloody mess, kept them warm in the winter and cool in the summer. He was the one who cleared their crappy mess up. But did they care? Did they bloody hell. They were all . . .

"Bastards," said Alec again, flipping over the last roll of carpet. Spiders and silverfish beat a hasty retreat into darker places. He reached into the gap and found what he had hidden there. A bottle of Famous Grouse. Standing again, with a protest of creaking joints, Alec groaned, coughed out a wad of phlegm and made his way to the rickety chair by one of the boilers. The heat from that boiler was good for the bones. Sitting again, with a loud and overly emphatic sigh, he screwed the top from the bottle and took a deep swallow, closing his eyes. *Have a good time, you bastards,* he thought. *Enjoy yourselves. Get drunk, get laid, get stuffed. I'll just sit here with Mr Grouse and squeeze you all out. What the hell do you know about life, any of you? I've been to places you'll never see. Seen things you wouldn't dream of. Done things you'll never experience.* Alec took another swallow, feeling and hearing the boiler next to him give out its gently throbbing rhythm . . . just like the engines of a tramp steamer at sea.

TWO

Upstairs, on Floor 3, the party in the architects' office was in full swing. The Junior Partner had finally decided, under the influence of one gin too many, that the firm's senior secretary was the girl he wanted to marry, after all. There were fifteen of them left now, the others had drifted away. But there was plenty of gin left, and he could wait. He sipped at his drink again, laughed at a joke that was being told by his colleague (even though he wasn't listening) and looked up at the ceiling. There was a party going on up there, too. He could hear the music throbbing through the floor as he looked back again at the object of his desires.

THREE

On Floor 4, above the architects' office, a party in one of the Chartered Accountants' offices was destined, it seemed, to go on for ever. There were fifty-five people there, the bosses had finally gone home, and the girls in the general office had rigged up a makeshift disco for the purpose. Bruce Springsteen was hammering out a song as the punchbowl was refilled, principally with another full bottle of vodka. Now, if they could only keep that bloody old fool of a caretaker out of the office and ignore his whining about having to close the place for the night this promised to be the best party *ever*.

Alec wiped a hand across his mouth and opened his eyes again. The fantasy dream was beginning to turn sour. He wasn't at sea, he wasn't a million miles from this Godforsaken place. He was sitting on a crappy old chair with a bottle of whisky, down in the bowels of this bloody office block. The dream wouldn't hold up today. He coughed again and spat on the floor, feeling the sickening pain inside and remembering what the doctor had told him about giving up the drink. He'd had a lung removed eighteen months earlier and he should be retired. But the pension on offer was laughable; not enough to keep him in booze, even though he shouldn't be drinking. But you had to have something to keep you happy, didn't you? He'd given up smoking . . . and that was all he was going to give up. Couldn't afford to drink *and* smoke, these days. Could barely survive on the money he was earning looking after these shite arses, let alone what the Government would let

12

him have for a pension. Alec drank again, winced away the pain and leaned against the chair back. Something scurried in a corner, but he ignored it. Ship's rats were worse. Something to worry about . . . but that was when you were at sea. And even though he wanted to pretend, he wasn't at sea, after all.

FOUR

On Floor 14, the thirty-five members of staff in the north-east branch of Magnus Shipping Inc, were dancing to the music which was coming through the floor from the Chartered Accountants' office below. Darlene had promised to bring a cassette radio with her, but had forgotten, and she had been apologising profusely ever since for having spoiled the party. Now that the disco downstairs had begun, everything had changed because of the excessive decibels.

Vincent Saville had been working for the same company for twelve years, even before they had moved into this office block. He liked Christmas just as much as the next man, but couldn't understand why management allowed the younger members of staff (and even the *not*-so-young members of staff!) to behave in such a way on Christmas Eve. He watched the cavorting that was taking place and sipped at his orange juice. They had cleared the desks and chairs back to create a dance floor, for goodness sake! And the new Senior Partner of the firm, Baker, was standing on the sidelines grinning his head off and encouraging them. This would never have happened in the old days. When the Senior Mr Baker had been alive, he would never have allowed his staff to behave in such a way. In those days, you knew who was boss. None of this "new management" rubbish. The Young Mr Baker had sent him on one such management course, but he had not been seduced by the waffle that they'd spouted. Business was business. There was a regime, after all. And Saville despaired that the old order was crumbling, and with it, his own status and credibility.

He was sure that the Young Mr Baker must be drunk. At 11.00 a.m. that morning, Saville had been dictating a series of shipment letters and, as Baker had passed his desk, he'd said with a smile: *Bah humbug, eh?*

Now what on earth did *that* mean?

FIVE

Somewhere outside, somewhere in the night beyond those ceiling-high windows, Alec heard a low grumbling.

"*Thunder,*" he said aloud, drinking again. He had listened to the weather forecast on breakfast television that morning, and they had promised that things might take a turn for the worse later on. The grumbling sound tailed away, and the sound of that distant thunder again reminded him of days long gone on foreign seas. He strove to recapture the fantasy again, but it obstinately remained at a distance. Even the familiar throbbing of the boilers seemed to be different.

And then Alec suddenly sat up straight, looking intently at the boiler next to him. He rubbed a hand across his mouth and shook his head, just to make sure that the booze wasn't befogging his senses. But he wasn't mistaken.

"Shit!"

Alec stood up and looked around.

The thrumming sound from the boilers had stopped. Somehow, they had switched themselves off.

"Shit!" said Alec again, replacing the whisky bottle on his seat and wiping his face again. The last thing he wanted tonight was any hassle with the heating system. Again, he heard that low grumbling somewhere outside that seemed this time to shake the foundations of the building.

But now the boilers had started again, giving out their familiar throbbing beat.

Alec moved to the others, checking the temperature readings and touching the metal, listening carefully. He hobbled around the room, checking the valves on each. Everything

16

was back to normal again, as if they had never stopped in the first place. He stood for a full minute in the centre of the boiler room looking around, convincing himself that everything was okay. Finally, sighing a massive sigh of relief, he moved back to the chair, picked up his whisky bottle again . . . and took a double-deep draft.

SIX

On Floor 3, the Junior Partner now made the move towards the girl he felt would be his partner for life. The gin and tonics had blinded him to the realities of their incompatibility; only the *now* of the moment, only the *now* of Christmas Eve mattered. He had never felt this way before about anything or anyone. For a dissatisfied man who needed the purity of feeling that only Christmas Eve and too many gin and tonics could bring him, *this* was the girl for him. And for a girl with too many shattered dreams, yearning for the better life that he might be able to give, she was prepared to ignore her better instincts about the reality of life and warm to his advances.

Now . . . in the stationery cupboard and away from the party, they shared desperate and mistaken passions. But it didn't matter. Not now. Not on Christmas Eve when everything was good, and real cares a million miles away.

Lightning flickered, casting a reflection of their coupling in the window. Thunder rumbled in the sky. The reflection was gone. Now, only the rain on the window and the wind buffeting the glass.

"Hear that?" he asked.

"Yes . . ."

"Am I making the earth move?"

"Try harder," she replied.

SEVEN

On the top floor of the office block, the management of the building society which occupied the entire level had decided on a sensible drinks-and-buffet celebration of Christmas Eve. No silly music. There was no need. Just a small collection from the management and staff to provide a bowl of punch; vol-au-vents, crisps and things-on-sticks. But the punch ended up being spiked with two bottles of vodka, and now people wished there was silly music, not just the ghosts of music from other parties echoing up through the air-conditioning shafts.

Not liking hard booze, Eleanor Parkins had opted to drink the punch instead of the illicit whisky and beer that the others had bought and brought to the party, bought and brought with the grudging but wilting approval of management. Unbeknownst to her, drinking the acceptable punch was more intoxicating than drinking the (grudgingly) acceptable whisky and beer.

"Having a good time?" asked one of the office juniors.

"Yes, Billy. Feel funny. But nice . . . you're a good lad."

"And you're a bloody good typist. Thanks for what you did."

"What do you mean?"

"That miscalculation in my report. You said it was a typing error. I'll never forget that . . . you, taking the blame."

"Listen, we all make mistakes."

"Come on, Eleanor, have a drink."

"It's alright for you. I've got to get home and start making a meal for six. They're expecting me. How's it

19

going to look when I stagger through the door singing Beatles' songs?"

"So what's wrong with The Beatles?"

"Nothing! I was around when The Beatles first came out, I'll have you know. I bet I know more lyrics than you do."

"Knew you were more trendy than I was, Eleanor. Come on, have one of *my* drinks."

"You monkey! Are you trying to get me tiddly?"

"Who, me? You're joking. I just want to say 'Happy Christmas'."

Eleanor looked out at the billowing grey and black clouds which were sweeping through the sky. She thought of the bad weather, the oncoming storm and the fact that Christmas could not begin at home without her. She thought about how long it might take her to get home on public transport tonight. Wouldn't the buses be crowded? She thought about the bad traffic, but didn't really care about that since she had a lovely home to go to. Geordie was working shifts tonight. He wouldn't be home until later. The "kids" would already be home. They'd said they could cope without her, that she should just enjoy herself at the office. She should leave the turkey to them and just enjoy herself, even though they didn't really know what to do with it.

Then she saw his young and grateful face and thought: *I'm worth something here. Another ten minutes won't matter.* She looked down at her glass, then out through the windows at the gathering clouds. She heard the rumbling of thunder in the skies.

"Alright," she said. "Just *one* of your drinks."

EIGHT

The whisky was not having its usual effect. Alec had struggled with himself to regain that fantasy, fuelling his depression with extra swigs of the bottle. He wanted to be away from this place, even though his job after the parties were done would be quite simple. All he had to do was regulate the heating, shut it down for the Christmas period and then check all the floors to make sure that all the bastards had gone home; check to make sure that they weren't still lying under desks asleep or screwing, and if they were, to send them packing . . . a job which, when he thought of it now, he quite relished, bearing in mind how they had snubbed him tonight. The basic shift of cleaners . . . all that could be obtained on Christmas Eve night . . . were due at seven o'clock for a basically perfunctory clean-up. The empty bottles and the plates of crisps, and the vomit . . . all of that could wait until the bastards got back to work again. There was nothing in anybody's contract that obliged them to clean up after *that* kind of mess − particularly since tips had been unforthcoming. After that . . . well, after that, Alec would make his way to the local working-men's club for a few drinks, and there-after on to home and a warm meal provided by his wife Mary. After that, no doubt they would both fall asleep in their chairs until it was time to switch off the buzzing, no-transmission television, and go to bed. Somewhere along the way, he would have to find a Christmas present for his missus; maybe one of the lads in the club would be selling something cheap "off the back of a lorry", as well as some of that cheapo Christmas wrapping paper.

The warmth and the cheapening, deadening effect of the whisky was at last reasserting the fantasy that had escaped him for a while. The *thrum, thrum, thrum* of the boilers and that penetrating, sub-tropical heat had overtaken him now. He drifted away into a blissful sleep.

That sleep was timeless. He was back on the tramp steamer, sailing through seas that had never been that colour in real life. Everything was fine . . . but something was making him uneasy now . . . something he could not quite place. What the hell was it? He looked around the ghostly engine room of his dreams, each detail so perfectly clear . . . and at last he had found the source of his disquiet. It was the bloody engines (boilers) again. They weren't making that oh-so-familiar, pleasant, lulling sound anymore. He rushed to the valves in his dream and began trying to adjust them. They were frozen solid. Angrily, aware that the dream might dissolve at any second, he began twisting at those valves; but they refused to budge.

"Come on, you bastard! Come on! Come . . . on!"

And Alec was suddenly awake again, down there in the suffocating heat of the boiler room beneath Fernley House. His hand was groping out at his side towards the boiler. It was still hot.

But the boiler had switched itself off again.

What kind of games were they bloody playing?

Oh God, no. Please. Please . . . not on Christmas Eve. If there's anything really wrong with these bloody things, then I'll have to try and get an engineer out.

Alec moved across on unsteady legs to the other boilers. They were all switched off and, although hot, already cooling.

Come on. Give me a break. Just switch yourselves on again for a little while longer. Just long enough to clear the building, then I can switch you over to timer and leave you for a nice little Christmas break. Then we can see to you after Christmas is over. Now wouldn't that be nice? Wouldn't it?

"Wouldn't it?" he shouted aloud.

22

And then the noise began.

At first, Alec thought that it was simply an echo somewhere in the boiler room, even though he knew that there were no echoes down here. Any sound made was swallowed up as if the place was lined with cotton wool. He stood still and listened. Was it someone outside perhaps, banging on the walls? Yeah, that's what it was. A bunch of drunken yobs outside, banging on the walls. But he *knew* that it was not that either.

The noise sounded like a door slamming somewhere; a large, heavy door. As he listened to it slam again, it seemed to him to be like a massive door on some huge safe in the vaults of the bank. The muffled, hollow-sounding *boom* came again.

And again.

The sound was repeating itself every ten seconds or so. Was he just imagining it, or was the sound getting louder . . . somehow closer?

Alec looked around again, moving now to the boilers and placing his hands on their hot sides. Was it coming from inside? Was that the reason that they had shut down? Yes, that had to be it. It was the mechanics of the bloody heating system. The whole bloody thing *was* breaking down after all.

The sound was becoming uncomfortably loud, uncomfortably close. Now they sounded like giant footsteps. Alec staggered around in a circle, trying to find exactly where the sounds were coming from. But it was impossible to pinpoint the source. The booming noise was coming from everywhere . . . and nowhere.

BOOM!

"*Jesus, that hurt!*" Alec clasped his hands to his ears, and spun around again.

BOOM!

"*OH MY GOD!!*"

The boiler-room walls seemed to be shivering with the sound of what were now terrible, eardrum-stretching explosions. The walls were not shivering, but the vibration had affected Alec's eyesight as he staggered back against the boiler and the whisky bottle rolled from his makeshift chair. It shattered on the floor, but the sound of it was completely lost as . . .

BOOM!

. . . Alec shrieked in pain, hands still clasped over his ears, and staggered to the stairs.

BOOM!

Pain was clutching and grabbing at his brain. He knew now in blind panic that first his eardrums and then his brain must burst.

BOOM!

Alec reeled against the wall, missing his footing on the first step. He twisted in agony to regain his balance, the breath now like molten lead in his one remaining lung as he crumpled to the boiler-room floor.

"No more!" he cried out again. "Please, no more, I can't . . ."

BOOM!

"I CAN'T STAND IT!!"

And then the noise stopped, leaving only one long and fading, impossible, echo; as if that great steel door had finally been slammed shut and locked. The crashing echoes inside Alec's head subsided. Gasping for breath, still feeling that molten lead in the ragged hollow where his lung had been, he rolled over. Hugging his side, he retched on to the floor at the foot of the steps. It was an almost-pure stream of whisky. Gagging, with nothing left inside now to get rid of, he looked around the boiler room. His vision was blurred; nothing seemed to make much sense. When at last his vision had cleared, he could see nothing to account for the terrible noises . . . but fear still remained. There must be something devastatingly wrong with the heating system and the boilers. Damn it all, he knew something about ships' boilers. The noises could only mean that there was some freakish pressure build-up in one or all of them. Maybe this calm was merely the calm before the storm . . . a brief pause before the bloody. pressure inside the things built up to an unbearable level.

There was bound to be an explosion in that boiler room at any second.

Still gagging, still hugging the unbearable pain inside his chest and his head, Alec pulled himself shakily to his feet and clambered up the steps towards the main doors as fast as he could manage.

"Please . . . please . . ."

At any second, he expected that blast; expected the sheering pain as he was blown to pieces.

But the boiler room was quiet; only the hiss and tick of the boilers as they cooled.

If they're cooling, there can't be a pressure build-up. There can't be . . . oh God, please . . . "PLEASE!"

Alec cried out aloud, afraid that the noise would start again. He squeezed his hands to his ears again, just in case. If it came again, he knew his brain must burst.

Alec fell against the outside door, forgetting in his confusion that it opened inwards, not outwards. Sobbing, he heaved it wide against the wall and stumbled out into the main ground-floor corridor. Leaning against the wall, he sucked in mouthfuls of air, waiting for the explosion. He stood crumpled against that wall for a full two minutes, trying to summon up reserves of strength to move. Still no explosion. At the far end of the clinically tiled corridor, he could see the main reception desk and the glass frontage of the building. There should be at least one night porter on duty. But he could see no one at the desk and no reflection in that glass frontage of any movement behind it. Outside, darkness had fallen heavily and sleet was being driven against the windows. Alec looked across to the elevators. There were two of them . . . the lights above each indicated that they were stationary on Floor 7. He willed one of them to descend. But they remained fixed there.

". . . anyone . . . ?"

Words would not come yet. The molten metal inside his chest swallowed them before he could speak.

25

Somewhere out there in the night, thunder rolled in black, mountainous skies.

Alec pushed himself away from the wall, casting one fearful look back at the boiler room and staggered down the corridor towards the main reception desk. Heaving himself around the corner to face the main desk, his first impression was confirmed. There was no one there.

Probably next door, getting pissed.

Lifting the "lid" on the counter, Alec stumbled through and let it crash down behind him. There was an ante-room behind that office and he bundled it roughly open as he entered.

"Look . . . there's something wrong with the . . ."

The office was empty.

"Shit!"

Alec blundered back to the desk and grabbed the telephone receiver, wincing again at the pain and tasting salt in his mouth.

The line was dead.

He rattled the receiver, trying to get a dialling tone. There was only a blank and seemingly bottomless hiss of static. For some reason, Alec almost expected to hear the dying, crashing echoes of that terrible sound from the basement on the line. The thought unnerved him enough to slam the telephone receiver down again. This was bloody ridiculous. He reached for the internal telephone, punching out the number for the maintenance room on the floor above. Even if there was nothing wrong with the boilers, he would still be remiss in his duty if he didn't arrange to have the building cleared. He waited for the ringing tone, but the line wasn't connecting; just that faraway, static hiss. Alec redialled . . . and then redialled again. The internal line was also dead. Again slamming down the receiver, Alec made his way cursing back down the corridor, pausing only briefly at the boiler room door to listen. There were no sounds from below. The elevator lights were still fixed on Floor 7. When he pressed the button, one of the lifts began an immediate descent. Should he use the elevator? Or should he use the stairs? What would happen if there was an explosion when he was in the elevator? When the elevator doors *pinged* open, Alec was already gone, standing in the blue-blackness of the staircase well; his hand on the rail.

Bent forward, hugging the pain, he sucked air into his remaining lung and listened to the sibilant, ghostly echoes of his breath rising up the empty stairwell; vanishing into dissipation fourteen storeys above. He stabbed at the master light switch beside him . . . and all the lights in the stairwell from the ground floor to the fourteenth floor came on. Alec tried to call out, but could not find the breath. He began a slow ascent of the stairs to the first floor.

Thunder grumbled ominously outside and Alec paused on the stairs; sick fear inside that the terrible sound might be returning. But the thunder rolled, bottomed out and subsided; like a giant turning in its sleep . . . and the other noises did not come again. Alec continued up, gripping the stair-rail tight and hauling himself up each step; his rasping breath now filling the stairwell with its sibilant echoes.

He rested again on the first landing; turning to look at the next flight of stairs which led to the first-floor double-doors. Beyond that, the loan firm and the building-society office which comprised the first floor. He could hear the distant throbbing of disco music; could see the faint red-green-blue reflection of lights on the glass-panelled door. Casting one fearful glance back downstairs to the bottom of the stairwell, expecting the walls to collapse inwards as the boilers exploded at last, Alec began to climb again; step by careful step, heart hammering.

He reached the first floor at last and groped for the interior door with a grip that felt as weak as a baby's. The door opened slightly, the disco music pulsed through the gap and then the door slapped back again from his fingers. He leaned against the door, breathing hard – and then tugged it open again, kicking his foot into the gap to keep it open. For a while, he remained there, staring at the toilet door opposite to him. Surely there must be someone in there; someone who would see him as they emerged on their way back to the party?

He couldn't wait too long. For God's sake, those *boilers* . . .

Afraid, angry and exhausted, Alec staggered to the frosted-glass door of the loan firm with its kaleidoscope of lights shining through. Beyond, some screeching bastard of a rock star was singing about how great it was at Christmas time.

Alec shouldered through the door. It swung back on its hinges and crashed against the wall.

The red, green and blue lights swirled from the improvised disco in the centre of the floor. There were bottles and plates of crisps and nuts on the tables. Christmas decorations fluttered from the ceiling; green tinsel climbed the walls like some strange growth from a Japanese science-fiction film. The voice from the turntable told Alec to . . .

Come on, come on . . . let's have a great time . . .

But there was no one in the office.

Now suffused with a rage that ignored his pain and his fear, Alec blundered into the middle of the room . . . and bellowed. For all the world, it sounded like an enraged bull looking for matadors to maul. Here he was, trying to save these bastards, and he couldn't find them. He was convinced that they were all somehow trying to keep out of his way. To hell with the boilers! Let them blow apart and kick out the floors of the office block. Let the whole bloody building collapse. Fourteen floors collapsing under the feet of these prancing, drinking, uncaring, selfish bastards. They'd all end up in the basement where they'd confined him. The whole bloody lot of 'em. Never mind who earned most, never mind upper, middle or lower working-class. Never mind all of that. They'd all end up in the bloody cellar, bloody-jam-packed in rubble. All the same. Why the hell should he care?

Alec strode with failing dignity to the glass-partitioned office marked "Chief Administrative Officer" and kicked the door open like a gunfighter. There was no one there.

28

Alec staggered back out into the corridor and headed towards the fluted-glass door which read "Underdown Building Society". Bracing himself on the lintel, he hammered against the glass with the flat of his hand. The sheet glass quivered and rattled. But no one answered. He banged again, harder, drawing in breath and grimacing at the pain.

"Come on, you . . ."

Alec shouldered it open, still consumed by rage. He burst into the office.

It was empty.

He could see a beer keg on one of the long collating tables. He could see plastic glasses, and a damp patch on the floor where the keg had spilled. He could see the Christmas decorations on the walls.

But there was no one in the room.

"You've got to get out!" he shouted, voice returning. "There's something wrong downstairs. In the boilers." His voice seemed flat. Next door, the disco music continued to thump through the walls.

"Come *on*!" he shouted again. "Where the hell is everyone!"

He stamped back out into the corridor, any threat of imminent danger pushed firmly to the back of his mind now as he caught sight of the elevators. One was still on Floor 7 . . . but the other was somehow sitting on Floor 1, waiting for him. He pushed inside and stabbed the button for Floor 2. The hell with it!

McEwan's Loans and Investments and Holsten Computer Inc occupied the bulk of the offices on Floor 2. Parties had been taking place in both of them . . . but both offices were empty.

Alec tried all of the floors until he had reached the top.

There was no trace of a single soul on any of the floors.

No one in the offices.

No one in the cupboards.

No one in the toilets.

No one.

29

But on the fourteenth floor, Alec found something lying on the carpet which sent him staggering in panic back to the elevators.

"Oh my *God* . . ."

He didn't like the way his voice sounded as he stabbed at the elevator buttons; didn't like the way his voice seemed to echo away and die. He didn't like the horrifying feeling which now overwhelmed him that, just as everyone else in this place had vanished . . . he might suddenly vanish too, and wake up in a place that was the last nightmarish place he wanted to be in.

Trying to control his ragged breathing and fighting to control nausea at his discovery, he reached the ground floor again.

He staggered out of the elevator into the corridor.

Don't run . . . Alec told himself, when he reached the reception area again.

Don't panic. And don't run.

Thunder rolled and grumbled in the skies again as he made his way towards the glass frontage. The lights flickered again, and Alec froze . . . as if waiting for something terrible to happen. Outside, he could see the wind and the sleet as it gusted at the window.

"Don't panic," he said aloud again, taking deep breaths. "And don't run."

He rolled up the collar on his boiler suit and headed for the main door.

Outside, the wind was bitterly cold and snapped at his face as he walked out into the sleet. Icy spasms racked him as he crossed the flagged forecourt of the office building. Through slitted eyes, he could just make out the rain-blurred headlights and darkened silhouettes of cars on the main highway, not fifty yards from where he walked. Should he go over there and try to flag a car down? No . . . no . . . he would do what he planned to do. He would play this by the book.

Still thinking of the thing that he'd found on the top floor, Alec struggled through the wind and the rain and the sleet towards the public telephone box which nestled in the concrete alcove beside the office-block car park. He hoped to God that it hadn't been vandalised like so many of the public boxes in the area.

Pausing only to lean against the red booth door to catch the breath which had been whipped away from his mouth by the icy wind, Alec yanked open the door and slid inside to the temporary respite that this small shelter could give.

NINE

"Nine nine nine. Which service do you require, please?"

"Police, get me the police. Quick!"

"Could I have your name please, sir?"

"Beaton. Alec Beaton. Look, tell them to get over . . ."

"And your address, sir?"

"What the hell has my address got to do with it?"

"Where are you calling from, please?"

"Oh, I see. Look . . . My name's Alec Beaton. I'm care-taker at Fernley House Office Complex on Fernley Road. And everyone's gone . . ."

The Civilian Receiver at Police Headquarters typed up the message on her video screen, shook her head, smiled and looked at her colleagues as the message was relayed to the Receiver in HQ Control Room.

"Another one?" asked her colleague.

"The seventh so far. And it's ages until the pubs are closed. What the hell are they putting in the beer these days?"

TEN

The Receiver slapped his thigh and leaned back in his seat. It had been a long day and his shift was due to end shortly.

"Why me? Why do I always get them?"

"A good one?" asked someone from the other side of the Control Room.

"Not bad. There's a guy here from Fernley who says that an entire office-block of people have gone missing."

"Nutcase?"

"Well ... yeah, I suppose. Says he's the caretaker at some office complex on Fernley Road."

"Crank."

"Yeah, but that's what they're paying me for, I suppose. Who's out on Fernley Division?"

The owner of the other voice began stabbing at his own console.

"Barry Lawrence and John Simpson," came the reply.

"I can imagine the response. They're due to finish shift themselves in twenty-five minutes."

"Time stops for no man. Not even on Christmas Eve."

"Okay, then. Here we go. This should be good for a laugh, if nothing else." The Receiver sat forward again, cleared his throat and stabbed at the console. "Hello, panda seven-nine-two. This is Control. We've got a 999 call from a Mr Alec Beaton, at ..."

ELEVEN

Sergeant Barry Lawrence and Police Constable John Simpson were not full of Christmas spirit. In fact, they had had enough of this particular Christmas Eve. The fact that the Division was short-staffed was taken for granted, and with teeth gritted they hadn't complained when they had been advised that they would have to work on Christmas Eve right through to Christmas Day, even though they'd had to do the same last year. But after three drunken punch-ups in pubs in the City Centre and two burglaries (one of which had involved the lifting of a single-parent mother's entire Christmas presents) their patience was wearing thin . . . and the weather was not helping matters one little bit. Every trip out in the panda car was an ordeal.

Now this.

How much did they expect?

The panda passed under a flyover and took the Fernley Division main road. The weather had closed in fast and thin snow slashed across the windscreen as they moved. The windscreen wipers could barely cope so that the way ahead was a blur. Once again, thunder grumbled somewhere in the sky.

"Bloody hell," said Simpson, who was driving. "This weather . . ."

Lawrence shifted in his seat but said nothing. He yawned and ran a hand across his face. He was forty-five, twenty years Simpson's senior and feeling more like retiring now than he'd ever done in his life. He was a big man and his close-cropped hair was a salt-and-pepper colour, giving credence to the description of "grizzled" which he'd once

34

heard applied to him in the police social club. He still wasn't sure whether it was an insult or a compliment. Lawrence had seen a great deal of hard street action in his time and was relied on by his seniors to show relative newcomers "the ropes" — and if it meant that as a result his constables ended up literally on those ropes with some drunken lunatic throwing body punches, then so be it. It was a hard job, and if they weren't able to accept that then they shouldn't be on the force.

The main Fernley Road became the dual carriageway which would lead to Fernley House, and now the rain was slashing at the windscreen in a continuous sheet. Lawrence watched PC Simpson grit his teeth as they pulled up at an intersection. Rain-blurred headlights swam against the windscreen. And then Simpson tugged hard at the wheel, swinging across the road and into the layby which led to Fernley House forecourt. He could tell by his tense white face that he expected at any moment to see twin headlights blazing through that murk towards them. Simpson was too nervous. Never mind, he'd straighten him out eventually. If they did get hit by an oncoming car, it would be the perfect end to a perfect bloody day.

In the forecourt, there was a little more shelter from the storm than they had on the road. The windscreen wipers cleared the slush away from the windscreen now as the panda swerved into the side pavement.

"Now where . . . ?" began Simpson.

And then a hunched figure scurried from the main reception doors of the office block. He had obviously been standing there in the shelter, looking out for them.

"If there's drink on his breath," said Lawrence wearily, "I'm taking him straight in."

The man, about sixty years old, scurried up to the driver's door, holding his boiler suit close up to his neck to ward off the cold. Simpson wound his window down, wincing and shivering as cold air stabbed into the car.

"Mr Beaton?"

"Yes, yes. That's me. What took you so long?"

Now it was the Sergeant's turn to wince at the whisky fumes that Beaton was breathing directly into the car.

I knew it. "It's Christmas Eve, Mr Beaton," said Lawrence. "And in case you didn't notice there's a storm. The roads are bad."

"But they've *gone*," babbled Beaton. "They've all gone. Did you get my message? That was the first thing I did after I checked the floors. The boilers, you see? God knows what's happening. I mean, they've . . ."

"Yes, Mr Beaton. Now if you'd care to just stand back, away from the door, we'll be able to get out of the car, won't we?"

The Constable had also picked up the telltale waft of alcohol as Beaton stood back nervously, and he climbed out of the car simultaneously with the Sergeant. The cold wind stabbed through his uniform. All he could think of now was a warm fire at home, a hot drink and the kids ogling the presents his wife had carefully placed around the Christmas tree that morning.

"All of them," continued Beaton again from the pavement, his words snatched in a blur from his mouth by the wind. "Every single one of them. Just all got up and gone and then when I checked the floors I . . ."

"Let's go inside, Mr Beaton," said the Sergeant. "It'll be better inside, in the warm."

". . . the boilers, see? Those bloody boilers were acting up. The noise. That bloody awful noise. Thought it would send me mad. I had to make sure, see? Make sure everyone was okay. That's my job, after all."

The Sergeant walked forward, holding out his hands in a "shooing" gesture. Still facing the Sergeant, Beaton backed away from him as they both moved towards the glass reception doors and windows, the Constable following behind.

". . . this noise they were making, see? But when I checked the floors, they weren't there, were they? The people, I mean. Then on the top floor I found that . . . that . . ."

The Sergeant gently shoved Beaton so that he bumped against the glass door. Suddenly seeing where they were, Beaton looked nervously behind and seemed alarmed to see his own shadowed reflection in the rain-streaked glass.

Somewhere above, thunder grumbled in the clouds and the Sergeant saw Beaton's nervous glance skywards. For a moment, it seemed as if Beaton was afraid not only to go inside but also to stay outside. Slowly, he pulled his collar tight around his throat again and said: "Let's go in."

Again, the Sergeant had a waft of whisky-tainted breath and exchanged a knowing glance with the Constable as Beaton pushed on through the glass double doors, glancing back to see if they were following.

They followed.

TWELVE

The dirty rain and snow slashing in runnels across the office window reminded him of things he could not forget, so he'd lowered the venetian blinds and sat back in his swivel chair again. Through the plastic slats, he could still see the snow and the rain but could not somehow find the energy to reach over, pull the nylon cord and block the winter out altogether.

There was no way, he knew, that he could block out the winter which was behind his eyes.

He swung around in the swivel seat and examined the empty office. Three untidy desks, covered in paperwork. Lever-Arch files on the floor-to-ceiling shelves and also lying in a jumble on the floor. Twenty-year-old Christmas decorations festooned the tops of cupboards and window frames: red and green tinsel in a rapid state of disintegration having been pulled from a battered cardboard box in the storeroom for the annual airing.

He was alone in the office.

He could hear the others next door, grabbing half an hour on-duty for an illicit drink; toasting-in Christmas off-the-record since they'd all drawn the short straw and had to work the Christmas Eve/Christmas Day shift.

"A policeman's lot . . ." he said to himself.

Beyond his office, through the partition wall, someone cracked a joke (probably dirty) and everyone guffawed. Glasses clinked.

". . . is not a happy one," he finished ruefully.

He had volunteered to man the DI office for the Christmas shift, and everyone knew why. Just as he'd volunteered to stay behind the emergency desk while the others went next door, just in case the phone rang. Again, they knew why he didn't want to join them in their Christmas toasts and they respected it, but secretly were relieved that he wasn't going to cast a pall over the proceedings. In truth, it had nothing to do with commitment to the job and everything to do with hating the hell out of Christmas and all the *bonhomie* that went with it. He leaned forward and picked up the plastic desk-sign on his desk, turned it over in his hands and looked at it.

Detective Inspector Jack Cardiff.

He grimaced. Someone had spilt Tipp-Ex on the lettering. It reminded him of snow. That's what it was, after all, wasn't it? Wasn't the trademark "Liquid Snow"? Christmas again! It wouldn't go away. He began to pick absently at the dried Tipp-Ex.

It was the third Christmas without Lisa and Jamie.

The photograph of them both was in his top left-hand drawer. It had been on the desk itself for the first year, but far from consoling him, it only made him feel worse. He had placed it carefully in that drawer, face down. But its presence always made itself felt. Sometimes, it was almost as if it was still there on the desk top, facing him. The effect was the same.

Cardiff dumped the name-sign unceremoniously down on the desk, turning his attention to the right-hand drawer. The presence of the something else in that drawer was also a life-balancing constant – a balance for the photograph on the left. No one knew it was there but him, although the inevitable inventory check of the Evidence Room drawers would show that it had been removed without authorisation.

More laughter from next door.

"Jingle all the way," he said, without emotion.

Cardiff opened the right-hand drawer of his desk, still looking at the outside door and prepared to slide it shut if someone came in. He picked the consoler out of the drawer and placed it on the desk so that it was hidden by a file and a pile of paperwork.

Cardiff held it up above the level of the desk, no longer obscured by the pile of paperwork.

It was a Browning Automatic. .38 Calibre.

Then he reached for the companion piece; a magazine clip of thirteen bullets. There were only six shots left in that magazine. The others had been used by a gun freak who had taken exception to the garage that had refused to honour an insurance policy on the second-hand car he had bought from them. Full of happy-hour whisky, he had rammed that car into the garage wall and then stormed inside, demanding that they pay for the damage. When they had refused, the gun had come out. Fortunately, no one had been hurt. The drunken shots had punctured the glass frontage of the shop and blasted a shelf behind it. The felon had then collapsed drunk on to the garage forecourt and lain there until collected by the police. The law had taken its course, and the felon was now serving four years in Durham Jail. After the trial, the physical evidence had been placed in Locker 53 of Fernley Divisional Police Headquarters. After the statutory time period, it would be transferred to Regional Divisional HQ, and disposed of thereafter.

Detective Inspector Jack Cardiff had been in charge of that job.

And on one particularly bleak September evening when the memories and the pain had been too much to bear, he had gone down to the Locker Room, opened Locker 53 without authorisation, and had taken the gun away.

It had stayed in his right-hand drawer now for three months. Its disappearance from the locker still undetected and its presence in his drawer always begging the same question.

Cardiff looked at the streamlined muzzle, watched his thumb move to the safety catch.

Outside, the wind moaned at the window. He looked at the outside door and then at the snow and rain flurrying against the window between the plastic slats of the venetian blind.

And then he looked back at the gun in his hand.

THIRTEEN

"And then the boilers, you see? The boilers . . . I thought . . ."

"Mr Beaton!" snapped the Sergeant at last, now that they were in the comparative warmth of the office-block reception. A fresh wave of rain rinsed against the blue-blackness of the sheet-glass windows. Beaton stood back, as if the words had slapped his face. Astonished, he seemed to see the Police Sergeant for the first time.

"Yes?"

"You're not making a great deal of sense. Your telephone call was garbled. And I have reason to believe that you've been drinking. Now, I want you to tell me. Clearly, calmly. Take your time. Just what is wrong?"

Beaton seemed to take half a step back as the policeman's words registered. He swallowed, looked at the Police Constable, took a breath and said: "Everyone's gone. And I think the boilers in the basement are going to blow up."

"Shit!"

Ten seconds later, the policeman had dragged Beaton back out on to the pavement and into the car. The car screeched in reverse away from the office-block frontage and into the car park one hundred and fifty yards away. Twenty seconds later, the Sergeant had radioed headquarters.

This was a job for the specialists.

Or . . . as the Sergeant so eloquently put it after the call had been made . . . it was a job for some other bloody idiot to go down into that boiler room and check things out.

FOURTEEN

"It's okay," said the guy in the blue boiler suit, emerging from the office-block frontage. "There's nothing whatever wrong with those boilers. I've checked and double-checked. They're working fine. No pressure build-up, no irregularities. No nothing."

The Police Sergeant and Constable sat back in relief. In the back seat of the car, Beaton still continued to stare straight up at the block, with that same glazed expression in his eyes. While they'd been waiting for the engineering operatives to arrive, he'd told them the story of what had happened, making more sense than previously; but with a tale that still sounded more drunk than sober.

"Tell you something, though," said the man in the blue boiler suit to the Sergeant, leaning in the panda-car window.

"What's that?"

"We don't get paid to come out and get blown up on Christmas Eve. That's what they pay you boys to do. Or the army."

The Sergeant grinned back, no hint of humour in his ragged smile.

"Claim double-time tonight. You're worth it."

The blue boiler suit grunted and turned away from the car, moving back to the two Land-Rovers and trailer of equipment they'd brought out with them. The Sergeant watched them go, muttered "Clever shits" under his breath and then turned back to Beaton in the back seat. "Alright, so you say everyone's gone."

"That's right."

"Been watching the windows, Sarge," said the Constable. "Doesn't seem to be anyone up there on any of the floors. At least, no one's come to the windows."

"Maybe they're all shagging on the floor. Out of sight. Know what Christmas parties are like."

"All gone," said Beaton again, his voice far away.

"And you say you found it on the top floor, is that right?"

Beaton nodded, eyes still fixed on that distant fourteenth floor.

"Well, if we're not going to get blown to Hell after all, let's take a look."

In the office block, on the ground floor, the Sergeant and the Constable ushered Beaton into the first elevator. The strip lights overhead flickered as they entered. Beaton pushed back against the wall, eyes wild.

"Steady, Dad," said the Sergeant. "Nothing to worry about now."

"Where to?" asked the Constable. "Top floor?"

The Sergeant nodded and Simpson stabbed at the button for the fourteenth floor. The elevator juddered and the doors slid closed. The Constable found his attention drawn to Beaton. There was sweat on his face, and his eyes were fixed glassily on the lights as the elevator began to climb. And now the Constable was beginning to feel uneasy himself as those lights ascended.

One . . . two . . . three . . .

Something about Beaton's manner, something about the way he was sweating, something about that fearful, glassy stare, something about the way he was pressed back against the wall of the elevator . . .

eight . . . nine . . . ten . . .

Something about the way he was licking dried lips.

. . . eleven . . . twelve . . .

Something about the way he was almost expecting the bottom to drop out of the elevator, sending all three of them hurtling downwards . . .

. . thirteen . . .

Something.

... *fourteen* ...

The elevator shuddered. The elevator light *pinged*. And Beaton moaned; a low, almost desperate and resigned sound. The Constable watched him look down and close his eyes. And the something that was so terrifying him now seemed to jump across to the Constable. For reasons he did not understand, Simpson preferred not to step out of the lift on to the fourteenth floor.

"Fourteenth floor. Jockstraps and ladies' knickers!" The Sergeant's harsh voice made them both jump.

The caretaker exchanged a look with the Constable. And when Simpson saw his fear reflected in those eyes, he was shamed into turning away, looking directly ahead ... and then following the Sergeant as he stepped out into the corridor.

Disco lights flashed blue, red and green against the pastel wall before them. Bryan Ferry was singing about a Hard Rain that was Gonna Fall.

The Constable almost collided with the Sergeant when he suddenly stopped and turned back. Beaton was still standing in the elevator, back to the wall.

"Mr Beaton," asked Lawrence, in as controlled and well-tempered a voice as he could muster. "Would you care to join us?"

Beaton swallowed hard and pushed himself away from the elevator wall and into the corridor.

"Maybe you'd care to show us where?"

"... straight ahead ..." Beaton's words were a croak in his throat. "Through the main door."

"Seems right so far, Sarge," said the Constable. "Not a sign of anyone."

The Sergeant gave him a sour look and pushed on through the glass double-doors and into the office area.

The room was as deserted as before.

Spinning lights from the makeshift disco in the centre of the room. Christmas party decorations on all the walls; red, green and blue. Posters of Santa and the Crib. Drinks on tables, small bowls of potato crisps and nuts. Cigarette ends stubbed out on floors. And Bryan Ferry singing to himself.

But no one in the room.

The Sergeant walked into the centre of the room. Water streaked the outside panes. Somewhere, thunder growled again.

"Christ," said Beaton at last. "Let's get out of here. I don't like it. Can't you feel it? Well, can't you?"

"Feel what?" the Constable heard himself say.

"There's something wrong here. Something *bad*. Can't you feel it in the air?"

Lightning flashed in the skies again, and as if in answer to Beaton's words, thunder rolled in the sky. The windows seemed to rattle.

"They *are* gone," said the Constable at last. The Sergeant stopped in his scanning of the room to give him a hard look. Turning to Beaton again, he said: "Alright, where is it?"

The caretaker's gaze remained fixed on the rattling windowpanes.

"Mr Beaton!" snapped the Sergeant. The caretaker looked wildly at him. "Where *is* it?"

"On the floor. Over there . . . beside the wall."

The Sergeant and Constable followed the track of his pointing finger to the far wall.

"Where?"

"Behind that office screen they've pulled to one side."

Impatiently, the Sergeant strode over towards the screen; a four-foot-high partition. There were others like it in the office, all pulled up to the walls to make space for the party. The screens acted, no doubt, to break the office up into units for typists and clerks. The Constable seemed less inclined to follow him, as thunder rolled again and a brief flash from outside gave them a momentary reflection of themselves in the windows.

The Sergeant reached the screen and pulled it aside.

"Jesus Christ . . ."

"What? What is it, Sarge?" The Constable hurried over to join him now.

"He was right."

Not wanting to look, not really wanting to have that crazy radio report verified, the Constable looked down anyway at the crumpled pale-white thing that lay on the carpet. And now the feeling of not-rightness was upon him with an undeniable reality, just as the crazy, drunken old caretaker had said.

"Don't throw up, son," said the Sergeant matter-of-factly. "You'll see worse than this on the job eventually."

"Yeah . . . I'm okay. It . . . I . . . just didn't think . . . thought it was a drunken call, that's all."

The Sergeant looked up to check if he was okay, and then back at what lay on the office floor.

It was a man's hand, severed at the wrist.

The fingers were curled inwards towards the palm, making it look like some large, dead, white spider.

FIFTEEN

Cardiff looked at the streaked glass again and heard something click. He wasn't aware that his thumb had moved on the safety catch but he wasn't surprised at the inevitability of it.

But he was shocked when someone said: "Jack?"

Startled, he looked across to the outside door. His colleague, DI Peter Johns was standing against the doorframe with a glass of whisky in his hand, looking at him. Cardiff hastily dropped the pistol below the desk line and into the drawer again, sliding it shut and turning in the swivel chair to face Johns.

"Yeah?"

Had he seen?

"Coming for a drink? We can put an intercept on the lines. You don't have to sit here by yourself."

"No . . . thanks, Pete. You go on. Have one for me."

Johns nodded at the spot where he had just shut the drawer.

"That's not the answer."

He has seen the gun!

"What . . . ?"

"Drinking alone, I mean. You don't have to hide a bottle in there."

Cardiff made a gesture; part relief, part acceptance of what Johns had wrongly assumed. "I'm okay, Pete."

"Alright, alright. If you say so. But I know what time of year it is. When we're done, we can go down to the club and have a few bevvies before we go home. Just me and you. Okay?"

"Thanks, Pete. I appreciate what you're saying. I'll give it some thought. But you go back and have another. Like you say . . . it's Christmas Eve."

Johns stood in the doorframe a while longer, swirling the whisky in his glass. He looked down into it for a long while, as if balancing something; maybe professional judgment, maybe whether he should let loose with a rash statement brought on by the booze . . . maybe even something to do with comradeship. After a while, he looked up.

"Don't say it," said Cardiff.

"You don't know what I was going to say."

"It doesn't matter, Pete. I respect you. Just don't say it."

Johns gave a fractured smile, looked down into his glass again, and thought of his own kids. Then he looked directly back at Cardiff, brought the glass up and gave a toast to him. He swung away from the doorframe, back to the party. The door snicked shut.

Cardiff looked at the snow again . . . and then back at the top right-hand drawer.

Then the telephone rang.

And the nightmare began.

SIXTEEN

She was fifty-four years old, five feet two inches tall, married with two grown-up kids — and she felt like hell.

She had been wandering the crowded street for well over two hours now. Late Christmas shoppers had bumped, jostled and cursed their way past her as she wandered aimlessly down the pavement. Her hair was awry, her coat was wet down one side and she seemed to have lost her handbag. She stopped for a moment and stared at her reflection in a shop window. That reflection was surrounded by an aura of Christmas lights; flashing blue, green and yellow. She put her hands on the glass and stared the reflection right in the face.

She did not recognise the anguished face that stared back at her.

Someone else in the crowd collided with her, spinning her away from the shop window — and she was lost again in that dizzying, bustling crowd.

She felt sure that she must have had a handbag when she set off. If she had it now, she could have hunted through it for the evidence she needed. She would have been able to find something with her name on it; perhaps an address.

The streets were unfamiliar to her.

She'd no idea how she'd got there.

Or where she had come from.

In fact, she didn't know who she was — or how she'd come to be wandering the streets like this.

"Excuse me ... I wonder if ... ? Excuse me ... ?"

The crowd hurried on past, ignoring her entreaties, full of Christmas spirit for themselves and their own; with none to spare for what seemed to be a white-faced, bedraggled old bag lady with dishevelled hair and a dirty coat. The figures she tried to catch by the sleeve or by the lapels side-stepped, pushed by or dragged past her, cursing.

This was a terrible nightmare.

Who was she? Why would no one help?

"Please . . . ?"

A young man was standing in a café doorway, coat collar pulled up around his neck, smoking a cigarette. He was unshaven, one lick of black hair hanging in his face. His eyes seemed feverish as he took another drag on the cigarette. Their eyes connected.

"Please . . . ?"

The man dropped the cigarette, stubbed it out with one foot and walked over to her through the crowd keeping the collar tight around his neck. He began chewing the fingernails of his other hand nervously. Those feverish eyes kept looking from side to side as he said: "How much?"

The words made no sense to her. But here was someone in the crowd who had noticed her plight; someone who would be able to help.

"Please help me. I think I'm lost . . ."

"Yeah, yeah. Lost. Right. But how much?"

"I don't know what you mean. Please help me. I don't know how I got here or where I came from or . . ."

"Come over here." The young man had taken her coat sleeve by the elbow and was guiding her out of the flow of the crowd towards the café entrance. She let herself be led. When they reached the comparative shelter of the entrance, he glanced nervously back inside over his shoulder as if fearing that someone he knew back in there would see him.

"Please . . ."

"Yeah, okay. You're lost. I heard you. But you look cold. Wet. Wouldn't you want to earn something to warm you up? Something to eat. Something hot to drink."

Everything was going to be alright now. He would help her. But what did he mean about earning? None of this made any sense.

51

"I just . . ." and now the tears were starting to form, "just . . . want to go home."

"Yeah, go home. But don't come on with the water-works, love. That won't help. Just come with me a minute." Again, that gentle tug on the elbow of her coat, leading her away from the café entrance and down the alley at the side. Again, she let herself be led, dabbing at her eyes with the other sleeve of her coat. What was *happening* to her?

There were ranks of overflowing dustbins back here. In places the garbage had spilled from the bins and on to the shining black pavements. A solitary street lamp at the end of the alley gave a stark blue-black lining on the bins, the railings and the smeared back-window panes. Steam gushed from a grating in the ground at the back of the café and her sense of smell was assailed by the odours of burned fat and grease. The young man continued to lead her on.

"Where are we going?"

"Just down here."

"Are you going to help me?"

The young man laughed. "Could say that."

At last they stopped in the shadows. The young man pulled her into a doorway and at first, she thought that he must live here; but then he stopped, pushed her into the alcove and stood back, looking again towards the street at the top of the alley. Content that they had not been seen, he stood up close to her again and she could smell his breath: sweet and unpleasant.

"How much, then?"

"I thought you were . . ."

"Okay, okay. A tenner. How's that, then? Wouldn't get much more. Not at your age."

Something was happening to her. She could feel it as he pulled the coat collar away from her neck and she could see, despite the biting winter cold, that he was naked underneath. She could see his skinny, ribbed and hairless chest; so unlike . . . unlike her husband's . . .

. . . *husband . . . Donald . . .*

... and below that, she should be horrified to see that this would-be rescuer was sexually aroused as he stepped up to her, eyes glittering, breath excited. She should be utterly horrified and try to beat him off when he began to unbutton her own coat from the neck downwards. But she was completely overcome now by a strange drifting sensation; a strange lassitude, as if this was all somehow inevitable; as if something alien inside her recognised what was going on and was, even now, responding accordingly.

"Changing..." she said vaguely, as her sensibilities began to slip back again to that nowhere place from which she'd come. "I'm changing."

"Aren't we all?" said the young man, eyes wide in anticipation as he pulled open her coat and blouse at last and then pushed up close.

The screaming began then.

She was aware that he was screaming directly into her face. And although she wasn't holding him, she was aware that *something* was holding the young man tight against her. Disinterested, uninvolved, uncaring and content only to drift away again, she listened as the screaming went on and on...

And then she ... and the screaming, drifted away.

SEVENTEEN

The outside door, leading back into the CID Christmas party had just snicked shut when the telephone rang. Turning back to look at the rain-streaked glass, Cardiff lifted the telephone.

"Cardiff speaking."

"Jack?"

"Who . . . Barry?"

"Yes, look. We've got something bloody funny going down here at Fernley House: the office complex."

"Who sent you up there?"

"Routine patrol. Me and young Simpson on short-straw panda duty. We got a call to investigate."

"You know the normal routine, Barry. You're supposed to radio straight into the Control Room. Then they get in touch with me."

"I'm not sure how to handle this one, Jack. Not sure I want anything formally recorded before I talk to you as my CO."

"Okay, better let me have it."

"Seems as if an entire office block of people has gone missing. Everybody on fourteen floors has just bloody vanished. There's only one guy left here. The caretaker. He was in the basement. Says he thought the boilers were going to blow and checked out the floors above to evacuate the place. Couldn't find a soul up there."

"Is this a wind-up, Barry?"

"You know me, Jack. And that's not all."

"What else?"

"Simpson and me checked the building ourselves. And

we found a hand. A man's hand on the top floor. Just lying on the carpet — chopped off at the wrist. No blood."

Cardiff swung back to the desk.

"Okay, Barry. Get the normal team . . ."

"Yeah, they've been. The boilers are okay. No problem, no danger."

"Alright. We need an ambulance for the caretaker. And you'll have to put the hand on ice — just in case we find the owner and he wants it back."

"On *ice*?"

"That's what I said."

"How do I . . . ?"

"Someone must have had a Christmas party somewhere in the building, mate. Find an ice bucket. Stick it in, until we get there."

"You're the CO, Jack."

"Okay, now ring off and telephone into control. I'll be there soon. Oh . . . and Barry?"

"Yeah?"

"Happy Christmas."

"Hah, hah," he said, without humour.

EIGHTEEN

Paul McNichol, fifty-nine, slightly overweight – but trying to ignore the fact in view of the anticipated food indulgences over the Christmas ahead – was watching television. It was typical British Christmas Eve TV: game shows, Christmas spectaculars and a three hour "Lawrence-of-Bloody-Arabia", as he put it. Retirement was a year away and he should be enjoying the prospect, but wasn't anymore. Not since his work colleague, Jackie Shaughnessy, had retired from the factory last year at sixty – and had promptly keeled over dead of a heart attack in the supermarket while shopping with his wife three weeks later.

Now, idly switching channels on the television with his remote control, he was sitting in an armchair while Miriam, his wife, pottered in the kitchen, basting a turkey in the oven. The kids (*kids*, hah? The boy was twenty-five, the girl thirty) and their families were coming over for Christmas dinner tomorrow. This would be their last real Christmas-time alone.

He had taken the Christmas Eve shift off, even though the others were either working for the bonus time, or simply going to the boozer to get pissed. He wanted this to be a good Christmas (your *last* Christmas? asked that pessimistic inner voice) so he'd done the last-minute shopping for Miriam while she got on with the work in the house. Now, at home, with a belly full of tea and soft drinks (you didn't need alcohol to get a high, after all), he just wanted to spend this Christmas Eve at home with his wife in their comfortable three-up, three-down semi-detached haven in Jarrow.

"Tea?" asked Miriam from the kitchen.

He patted his stomach and groaned.

"Okay." Miriam went back to basting the turkey. The bird, he had commented, was almost the size of a pterodactyl – which was just what they needed, bearing in mind the hungry mouths that would be crowding that dinner table tomorrow. Pretty soon, he would force himself to find the energy to start wrapping up the kids' Christmas presents. Maybe he would wait until Miriam was done, then they could perform the task together. Paul checked his watch. It was 7.10 p.m. He wondered whether Miriam was feeling tired, or whether he should go into the kitchen and grab her from behind.

Then something exploded in the garden with an almighty crash of glass.

"Bloody *hell*, what was that?"

Miriam shrieked and hopped back out of the kitchen. The turkey crashed from the oven on to the kitchen floor in a spray of boiling fat. Paul leaped from his seat and ran to her, grabbing her arms and pulling her out of the kitchen.

"Are you okay? Are you hurt? Are you burned?"

"No, no . . . I'm alright. But that *noise*. What on earth was it, Paul?"

His first instinctive concern had been that something had happened to Miriam. Now he knew that this wasn't the case. Paul's mind refocused in the three seconds it had taken for that reverberating crash to reach his ears.

The garden.

"I don't know, but it . . . sounded like . . ."

Paul hurried to the lounge windows and twitched back the curtains to look out at their garden. It was too dark. Rain and sleet were running diagonally across the glass. All he could see was the faint sodium glow of the street-lights on the motorway a mile away. He hurried into the hall, pulled on his coat from the peg on the back of the door and made for the back door leading out into the garden.

"A car crash," said Miriam, hurrying behind him. "It must be a car crash. That was glass breaking, wasn't it?"

"I don't know. Where's the torch?"

Miriam found the torch in the hall cupboard and gave it to him.

Seconds later, Paul was outside in the back garden, pulling the zipper up tight on his waterproof coat and swinging the torch beam across the garden.

He could see immediately what had happened.

The greenhouse standing by the fence had caved in on itself. Even from where he was standing, he could see that the roof had collapsed completely and that one of the main walls was also on the verge of falling apart. In this wind and with the rain coming down as it was, it could only be a matter of time before the entire thing collapsed. Glass shards littered his patio and the neatly trimmed grass of his lawn. The fragments of glass caught the torch beam as he swept it over the scene of devastation, and only one thought now came to mind.

"Kids!"

Something like this had happened last year. Those little swines from Collingwood Avenue had once prised up a flagstone from the main street and heaved it over the fence at his greenhouse. He had lost seven panes of expensive glass on that occasion. But tonight was worse. The whole greenhouse was a write-off.

Paul strode across the garden into the biting wind and rain, steadying the beam on the greenhouse.

"What is it, Paul?" asked Miriam nervously from the back door.

"Bloody kids again, I think," he replied. "Look at it!"

"Come back in. I'll get the police." Miriam's voice was resigned and weary.

"Christmas Eve! You'd think the little sods would have something better to do on a night like this."

He reached the greenhouse and fumbled with the latch on the main door. The glass was smeared, the torchlight reflecting back and obscuring his view. Well aware that by

58

opening the door, the whole place might fall apart, Paul pulled open the door anyway, intent on finding what it was that the little bastards had thrown through the roof to cause such damage. The glass panes shuddered as he wrenched it open.

"Be careful, love. You'll get cut . . ."

But now Paul had wrenched the door all the way open. The structure groaned and tilted a little in the wind, but remained intact.

He shone the torch beam into the centre of the greenhouse . . . and then recoiled.

There was a body lying in the middle of the greenhouse, covered in broken glass and wood.

There was a growing dark pool around it and splashes of black-red stuff all over the inside glass panes, as if someone had gone mad with a pot of paint. The entire inside of the greenhouse had been destroyed; shelves and plants, pots, roots and compost all in the centre of the greenhouse in a devastated pile. But there was no mistaking that huddled, dark, contorted shape lying in the middle of all that destruction.

It was a man.

The torchlight played on his face, and Paul nearly vomited when he saw the shattered extent of that face.

"What is it, Paul? What's happened?"

Paul swung away from the doorframe, bile rising. The structure groaned again and glass began to crack once more.

"Paul!"

He darted away from the greenhouse, just as the far wall caved in at last with a crackling explosion of glass. The remaining walls followed after it; slap-slap-slap. Rain hissed on the shattered ruin.

"What, Paul? *What?*"

"Ring for the police, Miriam." Paul pushed her back inside again, glad that she hadn't seen what had fallen through the roof. "Ring for them, *quick!*"

NINETEEN

Cardiff sat in the back of the panda, watching dark streets glide by as the car sliced through winter's tears towards Fernley House. It was bloody cold tonight, and he was beginning to wish now that he had tucked one or two whiskies under his belt to help him through the rest of the night.

What for? asked a small voice. *No use in doing that. Don't need anything warm where you're headed, pal. Don't you remember the right-hand drawer in your desk?* Yes, I remember it. *Well, what were you intending to do? Wasn't tonight the big night? Wasn't the climax of the Big Show going to take place right there, in the station? Right there in the office, with all your colleagues around?* No. Maybe not there. Wouldn't be fair on them. *When then?* Maybe later, maybe at home. *Don't bullshit me, Cardiff. If you really meant it, you would have taken that gun home.* Yeah? Well, there's a reason I haven't taken it home. It's the wrong place. *You're full of crap, Cardiff. So where's the right place? Not at work, not at home.* I don't know ... maybe somewhere out there on the street where ... But not at home.

Cardiff laughed at the word: "Home". It had really ceased to be a home almost four years ago. Now, it was ... what? Some kind of shrine. Some kind of memory chamber, where whisky turned to acid in his stomach and kept the ulcer fermenting.

Detective Sergeant Ken Pearce was sitting in the back seat next to Cardiff. He looked up at Cardiff's laugh, waiting to be let in on the joke. When it became clear that he

60

was not and that Cardiff had slipped back into some kind of reverie, Pearce gave him an unnoticed look of disdain and returned to window-watching. He was not looking at the streets, or the storm – but at himself. He straightened his tie and smiled.

Pearce was the same age as Cardiff, and had worked with him before. But he could identify a near burnt-out case when he saw one – and Cardiff was certainly heading that way. It was all a question of proportion. Pearce smiled at his reflection, dusting lapels on a jacket that was perhaps too expensive for a policeman's wages. He turned back to Cardiff, still in reverie. Just a matter of time . . . and Pearce could be standing for promotion again.

Cardiff watched the dark streets gliding by; peered at the blurred orange street lamps standing crooked in dirty back-alleys. The pavements glistened ebony black, refusing to give in to the light frosting of snow which was whipped from the skies by the rain and the wind and the oncoming storm. He heard the distant ratcheting echo of more thunder, even over the noise of the car engine and the slush sliding by under the wheels.

"Bad storm coming," said Evans, his Constable driver.

"Someone better let Santa know," replied Pearce. "Can't have the old bugger knocked off his sleigh."

"You really think all those people have vanished, sir?" asked Evans.

Cardiff laughed, returning from his thoughts. "No, just a pissed caretaker, that's all."

But the hand was another thing altogether.

Cardiff had known Sergeant Barry Lawrence for seven years. He was a good man; dependable, reliable and had seen a hell of a lot of street action in his time. He knew that he would have checked the place as thoroughly as he could and if he said he'd found a severed hand, well then . . . he'd found a severed hand.

Even now, the Control Room network were checking out the local hospitals for any notification of severe injury. Two further panda cars were right behind them now, containing a further six uniformed officers to begin a systematic check of the building. But they wouldn't be searching for lost people. Cardiff was pretty sure that there was nothing wrong there; nothing that a check on keyholders for the various offices and companies in the buildings wouldn't confirm. There would be at least three names of keyholders for each company. It was simply a matter of checking and it was also a safe bet that the caretaker had got pissed and slept while everyone had gone home. He'd woken up with his brain addled. No, the search was related to the hand and the possibility that the owner of the missing hand was lying in a cupboard somewhere, dead. In which case, there would be a whole new slant on the affair. At present, there was a grey area of who should be responsible for this particular incident. Was it a matter for CID or a matter for the uniformed bobbies to sort out? Cardiff had taken the first initiative. Once they'd arrived, a search would be made, the building checked and the caretaker interviewed properly, then the next stage of responsibility could be decided.

Morale was not good tonight. Not on Christmas Eve, with the regulars wanting to get home as soon as possible. Only the unlucky ones who had drawn the short straw for the Christmas Eve shift were deriving any pleasure from the reporting of the incident; a kind of gleeful sadism in the knowledge that they didn't have to suffer alone until the whole business had been cleared up. Christmas Eve always brought with it a plethora of drink-related incidents in the City Centre and suburbs, stretching already limited manpower and resources.

The procedures were locked in Cardiff's mind. He knew just exactly what he would do when he got there, knew how to react to the given situations. But nothing about the incident galvanised him, nothing was thawing that ice block inside . . . and his attention turned back to the street again.

The street . . . the street . . .

And he was thinking again, as he so often thought, of that day in June 1986.

It was Sunday. And the sun was shining; a kind of fresh, cleansing sunshine. Not warm enough for summer sun, but enough to make you feel good anyway, with the smell of a hot summer on the way ... just as surely as there was the smell of a bad storm on the streets tonight, bad and foul and very near. Just the opposite.

She had turned to him and laughed as they walked. He was holding Jamie in the crook of one arm while the kid played with the curls of hair on his father's neck. He was four and a half, and all the more dear because those idiotic doctors had told Lisa that, at forty years old, she could never have a child. Playfully, Lisa attributed the success to the fact that she had married a toyboy; then, at thirty-five years old and with a promising career ahead of him in the police force. A Detective Inspector, happily married to Lisa these past eight years. Theirs was a special marriage. Statistically, divorce was a high risk in the force, with long hours of work and the inevitable strains of a basically hideous job at times spilling over into many relationships.

But not for Jack Cardiff.

Not for Lisa Cardiff. What had held them so close and tight? Surely not "love"? No ... nothing so clichéd. A policeman's cynicism would not allow this sentimental term to apply to their marriage. A better word was ... strength. A strength in, and about, each other. A strength which bound them together. Affection without sentiment. A regenerating power between them whenever he came home from the scene of a murder investigation and she had turned over in bed to embrace him. The strength that it took to take those images of pain and mutilation and hideous death away and file it into the proper recess of his mind where it could do no damage. The strength to dispel any doubts or fears about humanity, when he was involved with and subject to all the desperation, misery and loneliness of the victims with whom he came into contact every day. She was his balance. She gave him everything he needed just by being what she was. An effortless gift, because she was who she was ... and they knew each other as lovers really must.

Jack and Lisa. A twee-sounding pair. A bit like Jack and Jill, that perennial pair from English reading primers. And a comparison that made her laugh a lot. "Don't break your crown," she would say. "I'm not coming tumbling after."

And then that Sunday.

How appropriate that the sun was so vivid on that day. They had walked and talked while Jamie twisted and burbled and laughed in Jack's arms. And they'd talked about nothing in particular; and Jack had felt that peculiar, joyful and invigorating strength flooding into him. He could hear her talking now.

"Okay," she'd said, throwing back her head and giving him a mock fierce look. "You're in a panda car on a lonely country road, and there's a car right behind you, chasing you. And it's full of criminals, armed to the teeth. Axe murderers, maniacs, cannibals, estate agents. And they're going to kill you. Their car is doing eighty miles per hour right behind you. What would you do?"

"Ninety," he'd replied ... and she'd blown a raspberry, taken his arm and laughed when Jamie had grabbed a strand of her red hair and began twisting it in a chubby fist.

And then she'd turned to him and said: "You know what I'd really like for Christmas ... ?" She'd paused then, her dark eyes were filled with a kind of mysterious amusement. He had turned towards her, hoisting the child further up on to his shoulder and began to ask her what she was going to say.

Then every nerve-ending inside him spasmed when that horrifying, shrieking noise began. The intensity of that high-pitched banshee-shriek was like a physical assault. He turned ... just in time to see the car, out of control, mounting the pavement like some kind of mechanical juggernaut. In a dream, unable to move, he could see that whoever or whatever was driving that car – *had no face*. In the split second before the car hit them, he could see only the blurred white mask of the shape behind the wheel.

The shrieking of tyres became another kind of shrieking as Cardiff smashed on to the bonnet of the car and the child was torn from his grasp. The shrieking continued as Cardiff whirled over the car roof, the knowledge of agony within his legs — but without *feeling* the agony as such. He was spinning in a black vortex and the shrieking was resolving itself into the sound of . . .

. . . ambulance sirens, as his pain suddenly focused into sick agony. He was on a stretcher; people were shouting, lights were flashing. His double vision focused into single vision and now he could see that car again. It was a wreck, its front end embedded in the wall, broken glass lying on the pavement and a pool of something dark running from under the devastated front of the car and into the gutter on the street.

His own screaming had started then.

Tyres screeched again — cutting deeply into Cardiff's memories with the same hideous effect. The shock of that familiar sound brought him back from that time with horrifying suddenness and immediacy. He started forward, clutching at the seat in front.

"Sorry, sir," said Evans — and Cardiff's mind was back again. He was in the car, travelling through Newcastle on a wild-goose chase. Rain slurried against the windscreen, the wipers barely having a chance to make a clear view. "This bloody weather. Didn't see him coming." And now the car was crossing the central reservation in a spray of slush. A car horn bleated angrily somewhere.

Cardiff wiped the sweat from his face. His heart was hammering. He swallowed deeply, took a breath and stared out of the side window as the car swung into the forecourt of Fernley House.

Pearce turned back to his own reflection in the side window and shook his head.

A burnt-out case.

Someone was moving out of the forecourt darkness to

meet the car as it slid to a halt. The cars behind were also pulling up as Cardiff shoved open the door and climbed out, expecting that huddled form to be Sergeant Lawrence.

But the figure was not in police uniform.

He was dressed in a greatcoat, collar pulled up tight against his throat against the weather; hair dancing in the wind. The man had a beard, flecked white – and Cardiff cursed when he eventually recognised the face.

"Evening, Mr Cardiff," said Farley Peters, local columnist for the *Evening Despatch*. "Hell of a night to be on duty, isn't it?"

In disgust, Pearce and Cardiff climbed out of the car. Cardiff turned back to Evans.

"Evans," said Cardiff.

"Yeah?"

"Kindly escort Mr Peters from the premises before he gets in the way."

"On what grounds?" asked Peters, quick anger rising to the surface.

"On the grounds that you're a pain in the arse and I don't want you interfering with us here."

"Well just give me a few details to be going on with. You can't keep something like this quiet for too long. The place'll be swarming with media people soon – even if it *is* Christmas Eve."

"You mean people like you, Peters? People who've got nothing better to do than monitor police shortwave radio broadcasts for juicy material – *even* on Christmas Eve?"

"Come on, Cardiff. Just tell me . . ."

"It's a crank call, that's all. Get him out of the way, Evans."

"You must be taking it seriously, Cardiff. I mean – all these coppers . . ."

"And if he resists, charge him with obstructing the police in the course of their duties."

"Thanks for nothing . . ." began Peters as Evans bundled him away and Cardiff headed towards the reception doors, the others not far behind.

"Happy Christmas," Cardiff mumbled grimly.

A vortex of ice wind was snapping at the base of the office block. It bit at their faces and hands as Cardiff and Pearce reached the doors.

And then they were in the comparative warmth of the office-block lobby and the nightmare was ready to escalate again.

TWENTY

"Okay, where is it?"

Nervously, PC Simpson pushed open the door behind the reception desk and beckoned weakly.

"Through here, sir."

Cardiff and Pearce walked past the old man slumped in the upholstered chair. Sergeant Lawrence was standing next to him, and the old guy was looking a little the worse for wear.

"Mr Beaton?" asked Cardiff as he passed.

"Yes sir," replied Lawrence. "He's a little . . ."

"Emotional?"

"Exactly."

Cardiff grunted as they walked briskly behind the reception desk. The other police officers were filing into the reception area, groaning at the cold as Cardiff stepped through the door into the waiting-room beyond.

"Where?"

"There's a sort of cupboard room over on the left, sir. It's in there . . . in a fridge," said Simpson sheepishly.

"The fridge." Cardiff and Pearce crossed the room, entering the storeroom. There was a plastic sink unit in here, shelves laden with cleaning materials and Domestos bottles. A row of mops and brushes stood to attention next to a rack of cleaners' smocks. The fridge lay beyond.

"You said somewhere . . . cold, sir," said Simpson.

Cardiff opened the fridge door.

The hand lay in a plastic tray surrounded by ice cubes . . . like some exotic dish prepared by a sadistic master chef. It was sliced cleanly at the wrist, dark meat and cartilage protruding from the skin. The fingers were curled inwards.

Cardiff knelt down, inspecting it without touching.

"A hand?" asked Pearce.

Cardiff closed the refrigerator door and stood again.

"It's a hand," he replied. "Now all we have to do is find out who it belongs to."

The reception door opened and Sergeant Lawrence leaned in.

"Dr Craig's here, boss."

"Yeah, I asked for him . . ."

A bulky man in a somewhat shabby overcoat, a trilby and a multi-coloured scarf pushed past Lawrence and into the ante-room. His face was florid, but not from the cold.

"And here I am. Got the call. Not two blocks away. *Handy*, eh?"

Cardiff gave a sour grimace and pointed backwards to the fridge. "It's in there."

"Got a small army out there, Cardiff. All *hands* to the job, no doubt."

"Spare us," said Cardiff, moving past him towards the main reception area again. Craig was carrying a specimen bag. With something approaching glee, he opened it, dropped it on the floor and swung open the fridge door as if expecting to make himself a snack. "Now then . . ."

Back in the main reception area, Sergeant Lawrence and the six uniformed policemen were waiting for their next instructions. Beaton looked exhausted and on the point of sleep. He was rubbing his hand over his face. Cardiff had smelled the whisky and was prepared to listen to a bullshit story. Quite why Lawrence and Simpson had found record players still playing and disco lights spinning upstairs when everyone else had obviously gone home for Christmas or to the boozer to continue the parties, could no doubt be cleared up fairly easily. Maybe Beaton had got drunk and lonely and decided to set them all away himself. But the severed hand could not be ignored.

"Okay," said Cardiff briskly. "Barry . . . is there somewhere we can interview Mr Beaton properly?"

"There's a small office at the bottom of the corridor," replied the Sergeant.

"Good, Sergeant Pearce and I will take care of that. There are three keyholders for the building so we're waiting to hear from them. In the meantime Barry, I want you and PC . . ."

"Simpson, sir," replied the Constable, still trying to forget the ghoulish look on the police surgeon's face and trying to ignore the silly part of his mind that told him the bastard was going to eat that hand or something.

"Okay . . . you and Simpson, and the other lads, I want a preliminary search of the floors starting at the top where the hand was found, usual procedures, photos . . . then work your way down. Give HQ a situation report."

"Yes, boss."

"Hang on . . . better still. Simpson?"

"Yes, sir."

"I want you to take down the licence-plate numbers of all the cars left in the car park at back. Radio 'em in and run a check on them all through the PNC. That'll give us the names and addresses of our so-called missing persons while we're waiting for the keyholders."

"Yes, sir." Simpson headed for the outside doors while Sergeant Lawrence and the other uniformed officers headed for the elevators, just as Craig emerged from the ante-room.

"Got to *hand* it to you, Cardiff. Interesting little case for Christmas Eve."

"You're sick, Craig. Always said so."

"Only way to survive in police work. You should know that."

"You've got the hand, then?"

"It's in the bag — as they say. Male. Middle-aged I think. The fingers are calloused. Be able to tell more once I get it back."

Pearce was already helping Beaton to his feet, a little too forcibly for Cardiff's taste.

"Cardiff?" called Dr Craig.

He looked back to the police surgeon who was following Simpson out into the storm.

"*Hands* up!" Craig was pointing a finger at him with his thumb cocked, like a gun.

"Sick, Craig. Just sick."

The police surgeon exited laughing and Cardiff turned his attention to the old soak who was being helped towards him.

"Now then, Mr Beaton," said Pearce. "Let's find that office, get a cup of tea on the brew. And then you can try and remember where you've misplaced all these people."

TWENTY-ONE

"Emergency, which service please?"

"Police, please . . . and, I don't know . . . maybe an ambulance . . ."

"Your name and address, please."

"McNichol, 67 Collingwood Avenue, Jarrow. There's a man . . . oh God . . ."

"Connecting you."

"*Area Operations. This is Nightingale Division. Message on screen: 'Man fallen through greenhouse, presumed dead – despatch nearest panda car and inform Duty Inspector at Jarrow station to attend scene with Patrol Sergeant.'*"

TWENTY-TWO

Miriam stood in the doorway of the kitchen with Paul, near to tears. Those policemen hadn't even wiped their feet and there was mud all over the passage and living-room carpets. Outside on the main street, blue lights spun on police panda cars and scratchy radio messages cut through the growing sound of the rain and the oncoming storm. She had seen the curtains twitching across the way, and it infuriated and distressed her. What would people be thinking? And on top of everything else, in all the upset, the turkey had been ruined.

In the back garden, policemen and men in civilian clothes were lifting sheets of cracking glass from the ruin of the greenhouse. Rain glinted on bright-yellow police mackintoshes and waterproofs. Apart from the huddle of figures around the greenhouse, another half-dozen men in waterproofs were searching the rest of the garden, torch beams scanning the soaking grass. A sergeant, standing nearby, conferred with the police pathologist, who was kneeling down and examining what lay beneath the detritus. The pathologist shook his head.

One of the overcoated men began to take flash pictures of what they'd uncovered. The stark white flashes momentarily lit up the garden and its occupants brilliantly, like silent thunderflashes from the oncoming storm. The Sergeant and the man bending over the body exchanged words, lost in the sounds of the wind and the rain. Moving away from the scene of the examination, the Sergeant reached into his inside overcoat pocket and spoke into his radio.

"Foxtrot Four. Sit rep. We've definitely got a dead'un. Need Superintendent at Jarrow informed."

The senior officer-in-charge — the McNichols hadn't caught the Superintendent's name — took the Sergeant by the sleeve and said something. The Sergeant listened and then continued with his situation report. "Scene of crime officers almost complete. Search pending. Over." The Superintendent moved back to the pathologist, gesturing to the other uniformed men nearby. They started to move the body and search the pockets.

The McNichols watched it all from the back door overlooking the garden. Paul suddenly became aware that his wife was shivering. They were getting wet and chilled. Paul saw the Sergeant begin to move towards them as he closed the door, and guided Miriam back into the kitchen. He seated her at the table.

"I'll make something hot. Tea, maybe."

Miriam buried her face in her hands and began to weep. He moved quickly to her and consoled her while the kettle began to hiss on the bench. The kitchen door opened again and the Sergeant came into the room. Not wanting to be seen weeping in company, Miriam dried her tears on her sleeve and rallied.

"You okay, love?" asked the Sergeant, now self-consciously aware of the muddy bootprints on the linoleum and well aware of the hell his own wife would give him if he didn't wipe his feet. Six foot four inches tall and hard as nails, the Sergeant nervously wiped his shoes on the mat.

"Yes . . . yes . . . It's just such a *terrible* thing to happen."

"I know, I know . . . but it's nearly all over now."

"Tea?" asked Paul.

"Yeah . . ." replied the Sergeant, looking through the kitchen curtains at the scene outside. "Thanks. Just a cup."

"So who is it? Do you know? What's happened?" asked Paul, pouring another cup.

"Don't know who he is. But it's a bloody peculiar one."

"Peculiar?"

"Well, you've seen your greenhouse. It's demolished. That fella, whoever he is, didn't just come flying over the fence. He fell. Fell from a helluva height. Terrible."

"From a height? But I don't understand that. How? There's nothing over us, unless he fell out of . . ."

"That's what they think."

"What? What do you mean?" asked Miriam.

"He must have fallen out of an aeroplane or something. Body's in a terrible state."

"Oh dear . . ." Miriam began to feel the tears welling up again. "Why are those other men searching the garden? What are they looking for?"

"He's not . . . well, the guy out there in your greenhouse. Well . . . he's not . . . complete."

"Complete?"

"They can't find his right hand."

Miriam dissolved into tears again while Paul poured the tea.

TWENTY-THREE

". . . and then your policemen came," finished Beaton. "That's it."

Cardiff exchanged a look with Pearce.

"How much have you been drinking?"

"Look . . . I've had a little, that's all. It's Christmas Eve."

Beaton looked up with haggard eyes and could see the blank look on the faces of his interrogators. "Why in hell would I make something up like this?"

"How much?" repeated Pearce.

"I don't know. Maybe three-quarters of a bottle."

"That's a lot of booze, Mr Beaton," said Cardiff.

"I'm telling you. I came out of the basement after that . . . that . . . noise. And they were all gone."

"Doesn't sound very good, does it?" said Pearce. "Lots of booze. Strange noises. Seeing things . . . or should I say *not* seeing things."

"Sounds like delirium tremens to me," said Cardiff.

"What?"

"Delirium tremens, Mr Beaton. The shakes. Pink elephants and psychedelic crocodiles."

Beaton groaned and held his head in his hands. "I need a drink."

Cardiff stood up. "I think it's time we had a look at where the funny noises came from."

TWENTY-FOUR

Light from the opened door spilled down the stairs and into the basement. Cardiff could barely see the boilers. He flicked the light switch, but nothing happened.

"It won't work," said Beaton. "The bulb blew out when that noise began. Wait a minute..." The caretaker fumbled in the darkness at the outside wall until his fingers found a wooden plinth. There were half a dozen rubber-encased torches hanging there. He unclipped one and stepped forward, swinging the beam slowly around so that Cardiff and Pearce could see the layout. After thirty seconds or so, he switched off and turned away.

"Wait a minute," said Cardiff, taking his arm. "We want to take a look down there."

"Not bloody likely," said Beaton, stepping back and pulling out of Cardiff's grasp. "Not after what I've been through. I'm not going down into that Hellhole again."

"Our engineers have examined the boilers. They're switched off and there's no danger."

"Some bloody engineers. Couldn't even put a new bulb in."

"Mr Beaton, I want you to come downstairs and show me exactly where you were and what you were doing when the noise started."

"I've *told* you . . ."

"You don't really want your employers to know that you were drinking on duty, do you?" said Pearce.

Beaton scowled, hesitated . . . and then pushed past, switching on the flashlight again and stomping down the

77

stairs. Cardiff and Pearce followed, their shoes crunching on the broken glass from the exploded bulb.

"How much bloody evidence do you want?" grumbled Beaton as he made his way down. "Watch your step on that last step there, unless you want to break your neck. That's where I puked up. Maybe you want to scrape it up and put it in a plastic bag for analysis, then?"

"Be nice, Mr Beaton," said Cardiff. "This won't take long."

At the foot of the steps, Cardiff took the torch from him and swung the beam around the basement. The light reflected back from the dull copper boilers and pipes and then lingered on Beaton's broken whisky bottle. The caretaker saw the look on Cardiff's face and said: "I *didn't* drink it all. The rest of it spilled out, that's all."

They walked into the centre of the basement, their figures stark against the backdrop of the light from above, still spilling down the stairs.

"And you were sitting here when the noise started?" asked Cardiff, pointing with the torch at the small wicker chair which lay overturned beside one of the boilers.

"Yeah . . ." said Beaton, wiping a nervous arm across his mouth and with his eyes scanning the stark shadows thrown by the beam. "Just there. Thought my eardrums would bust." Outside, thunder grumbled in the sky again; seeming to shake the foundations . . . and Beaton flinched back in alarm.

"Just the storm," said Pearce, moving to the chair and setting it upright. He tapped with his knuckles against the nearest boiler. The sound echoed.

"Keeps on like this, we'll be snowbound."

Beaton snorted in derision. "Seen the human filth out there on the streets? Nothing white ever sticks here."

"Must get hot down here, Mr Beaton. Sitting right next to the boiler like that. Make you feverish, does it?"

"No. And I haven't seen any pink elephants down here, either. Now is that it? I want to get out of here. It gives me the creeps."

Something flashed at the windows near the ceiling and the sky grumbled again. Cardiff guessed that those windows were at street-level up above. Rain and slush were streaking across the panes.

"Mr Beaton. Are you sure it wasn't just the thunder that you heard?" asked Cardiff. "Perhaps . . . you know, a really loud thunderclap?" Cardiff kicked a nearby boiler. It made a hollow booming sound. "Peculiar acoustics in here. Could have made a lot of echoes. Or at least it could have sounded like a lot of echoes after you'd had a few drinks."

"It *wasn't* a thunderclap."

"What then?"

"Well if it wasn't the boilers, I don't know what the hell it was. All I know is that my head's still ringing with it and I'd rather we didn't stay down here too long, thanks very much, if it's all the same to you."

The windows at ceiling-level flickered again. Two seconds later, the sky grumbled, not unlike the hollow booming sound made by the boiler, and the panes rattled.

"Funny bloody storm," said Pearce. "Always seems to be coming, but never seems to get here."

"Alright, Mr Beaton," said Cardiff at last. "I don't think there's any further reason to stay down here."

Beaton was almost at the stairs again, anxious to get away, when the windows flashed and rattled again.

"Storm *is* getting closer . . ." began Cardiff.

And then the windows exploded with ferocious impact and a detonating roar of noise.

Beaton shrieked as he was knocked flat on the stairs. Cardiff and Pearce staggered backwards in the blast, hands flung to their faces. Cardiff had been closer to the windows, and felt flecks of glass whicker across his fingers. The torch was torn from his grasp, falling somewhere on the floor and rolling crazily, casting huge dancing shadows in the basement.

Rain gusted in through the shattered windows.

"What the bloody *hell* . . ." began Cardiff, then saw

even in the darkness the flecks of blood on his hands.

"A lightning strike!" exclaimed Pearce, reorientating himself again. "Must have hit the building!"

Beaton was scrabbling on the stairs, looking for something that he had dropped and making a low moaning noise. He found them . . . his false teeth had fallen out on to the stairs, and Cardiff didn't know whether it was comic or tragic. Runnels of drain water from the pavements began to splatter in through the windows.

And they all heard the noise.

Distant at first, following on from the explosive roar of the lightning strike, but now growing. Like a distant, muffled explosion. Like the beginning of a faraway mortar bombardment. Like the slamming of a great steel door in a crypt.

Once . . . twice . . . three times.

Growing louder.

And now Beaton's nerve had completely snapped. Howling like a wounded animal, teeth back in place, and hands clamped firmly over his ears, he scrabbled up the stairs towards the opened doorway.

Cardiff and Pearce exchanged glances. The fourth "echo" . . . if that was what it was . . . resounded even louder, and Pearce moved quickly to the nearest boiler and placed his hand on it. The fifth crash made their ears ring and Beaton was out of the basement and away from sight. Pearce shook his head in confirmation that the sound was not coming from the boiler.

The sixth explosion was like a hand grenade exploding in the basement. The sound of it pierced their eardrums. Cardiff bent double, hugging his hands to his head. The shock of it flung Pearce back against the boiler.

"Get out! *Get out!*" yelled Cardiff and seized Pearce by the sleeve, dragging him to the stairs.

Cardiff's foot skidded on Beaton's vomit. He struggled for balance and threw Pearce ahead of him as a seventh detonation shook his optic nerves and threatened to make him keel over off the stairs. He shouted — a wordless yell of anger – and pushed hard at Pearce's rear, aware that his Sergeant was also crying out in pain. Cardiff was a powerful man and Pearce was pushed to the top of the staircase. He braced himself in the doorway, whirled around, grabbed Cardiff as he blundered upwards and pulled him clear away from the doorframe and back into the reception area.

Ears ringing, Cardiff braced himself against the cold tiles of the reception wall; waiting for the next literally deafening blast. But up here, on the ground floor, there was no further eruption of that noise. He clasped his hand to his head again. There was a ringing, singing, hissing sound in there; just like the sound he heard after he'd got drunk and put on the headphones with the volume up too loud, to drown out the sorrow. Pearce had staggered over to the elevators, directly opposite, and was suffering from the same kind of side effects. There was no sign of Beaton.

Cardiff moved back to the basement door and looked down.

The rain still hissed and runnelled into the room. The torch had come to rest beneath a boiler, its beam casting bizarre and surreal light and shadow.

But the noise had gone.

Somewhere beyond, thunder groaned in the sky. But the ear-splitting detonations had ceased.

"Been drinking, Pearce?" asked Cardiff.

"No." Pearce moved to join him at the door.

"Think it was just echoes?"

"Nope."

"Then I think we've just heard the funny noise that Mr Beaton heard."

Something scuffled behind them, and they turned from the basement to see Beaton on all fours emerging round the corner from the main reception desk. He stood up, leaned against the wall and gave a painful-to-hear, racking cough. Using the wall to keep him erect, he staggered towards them.

"You bastards . . . I told you about that noise . . . but

81

you thought I was just bloody drunk, didn't you? Well, I tell you . . . I tell you . . . there were times at sea when I would have kicked the living shit out of anyone who called me a liar . . . the living *shit* . . ."

Beaton launched himself from the wall in a feeble attack, which turned into a dive for the floor when gravity took over. Pearce was nearest; he was able to catch him by both feeble arms. Cardiff quickly joined them, helping Pearce to lift him back down the reception corridor and into the main reception area. He gave a quick look back in the direction of the basement door. But there was no more sound other than the hiss and splatter of rain and the groaning rumble of the sky. They manoeuvred Beaton back into the chair where Cardiff had first seen him slumped. Beaton seemed to accept the position gratefully, putting his hands to his head just as Cardiff first remembered seeing him.

"Sir?"

Cardiff looked up to see PC Simpson standing at the main doors, rain glinting black on his waterproofs.

"Sergeant Lawrence is outside, sir. He had to leave the others. He tried to give a sit rep but his radio wouldn't work upstairs. So he popped out to use the car radio. Still too much static interference so we can't . . ." And then Simpson realised that something had happened, and shut up.

"Lawrence is outside?" snapped Cardiff.

"Giving a sit rep like you said, sir . . ."

"Get him in here straightaway."

Simpson turned to open the door and shout for Lawrence, still unaware of what was happening. A cold gust of winter wind sent a spray of water into the reception area.

"Did you hear it?" asked Pearce as the Constable joined them again.

"Hear what, sir?" asked Simpson.

"I was afraid you were going to say that," said Pearce.

"You mean you didn't hear *anything*?" rejoined Cardiff. Beaton was flopping back in his seat now and moaning.

He didn't like the caretaker's chalk-white complexion.

"Nothing, sir . . . apart from a lightning crack. A pretty loud one."

"Loud enough to blow in the basement windows without your seeing," said Cardiff impatiently, loosening Beaton's collar. "But nothing else? You didn't hear any other loud noises — like explosions?"

"No, sir," replied Simpson, now completely confused as Lawrence appeared through the reception doors again. "Nothing else. We can't see the basement windows. They're screened off to the side. Blown in you say?"

"And how. Barry . . . did you get through?"

"Yes, boss. Pretty bad reception, though. Must be the storm."

"We need another sit rep," said Cardiff. "Where the hell's that ambulance for Beaton?"

Lawrence reached automatically for his personal radio, remembered that he couldn't use it indoors because of the electrical interference caused by the storm and cursed again as he pushed back outside into the rain.

"Pearce," said Cardiff. "I want you and Simpson to recall the lads searching the upstairs floors. I want to know if they heard anything."

Pearce nodded and headed for the elevators with the Constable following.

"The living shit . . ." mumbled Beaton again as Cardiff tried to hold him in his seat.

"Yeah. I know," said Cardiff, ears still ringing from the noise-that-hadn't-been-heard. "When you were at sea."

Not the only one at sea, he thought. *Just what in hell is going on here?*

TWENTY-FIVE

Farley Peters – columnist, interviewer, *nom de plume* and would-be novelist – had been just about to give up this ridiculous vigil at the office block, when interesting things had started to happen.

Nothing better to do on Christmas Eve, Cardiff had said – and he had been right. Peters had been idly monitoring the police air waves in accordance with the usual eavesdropping procedure, on the shortwave he kept in the office for just such occasions. It was a useful way of picking up juicy stories and getting people out into the field. Tonight's idle Christmas Eve had picked up a *really* juicy one.

Some frantic old caretaker with a piss-crazy story about an entire office-block of people vanishing. A crazy enough scenario. Worth ignoring perhaps as the fantasy of some alcoholically deranged old fart or a prankster. But something about the report, something about the bizarre nature of it had caught Peters' attention. Maybe there was something in this story. Most of Peters' colleagues would be in the boozer at the moment; the others working shift. If this *was* a scoop . . . and he laughed at the clichéd way the word sounded . . . then he would have it.

He hadn't been at the office block for more than two or three minutes, sheltering from the storm behind the workmen's hut in the car park which fronted the office block, when the first panda car had pulled up and the old man inside had rushed out to meet them. Through rain-blurred windows, Peters had been unable to make out what was going on inside except that the old man – presumably the caretaker who had made the call from the public telephone box at the car park entrance – was extremely agitated.

Peters scanned each of the fourteen floors for signs of movement. Lights were shining on most floors but he couldn't see a damn thing.

The storm had continued to build and the chill of the winter night and the acid-cold bite of the rain on Peters' face had convinced him after a further hour that he really was wasting his time here. Look at him. A forty-five-year-old professional man with a wife and three kids at home waiting excitedly for Christmas – and here he was, standing in a bloody car park in the freezing rain while his mates were partying in their local boozer. He had continued to use his shortwave radio, but the interference had been bad; a mad crackling of static, no doubt caused by the storm. He had furiously tried to zero in when the Sergeant had emerged and given a situation report from one of the panda cars. But his own radio was less sophisticated than the police model, and the snatches of words he'd picked up in no way enlightened him. He cursed in the wind; the words snatched away from his lips.

Maybe it was time to pack it all in.

Twenty angry minutes later he began to walk back to the car park entrance.

And all because of – his laugh held a trace of bitterness and self contempt – a so-called "scoop".

Then the Incident Squad van had pulled up in a spray of dirty water and Peters' self-contempt had vanished. He dashed back to the workmen's hut. Four men clad in yellow waterproofs and carrying equipment of some kind had hurried through the reception doors.

Maybe something *was* going on.

Peters' new-found enthusiasm and self-justification was further fuelled when further panda cars had arrived and officers had climbed out on to the pavement under grumbling skies.

When he recognised Cardiff, Peters had broken cover and made his approach – only to be threatened with arrest.

He knew Cardiff of old. He was a hard bastard and it wasn't a threat to be taken lightly.

But all of Peters' suspicions had been confirmed.

Something *big* was happening and he knew that by now, others with a vague interest in the police call — being monitored in at least half a dozen other places of which he knew — would now have listened intently to the further calls which he knew must have taken place.

The police were too absorbed in what they were doing to take a real interest in him once he had been given the bum's rush. Once they had vanished into the reception area, he had slipped back across the road and resumed his former vantage point behind the workmen's hut.

From there, he had seen the arrival of the police pathologist — and wished he'd known what the man had taken away. There was now too much static on his radio to even pick up garbled words — just a maddening electric hiss. Peters wiped water from his face to see the police in the main reception moving to the elevators — and knew that a search was underway. He crept forward, sheltering behind a car.

Cars?

He looked back. There were thirty or forty cars in the park; presumably owned by those in the office block. He looked back up to the office block.

All vanished?

Where the bloody hell had they gone?

And now, Peters realised that his vantage point might soon be under threat. It was only a matter of time before the police started to check the licence plates of the cars in this park in an attempt to identify the missing people.

He waited, watching the office block and ready to move. A Police Constable emerged on the pavement and headed for one of the pandas.

Overhead, there was a terrific crack of thunder. The sky blazed blue-white for an instant and Peters seemed to feel the ground tremble under his feet.

That was bloody close!

Peters knew that it was now or never.

He broke away from the shelter of the car and ran into the teeth of that biting wind and slashing rain, keeping his eye on the Constable.

Rain-soaked in slush water, he sprinted across the car park forecourt and around the side of the building. The builders had been landscaping there in the summer, and young saplings in wire cages thrashed in the wind.

In the shadows of the office block, Peters found the rear access to the building where large van deliveries were made.

He clambered over a small brick wall, cursing again at how out of condition he had become, and skirted around an outside generator.

The service door set into the office block before him was marked "Staff Only" and Peters considered whether the back doors would be burglar-alarmed. Using the keys he held for just such a purpose, Peters tried four before he found the right one.

The service door snicked open.

Only blackness within.

Excited in a way he had never been before, he let himself in and closed the door behind him. There were so many questions.

Wondering what the police search party might have found, Peters felt his way along a wall in blackness, hunting for a light switch.

TWENTY-SIX

"Radio?" said Cardiff when Sergeant Lawrence re-entered again, soaking wet.

"Nothing, boss. Just bloody static. How's Beaton?"

"Not good." Cardiff checked the caretaker's pulse again. His breath was ragged. "Look, Barry. I don't know why the hell it's taking Pearce and Simpson so long. But I don't think Beaton can wait. I want you to drive him to hospital now. Then I want you to . . ."

The elevator doors pinged open.

Pearce and Simpson emerged.

"Wait a second, Barry. That you, Pearce?"

When the Detective Sergeant and Constable turned the corner from the corridor into the main reception area, Cardiff saw the joint expression on their faces; a bewildering mixture of doubt, embarrassment and outright confusion.

"What's happened?"

Simpson turned to Pearce, acceding to authority to make some sense of what was happening tonight.

"The others," said Pearce. "The others searching the floors."

"Well, come on, then. What have they found?"

"Well, well . . . nothing *they've* found. Just that . . ."

"What?"

"We can't find *them*, sir. They've all gone. We can't find them anywhere in the block."

Thunder grumbled in the skies again and the window-panes in the reception rattled.

"They've gone," continued Pearce. "They've just bloody vanished into the woodwork."

Cardiff stood in rage, scrutinising both Pearce and Simpson's faces. Now the rage was subsiding and for the first time, Cardiff could sense the overwhelming feeling that they were conveying to him.

Fear.

He beat down the knots that were tightening in his gut, and turned back to Sergeant Lawrence.

"Barry. I want you and Simpson to get Mr Beaton to hospital. Pearce. The radios are no good here. We're going back to HQ smartish. I want a full-scale op and back-up here. Urgent. I want another squad for full-scale supervised search. The office block has to be cordoned off, manned and patrolled. Simpson. How far did you get with the licence plates?"

"Not very far . . ." said the Constable.

"Alright. It doesn't matter for now. When we get back, I want the licence plates in the car park identified and the men from the lab here pronto."

Nervously, Lawrence and Simpson helped Beaton to his feet. They headed for the reception door – and for an unreasoning, terrifying instant – Simpson felt sure that the doors would be locked and they wouldn't be able to get out. They would be locked in this Godawful place until whatever had happened to the office workers – and now the police search party – had happened to them. Terror made his stomach lurch when the door wouldn't open.

But it was only the force of the wind and rain holding it shut. Seconds later, they were out on the pavement, with Beaton hanging between them, heading for the panda car.

Cardiff exchanged a glance with Pearce when they saw the other empty panda cars parked across the way and then they too were out in the storm and heading for their car. When they had climbed in, Cardiff reached for the ignition, paused and looked back at Pearce again.

Pearce knew what the unasked question would be and replied: "Gone, boss. I'm telling you – they're just not there anymore."

Into the woodwork, thought Cardiff.

Both cars pulled away from the office block.

For some reason, Cardiff could not get a horrifying image out of his mind; an image that had haunted his dreams since the tragedy that had taken Lisa and Jamie away from him. It was the image of the driver of that car. The image of that terrible *blank* face; no features, no eyes or mouth. Just a blank mask of flesh. The police had never been able to trace the driver. The car had been stolen earlier on that terrible June day, presumably for a "joyride". Ever since then Cardiff had been haunted by what he'd seen – or what he thought he *hadn't* seen. That face seemed to be specially significant to him now for reasons he could not fathom. He tried to shake it from his mind as Lawrence's panda moved out on to the main road and vanished in a hissing blur of rain.

Cardiff's ghostly reflection in the side window seemed to leer at him. Shrugging down the feeling that if he looked at the reflection it would turn into that ghastly no-face, he turned to look at Pearce in the driving seat, as he followed Lawrence's panda.

Evans was sitting in that driving seat. Now he's gone. Just vanished like the others. What the hell is going on?

On impulse, Cardiff tried the car radio again.

Back on the motorway, heading for the town centre, Sergeant Lawrence's car radio crackled back into life.

"Panda nine to panda four."

Lawrence grabbed at the microphone. "Panda four. Come in."

"Cardiff here, Barry. Right behind you. Now that we're away from the block, the bloody radio's working again. Are you receiving, over?"

"Loud and clear, boss. That storm must have been right over us or something. Over."

"Look, Barry. Get Beaton to hospital as fast as you can. We're going back to HQ to get everything sorted for a proper operation at Fernley House. After everything that's happened, I don't want the place left unattended so I'm having the place cordoned off. Then we're going back there

90

to find out just what the hell is going on. Got that? Over."

"Got it all, panda nine. Jack? Just what in hell *is* going on up there? Over."

Cardiff had chosen to ignore the question, but his next statement only seemed to confuse Pearce completely.

"Remember Jimmy Devlin, Barry? Small-time crook. Did two years for doing-over a jewellery store in the shopping mall. He's back out now, I think. Over."

"Devlin? Yeah. I know him, alright. Hard case. It was Sergeant Pearce who pulled him in for that job. Over."

"And Pearce and me who got him put away. Think you could find him for me after you've got Beaton to hospital and completed your report?"

"Yes, I think I could find him. I know our Jimmy pretty well. I think I know which pub he may be drinking in tonight. Over."

"Good. When you've got him, I want you to bring him back to Fernley House. I'd like to talk to him. Over."

"On a charge? Over."

"No charge, Barry."

"Then he won't come, boss. Simple as that. Over."

"It's important I talk to him. Over."

"Okay, boss. Leave it to me. Over and out."

The two cars parted company at a junction. After a while, Pearce turned to Cardiff.

"Devlin?" he asked.

Cardiff didn't answer.

TWENTY-SEVEN

Feeling more than a little foolish but still nevertheless excited in a way that he hadn't felt for years since becoming a professional cynic, Peters continued to grope his way blindly along what felt like a cold, plaster wall in the darkness.

Moving one hand carefully up and down the wall before him, and with the fingers of the other hand braced against that wall for balance, he moved like a blind man.

He came to a door and felt sure that there must be a light switch somewhere nearby on the wall. He groped eagerly forward and pain stabbed into his skin as he collided with something that fell over with a flat, metallic clatter. Wincing in pain, Peters held his breath, feeling sure that someone must have heard that noise and would be coming to investigate. He exhaled slowly in the darkness, heart hammering. With what could the police charge him? Breaking and entering? Probably. Cardiff wasn't likely to let him off if he'd already given one warning. On one job recently where Peters had shown up, the bastard really had tried to get him done for obstructing the police in the course of their duties. Excuses, apologies and just plain begging stories raced through Peters' mind, and it was only after several minutes that he realised: no one was coming. He hadn't been heard. Breathing out softly in relief, he realised by the sound of it that he was in some kind of confined space. Maybe a cleaners' room, or a corridor. He fumbled for the handle of a door and found one, but the door was locked. He continued onwards, still groping at the wall, and still unable to see anything in the utter blackness. Another door . . . and this one was also locked. Cursing again, he moved on.

But the third door was unlocked and when he carefully opened it one inch, there was no glimmering of light from beyond. He fumbled around the door and at last found a switch. He flicked it.

A cleaners' cupboard lay beyond. He could see a stack of cardboard boxes filled with bottles of cleaning fluid and detergents. Looking back, he could also see that he had guessed correctly. He was in a corridor that led off to three doors on either side of him. More cleaning cupboards and storage space, no doubt. With surprise he could see that he hadn't moved more than thirty feet from the Exit door. It had seemed a great deal further in the dark. There were three large paint tins on the floor, where he'd knocked them over. But they were sealed, and there had been no spillages.

Now he could see the light switch in the corridor wall and couldn't understand how he'd missed it. Deciding to use the light of the cleaners' room to guide him, rather than from the corridor, Peters skipped back down the corridor and retrieved one of the paint tins; returning to prop open the cleaners' room door with it. Turning, he could see a small flight of three concrete stairs leading to a main door at the far end of the corridor. He crept to it and listened at the woodwork for any sign of movement or voices on the other side. There were none.

Carefully, he eased the door open.

Beyond lay a tiled wall and floor. Pushing further, he peered through the slit in the door jamb to see that the main corridor leading away from the reception area lay beyond; the same corridor he had been trying to watch from the workmen's hut. Rain was pounding against those glass reception windows now, and from where he stood he would be able to see in those windows the reflections of anyone around the corner from him. He could see the reception desk. But there was no sign of anyone there. Had they *all* gone to search the floors above?

Blast!

It would have been far better if they'd stayed put. Then he could stay where he was and hope to overhear something. After a juicy lowdown, he could have sneaked back the way he'd come and got out of there before anyone knew. He'd have to move.

Peters pushed the door open carefully. Still no sign of anyone. Stepping into the corridor, he eased the door quietly shut behind him and listened again.

Nothing.

On his right, he could see the elevators. Two of them both on the ground floor. Directly opposite to them, and a little farther down on the opposite wall to him were two doors. One marked "Basement" and the other marked "Stairs". Peters crept across the corridor, aware of the ridiculous fact that he must look like Sylvester the Cat, stalking Tweety Pie. In the centre of the corridor, he caught movement directly on his right and froze on the spot, heart hammering.

It was only his reflection in the reception windows.

Quickly, he reached the door to the stairs, opened it and stepped into the stairwell which Beaton, not too long ago, had ascended. The door was spring-loaded and slapped back quickly. Peters lunged for it, and caught it before crashing echoes could bounce up that stairwell. Slowly, he eased it shut and moved forward to look up the stairs. Somewhere outside, thunder cracked and grumbled. Inside the stairwell, he seemed able to hear the hiss and splatter of rain against an unseen skylight.

This is crazy! I'm bound to be found out.

Peters stayed in the shadows, deliberating his next move. Up the stairs? Waiting for the first sound? What?

Ah, sod it . . .

This was ludicrous. He was the writer of a popular and well-regarded local newspaper column. He was reasonably well off for someone in his profession. Just what the hell did he think he was doing? He was Farley Peters, well, he wasn't really, not his *real* name . . . but he certainly wasn't Dick Tracy.

He had almost decided to slip back into the corridor and make good his escape back the way he had come . . . when he heard the noise.

He paused, with his hand on the door, and listened again.

He could hear the storm somewhere above, venting its anger in the clouds.

He could hear that hissing of rain.

But had he really heard a . . . ?

Help me . . . please . . .

A voice? A whispered, pained voice that seemed to be a part of that hissing rain-sound? A voice that echoed sibilantly up the staircase? Peters let the door close quietly again and listened.

Please . . . God in Heaven . . . please . . .

It *was* a voice.

Peters moved to the bottom of the stairwell again. The voice was whispered, but seemed to carry a peculiar sibilant force — and it was the sound of someone in agony.

HELP ME!!

The suddenly loud cry of agony and distress made Peters reel back in shock. The echoes of its dying entreaty seemed to shriek to the top of the stairwell and back again. Discarding all notions of stealth, all notions of the sleuth/newshound, all notions of self, Peters lunged to the bottom of the staircase and began to ascend quickly. Innately decent and less the selfish pessimist than he could ever have believed himself, Peters reached the first floor and called out.

"Where are you? Tell me!"

His own voice sounded somehow flat and dead, completely unlike the acoustic effect of the agonised scream he had just heard.

God . . . I'm here . . . here . . . HERE!

The voice was coming from somewhere up above. Maybe the third or fourth floor.

"Hang on! I'm coming . . ." Peters clattered up the staircase, wheezing, the pace of his flight giving him no real time to think what could be happening or what could be wrong.

Please, oh please! I can't stand it . . .

Peters paused only briefly in his ascent. This was a different voice, surely. The first voice had belonged to a man . . . but this new voice was a woman. But it still contained that peculiar, whispered, echoing quality that was so unlike his own voice when he shouted. And it also contained the same dreadful agony. Peters reached the fourth floor. There was no one on the landing, but he was sure that this was where the voice . . . the voices? . . . had come from.

"Where . . . ?"

IT HURTS! OH SWEET GOD, IT HURRRTS MEEEE!

But now the dreadfully agonised voice seemed to be both below and above him; echoes bouncing like tortured banshees. The pain in that scream filled Peters with an intense horror. He ran to the rail and looked down. He could see nothing on the stairs below or above.

. . . helllllllpppp . . .

This time, the fading voice of the man was coming to him from behind the fourth-floor landing door. He ran to it and flung it wide. There was no one in the main landing. Throwing open the main door leading into the office area, Peters looked down another darkened corridor with offices leading off at either side. He felt sure now that the voice or voices had come from here, despite the nearness of those terrible entreaties in the stairway.

. . . pleassssse . . .

And this time, it was the voice of the woman pleading to him. It had come from somewhere near the bottom of that corridor. It was plain to him that the woman must be dying.

"Wait! Don't move! I'm here to help you."

Peters moved quickly down the darkened corridor towards the sound of the voice, breath wheezing in his lungs. As he moved, his shadowed reflection passed by on either side of him in glass partitioned walls.

I don't want to be here! implored the man's voice. He was obviously down there with the woman.

"Wait!"

Peters could see movement at the bottom of the corridor now, in the shadows. Surely someone was crouched against a wall there in the shadows, as if in pain. The shadows were darkening as he finally reached the strangely crouched and half-formed shape pressed so closely against the wall.

Something was terribly, terribly wrong.

He couldn't move, couldn't breathe, when the shadow crouched tight in that wall turned its face to see him . . . and smiled its smile of insanity.

It reached out to him from the shadow.

And this time, Peters found the strength to turn and run from the horror which he had been trying to help. Crashing against the partition walls in his desperate plight, he seemed to hear its imploring cries of anguish; then realised that the voice was his own.

Peters burst through the door at the end of the corridor and on to the fourth-floor landing. He reached for the stairway door, and then recoiled from it. The last thing he wanted to do was go back in there again. Because now he realised that there was more than one of the terrible things he'd found. And that the others were probably in the stairway waiting for him.

Something *pinged!* and Peters turned to see that one of the elevator doors had slid open. Gasping, he hurtled across the landing and into it with such force that the entire cage seemed to shake. He stabbed both hands on the Ground Floor button, eyes still glued to the door at the far end of the landing.

Whimpering, Peters stabbed and stabbed at the button.

The door began to open . . . just as the elevator doors slid shut and masked from sight whatever it was that might be, even now, coming through the landing doors after him. The elevator began to descend. Peters staggered back and braced himself against the far wall, watching the floor panel lights above him move downwards from four . . . to three . . . to two . . . to one.

And then the elevator shuddered and stopped between floors.

Peters began to scream hoarsely for help. If that elevator started to ascend again, and if the doors opened on floor four to reveal what he thought he had seen . . . then he must surely go mad. Frantically, he began to beat against the elevator doors.

The elevator lights went out.

Moaning and sobbing, Peters began once again to feel his way around the wall of the elevator, just as he had done in the pitch-blackness of the corridor downstairs. If this elevator was like the one in his newspaper offices, there was a metal panel just above the lift buttons. Inside that panel would be an emergency light, a telephone and an emergency button. Hand over hand, weeping in terror, he fumbled his way towards where he thought that panel would be.

And put his hands on a face in the darkness.

A face that was somehow almost flush with the wall.

You've found me, it said in a liquid-croak of a voice. *Thank God, you've found me.*

Peters screamed aloud and tried to pull away, but the owner of that face had somehow gripped him around both wrists with what seemed to be concrete-hard hands, like manacles.

Come join us, the face in the darkness said . . . and began to pull him back towards it.

Peters screamed and kicked, but could not break free.

At the last, he realised with an insane and desperate terror, that the thing in the elevator wall meant to kiss him. And then it meant to hold him there until the next lightning strike. Because only with the next lightning strike could he join it.

Much later, the elevator juddered and moved down to the ground floor.

The light in the floor panel above the doors *pinged!* and the doors slid open.

The elevator was empty.

TWENTY-EIGHT

"One more," said Jimmy Devlin. "And then I'm going home."

The barman laughed ruefully and lifted Jimmy's glass from the beer-rinsed bar. He tapped the face of his wristwatch with the bottom of the glass and held it up to him. "Remember what you said? You had to be home by six and you'd give me bother if I didn't remind you."

The other three men at the bar began to laugh; a little too loud bearing in mind that they'd all drunk six pints of beer each. Jimmy grinned and ran a hand through dark, cropped hair.

"Just one. Go on, Frank."

The barman began to refill the glasses, shaking his head.

Jimmy was six foot three inches tall; his tallest companion reaching only to his shoulders, explaining the reason that, one foot on the bar rail, he was leaning across the bar itself while they talked.

In the popular vernacular of the area, they were in a working-men's club. No fancy spinning lights; no chrome; no brass bar fittings. Just the bar, a few battered chairs and fitted drinking stalls with a threadbare, faded carpet that had seen too much spillage in its time.

Jimmy's face was almost boyishly handsome for his twenty-three years of age; an effect which was spectacularly ruined by a nose badly broken in a street fight years ago. Jimmy took a deep draft from his fresh pint before rejoining the argument with a carefully chosen and definitively delivered statement: "Bollocks!"

"What?" said the man with the moustache and the cap.

"Bollocks. No such thing as Christmas anymore."

"How do you mean?"

"It's just been commercialised to hell, hasn't it? Bloody television adverts just *tell* everybody what they're supposed to want. And all this Goodwill crap. That's a joke, as well. One or two pints of Newcastle Brown Ale in the boozer, a couple of choruses of 'Auld Lang Syne' on New Year's Eve — and everybody's supposed to change in the morning. Everybody's supposed to be bosom buddies again. Does it happen like that? No — after the booze and the turkey wears off everybody just goes back to being the same selfish, grasping bastards they were before the pubs opened."

"What about those, then?" said another of Jimmy's companions, poking with a foot at one of two parcels beside Jimmy's feet; all wrapped in Christmas paper with plastic bows. Jimmy looked down.

"Ah, well . . . that's the kids, isn't it? Gotta have presents for the kids."

"But if you don't believe in any of this Christmas stuff you wouldn't buy presents for the kids, would you?"

Jimmy drank again, wiped his lips and delivered the catchphrase that he always used in a difficult situation and which always got a laugh from his pub mates.

"Not necessarily."

The catchphrase worked again. Jimmy's friends were still laughing when the club's double-doors opened and two policemen entered in a flurry of snow, wind and oaths from the other customers in the bar, complaining at the entry of cold winter air.

Sergeant Lawrence and Constable Simpson shook snow from their uniforms and scanned the bar. The Sergeant spotted Jimmy and nudged his companion. The bar was perceptibly quieter now as the policemen moved towards them; only the sounds of Jimmy's mates' laughter, now dying away completely as the two policemen drew level with the bar.

Jimmy's companions moved aside, creating a clear space

between Jimmy and the new arrivals. Jimmy remained leaning on the bar, lifting the drink to his lips again, face set. He had seen them but refused to acknowledge their presence. There was an air of open contempt.

"Evening, Mr Devlin," said the Sergeant.

Jimmy turned slowly on his elbow and eyed the policemen carefully, sipping at his pint of beer again. The Sergeant looked like a boxer in a uniform. He also looked as if he had seen as much, if not more, street action than Jimmy. Eyebrow scars had all but eliminated those eyebrows.

"Yeah, it's that alright," said Jimmy. The Constable shuffled uneasily.

"We've been looking for you tonight, Jimmy," said Sergeant Lawrence. "This is the fourth pub we've tried. You like to move around a lot on Christmas Eve, don't you?"

"Shouldn't you be out there catching rapists and murderers, or something?"

"Mr Cardiff would like to have a word with you."

Jimmy slammed his beer glass down hard on the bar counter with a flat *snap!* His drinking companions recoiled in alarm at the sound. The beer frothed and slopped over the rim of the glass and the pub became deathly quiet.

"Now, now, Jimmy," said Lawrence. "No need for aggro."

"Cardiff up to his tricks again, is he?" asked Jimmy. "What does he want to set me up for this time?"

"All we want . . ."

"All you want, copper. All you *want* . . . is a fucking warrant. Right?"

"Like I said, no need for aggro, Jimmy. We just want to talk."

"What's the charge?"

"No charge."

"Then you can get lost. The pair of you. Back to Cardiff and tell him from me what he can do, if you haven't already guessed. He's not pulling me in on Christmas Eve."

"Look, Jimmy . . ." PC Simpson stepped forward and

put a hand on Jimmy's arm. And then he saw something spark in his eyes at that touch; something dangerous ... and he knew that he had made a mistake. A line had been crossed. He knew that he should react, but couldn't react fast enough as Jimmy swung away from the bar with a solid, jabbing punch that caught the policeman on the bridge of his nose.

The Constable's nose exploded. He blundered backwards into a table, knocking glasses to the floor in a crashing spray of beer. Jimmy snatched his pint glass and smashed it on the bar, ready to use the jagged shard left in his hand if he must, to prevent them taking him away. But the older policeman had been brought up on the same streets as Jimmy. Moving quickly, he pinned Jimmy's forearm and weapon to the bar with a meaty left hand and jabbed a tight, hard uppercut to Jimmy's chin. Jimmy sagged instantly and the broken glass fell to the floor in disintegrating, tinkling shards as the Sergeant held him against the bar. Simpson staggered back to the bar with blood streaming from his nose. He seized Jimmy's left arm, pinioning him backwards over the bar. There was no need. Jimmy was semi-conscious.

"I ... see what you mean ... about Jimmy Devlin," said the younger man.

Jimmy was trying to shake his head now, struggling weakly. His drinking companions had shrunk away from the bar.

"I'm not ... going in ... there's *no* charge ..."

"There is now," said the Sergeant, pulling him away from the bar. "Assaulting a police officer in the course of his duties." He shoved Jimmy's unresisting arm up his back and, with his bleeding companion, frogmarched him across the club to the double-doors.

"Gotta ..." said Jimmy, still dazed from the blow to his jaw. "Gotta get home. It's Christmas Eve, you bastards. The kids are expecting ... the kids ..."

The two policemen bundled Jimmy out into the street and across the frosted pavement to their nearby panda car.

". . . the kids . . ."

The panda car pulled away from the club into the near vertical torrent of sleet, wind and rain.

Two brightly wrapped Christmas presents remained by the bar rail in the club.

TWENTY-NINE

She was different . . . and knew it.

But that change horrified and delighted her by turns as her mind spun and twisted in new ways. She could still not recall who . . . or even what . . . she was, or where she had come from. She still staggered down these unfamiliar streets, bustling with what at times she knew to be late Christmas shoppers, at other times to be strange, alien multitudes that sometimes frightened her . . . and at other times made her feel horribly hungry for something, she knew not what.

As she blundered along those streets, with the crowds of people parting before her — some of them with looks of disgust or horror on their faces — she was aware that she was soaked and that an icy wind was biting at her face and hands. Sometimes the feeling was bliss, at other times agony. Shades of emotion swept through her like stormclouds; hunger, then fear, then hate, then hunger again. Those emotions seemed mirrored and somehow intimately connected with the blue-black stormclouds that surged in the sky overhead.

She remembered the back alley, and the young boy who had offered to help her. Nothing before that. She had felt sure that the boy would be able to make sense of what was happening to her. When he had pulled her into the doorway and said those words that made no sense, she had felt a new and uncontrollable impulse surging inside. It was a ravenous, engulfing hunger . . . for something. She could not remember clearly what had happened, other than that she was satisfying that hunger, fulfilling herself in a strange and alien way. Somewhere deep inside her, somewhere deep inside that frightened, lost woman — was another person. A new *her*. And that new person had taken over completely in the shop doorway, in a way that she could not describe. It was as if she had gone to sleep and let the new *her* take over. In that sleep, she seemed to hear other, less pleasant noises. Noises that sounded . . . liquid . . . and a faraway, unconnected screaming.

After the boy had provided the fulfilment that she could not explain, she had woken from the dream to find herself back on the streets again; back amongst the throng. The new *her* had departed, leaving the old, lost and frightened *her* behind.

"Please," she begged, of no one in particular and everyone in general. "Please help. I don't know where . . . I'm lost . . ."

One older man, with a Marks and Spencer's carrier bag in each hand, stopped in front of her, genuine concern in his eyes. He started to speak, but she held her arms apart in a plea . . . and for some reason the man's face was now horrorstruck. Pale-faced and trembling, he had uttered an apology and hurried on past her. She watched him go, as he hurriedly bustled into the crowd. Her emotions were changing again. Now she was not only unaware of her whereabouts, but did not even recognise the species of animal which moved past her on all sides as human beings. These things were something else. Something to be hated, something to be used somehow to appease that hideous appetite. With that rage, came a great sense of strength, the new *her* surging through her body again. If she lashed out and seized one of them, then . . . things . . . would start to happen. Things that she could not explain but which would only serve to make her stronger still and eventually make sense of this strange dream she found herself in.

Come on, Eleanor. A voice seemed to be saying in her head. *Have another drink.* And the sound of that voice swept away the hate and the strength and brought back the fear and the hopelessness of being lost in this night-

106

mare. *Knew you were more trendy than I was, Eleanor. Come on, have one of my drinks. Just one more. It's not as if you have to drive home or anything, is it? Go on . . . it's Christmas.*

"Help me!" screamed Eleanor into the night. "Come out of my head and help me find my way home!"

She staggered into the middle of the road.

Horn blaring, a car swerved to avoid her and rammed head on into another car coming in the opposite direction. Glass flew in a hissing spray. Eleanor whirled untouched in the road as the rammed car mounted the pavement, missing passers-by but ploughing into a Thornton's Toffee Kabin window. A shroud of broken glass cracked and shivered around it as people leaped and screamed out of the way. The other car slewed to the other side of the road, horn still blaring. It hit the pavement hard and rocked on its suspension, coming to a stop. The car horn continued to blare. Shoppers on either side of the road were screaming.

And their screaming dispelled Eleanor's fear again, bringing back the hate and the same ravening hunger that she had experienced with the young man in the back alley.

She staggered to the rammed car on the pavement next to the Toffee Kabin. Two men were already trying to pull open a car door to rescue the driver, who lay slumped forward over his wheel. There was a dark stain on the windscreen in front of him. Filled with a loathing for those that screamed around her and those that tugged at the far side door, Eleanor reached the other front door and tugged at the handle. The door swung wide, and now Eleanor was climbing into the passenger seat, eyes riveted on the man at the wheel. His eyes were staring downwards, through the spokes of the driving wheel – as if something terribly interesting was happening at his feet. There was a crimson splash on his face, and more of that crimson was dripping thick as Thornton's toffee from the end of his nose and from his mouth.

She leaned forward, oblivious of the men on the other side of the driver's window who looked at her and cried out in disgust: "Oh bloody hell, *missus* ... !" as she dipped her fingers greedily into his face and began to bring it to her mouth.

There was more screaming now, and someone was retching as she pulled the man back from the wheel so that his head was tilting backwards and more easily accessible. She continued to feed that ravenous, terrible hunger. When she had finished here, there would be many more on the streets from which she could get strength when she needed it.

"Get the hell *away* from him!" something screamed into her face. She felt the blow on her face, lashed out with the new-found strength and felt a part of the attacker come away in her hand. There was a new shrieking, and the sound of it served to fuel her appetite.

A long time later, she could hear the screaming become the monotonous, shrill whine of a police siren. But she neither knew what it was or cared as she continued to grow strong.

THIRTY

"Seven twenty-one? Here's a nice little Christmas story for the kids. Seems we've got a cannibal on Regent Street."

"Say again, thirty-one. A carnival?"

"That's cannibal. Know what I mean. Eats people."

"Nice try, thirty-one. But this is Christmas. Not April Fools' Day. Get on with it or clear the line."

"No need for temper, twenty-one. Straight up. Car accident on Regent Street. Little old lady covered in blood. Except it's not hers."

"Details please, thirty-one."

"Bringing her in under restraint. Medical assistance required. Reason I'm ringing is that her name's on the PNC as missing since . . . here, hang on . . . that's not right . . ."

"Say again, thirty-one."

"Error on PNC, twenty-one. It says here that Mrs Eleanor Parkins has only been reported as missing for . . . two hours? That can't be right."

"Wait a second. Is that the PNC relay on an incident at Fernley House, Newcastle?"

"Wait on . . . Yeah . . . that's it."

"No mistake, thirty-one. Address please?"

"23 Wellingbroke Gardens, Jesmond."

"Mrs Eleanor Parkins from main listing of eighty-four persons. Reference 65498. Age fifty-four. Married. Two children."

"That's the one."

"Definitely no mistake. Relay all details through, thirty-one. I'll have to convey this to Operations Unit at Fernley House."

"Reported missing in Newcastle this evening? But we picked her up in London not an hour ago. She got wings or something?"

"Relay, through, thirty-one. I sense that someone somewhere has made a major cock-up and is in for a hiding from Santa's little helpers . . ."

THIRTY-ONE

Cardiff stared at his blue-white reflection in the window. He was in the ante-room/office behind the reception desk of Fernley House and there was nothing to see out there now; no amber lights from passing cars on the motorway, as the ever-building storm had blocked the roads and stopped the traffic. He could see no details of the car park beyond. Just a void of blackness slashed by dirty city rain and slush which was driving with ever-increasing force at the windows. His face looked ghostly and those unbidden thoughts which were so frequent now, came to him again as he looked at that face.

Is that me? Is that what I've become?

And then, worst of all: *Will I look like that when I'm dead?*

The image of that faceless man behind the wheel of the car that had killed his family came to him again. He wiped it away and strained to look further around to the right. At last he saw the smudged yellow beacons of the police cordon which had been established in the office forecourt and which blocked off the entrance to the building. On return to Fernley House, Cardiff had taken this office on the ground floor – an area set back from the main reception area on the left-hand side overlooking the motorway. The full team requested and confirmed by Central Headquarters was somewhat less than "full", but it *was* Christmas Eve, staff resources *were* limited and the team would be supplemented as soon as possible.

Secondary keyholders for the alarms on the various premises in Fernley House had been contacted at last; all the "out of hours" contacts for emergencies such as fires or burglaries. Preliminary and still incomplete lists of staff had been obtained and enquiries so far had revealed what Cardiff had at last begun to suspect. People who worked there, and who had stayed for Christmas parties – had still not arrived home. The car park had been checked, again with great difficulty, as the severity of the storm had increased. A substantial number of licence-plate numbers checked on the Police National Computer had been cross-referenced, confirming that a substantial number of the car owners should – by rights – still be partaking of the Christmas spirit in Fernley House.

Cardiff stood back from the window and watched the seven main personnel – including Pearce – who formed his Incident Team and (perhaps) Casualty Bureau (if they could *find* anyone that was), quickly establishing the portable computer terminals in his "office" for linkage with Central Headquarters.

His team were not happy.

The storm continued to play havoc with shortwave radio, and now showed signs of interfering with the computer performance and interface. Two of the personnel involved in establishing the Casualty Bureau which would provide information and input/output for members of the families of missing persons were having particular difficulty with a VDU which insisted on giving a crazy-paving display rather than the necessary information.

Arrangements were underway at Headquarters for an early police conference for full briefing and debriefing as well as a potential press conference. Already Central Office was considering the release of partial information internally on a strict "need to know" basis – which always rankled within the force. Cardiff hoped that it wouldn't lead to internal conflict and further breakdown in communications.

A secondary search of all floors had been undertaken.

A pathology squad of three officers were even now re-examining the placc where the severed hand had been

112

found. Cardiff had still to hear from the police pathologist who had collected the severed hand.

And very soon now, Cardiff knew, the press would arrive – even though the ferocity of the storm was managing to keep everyone else away.

The disappearance of the original seven policemen searching the building had not been taken too seriously by Central Office. The reaction of Cardiff's seniors had been typical: *Probably found another Christmas party somewhere.* But there was no time. He had deliberately downplayed it, even though it was already causing communication difficulties at Central Headquarters. He had also instructed Pearce to play down the "noise" they had heard in the basement until the Incident Team was established. Police technicians had checked over the basement again. They had checked the boilers and boarded up the shattered windows. It had been a lightning strike, pure and simple. A *second* lightning strike, in fact. The first had shaken Beaton up with the peculiar acoustic effects the strike had caused beneath ground level. Stranger things had happened.

And yet . . . ?

The seriousness of the actual vanishings and the discovery of the grisly item on the fourteenth floor seemed to have focused a familiar kind of schizophrenia among the police personnel in the building, a schizophrenia which Cardiff had seen before: the depressed sympathy and total sarcasm which seemed to keep the police going in hazardous or harrowing situations.

"Bloody hell."

Cardiff turned to look at Pearce. He was leaning over the shoulder of one of the policewomen who had linked up a computer terminal and was collating initial information. "We've got a link-up here, sir. We're getting this direct . . . it says here . . . because they couldn't telephone it through. Well of course they bloody couldn't, could they! The phones are off! And the . . . hang on . . ." Pearce stubbed out his cigarette and asked the policewoman to copy the

113

information. Again, something else was appearing on screen as the computer printer began to chatter and the information printed out. Pearce's breath hissed through clenched teeth, a familiar habit when it was obvious that something really peculiar was happening.

"What is it?"

"One for Sherlock Holmes I think."

"Come on then, Pearce. Be my Dr Watson."

Pearce tore the print-out sheet from the printer and read out loud as he walked over to join Cardiff.

"Craig's report on the hand is through. He fingerprinted it and he came up trumps. The owner's prints were on record for a drink driving offence in 1988. 'Very handy' it says here."

"Sick, Craig. Sick. And the name?"

"Vincent Saville. An administration and finance officer for Magnus Inc – that's the shipping firm."

"On Floor Fourteen. Where we found the hand."

"That's not the end of it. They've found the body."

"He's dead . . . ?"

". . . and bloody how. We've got a separate report tied in from Jarrow division. Fell through a greenhouse roof in somebody's back garden and . . . this just gets more idiotic . . . it says here the injuries of the body were 'consistent with a fall from a great height, perhaps three or four thousand feet'. They've been checking the local and regional airports for flights passing overhead. But there've been none."

"What the bloody *hell* is going on here?"

"He loses his hand upstairs. Then he runs out, gets a plane somewhere, jumps out and . . ."

"What time was the Jarrow incident reported?"

"Not sure." Pearce nodded to the policewoman, who began immediately to access information on the computer keyboard.

"What I want is the time of the 999 call. I presume that first notification was a police response to an emergency call?"

"Yes sir," said the policewoman. "6.15 p.m. Call received and logged."

"I thought so," said Cardiff. "More impossibilities."

"Sir?" Parker lit up another cigarette.

"Not possible. Beaton – our caretaker. His 999 call was logged in at 6.32 p.m. How can Victor Saville lose a hand here in Newcastle at – let's say 6.00 p.m. – and crash through a greenhouse fifteen minutes later in Jarrow which Dr Watson, as you know, is . . ."

"More than ten miles away . . ." The match burned Pearce's hand and he hastily shook it out.

"Know what?" said Cardiff.

"What?"

"This is more like Hallowe'en than Christmas Eve."

Pearce moved back to the policewoman operating the computer terminal. She was nervous. And Cardiff could see that tension in the others. It was more than having to cancel shifts, bring in people who'd thought they were going home for Christmas Eve with their families. The disappearances were . . . simply put . . . unnerving. Even for the professionals. What should have been treated as a great big stupid Christmas Eve joke was being treated seriously by the people at the top.

Eighty-four people did not just suddenly go missing.

Not tonight.

Not here.

Already, the staff on the ground knew that a first search party of seven policemen suddenly weren't around anymore and that no one was talking about it.

Thunder grumbled in the sky and a brilliant blue-white flash fizzled at the windows, making the panes rattle. Overhead, the strobe lights began to flicker. Cardiff exchanged a glance with Pearce, and then cursed himself silently when he saw that the policewoman had seen their own tension.

No one wanted to be in *this* office block.

"Getting scrambled again here, sir," said the policewoman.

"Storm interference?"

"Yeah . . . but the input is clogging up on file with family requests, asking where their people have gone."

Pearce shrugged, sitting on the desk and looking out into the storm. "Haven't we got a Bureau for Missing Persons? Maybe we could just let them have all the bumph on the case and bugger off down to the boozer."

"New one coming in, sir," said the policewoman in a voice which was so calm that it betrayed how nervous she was feeling.

"On line over here, boss," said one of the other uniformed men from behind her. They had successfully connected their equipment; another direct feed-line on computer, assessing the data being relayed from other national offices. This second model was much more sophisticated than the one which they had so far been using.

"Over to you," said the policewoman, and Cardiff couldn't help but think that the whole thing was like some small combo orchestra, with each instrumentalist allowed their own "solo" input to some bizarre musical piece.

"So long as we *get* it!" said Pearce sarcastically and moved to the man on the newly connected relay.

Cardiff turned back to the window again; feeling less in control than he wanted to be. He looked at his face again. The rain on the window outside was trying to tell him that he was crying. But it was a trick with which he was familiar. He listened to the buzzing and clattering of the word processors and computers behind him. He didn't trust computers. He didn't trust what they told him.

It was much better to talk to people face to face; be it subordinates, victims or criminals. Because when he could see their faces he could use his own instincts, could see subtle things that a machine could never, ever see. But once again, he was in an isolated situation and relying on what the computer told him without being able to look at the faces of the people supplying that information.

He had started this night in the hope that its complexities would take his mind away from something that had been encroaching on him for four years. Something that every

116

policeman was trained to keep in perspective. But this was a perspective he had lost when Lisa and Jamie . . . had been . . .

Murdered! his mind screamed, and he turned back again to the windows, which were still trying to convince him that he was crying. Already he could dimly see that three cars had been stopped at the police cordon and knew instinctively that the media hounds and the newspapermen had finally got the scent. *Even on Christmas Eve. Even on a stinking night like tonight. They can still smell the potential blood of . . .*

Victims, he thought.

Victims and murderers.

It was the policeman's job, whatever the grade, never to allow contact with either to affect him personally or to interfere with the sacrosanct *job.* Now he didn't know whether the job was helping to keep him alive or helping to kill him. Because after Lisa and Jamie's death, the plight of each victim with whom he came into contact *had* affected him — profoundly. His professional distance was lost, and he could feel each case he dealt with killing him inside. Each contact with grief also became his grief; eating away at his soul, destroying him inside. And then there were the others: those who preyed on others, those who killed . . . and Cardiff's dealings with them were also destroying something else inside, his faith in humanity, and any sense of meaning to life.

He thought again of Lisa and Jamie . . . of the man without a face who had killed them . . . and then of the potential answer to his problem in the top right-hand drawer of his desk.

"We're getting scrambled on this one, sir," said Pearce again. "But it seems we've picked up one of the missing people. Mrs Eleanor Parkins. Employed by . . ."

"Found where?"

"Hang on. Employed by 'Johnson and . . .' Shit!" The woman operator sighed in exasperation and sat back. "We've lost it. Lost the whole screen."

"This bloody storm," said the operator. "Let's try again. Anything on line?" she asked the other operator behind her.

"Garbage. But we're still trying. We keep getting it and losing it."

Overhead, the strobe lights flickered again and thunder rolled outside.

"Sir?"

Cardiff turned back to the male operator. "Yes?"

"There's something else coming through here now. I think you should see it."

Cardiff crossed to the VDU and watched as bright-green lettering grew on the screen before his eyes:

Cardiff. Re Fernley House.

Divisional Commander has met with Head of CID. Police Conference pending: Assistant Chief Constable (Crime), Divisional Commanders of Newcastle and Sunderland, Sub Divisional Commanders of above Divisions, Detective Superintendents and Police Press Officer.

Cardiff had expected as much: a conference to collate and evaluate the information received so far, followed by speculation and theory with plans for strategy and action.

"Okay," said Cardiff. "But we need to have these computer links sorted out if we're going to be of any use here. What's the latest on British Telecom, Parker? Any news on when we can expect the telephones to be working again . . ."

"There's more here, sir," said the operator.

Cardiff looked back at the screen.

Incident Squad en route. Code: Darkfall. Restate: Darkfall. To assist in forensic and other scientific investigation. Overall hands-on responsibility to remain . . . And then the words dissolved into a jumbled, meaningless tapestry.

"Storm again, sir."

"Incident Squad?" said Cardiff, realising now with some irritation that Pearce had been standing behind him, reading the message on the screen from over his shoulder. "What the hell's *that* about?"

118

"Darkfall?" echoed Pearce.

"Mean nothing to you?" asked Cardiff.

"No, sir."

"Even less to me."

"What the bloody hell is going on here? I'm either in charge of this investigation or not. Get me a message through."

"I'll try, sir. But the storm . . ."

"Hell, I'll use one of the car radios outside. Bloody modern technology."

"Yes, sir," grimaced the operator, returning to his VDU.

"Car radio's no good," said Pearce. "Just static. I tried again five minutes back. We'll have to reply on the computer for the time being – or send courier back by car."

"Keep on trying, then."

The operator nodded and continued stabbing his fingers at the console keyboard.

"Darkfall," said Cardiff again, and walked back to the window. "What in hell is *that* supposed to be?"

Thunder cracked and lightning sizzled across the sky, making the strobe lights in the ceiling flicker again.

"Darkfall . . ."

THIRTY-TWO

She sat alone in the police cell on a scarred and battered plastic chair. She was looking at the palms of her hands, shoulders hunched and staring down at them — and had been doing so for the past twenty-five minutes. There had been blood on those hands when they'd first brought her to the police station, but she had licked her hands clean since then. The taste was a pleasant memory. Soon, she knew, she would be hungry again.

She looked up at the tiled walls of the cell. There was felt-tip pen graffiti on those walls, and some deep part of her knew that they were *words*, but she did not know what they meant; did not know what words were anymore. The echoes of some unfocused anger behind the meaningless scrawl reflected back to her newborn instincts. She scanned the walls, her gaze resting only briefly on the spare cell bed. The mattress was torn and shredded; plastic foam rubber and tattered fluff lay scattered on the floor. There had been blood on the floor, too . . . but she had licked that up as well when she'd been hungry.

Clean enough to eat your dinner off the floor, Eleanor, said a voice in her head. Those voices kept coming back to her occasionally, but the meaning of those "words" was less and less clear as the minutes ticked by. She looked at the locked cell door, and then at the ceiling. She smiled when she felt an affinity there; with the tiles, and the plaster and the concrete.

She was getting stronger all the time . . . and those outside didn't know it.

When she was hungry, she fed. And when she fed, it

hastened the great changes that were taking place inside her. They thought she was locked up in here. Her smile spread, and she giggled. Her gaze drifted back to the hands in her lap, to her outstretched palms. The skin was white and cement hard; the top layers of skin crumbling like plaster when she flexed her fingers. With more food that crumbling would cease.

Just one more drink, Eleanor, said the voice in her head again. *It's not as if they're kids anymore, is it? They can look after themselves until you get back*. That voice generated a pang of doubt and fear, a fleeting remembrance of another, vague life. It was quickly swamped by the reassertion of her new "mind".

She giggled again, and this time it rattled and wheezed in her rib cage. She coughed, and plaster dust curled from her lips and nostrils, settling like dandruff on her shoulders and clothes. When she shifted in her seat, her innards rustled and crackled like newspaper.

"What is she doing now?" asked a voice, and Eleanor knew that this was not one of the voices from her head. This voice was coming from the other side of one of the cell walls. Her hearing now supernaturally enhanced, she turned with a grin to look at the wall. The grinding of her teeth sounded like sandpaper on marble.

"Nothing, just sitting there."

"Let me see."

A pause. And then Eleanor heard the viewing hatch on the cell door open. She cocked her head sideways to watch and grinned again.

"Bloody hell," said the same voice.

"Look, this is just a police station," said a third voice. "And I don't know what the hell is going on here, but I want that . . . that thing . . . out of here into somewhere more secure. God knows how long she'll stay quiet like that, and I can't risk any more of my people if she suddenly . . . *turns* . . . again."

"Let's get this straight," said the other voice. "She attacked three of your men on the initial callout?"

"Hospital jobs, all of them. I've never seen anything like it. I don't think Jackson is going to make it."

"And then . . . ?"

"Look, you've seen the report . . ."

"And *then*?"

"We sent a squad. But she was as meek as a kitten. Just allowed herself to be led into the van. Said something about having to get home and check on the dinner. Mumbling on about how she shouldn't have stayed for that last drink. Then when we got her back here, she *turned* again. Like a bloody wild animal. We just managed to get her in here and lock the door. Another two of my people . . . God . . . she's . . . it's not human. Just get it out of here . . ."

"And she's been quiet since then?"

Eleanor heard hurried footsteps on the other side of that wall, heading towards the cell door. She smiled again. Food was on its way. A fourth man joined them.

Breathless: "Okay, I've got it. And our people are standing by with the security van."

"Alright, let's get ready."

"You mean the two of you are going in there alone?"

"That's the idea. We've got something here that should keep her quiet."

"Look, I've seen your clearances and I know I'm not supposed to ask questions . . . hell, I've never even *heard* of Darkfall . . . but you're going to need more than just two . . ."

"Just keep out of the way. We know what we're doing."

Even from where she sat, head cocked and smiling her teeth-grinding smile, Eleanor could hear the rumpling of a bag being opened, the metallic chink of something being taken out. There was a pause. The bag was snapped shut again, and the viewing hatch was slid back into place.

"Ready?"

Someone grunted assent . . . and the cell door opened.

Eleanor giggled: a brittle rasp. More plaster dust curled from her mouth like talcum powder.

Two men stepped into the room. One was short and

122

tubby, with thinning hair and a pink face. He was wearing thick-lensed spectacles which enlarged his eyes. The other man was much taller, with a dark coat and blond hair. They moved slowly into the room. The door closed behind them.

"*Food,*" said Eleanor and giggled again.

The taller man with the blond hair moved forward and smiled at her. Behind him, she could see that the man with the pink face was holding a hypodermic in one hand . . . and he looked afraid as the other continued to advance slowly all the while.

"Mrs Parkins?" said the blond man. "Can you hear me, Mrs Parkins? The doctor and I are only here to help you. There's no need . . ."

Eleanor laughed this time; a braying cackle that rattled her rib cage. She raised her hands and flexed her fingers; dry white powder crackled and drifted to the floor.

"Oh, God," said the doctor in a dry voice.

". . . to be afraid," finished the blond man. He looked behind him to check that the doctor was still following. The doctor's face was ashen. Angrily, then: "Come on, Gilbert. You've seen this before . . ." The doctor's eyes were popping, and now the blond man realised that something had begun to happen when he turned away from her. He jerked back.

The woman had risen from her seat and was walking awkwardly towards him. Her limbs made an obscene crackling and rustling as she moved. There was white powder all around the chair she had been sitting on, and she made footprints in it as she moved towards him, raising her arms and smiling that hideous, parchment-faced smile of decay.

"If you want to help me," she said, "give me something to *eat.*"

The tall man moved quickly back to where the doctor was fumbling with the hypodermic and took it from him. But the woman was moving more quickly now and the blond man moved around to her right. The doctor dodged

123

to her left and was swamped with a feeling of sick horror when he saw that she seemed to be more interested in him than in the blond man.

"Mrs Parkins, Mrs Parkins . . ." breathed the pink man, still weaving away from the old lady as she advanced jerkily towards him. She was throwing backward glances at the blond man now, but was still intent on following the doctor with a chilling single-mindedness.

"Come *on*, Rohmer!" moaned the doctor. "For God's sake."

"What the hell have you done with this damned hypodermic?"

"I shouldn't be here. This is Duvall's job — not mine."

"You've *jammed* the hypo . . ."

"Just get the bloody thing into her!"

The pink man was holding out one hand towards her as she advanced, and now Eleanor snatched for that hand as if it was some piece of meat proffered to a wild animal on the end of a zookeeper's pole. Gilbert snatched his hand back and now Eleanor was making a high-pitched keening sound, like some monstrous child deprived of a favourite snack. The whining turned to a mocking laugh and the pink man's face was a mask of horror as she launched herself at him like a screaming banshee. The pink man slithered away down the wall on to one knee as Eleanor connected with the wall, both hands smacking flat against the tiles, cracking the lamination.

Rohmer was behind her now, stabbing the hypodermic into the back of her neck and ramming down the plunger. Eleanor shrieked, whirling back from the wall and slashing out at him. Rohmer felt a claw-fingernail gouging a ragged track across his face as he recoiled. Gilbert fell to the cell floor, vision blurred, and saw the old woman twisting and writhing to grab at the hypodermic, which was still imbedded in the back of her neck. Scrabbling backwards away from her, Gilbert heard a brittle *snap!* as she finally yanked the broken hypodermic free. She began to make that hideous, hysterical, crackling sound of laughter as she held the needle in both claw-like hands, examining it now as if it was some mysterious toy. Now, the old woman was crumpling the hypodermic in her concrete-hard hands as if it was newspaper. Giggling again, she stuffed the broken shards into her mouth and began to chew. Glass and plastic splintered and cracked between those hideous teeth.

"Want *softer* food," she giggled again, and tottered back towards Gilbert – white-powdered, gnarled claws held out towards him.

"Oh Jesus . . ." said Gilbert as those claws reached down for him. Still on the floor he scrambled away from her.

"Mrs Parkins," said Rohmer in a voice that was too calm, and the thing cocked its head to grin at the blond man.

And then something exploded with a detonating roar in the cell, almost bursting Gilbert's eardrums. The old woman's face blew apart in front of him and Gilbert screamed aloud as she fell across his body in a liquid embrace. He struggled to push the monstrosity from his body. Wiping blood from his eyes, he could see Rohmer still looking at the body, with his service automatic weapon still held outwards.

"Shit," he said quietly. "That's *another* one we've lost."

PART TWO

STORMBOUND

"I have felt the wind of the wing of madness"

Baudelaire

ONE

Jimmy sat in the back seat of the panda car, senses returned. The alcohol inside was now only faintly blurring out the throbbing pain in his jaw. He tried to rub it, and then realised that he was handcuffed to the Police Constable sitting next to him. The Sergeant was driving, and the windscreen wipers were waving crescents of slush away from the glass as they headed on into the teeth of the storm.

"So I'm arrested, then?" asked Jimmy at last, shaking his handcuffed wrist so that the policeman's hand also jerked upwards. Simpson angrily jerked their manacled hands down again.

"Depends," said Sergeant Lawrence from the driving seat.

"On what?"

"On your being a good boy, Jimmy."

Simpson blew his nose again, and Jimmy saw with satisfaction from the handkerchief that it was still bleeding.

"This going to take long, then?"

"Not long. Maybe an hour at most," lied Lawrence, not knowing what the hell Cardiff wanted him for anyway.

"Is that *before* or *after* we've stopped in some back alley somewhere?"

"What?"

"You mean you're not going to work me over as usual? Not going to pay me back for the bloody nose, even if you did nearly knock my head off?"

"Don't tempt me," mumbled Simpson into his handkerchief.

129

"Enough of that!" snapped Lawrence. And then, to Devlin: "You know me better than that, Jimmy."

"Yeah, I suppose so," said Jimmy grudgingly. "But I wish I could say the same for your superiors."

"What's he mean?" asked Simpson.

"Never mind," replied Lawrence.

Jimmy gave a quiet, derisive laugh. He looked out into the night at the rain-soaked pavement and the ravaged brickwork of empty and derelict factories, as if trying to recognise something. His attention turned back to Lawrence. He looked at the back of his head carefully for a while before speaking again.

"Two years inside, Sergeant."

"You probably deserved it."

Jimmy laughed again: "Before that, I had two years' apprenticeship in the shipyards. Then the shipyards sank without trace, and it was three years on the dole. Suppose I deserved that as well?"

"Nobody deserves that, Jimmy."

"Oh yes, I forgot. You used to be a welder in the yards didn't you, Sergeant?" Jimmy looked hard at the man who was driving. Simpson could see that they knew each other much better than he'd presumed.

"Thirteen years, son. But you know all about that."

"Maybe I should have joined the force like you. That would have been a laugh, wouldn't it?"

"A scream, Jimmy. An absolute scream."

Jimmy's eyes were drawn to the garish reflection of neon on the pavement outside a working-men's club. He had a fleeting image of a bar, of the people inside, of someone singing Chris Rea's: "Joys of Christmas, Northern Style", and then it had all flashed by in less than a second. Now they were in darker, dirtier streets. But the fleeting images brought back piercing emotions. And like the slide-show slats of light and darkness that washed into the car from passing streetlights as they sped onwards, those emotions were good and bad by turns.

He had met Pamela at a club. She was a singer. Not one

130

of those warbling songstresses who made endless rounds of the clubs with an anonymous backing group. Pamela considered herself "Solo", playing her own keyboards and singing cover versions of songs that, to Jimmy, were better than the originals. From the very start, he had been in love with her, following her act around the clubs. Too shy (and now, he smiled at the word *shy* ever applying to him) to approach her directly in the way that he usually did with women he found attractive. Pamela was special. Deep down, he knew that she would be put off by any direct approach. He had seen others doing that to her in the clubs, and even though he'd felt like stepping in when their attentions were becoming too direct, he had watched her superbly effective "put downs" and stood back in awe. How could he let her think that he was one of them? Eventually, she had noticed him. And it had made him feel big in a way that had nothing to do with macho trappings. She was special – and they had been good together. She had been married before, of course, and he hadn't been surprised to find out. She had two children: Cathy and Noel, seven and five. Her ex-husband had walked out one day for unspecified reasons, never to be seen again. Jimmy cursed him for a fool and thanked him for standing aside. Pamela and he had been living together for a while and, until recently, Jimmy had been close to a happiness previously denied him; both as lover and as surrogate father.

But things had changed. And the change had been with Pamela, not with him.

She'd visited him regularly when he was in prison; but he could see as the months went by that whatever that special something they'd had, it was withering away. Pamela had been the reason he'd been put away. She was the one with the debts and money problems; the one who'd suggested the jeweller's shop job.

But on his release and return, he knew that the time away had ruined everything.

And then one day he'd come home early and found her in bed with someone else. The kids had been sent to her mother's house, and now it seemed that they had a new surrogate father.

And then he remembered the presents.

"Where's the presents?"

"What presents?" asked Simpson through the bloodied handkerchief.

"The Christmas presents I bought for the kids. You've left them behind in that bloody bar, haven't you? I should . . ."

"Calm down." Lawrence picked up the handset and radioed into central headquarters, asking for a policeman to go back to the club.

"Bloody idiots," muttered Jimmy. "If I know *that* club, they'll have been stolen by now."

"Sue us," said Lawrence, and the car swerved left off the highway and pulled into the forecourt of Fernley House.

Jimmy was temporarily blinded by the orange light which suddenly illuminated the car windscreen. The orange light resolved itself into four roadwork lanterns – and then he saw the cordon and roadblock with its black-and-white wooden pole which had been set up ahead, blocking off the entrance road which led up to the office-block frontage and car park. Now he could see a small knot of people in front of that roadblock, dressed in overcoats, caps and hats; attempting, it seemed, to talk their way past half a dozen yellow-anoraked policemen on the other side of that barrier. The huddled knot of men and women saw the car approach and stop. There was an unheard babble of excited conversation and now they were hurrying through the rain towards the car.

"What the hell is going on?" asked Jimmy.

And now the first of the small crowd had reached the car. Faces were peering in on them, voices raised above the sound of the rain and the wind. Knuckles were rapping on the car windows, breath steaming the glass. Somewhere, a camera-bulb flashed and at last he knew who these people were.

"Bloody press," muttered Sergeant Lawrence.

One of the yellow-jacketed policemen elbowed his way to Lawrence's window. The Sergeant wound down the window, and now they could hear the clamouring questions as he showed the policeman his ID. Ice-chilled air flooded the car.

"Come on, Sergeant. What's going on in there?"

"Is it true that *all* of the people in there have vanished?"

"You can't keep a mass murder quiet for long . . ."

"Piss off!" said the policeman examining Lawrence's ID.

"Can we quote you on that?" asked a white-faced, red-nosed newsman.

"Look, come on, you've got to . . ."

"We've got Jimmy Devlin in the back," said Lawrence. The policeman stuck his head through the opened window and examined Jimmy as if he was some strange zoological specimen.

"That's him, is it?" said the policeman unnecessarily.

Lawrence grunted, and the camera bulb flashed again, immediately answered by a fizzling flash of blue-white electricity in the sky and a rumbling of thunder.

Too late, Jimmy quickly raised his non-manacled hand in front of his face.

"We'll raise the barrier. You can take him straight in."

"Whatever's going on," said Jimmy in awe, "I didn't do it."

TWO

By the time that Jimmy had considered making a run for it, it was too late. Hustled through the storm and into the reception area he felt like someone on their way to a firing squad. Chilled and soaked, he was led past the reception desk and the hurried police activity (*had* there been a murder here? Was that what this was all about?) and into the ante-room/office that was being used as the base for the investigation.

A gesture from Lawrence, and Simpson had unfastened the handcuffs. For an instant, Jimmy wondered whether he should hurl himself at the plate-glass windows. Then he saw the reflections there of computer equipment, green VDU screens and police personnel. Lawrence pushed forward to another interior office, knocked and pushed the door open.

Jimmy halted between the two policemen when he saw Cardiff sitting behind a desk, rain pelting against the outside window. The Sergeant and the Constable had continued on for two steps through the door towards their senior officer without realising that they had left Jimmy behind. They started back for him, slightly embarrassed and anxious that he might decide to make a break for it — but there was no need. Jimmy wasn't going anywhere.

"You," said Jimmy, hand held to one side, a crooked smile on his face which contained no humour.

"Hello Jimmy," said Cardiff.

They held each other's look for a long five seconds. And then the Sergeant nudged Devlin and he walked up to the desk where Cardiff was sitting.

"Alright, Cardiff. You going to read me my rights?"

Cardiff leaned forward. "Depends on whether you're arrested or not, doesn't it, Jimmy?"

"What do you mean?"

"Well as far as I'm concerned you're just here assisting with enquiries. After we've had a talk you're welcome to go back home to the wife and kids, enjoy your Christmas. On the other hand, if you want to be awkward then we *will* press charges for assault. I'll read you your rights, you can make a call and then spend Christmas in the cells."

"You're a bastard, Cardiff. Always were."

"Well?"

"Alright . . . but I'm due home soon."

"To wrap up the presents?"

"Watch your mouth, Cardiff. If I do have to stay in the cells over Christmas I'll make sure I ruin your wedding tackle before they take me down."

"Alright, Jimmy. Alright. Let's be polite with each other, then." Cardiff pointed to the seat opposite his desk and Jimmy grudgingly sat down.

"Want this taped, sir?" asked the Sergeant.

"No, I don't think so," Cardiff replied, eyes still on Jimmy. "Not yet." Cardiff looked up then at the Constable, still dabbing at a fresh nosebleed with his now-crimson handkerchief. "Better get that nose seen to."

"Yes, sir." The Constable moved to the door. Jimmy watched him, wondering how long it would be before he met up with this guy again on the street. No doubt he thought that there was a debt to be collected there. It had happened to Jimmy before. He was used to it.

Jimmy turned back to Cardiff. "Okay, I'm here like a good boy. And I'm co-operating. What do you want to know?"

"July 13th, 1988. Fernley Shopping Centre."

"Shit!" Partly in anger, partly in contempt, Jimmy turned away from him again and stared at the outside door, attempting to control his emotions. "So that's . . ." Jimmy dried up in anger again. Then, calmly: "We went through

135

all of that when it happened, Cardiff. There's nothing else to say. It's all . . . what do you call it? . . . part of the official record."

Cardiff opened a cardboard file on his desk. "Jimmy Devlin. Andrew MacAndrews, known as Mac. And Donald Flannery. All three with criminal records. On July 13th, 1988 at 11.32 p.m. Devlin was apprehended in the course of robbing a jeweller's shop in Fernley Shopping Centre . . ."

"Apprehended?"

"That's what it says here."

"Bollocks. You and Pearce were in charge that night. And I telephoned your lot when . . . it happened."

"Telephoned in a panic. Some kind of garbled nonsense over the phone about something that had happened while you were robbing the place."

Jimmy paused, waiting for Cardiff to continue. But Cardiff sat implacably, looking at him.

"Okay," Jimmy continued. "So for no apparent reason, I ring the cops and tell them to get over to Fernley Shopping Centre because something bad has happened. Because Mac and Flannery are dead . . ."

"And while you're getting out of there, you run straight into a patrol car and they arrest you after a chase. It's only then you say you were the person who telephoned. It was an anonymous call. Remember that part of the story? You left all those parts out, Jimmy."

"You stitched me up, you bastard. Stitched me up good and proper."

"My heart bleeds for you."

"You and your bloody mates fingered me for those three other burglaries. And I didn't do them. That's what got me the two years inside, pal. Not the jewellery job."

"Poor Jimmy. Victimised by the police."

"Look . . . what the hell do you want me here for, Cardiff? I've done my time for that job, and the other jobs you laid on me. So what the hell is all this about?"

"MacAndrews and Flannery."

136

"What . . . you mean they've turned up again? But they can't have done. I saw what happened to them. They *must* be dead after that . . ."

"No, they're still missing, Jimmy. I just want you to tell me what happened to them again."

"I've told you! Told you all then and no one would believe me, so I changed my story."

"So tell me again. The *original* story."

"Yeah, well . . . we went over that at the time, didn't we?"

"Then you changed your story."

"No one believed me, Cardiff. Least of all you. Thought I was copping a plea on . . . diminished responsibility. Trying to get out of a prosecution and into a cosy mental home."

"And your accomplices got away — never to be seen again."

Jimmy gritted his teeth. Cardiff could see that the knuckles on his right hand were white where he clenched the chair rest. When he spoke again, his voice was bitter and guttural.

"That's because they're dead."

"So you say. But where are the bodies? The way we see it, they both did a runner and they've been in hiding ever since."

"For two years?"

"They both had form, Jimmy. More form than you. And there were other reasons why we wanted those two. Other jobs they'd pulled off over the years that we can nail them for."

"Like the way you nailed me? I did two years on account of you, Cardiff."

"An innocent man, eh? So you're *not* a thief, then?"

"Look, Cardiff. We were robbing that jeweller's. No use denying that. Then that . . . that *thing* happened. And they were both killed, whatever you say. I telephoned you. *Me!* Now what the bloody hell would I have done something like that for unless something bad had happened? We could

137

have just done the place over and that would have been that. We'd got past the security and into the shop for the stuff. Believe me, it was an easy job. We were ready to do a bunk. Doesn't make sense, does it?"

Jimmy was silent for a while, and Cardiff could see that he was reappraising the situation. Finally, he spoke again: "Look, Cardiff. It was dark. There was a storm that night. Just like tonight. Lights and shadows. I don't know. Maybe I *did* see things. Maybe what I thought I saw happen to them both didn't really happen at all."

Jimmy's words seemed to stick and hold inside Cardiff's mind. *There was a storm that night. Just like tonight.* "So tell me again. What happened to MacAndrews and Flannery?"

"They . . ."

From somewhere outside came the sounds of some kind of commotion; raised voices and the clattering of a glass door. The "interview room" door opened again and Sergeant Lawrence poked his head around the corner.

"Sir . . . ?"

The sound of raised, angry voices was louder.

"What the hell's going on?" asked Cardiff.

"I think you'd better come, sir. We've got visitors."

Cursing, Cardiff rose from his seat as PC Simpson entered the room again.

"What about me?" asked Jimmy in exasperation.

"You just stay," said Cardiff. "Keep an eye on him, Simpson."

The Police Constable with the bloodied nose blew into his handkerchief, glaring at Jimmy as Cardiff left the room with Lawrence.

Jimmy smiled at him, lounging back into his chair and crossing his hands on his belly.

"You would have used that broken pint glass on me, wouldn't you?" said Simpson.

"No . . ." replied Jimmy. "I'm just a big noise, that's all. But I dare say you won't believe that. So what the hell, eh?"

138

"Not all police are bastards."

Jimmy smiled.

"So what's Santa bringing you this year, then?" he asked.

Simpson grimaced, and blew his nose again.

THREE

Cardiff reached the corridor leading to the reception area and saw the source of the disturbance immediately.

A tall blond man wearing a greatcoat was standing by the glass reception doors, stroking rain and slush from his sleeves. Pearce was standing in front of him, talking angrily and pointing to those doors as two other men began to push clumsily inside, admitting a gale of icy air that even Cardiff could feel from his position. The men were carrying large metal cases of some kind, like metallic suitcases, and Cardiff heard Pearce exclaim . . .

"Who the hell *are* these people?"

. . . as the blond man continued to brush the rain from his coat, seeming to ignore Pearce completely. A yellow-jacketed police constable – one of the men at the security barrier – followed sheepishly behind the two men with the cases as they moved into the reception area. Pearce rounded on him fiercely and the policeman held his arms wide in supplication.

Cardiff strode down the corridor towards them, followed by Lawrence.

The outside door banged open again and a fourth stranger, also wearing a greatcoat, pushed inside and squeezed past Pearce and the Constable.

"And who the hell is *that*?" demanded Pearce of the Police Constable. "That thing outside . . . the thing you're supposed to be supervising, in case you didn't know . . . is a security cordon. But for all the bloody good it's doing it might as well not be there!"

"They had ID, sir," said the Police Constable weakly. "They're men from . . ."

"I don't care if they're the Men from Uncle, you should be keeping everyone . . ."

"It's okay, Pearce," said Cardiff as he strode to meet them.

The blond man looked up at last — and his eyes latched on to Cardiff.

Something seemed to happen then.

Something that Cardiff could not explain, but which had a peculiar clarity and depth which shook him. Because he seemed to feel the question emanating from this tall blond stranger's icy-blue eyes.

Is it you?

Outside, lightning flickered and lit up the glass reception doors. The crack and hollow booming of the thunder rattled the panes. And Cardiff seemed to hear that unspoken question again:

Is it you?

Cardiff retained eye contact with the blond man as he drew level.

When the stranger spoke, it was in a perfectly modulated and even tone. Cardiff was now somehow not surprised to find that the sound of the man's voice was familiar — even though they had never met before.

"My name's Rohmer."

He brushed more snow from his sleeve and gave a curious half-smile.

"I'm from D21. And these are my men." Rohmer brought out an ID card and showed it to Cardiff. Cardiff had seen similar identification only four times in his professional life. On each occasion, it had meant that the operation on which he was engaged would soon be taken out of his hands. "The man behind me here is Duvall." The other man in the greatcoat gave a perfunctory flip of his ID wallet. He had short, black hair with a brutally regimented parting and a somewhat effete face that failed to conceal an undeniably hard and no-nonsense efficiency.

141

Pearce appeared on Cardiff's left. "Sorry, sir. They should have been stopped at the block . . ."

"Never mind." Cardiff looked over to where the other two strangers were laying their metal suitcases carefully down in the main reception area under the watchful eye of Pearce's men. The yellow-jacketed policeman shuffled uneasily from foot to foot, uncertain of what they should be doing now.

"And the other two?" asked Cardiff.

"Gilbert and Frye. They're . . . scientists." Rohmer turned away from Cardiff and began to walk over to them. There were too many questions. It was too soon for the operation to be taken away from Cardiff before he found out just what was going on in this hellish office block.

"Rohmer?"

The blond man turned back.

"That's not enough."

Rohmer smiled that half-smile again and returned.

"You'll have been given a directive from D21?"

"No."

Rohmer paused again, as if weighing Cardiff up. Thunder grumbled somewhere in the sky again and rain hissed at the windows.

"Top security clearance from your Central HQ? We have a code name for our operation."

Cardiff shook his head, and this time the half-humour in Rohmer's eyes had gone. When he spoke again, his voice was harsh and clipped.

"Darkfall."

"Don't know what you're talking about," said Cardiff, seeing from the corner of his eye that Pearce was looking at him quizzically. *Darkfall.* The word on the computer screen just before the message broke up.

"That's not possible," continued Rohmer. "You must have received instructions."

"This storm has knocked out the telephones. Our radios are screwed up." From the reception area, the other two newcomers looked up sharply.

"And your computer link?"

"The messages are scrambled. Like I said – the storm."

Rohmer smiled again, and this time it was as if he'd just heard the best news of the evening. One of the other newcomers was hurrying over.

"Then I suggest you send one of your people back to HQ and receive your orders by hand."

"I've done that. We're waiting."

Cardiff watched the other newcomer's hurried approach. The man was slight, with stooped shoulders, a pink face and thick spectacles that magnified his eyes, making the sockets look like deep pits in his skull. He was plastering wet threads of hair over a balding pate, and there was a look of alarm in those magnified eyes.

"Telephones and radio out?" he asked.

"Yes," said Rohmer, without taking his eyes from Cardiff.

"And you ... you said the computer messages were ..."

"Scrambled," finished Rohmer for him. "That's what the man said."

"Look, Rohmer. We were advised ..."

"Check with Frye."

"If what he says is true, this can't be residual weather effects."

"We took readings beforehand, didn't we?"

"Well, yes ..."

"And Frye is taking readings now, isn't he?"

"They're negative," said the man from the reception area. Cardiff looked back to see that the other man had opened one of the metallic cases and taken out what seemed to be earphones, which he was now wearing. The metal case was a portable computer.

"The readings are all negative."

"You see, Gilbert? Nothing to worry about."

"Maybe you can start telling me what this is all about, Rohmer?" said Cardiff. "We're in the middle of an investigation and, quite frankly, we don't want anyone from Central HQ getting in the way."

"We're part of your investigation now."

"Explain."

"For the time being you're still in charge, Cardiff. We'll be conducting a series of scientific tests — quite separately from your own forensic people. When you do get your orders back from HQ, you'll see that you're to withdraw your people and leave everything to us. For the time being you will retain hands-on responsibility for the operation but afford us any assistance we require. No questions, no hindrance. Just allow us to continue."

"No questions, no hindrance?"

"That's right. Your new orders will also confirm that I am to assume overall charge of the investigation. We represent the preliminary research team. Another unit of Central Government operatives and forensics are already on their way here to replace your people."

"Not good enough, Rohmer."

"For the time being, you're to carry on as normal."

"Still not good enough."

Rohmer half-smiled again.

"I've only your word," continued Cardiff. "That's not good enough. If you do want assistance, and no hindrance, then you'll have to answer some questions."

"You could be in serious trouble, Cardiff. These instructions . . ."

"*When* they arrive."

"As you say, when these instructions arrive, you'll find that they come from the very top. I don't believe that any obstruction on your behalf at this stage will be looked on kindly."

"Let me put it another way. Answer some questions . . . or else I'll make my own arrangements."

"And what arrangements would they be?" smiled Rohmer.

"I'll have you thrown out into the fucking snow until my new orders arrive."

"Gilbert!" The man with the headphones was beckoning urgently. Gilbert turned and scurried back to him.

"Then it seems we're at an impasse until . . ." began Rohmer.

And then the screaming began.

Cardiff spun around in shock, seeing all of the others reacting in exactly the same way, as the hideous, agonised cacophony echoed and reverberated around them. It was a deafening chorus of human agony; a shrieking cacophony of men and women's voices, dozens — perhaps hundreds of them — all wailing and shrieking in mortal torment.

But there was no one to be seen.

Cardiff whirled, searching the corridor and the surrounding area, as the screaming continued. It seemed to be coming from everywhere — and nowhere — at once. But the dreadfulness of the sounds was intensified by the horrifying *nearness* of those agonised voices. Cardiff ran to the glass doors, wiped the moisture from the pane and looked out into the night at the blurred orange glow of the traffic cordon — but could see nothing else. Pearce moved quickly behind the reception desk and flung open the door. Beyond, the computer personnel were looking around in horror, some with hands over their ears as the screaming went on and on.

Cardiff swung back into the lobby. Only Rohmer appeared to remain unmoved by the hideous cacophony as Cardiff strode hurriedly past him. The Operations Room door banged open again and Simpson burst out into the reception area, with Jimmy Devlin close behind him.

"What the hell . . . ?" said Simpson, gazing around in shock and horror.

They were the first words spoken since the horrifying, shrieking tumult had begun and the word registered strongly with Cardiff for those shrieking, howling, tormented voices indeed sounded like a horde of the damned from Hell. Someone, somewhere had opened a door into Hades — and they were hearing the torment of the damned.

"Where is it *coming* from?" shouted Pearce over the cacophony.

Oh God help me. GOD HELP ME, wailed one voice louder than the rest. *IT HURRRTTSS!*

Thunder crashed in the sky, and Cardiff felt the vibrations in his feet. And then he heard something else which utterly horrified him. Another voice, another man's voice rose louder in agony from the dreadful screaming and echoed plainly in the reception area.

Help me! Help me! HELP ME, CARDIFF!

It was a voice that he recognised.

The shock was redoubled when Cardiff recognised yet *another* voice in that bedlam of torment.

Let me go! LET ME OUT! LET MEEEE . . .

And then thunder crashed again, its impact slamming shut that door into Hell. The voices were abruptly cut off.

Everyone remained frozen in their positions, looking at each other, waiting for the hellish sounds to begin again.

Now, Cardiff could hear a hubbub coming from the Operations Room behind the reception area as people emerged from their shocked silence. Through the open door he could see the computer personnel; some with hands still over their ears, others looking around at the walls and ceiling.

"Everyone okay in there, Simpson?"

"Yes . . . yes . . ." replied the Constable. "I think so, but . . ."

"My God, Jack," said Sergeant Lawrence. "What was it?"

Everyone was coming out of it now. Pearce moved quickly to join Cardiff.

"Well?" shouted Jimmy. "What the hell was *that*?" as he tried to push past Simpson and into the lobby. Simpson tried his best to restrain him. His nose was bleeding again.

"Devlin!" snapped Cardiff. "Behave yourself if you want to go home."

Rohmer turned quickly and looked in Jimmy's direction.

"Devlin," he said in wonder, under his breath.

146

Pearce took Cardiff by the sleeve. There was a wildness in his eyes that hadn't been there before.

"One of them called your name," he said.

"I know . . ."

And now Rohmer and Gilbert were beside them.

"You know who it was?" asked Rohmer in that quiet, modulated voice. Cardiff turned to see that Rohmer was the only one apparently unaffected by what they'd all just heard. Unruffled, his face was now a mask of deep interest.

"Yes," said Cardiff. "The one who called me by name was Evans, my driver – one of the police constables who went missing earlier. The other was Farley Peters – a journalist."

"You mean you've had *more* disappearances?" gasped Gilbert. His face was wet with perspiration, and there was fear on that face. Cardiff saw that he was wearing gloves and that he was pulling at them nervously, as if afraid that they might come off. "I mean . . . since the initial disappearance?"

And then it occurred to Cardiff: "Oh Christ. The forensic people upstairs. They're looking at the same place where . . ."

Pearce rushed to the elevator.

"Someone's coming down."

Cardiff pushed past Rohmer and Gilbert to join him, and they both watched as the elevator light above the main double-doors began to descend from fourteen.

. . . nine . . . eight . . . seven . . .

And behind him, Cardiff listened to Rohmer and Gilbert speaking *sotto voce.*

"Frye had a reading," said Gilbert in his cracked voice. "Just briefly, before those . . . noises . . . began. It's stopped now. But it could have been a strike. Couldn't it, Rohmer?"

. . . six . . . five . . . four . . .

"Rohmer," continued Gilbert. "Were you lying? It's still happening, isn't it?"

"No, it's not. We're quite safe."

147

... three ... two ...

"But what if we get a Returner?"

"That's what Duvall's for."

Cardiff turned to see Duvall loosening his overcoat slowly as he moved to draw level behind them as they watched the elevator doors.

... one ... Ground ...

"Stand away from the elevators, please," said Duvall. It was the first time that he had spoken. His voice was cultured Oxbridge, and the grim intent in that voice made Cardiff and Pearce stand obediently aside. Something like resentment was beginning to swell in Cardiff; a resentment that he was now doing as he was told by these newcomers – these newcomers who seemed to have more answers than he did for whatever in hell was going on here.

"What the hell are you ... ?" began Cardiff, and then he saw Duvall reaching into his overcoat pocket, sensing his tension as the elevator light *pinged!* and the doubledoors slid open.

"Christ, look out!" shouted Pearce as a figure blundered out of the elevator. Cardiff elbowed Duvall aside when he recognised that figure immediately. It was one of the laboratory people: Edgar.

"Those noises!" gasped Edgar as he reeled into the corridor.

Duvall untensed, standing aside as the three other members of the forensic team blundered out into the corridor. Now, resentment exploded in Cardiff as he rounded on Rohmer.

"What the hell is wrong with you people? What were you expecting?" Rohmer remained silent.

"What in God's name made those noises?" blurted Edgar, looking around, as if expecting to see some scene of carnage.

"You heard them as well?" asked Pearce. "Up there?"

"Bloody horrible. All around us. Sounded like a bloody slaughter. What's going on, Cardiff?"

Cardiff turned to Pearce as the elevator doors slid shut

again, pausing only briefly to see that Rohmer was standing almost nonchalantly with his back to the corridor wall and with that infuriating half-smile on his face again. He struggled to contain his burgeoning resentment. "Alright, Pearce. I want everyone out of here before there's a panic. Get the computer people to clear out as quickly as possible. Edgar, I don't know how far your people got upstairs . . ."

"Nothing. Just minor bloodstains on the carpet where you found the hand. That was it."

"Okay. Then you don't need a second telling. I want you all out."

Rohmer pushed himself away from the corridor wall, smiling.

"Very sensible, Cardiff. You second-guessed me."

"Don't patronise me," said Cardiff tightly. "I still want some answers."

"Maybe you will get them after all."

Cardiff turned back to Pearce. "I want the whole building cleared. These people are taking over. But I want the roadblock maintained . . ." Cardiff turned and looked squarely at Rohmer, ". . . and I'm staying."

Pearce gestured to Simpson, still trying his best to restrain Jimmy Devlin. "Come on, you heard him." Simpson started forward, pulling Jimmy by the sleeve.

"He's staying," said Rohmer calmly.

Cardiff turned back. "What?"

"Jimmy Devlin. Twenty-three years old. Petty thief. Robbed Hanson's Jewellers in 1988."

"Always wanted to be a celebrity," said Jimmy. And then to Cardiff: "And who the hell is blondie, anyway?"

"Maybe you *do* know more than I'm giving you credit for, Cardiff," said Rohmer. "He stays."

"Like hell I do," said Jimmy, pulling away from Simpson's grasp.

"He's assisting with enquiries," said Cardiff. "He's not under arrest."

"So he can stay and assist me with my enquiries."

"Get fucked," said Jimmy.

149

"In that case, Mr Devlin," said Rohmer, "you're under arrest."

"On what charge?" asked Cardiff.

"Bad language in a built-up area."

Cardiff looked long and hard at Rohmer as Duvall drew level, reinforcing his authority.

"Okay, Simpson," said Cardiff. "You join the others. Looks like you and I are staying, Jimmy."

Duvall moved to take charge of Jimmy while Simpson slipped resentfully away, dabbing at his nose. Jimmy slouched back against the wall, and Cardiff was surprised to see a look of real concern on Rohmer's face as he moved forward and pulled Jimmy away from it. The concern melted into humour again, when Rohmer saw that Cardiff was watching.

"Bad posture," said the blond man. "Not good for the health."

"When the building's cleared," said Cardiff, "we talk."

Rohmer smiled . . . and nodded.

FOUR

Cardiff watched as the three policemen on the cordon-barrier lifted the wooden pole and the last of the police cars slid past and vanished into the storm. No matter how much he wiped at the condensation on the window, he could still barely see what was going on out there. The storm was reaching a savage pitch. The snow was driving down now but even through that whirling vortex of frozen city detritus, none of it seemed to be making any impression on those glistening black pavements or the tarmac. Cardiff couldn't help but remember Beaton's words: *Nothing white ever sticks here*. Visibility was severely restricted and the policemen still on duty at that cordon were dim blurs, as indeed was Pearce, who was out there now, supervising the departure of what had become, in essence, a rather ineffective investigation team.

Thunder rattled the windowpane through which Cardiff was looking and the strobe lights fizzled and flickered yet again.

The effect unsettled him, and he found the fact that he could still be unsettled somehow curious. He recalled the incident in the boiler room when both Pearce and he had been assailed by the same noises that Beaton had heard. A lightning strike? Well, yes . . . it must have been. That was the obvious answer. But why did he feel that there was something more, and why wasn't he acting on that instinct, the way that he'd always acted? Why did he want to hold his peace? Why had he kept Pearce quiet about their experience? And what the hell had happened when he'd first met Rohmer?

151

Is it you?

The depth of semi-recognition, even though they'd never met, was puzzling and disturbing. The potency of that question and those three words had affected Cardiff profoundly.

Is it you?

What the hell did it mean? And had Rohmer really felt the same thing?

"Maybe not," Cardiff said to himself. "Maybe it's all part of the process of cracking up."

Cardiff had supervised the clearance of the office block, noting wryly that it seemed easier to clear everyone out than it had been to get his original team established.

The noises ... the screaming ... had unnerved everyone.

Pearce had given the necessary instructions to a depressed, disillusioned and just plain pissed-off police cordon outside that the "block" had to be maintained. Two men would remain "on shift", to be relieved by two others when all of the team had returned through this furious storm to Central Headquarters. The two men already there had been on duty now for two hours. Even their police greatcoats had been insufficient to keep out the chill and the wet of this storm. The waiting outside in the wind and the snow had been too much for a majority of the newsmen who had shown up originally. As the storm had increased in strength, so it seemed that the enthusiasm of the pressmen on the "public's right to know", coupled with the fact that the pubs were still open in town, had served to weaken their resolve somewhat. Only a smattering of perversely conscientious newsmen and women remained outside the cordon ... and their resolve seemed to have paid off when the police began to leave the building, climbing hurriedly into their cars and vans.

The policemen on the cordon had lifted the barrier-pole to let the small convoy of police cars and vans past, ignoring with more than a little impatience the fusillade of questions thrown at them by the remaining newspeople.

"Why are they leaving?"

"Who are the new people? Have they found out what's happened to everyone inside yet?"

"There still seem to be others inside. Can you tell us what's . . . ?"

Anxious to get news of this latest development back to their own offices and realising that there was unlikely to be any more to be gleaned from this unpleasant vigil, the remaining newspeople departed as the small convoy of police traffic vanished into the maw of the blizzard.

They were to be the last to escape from the Teeth of the Storm.

Cardiff turned away from the rain-streaked window as the policemen on cordon-duty lifted the wooden pole and the last of the cars slid away into the night.

His attention was drawn away from the rain-streaked windows by the sound of Gilbert's voice, again nervously asking questions of Rohmer.

"Are you sure, Rohmer? You must be *sure* that it's over . . . ?"

Cardiff turned back and when Gilbert saw that he was watching, he became instantly silent. He returned to assist Frye, who was standing now with a frown of concentration on his face. Cardiff could see that he had attached a microphone of some kind to the metal container which still rested on the chair and which had been giving the so-called mysterious "readings". Now, he was holding that microphone up to the nearest wall and scanning it, adjusting his headphones. Cardiff watched him scan the wall, and then hold it up to the ceiling. Instantly, the metal container began to emit a clicking sound.

A Geiger counter? Is that what he's doing . . . registering radioactivity?

Rohmer seemed to be reading his mind. He had been watching Cardiff, and now that infuriating secret smile registered again. He shook his head.

"No, Cardiff. Not a Geiger counter . . ."

"Look," said Jimmy. "How long do you intend to keep me here?"

Since Simpson had left the building with the others, Duvall seemed to have acquired the position of Jimmy Devlin's personal guard. While Jimmy stood at the reception desk counter, both arms spread out on it backwards in the same pose that he had adopted at the bar counter earlier that evening, Duvall simply stood two feet by his side, watching him. For all the world, he reminded Cardiff of some kind of Gestapo officer. Well dressed, well groomed with that clipped, perfect accent . . . but enough about him to make anyone realise that Duvall, whoever in hell's interest he represented or whatever in hell he was doing here, was a dangerous man. Jimmy seemed aware of that too, and kept a wary eye on him while he addressed Cardiff.

Rohmer turned his attention back to Jimmy as Gilbert and Frye continued taking their mysterious readings. Cardiff noticed that they had turned the microphone towards the floor now, but the clicking from the metal container had stopped.

"Those screams," said Rohmer. "You've heard something like that before. Haven't you, Jimmy?"

Jimmy had been shaken by those sounds, more shaken than the others, for good reason, but Cardiff could see that he was unprepared to show it as he pushed himself away from the reception counter. Cardiff remained silent. It seemed that Cardiff's curious patchwork quilt of instinct and gut feeling was about to be sewn together by Rohmer.

"Yeah," said Jimmy. "I've heard something like it before. Same kind of . . . echo. Same kind of bloody pain – like people being torn apart. Except that time it was . . . my friends."

"MacAndrews and Flannery," said Cardiff simply.

"Yeah. Like I've been trying to tell everyone from the beginning."

"You heard those noises on the night you were robbing

the jeweller's," continued Rohmer. "On the night your friends . . ."

"Look," said Cardiff impatiently. Rohmer was spreading this game out too long. "Where *are* they, Rohmer? There were eighty-four people in here two hours ago. Apart from Saville and Mrs Parkins, who turn up bloody miles and miles away . . . the others have just vanished. So where the hell have they gone?"

"So you do know about those two? I thought that information had been suppressed."

"Suppressed? *Suppressed?* Just what the hell are you talking about?"

The reception doors banged open again. Cardiff started, turning in alarm to see that it was Pearce, now pushing into the comparative warmth of the reception area from outside. He was soaked. Angry at the interruption, Cardiff turned back to Rohmer.

"Answers, Rohmer. *Answers!* Where the hell have they all gone?"

"You know, don't you, Jimmy? You've told them all what happened to your friends in the jeweller's. You've told Mr Cardiff and Mr Pearce before. Tell them again."

"Bit of a bastard, aren't you, blondie?" said Jimmy and Duvall moved forward threateningly. Without moving or even looking at his new escort, Jimmy said: "If he wants to start a fight in here, I'm ready to oblige."

"Tell us again, Jimmy," said Rohmer in a gentle voice.

"Want the truth? Well, I'll tell you."

Duvall settled back against the reception counter as Pearce continued to shake water from his greatcoat, but the others were silent. Even Frye and Gilbert had stopped their "scanning" to listen. Somewhere in the sky, thunder groaned. Jimmy looked up at the ceiling when he heard it.

"There was a storm on that night. Just like this one. I was working on the safe. The others were leaning against the wall, just waiting for me to finish. Then there was a sound, like an explosion. The whole building seemed to shake. It must have been a lightning strike. They were

155

leaning against the wall when it started to happen . . ."

Thunder crashed again. Black and white sizzled at the windows. It sounded now as if the storm must be directly overhead.

"They began to scream," continued Jimmy. "As if something was . . . *killing* them. I was frozen there, I couldn't move — just watching them. They were . . . sort of . . . writhing around . . . struggling . . . trying to push themselves away from the wall.

"But they were stuck there. They were *stuck to the wall* — like flies on a flypaper."

Cardiff could see the sweat on Jimmy's brow.

"Mac started to scream at me, yelling 'Help me, Jimmy! I'm stuck!' But I couldn't move. I could only watch as the lightning lit up the windows and they struggled to get off that wall."

"Bollocks," said Pearce at last.

Jimmy glowered at him in hate. "*The wall swallowed them up*. I saw it happen, and I couldn't do a thing to help them. It just sucked them in as if that wall was made of . . . mud or something. They thrashed around, kicked and screamed and begged me to help . . . but I couldn't move. Flannery was the first to go completely. His face was stuck to the wall. When it sucked in his head he couldn't scream anymore. It took him quickly. But Mac was fighting harder. His arms had sunk in and he was twisting around, thrashing his head to keep it away from the wall — but it still sucked him in."

"Just like the tar baby, eh?" said Pearce.

"Shut up," said Cardiff, and Rohmer was smiling again when he saw Cardiff's grim expression. "Go on, Jimmy. Then what happened?" At last, Jimmy was telling the story that had first prompted Cardiff to seek him out and bring him here. Pearce's words when the six policemen had vanished had reminded him about Jimmy Devlin and his bizarre story of what had happened two years ago.

They've just vanished into the woodwork, Pearce had said.

"I ran," continued Jimmy. "I just broke and ran — with Mac screaming for help. I burst out through that jeweller's door and back into the shopping mall. Behind me, I could hear Mac's screaming turn . . . *muffled* . . . must have been when . . . when his face was sucked into the wall. Then it sort of . . . gargled away . . . and I kept on running."

"But it started again, didn't it?" said Rohmer.

Jimmy eyed Rohmer carefully. "Know all about me, don't you?"

"Everything."

"Yes, it started again while I was running to get out of that place. Mac and Flannery, screaming my name, screaming for help. They were in agony — and the sounds . . . kind of . . . *echoed*."

"And where were the screams coming from, Jimmy?"

Jimmy paused, swallowing hard.

"From the walls, from the floors . . . from the bloody ceiling. Like the noises we've just heard." Jimmy stood back again. "That's it. That's all there is."

"Bloody stupid," said Pearce.

"No, it's not," said Cardiff quietly. "That's why I wanted Devlin here. God knows why I should have thought of his crazy story again. Maybe something about the way he told it, as if *he* believed it . . . maybe the disappearances . . . or the storm . . ."

"Or maybe you're just a better policeman than you think you are," said Rohmer. "A man of instinct, eh, Cardiff? And here's me thinking you knew more than you do."

The Nightmare had taken further shape. His gut instinct about Jimmy had been right — even if none of this made any real sense yet.

"You see, Cardiff?" said Rohmer, apparently pleased with himself. He ran a hand through his blond hair, turning to look at Gilbert and Frye. "You see? It's the same."

"Am I missing something?" asked Pearce.

"The people in this office block," continued Rohmer. "All eighty-four of them. They never really disappeared, because they're still here." Rohmer spread his arms wide, turning to encompass the entire reception area with a kind of mad glee. "In the walls, the ceiling, the floor. They've been absorbed . . . and we heard their screams — because they're still here!"

Gilbert now seemed even more agitated than before. Plucking at his gloves again, he said: "What are you doing, Rohmer? This is all classified information and I *know* that these people haven't clearance."

"Gilbert, Gilbert . . ." said Rohmer, as if pacifying some nervous child. "You worry too much."

"But I don't understand why . . ."

"Trust me, trust me."

"Explanations?" said Cardiff tightly.

Rohmer looked over and smiled his infuriating smile again.

"Very well."

FIVE

"Fernley House is not an isolated incident," said Rohmer.

He was sitting on the edge of the desk used to interrogate Jimmy Devlin earlier, having retired to that room for explanations. Duvall, Gilbert and Frye had remained in the reception area on Rohmer's instructions. Cardiff, Jimmy and Pearce sat on uncomfortable plastic chairs while Rohmer talked. "There have been disappearances like this before."

"I knew it," said Jimmy quietly. "I knew I wasn't going out of my head."

"Just recently," continued Rohmer. "A similar thing has happened at a school in Norfolk and a factory in Leeds. But this has a history stretching as far back ... well, to tell you the truth – to when records began. There's been an acceleration of incidents in the last five years. But prior to that ... all the famous disappearances you've read about in the Sunday tabloids are all part of the same phenomenon. The Marie Celeste in 1852, when an entire ship's crew vanished. The disappearance of Flight 19 just off Bermuda ..."

"Come on," said Jimmy in disdain. "You're not saying this is Bermuda triangle stuff."

"It happens there, yes. Frequently. But the phenomenon is not restricted to that area. It's been happening all over the world for quite some time."

"Who *are* you, Rohmer?" asked Cardiff.

"The Ministry of Defence and Central Government established a team ten years ago when the disappearances became too frequent and too alarming to be ignored. That team is split into three Divisions and I'm in charge of one of them. Gilbert and Frye are scientists involved in analysis. The rest of the team are on their way . . ."

"And Duvall?" asked Cardiff. "What does he do?"

Rohmer smiled, ignoring the question as he continued.

"We know what's happening. But not why it's happening. And even though we've issued 'D' notices on these events, it's only a matter of time before we have a panic on our hands."

"D notice?" said Jimmy.

"It's a clampdown on press reports," said Cardiff. "A joint agreement by the media and the Government not to report on particular matters."

"Which is why none of the reporters clamouring around your office block earlier tonight will see their stories in print."

"You say you don't know why this is happening," said Cardiff. "*How* is it happening, then?"

"You know that the code name for our operation is Darkfall. Well, that's the name of our tri-partite investigation team: a team with statutory powers to override investigations such as yours, Cardiff. It's also the term we've applied to the phenomenon which results in these disappearances."

Thunder boomed in the sky overhead and Rohmer looked at the ceiling again. He had a look of intense concentration for several seconds. And when he spoke again, it was almost as if in reverence.

"*That's* what a Darkfall sounds like."

He paused, while the thunder died away — and this time his voice was clipped, precise and businesslike.

"A Darkfall is a particular kind of storm. Quite how the storm is generated is still something that we're investigating, although we have some idea of what causes its generation. All storms contain a force which we take for granted. A force that provides us with food and warmth and light . . . and upon which we've become very dependent, maybe to our cost. Because although we've harnessed that force,

160

know how to generate it and use it – it is still essentially a force about which little is known in terms of its effects on *us*.

"I'm talking about electricity.

"There's a positive side to that force. The elements I've just mentioned. But there's a dark side to that force, too. And a Darkfall storm seems to embody those dark elements."

"A Darkfall is an electrical storm?"

"Basically, yes. But it has particular characteristics. It builds and remains in a very localised position. It is particularly fierce and is accompanied by a peculiar state of darkness. By meteorological means we're now able to identify where such a storm will occur with greater efficiency and to take steps for keeping that area clear of people – or to arrange for controlled evacuation. But there are still occasions – such as this – where the phenomenon eludes us. The storm builds to a particular intensity. Its central 'core' is where the phenomenon occurs. And anything within the storm 'funnel', as we call it, can be subject to the phenomenon or anything which passes through it. The electricity within that storm is released by lightning. We believe that the phenomenon occurs when there is a lightning strike."

"Lightning struck this building?"

"Yes, I believe so. More than once. On the first occasion, your partygoers disappeared. On the second, your forensic team upstairs."

"What the hell happened to them?" asked Jimmy.

"The Darkfall strike generates what we can only call at this stage a chemical reaction. It's a chemical reaction which affects inert compounds such as concrete, steel, plastic – and living tissue.

"Skin contact is the means of absorption. Anyone who is unprotected and is touching anything connected with the building would be absorbed. The inert compounds react with living tissue and absorb the entire body. Can you imagine what happened here? The Darkfall storm had been building for quite some time, generating itself, growing stronger. Energy was released into the building by a lightning strike. Anyone in direct flesh contact with a wall or a floor would have been affected – sucked into the fabric of the building in just the way that Mr Devlin described."

"But not everyone would be touching . . ." began Cardiff.

"There would have been a panic. People would have grabbed door handles to get out and been sucked into the fabric of the door. No one would have realised what was happening."

"It must have been like Hell in here," said Jimmy.

"Flesh contact," said Cardiff. "But what about their clothes . . . ?"

"The chemical effect extends to what a person is wearing once the effect begins. And once it begins, their clothes, bones, teeth – all of it will be absorbed. But there would be no effect, say, on the shoes on your feet or the gloves on your hands if you weren't already in flesh contact with a door or a wall . . . or even a light switch . . . when the lightning strikes. In fact, all a person would need to do in the middle of a Darkfall storm would be to remain calm, not touch anything – unless he or she is wearing gloves – and wait for the effect to pass. Gloves or shoes would effectively protect one from the effects. But have only one centimetre of bare flesh in contact – and the building would absorb you. You'd be sucked in, absorbed and fused with the steel and the plastic and the concrete – fused into the very fabric of the building itself."

"But those screams we heard?" said Cardiff. "I heard one of my men calling my name. They're still somehow alive after that, Rohmer. How the hell can that be?"

"Oh yes . . . they're alive. Absorbed, bonded in the building in a way we've yet to establish. But they're still alive. Occasionally . . . very, very rarely in fact . . . there is a vocal effect such as the one we've heard, such as the one that Mr Devlin heard. We don't understand it. It happened in the Leeds factory . . . and we took a wall to pieces

162

after receiving positive readings of a 'presence' in the fabric of it. (You saw Frye taking readings earlier, did you not?) We took that wall to pieces with supreme care, with an almost surgical skill. Brick by brick, plasterboard by plasterboard . . . until all we had left was a pile of rubble. And no sign of anything living within it. And yet . . . and yet . . . we still had a life-form reading from that pile of rubble. Whoever had been absorbed into that wall, was still somehow there . . . was still somehow *alive*."

"Hellish," said Cardiff.

"Yes, it is Hell. Have you read Aldous Huxley's *Heaven and Hell*?" Rohmer smiled indulgently. "No, perhaps not. Well, he points out that many of the punishments described in the various accounts of Hell are punishments of pressure and constriction. Dante's sinners are buried in mud, shut up in the trunks of trees, frozen solid in blocks of ice, crushed beneath stones. The 'Inferno' may be psychologically true – Darkfall, Cardiff, is a literal Hell. But I believe this Darkfall effect can also explain a lot to us about our superstitious past. I believe that the cases of hauntings recorded over the centuries are actually the results of a Darkfall. Imagine it. A Darkfall storm on or near some kind of human habitation; let's say . . . an old country house. The owners disappear . . . sucked into the fabric of the building. Fused into the brick and the stone for an eternity. Over the years, that 'vocal' effect is heard. Sounds of torment from the people imprisoned there. The sounds of screams from an invisible source. What is our average listener to believe? What else but that the sound is being made by a ghost . . . by a haunting."

"Why is Gilbert so frightened?" asked Cardiff at last.

"He's always frightened on these investigations."

"The Darkfall's still active, isn't it? That's what he's frightened about?"

Jimmy shuffled uneasily in his seat.

"No, the Darkfall phenomenon has dissipated. We would have picked up readings on arrival. And if we had, we would certainly have cleared the building and got out of here until it dissipated."

"That storm still looks as if it's building up to me," said Jimmy.

"It's just a storm now," replied Rohmer. "Not a Darkfall."

"Gilbert is keeping his gloves on," said Cardiff.

"Like I said to you — he's always nervous."

Jimmy was looking long and hard at Pearce, who had retained an expression of disdain and scorn throughout.

"Who's the lunatic now, Pearce?" he said.

Pearce returned a hard stare, pushed himself from his seat and held out a hand to Rohmer. "Let me see your ID again." Rohmer proffered it nonchalantly and Pearce sat again, scrutinising it as if examining the small print.

"So anyone touching the wall . . . ?" said Cardiff.

"Or any of the inert material within it," continued Rohmer.

". . . would be . . . just, sucked into . . ."

"The wall, the floor, the furniture . . . whatever. Yes."

"Living flesh, bone, tissue . . . even clothes, fused into the building fabric. Sounds . . . bloody ridiculous."

"Plastic surgeons use titanium for accident reconstruction work. The bone fuses with the metal. That's a scientific fact. So it's not so unbelievable as you think."

"But how are they still alive?" asked Cardiff. "The process should kill them, surely."

"That's what we'd like to know."

"The hand," began Pearce, handing back Rohmer's identification. "What about the severed hand upstairs . . . ?"

And then something exploded outside.

Something that was most definitely not thunder and lightning.

Something that exploded with a sound of rending metal and shattering glass.

"It's another bloody lightning strike!" exclaimed Pearce as they leapt from their chairs.

"No," said Rohmer tightly, striding to the door. "Not a lightning strike. This is something else."

And then they were all in the corridor, heading for the reception area.

SIX

Gilbert and Frye were standing up against the glass panes of the reception area, staring out into the storm-ravaged night. Duvall was already pulling open one of the main doors when Rohmer and the others rushed down the corridor towards them. Wind whipped at Duvall's hair and the lapels of his greatcoat as he squinted out into the rain-slashed darkness, trying to see what in hell had happened.

"Duvall?" snapped Rohmer as they drew level.

"Outside," replied Duvall. "Something's happened outside at the police cordon."

Cardiff rushed to one of the reception windows, closely followed by Jimmy Devlin. Pearce seized Jimmy by the cuff to haul him back. Jimmy pulled sharply away.

"I'm not going to make a break for it, Pearce. You don't have to worry."

"Christ . . ." said Cardiff in a hollow voice, when he saw what had happened out in the storm.

"What is it?" asked Pearce, in a tone of voice which suggested that he didn't really want to know.

"Keep Jimmy here," said Cardiff. Rohmer was already pushing out through the front door after Duvall.

"Like hell," began Jimmy.

Pearce restrained him with a hand on his chest, and for an instant it looked as if long-awaited violence might flare up.

"Be a good boy, Jimmy," said Cardiff — and vanished out into the storm.

Jimmy pulled away again and joined Gilbert and Frye at

the windows. When he saw the devastation, his mouth dropped open.

"Bloody hell . . ."

At first, as he battled across the outside pavement and through the raging wind, Cardiff was convinced that a bomb had been detonated on the forecourt outside the office block. There was a ruined tangle of what seemed to be exploded machinery lying where the police cordon had been; a jumble of twisted wreckage wreathed in guttering blue-yellow flame which suggested petrol leakage.

A car! thought Cardiff as he battled across the road, the blurred figures of Rohmer and Duvall just ahead. *It's a bloody car bomb.*

There was no sign of the two policemen who had been on duty at the cordon. The car seemed to have been driven directly at that cordon, where it had exploded. Apart from the tangled wreck of the main body of the car, Cardiff could see twisted chunks of metal lying in the roadway and in the pavement. The black and white wooden pole used as the cordon had been completely shattered; shreds of wood lay scattered in the rain. Cardiff screened his eyes from the rain as he drew level at last with the other two men. The guttering blue-yellow flame within the shattered shell of the car was snuffed out at last by the rain and the storm-wind. Smoke and steam gushed and hissed from the shattered windscreen and side windows.

"Who would want to drive a car bomb at the cordon?" shouted Cardiff above the sound of the storm.

"Not a car bomb . . ." mouthed Duvall.

"What?"

"It's not a car bomb. Look . . ." He pointed back to the office block, and Cardiff could see the indistinct blurs of the other faces in reception, looking out. "If it had been a car bomb, it would have blown in those windows."

"But it's a *car*, isn't it?"

"Yes," shouted Rohmer. "It's a car. But it didn't blow up."

"Then what . . . ?"

167

"It fell," shouted Rohmer. "It fell from a great height."

Vincent Saville, thought Cardiff. *Injuries consistent with a fall from a great height.*

"And my men?"

"Dead," said Duvall, moving closer to the wreck. "It fell directly on top of the cordon." He wafted smoke from the side window as he peered into the devastated car. The smoke and steam was being sucked from the wreck by the storm wind anyway, and as it cleared Duvall suddenly shrank back from the shattered car window.

"Rohmer . . ."

Cardiff could see for himself what Duvall had discovered.

There was a charred and blackened figure in the driving seat crouched behind the wheel.

"God . . ."

The shape seemed too big for the seat; hunched, gnarled and blackened, it was still shrouded in hissing steam, but despite its swollen size the shape of a man or woman for all that. Charcoaled fingers still gripped the wheel . . . and the stench of cooking flesh would have been unbearable, if not for the greedily sucking wind of the storm.

Once, Cardiff could have imagined himself throwing up at the sight of that horror behind the wheel. Some secret part of him wished that he could, because in that recognisably human act of revulsion, his own humanity would be reaffirmed. But the horror was only doing to him what it always did. It registered the further damage being done to him. But his initial feeling about this office-block incident was reaffirmed.

Death was here.

Madness and Death.

Perhaps soon, he would meet them both and ask that one question that he longed to ask: *Why?*

Within one eye socket of the indeterminate monstrosity behind the wheel something that could have been an eye popped loudly and viscous yellow fluid streamed down the corpse's ravaged face.

"Shit!" Duvall recoiled further from the car in disgust; his cool, hard demeanour slipping for an instant.

Rohmer was looking up into the sky as the vortex of smoke and steam was greedily sucked skywards into the black roiling clouds of the storm.

"It fell?" shouted Cardiff angrily.

"Yes." Rohmer still searched the ravaged sky.

"How can . . . ?" And now Cardiff's anger really flared. He grabbed Rohmer by the arm and swung him around so that he was forced to look him in the face. "Two of my men are dead! Dead! So how can a fucking car fall out of the fucking sky, Rohmer? You mean it was blown off the motorway over there and into the forecourt. Don't you? *Don't you?*"

"It fell," said Rohmer simply.

Duvall broke Cardiff's grip on Rohmer.

"People and cars don't fall out of the sky," said Cardiff.

"In a Darkfall – they do," replied Rohmer – and now he was striding back through the biting wind towards the office block. Duvall followed closely behind, coat flapping in the wind and the rain.

Cardiff turned back to the car. The swollen monstrosity behind the wheel shrouded in the smoke and steam of its own cooling was surely much too large to have once been human. Surely that hideously charcoaled horror should have *shrunk* as it cooked and disintegrated.

Vincent Saville, said the voice in Cardiff's head. *He just fell out of the sky.*

Angry at his ineffectiveness and at the way Rohmer had made him a bystander in this nightmare, Cardiff followed them back through the savage whirlwinds towards the office block.

SEVEN

"It wasn't Cardiff at all, was it?" said Jimmy. "It was you."

"What?" Pearce had shoved Devlin back into one of the upholstered reception seats; keeping one eye on him, the other on what was going on outside. Gilbert and Frye were still glued to the rain-streaked glass.

"You're the one who set me up. Fingered me for those burglaries. Cardiff might have been in charge, but you're the one who provided the evidence."

Pearce walked over to him, looking down. There was undisguised contempt on his face.

"Don't get cocky with me, Devlin. That Rohmer fella might have the proper ID and he might corroborate your funny story, but don't think I'm falling for any of this crap."

"All that time inside for something I didn't do."

"You were robbing that jeweller's, in case you'd forgotten."

"No use denying that. But I didn't do the other jobs you accused me of, Pearce. What was wrong? Did you have a few unsolved crimes that needed tying up?"

"You're a thief, Devlin. Always were, always will be. And it's my job to catch thieves and lock them away."

"Even if it means planting evidence?"

Pearce cast a look back at Gilbert and Frye, to make sure that they weren't listening. When he looked back at Jimmy, he had a smile of disdain.

"Even that."

"They're coming back," said Frye.

All attention turned to the main reception doors again.

Jimmy felt curiously detached from what was going on; detached from whatever in hell had happened outside. This was just another jigsaw piece in the bizarre events of the night. He had known all along of his innocence of the crimes for which he had been committed. Now that Pearce had openly stated that the evidence had been planted, he wasn't reacting in the way that he'd ever have guessed. Far from leaping from his chair and seizing Pearce by the throat, a curious fatigue seemed to have settled in his bones. Perhaps it was also something to do with the fact that this tall, blond Government man had corroborated his story about what had happened in the jeweller's on that night. The knowledge that someone, somewhere in Government circles, had known that what he'd seen and experienced *had* really happened, should have been enough in itself to send Jimmy into a righteous rage. There had been times, after all, while he'd been serving his stretch in prison that he really had wondered whether he had hallucinated it all; wondered whether he was losing his mind. Even now, he had never returned to the shopping mall. The walls of his cell had given him nightmares. The echoing sounds of Mac's voice coming from those walls in his dreams had shaken him awake, clutching at the sheets, sweat oozing from every pore.

But the rage would not come. The rage that had eaten at his guts for so long, and had launched him at Sergeant Lawrence – who even Jimmy knew was a good man at heart – would not serve him now.

The reception doors juddered open again. The storm breathed its ragged, ice-breath into the corridors. Rohmer pushed through, followed by Duvall. Rohmer zeroed in on Pearce straight away.

"The caretaker's room in the basement. Where is it?"

Gilbert stood between them. From his viewpoint in his seat, enervated by this strange sapped feeling, Jimmy could see that Gilbert's previous nervousness had now reached a new pitch. He clutched at Rohmer's lapels.

171

"It's a Return, isn't it, Rohmer? You've been lying to me all along."

"Get out of the way," snapped Rohmer, pushing him to one side as he moved towards Pearce. "The basement room?"

"What the hell happened outside?" asked Pearce.

"The basement room. *Now!* Where is it?"

The reception doors opened again and Jimmy felt the ice-cold blast on his face with curious detachment as Cardiff pushed through.

"Down the corridor. First door on the right," said Pearce. "But you won't get me going into that basement again after those bloody noises we heard down there. Thought my eardrums would burst."

Rohmer turned quickly, striding away down the corridor with Duvall close behind. But now Gilbert was fumbling at Pearce's lapels, eyes glittering with what Pearce could now see was naked fear.

"Noises? What noises? You mean screaming voices like we heard before, don't you? Don't you?"

"No . . . look, get *off* me you crazy old bastard."

"What kind of noises? Please, you must tell me."

Pearce shoved Gilbert away from him. "Noises like . . . explosions. Like thunderclaps, echoing over and over. Cardiff heard them too. Blew the bloody windows in downstairs."

"This caretaker's room . . . the basement . . . is downstairs? Below ground?"

"Yes, but . . ."

Gilbert backed away, face white, fumbling at his gloves again. "He *was* lying. He's known all along."

Somewhere in the corridor, the basement door slammed and Jimmy watched everything as if it was taking place on a stage, and he was a member of the audience. He watched as Gilbert exchanged a look with an equally shell-shocked Frye . . . and then hurried quickly towards the reception door.

Cardiff seized him by both arms, preventing his escape.

172

"Let me out of here, you bloody fool!"

"Why? What the hell is happening *now*?" snapped Cardiff directly in his face. Gilbert tried to push past him, but Cardiff held firm. "You're not going anywhere until you tell me what . . ."

"Look . . . look . . ." Gilbert ceased struggling, realising that Cardiff would not let him go until he knew more. Gilbert forced himself to become calm, drew a deep breath and then the words came out in a torrent. "Rohmer is lying. He must have told you about a Darkfall back there. Maybe not everything . . . but he's lying when he says the Darkfall has passed. It hasn't passed. It's still happening."

"Oh my Good Christ . . ." said Frye.

"Those noises," continued Gilbert. "The explosive noises you heard in the basement. Well that's symptomatic of a Darkfall strike."

"We're in a *Secondary* Darkfall?" said Frye in sudden realisation, and a voice that wavered.

"A what?" snapped Cardiff.

"We've experience of two kinds of Darkfall," continued Gilbert, still looking to find a way around Cardiff, the words still spilling out of him. "A Primary Darkfall is where the storm builds to a pitch and there is one strike. There may or may not be a disappearance depending on the circumstances. But there is also a Secondary Darkfall. We've only had experience of two — that's where the effect continues to build, continues to escalate, with continuous Darkfall strikes. The effects can be horrendous. On both of the previous occasions, the area was evacuated and isolated until the storm blew itself apart. That's what's happening now . . . and why we have to get away from here. The noises you heard — the explosive noises — were the acoustic effects of a second Darkfall strike. That's when your second disappearance occurred. And that second strike means that this is a Secondary Darkfall. So let me past — the Darkfall's still active!"

"Then why didn't we get sucked into the building like the others?" said Cardiff, still holding on to him. "We were

173

here. We touched things, were in flesh-contact down there in the basement. But the Darkfall didn't affect us."

Continually frustrated in his attempts to get past Cardiff, Gilbert exploded in rage.

"Because you were *below ground*! Look . . . we've seen the early report on this incident. There was a caretaker here, in the basement, when the first strike occurred. The man who raised the alarm . . ."

"Beaton?"

"Yes, yes, yes. The reason he survived the first strike is the reason that you all escaped the second. You were below ground when it happened. And we do know that for some gravitational reason we've yet to fathom, the absorption effect is nullified below ground-level. Those outside the building remained unaffected by the strike. Now, let me past . . ."

"We're *here*," gasped Frye, still hardly daring to accept the fact. "In a *Secondary* Darkfall. But why? Why would Rohmer withhold that information from us. It doesn't make any sense. Why would he endanger himself?"

"There is no danger," said Rohmer. And they all turned to see that Rohmer and Duvall had returned. They were standing listening in the corridor.

Duvall was carrying two plastic containers. Cardiff could read the label on one of them: "Paraffin".

"You knew that there was still Darkfall activity when you sent us in?" Gilbert whirled to face him.

"Yes, there were readings."

"For God's sake, why?" bleated Frye, returning to the window and looking out briefly into the night at the blurred wreck of the car in the forecourt. "That's a Returner out there, Rohmer."

"Duvall is here to handle it."

"But why? We must get away from here."

"We're not going anywhere," Rohmer smiled. "We're going to ride out the storm."

"What's a Returner?" asked Cardiff.

"Sometimes," said Rohmer, "they come back. We don't

174

know yet how it happens. The inert structures, the buildings, whatever . . . can occasionally . . ." He hunted for a word. "Can . . . *cough* out what they've absorbed. Sometimes literally on the spot where the absorption occurred. On other occasions, people are spewed out into the atmosphere and turn up hundreds of miles away. Their molecular structure is changed. That may account for their ability to survive such an ejection. It's been happening for hundreds of years. Maybe you've heard of Kasper Hauser in Germany? Then again . . . maybe not. It's already happened twice with your office-block incident. Once with Eleanor Parkins, in London and twice with . . ."

"Vincent Saville," finished Cardiff.

"Coughed out again," said Rohmer. "Sometimes they're dead . . . sometimes they're alive, if you can call it that. But when they return, they're . . . how shall I say it? . . . not themselves."

"Transmuted," said Gilbert. "Their molecular structure is transmuted with the inert material in which they were absorbed."

"And what the hell does all *that* mean?" asked Pearce.

"It means," said Duvall holding up one of the paraffin cans, "that we have to burn what we found in that car wreck outside."

"It may be still alive," said Rohmer matter-of-factly. "And if it is, things could become . . . fraught, shall we say."

Duvall moved forward with the two paraffin cans.

"The car," said Pearce. "I hear what you're saying about bodies being sucked into walls . . . and sometimes spat out again. But how does a car fit into all of this? You trying to say a *car* was sucked into the building? Human flesh, you said . . ."

"I don't know," said Rohmer. "There's a lot we don't know. That's why we're here. Duvall — see to that business outside."

"I want to see," said Pearce, without taking his eyes off

175

Rohmer. "I hear these fairytales, but I can't swallow them. I want to see what's outside in the car."

"Want to give it a parking ticket?" said Jimmy from his chair.

"Quiet, Jimmy," said Cardiff. "Okay, Pearce. If that's what you want. But you won't need to burn that thing, Rohmer. It's already been burned."

"Humour me," said Rohmer and gestured to Duvall again. The storm intruded once more as Pearce and Duvall exited. Gilbert and Frye watched them leave and for an instant it seemed as if Gilbert wanted to dash out after them again. Rohmer took him by the coat sleeve, leading him to one of the upholstered seats beside Jimmy.

"Why, Rohmer?" asked Gilbert. "Why didn't you tell us that this is a Secondary Darkfall? What are we *doing* here?"

"You're both here to assess and observe," said Rohmer. "But you're also weak and you frighten easily. There have been two strikes here, that's true. But you know that the accelerating effect on a Secondary Darkfall starts slowly and gains momentum. There hasn't been any danger to us. And there won't be any danger."

"Thanks for the warning, Rohmer," said Cardiff. "There may have been no danger to you. But there certainly was to *us*, you bastard. If any one of us had been touching a wall above ground we'd have been part of the bloody architecture by now."

"But you should have told me . . ." continued Gilbert.

"And me." Frye had moved back to the windows again, to watch Duvall and Pearce battling their way through the storm to the car wreck.

"I needed you both," said Rohmer. "You're the best we have. And I didn't have time to pussyfoot around. As for you, Cardiff. You were sent instructions to evacuate but your own computer equipment was unable to receive our instructions and advice, as you very well know. The Secondary Darkfall effect escalates. There has been no danger to you or your people since the second strike. There won't

176

be another strike for a further forty minutes or so at least, which is why I want you and Pearce out of here now. You're not part of this investigation."

"And me?" asked Jimmy.

"As I said before. You stay."

"Like hell he does," said Cardiff. "He's a civilian – and he's in my jurisdiction, not yours. He leaves with us – and you can stay in this bloody office block if you like."

"You've seen my identification papers. You know I have the authority."

"Do I hell. I want corroboration from central office."

"And how do we do that with radios and telephone knocked out by the storm?"

"Exactly," replied Cardiff. "No corroboration, no over-all authority. You're not telling me what to do, and you're not keeping Devlin here."

"Never knew you cared so much," said Jimmy, emerging from his lethargy and rising from his chair at last to join Frye at the black, rain-blurred windows. Gilbert was rubbing his face with both hands as if trying to wash away bad dreams.

"Shut up, Jimmy. When Pearce and I leave, so do you."

"I think not," said Rohmer.

Lightning jarred the heavens once more, briefly illuminating the reception windows as Rohmer and Cardiff faced each other. Neither was going to back down.

"Nice car," said Jimmy, wiping the condensation from his patch of window, but still giving himself only a blurred view. "Or at least it *was* a nice car." Pearce and Duvall were blurred figures beside the wreck, distinguishable only in that Duvall was carrying the paraffin containers, which he was setting down on the pavement. Rain was hissing on the roof of the car wreck, fogging the scene still further. The figures blurred completely out of view in that mist.

"That's a Ford Zodiac," said Jimmy. "Or it *was*. You can tell by the wings on the back. About 1964 I'd say. Not a lot of them about. One less now, that's for sure."

"Are you sure that thing is dead?" bleated Frye. "The thing in the car?"

"No," said Rohmer, without taking his eyes off Cardiff. "That's why Duvall is going to soak it in paraffin and set fire to it if they're able to in this storm."

"Nice car," said Jimmy. "Bet it had whitewall tyres. Two-tone, green and cream bodywork."

"I've got a job to do," said Cardiff, also staring out Rohmer. "If it's dangerous, we all should be out of here. But you talk as if these . . . Returners . . . were freaks, or movie monsters or something," said Cardiff.

"They are," said Rohmer. "Eleanor Parkins. One of your own Returners. Her body had been fused with concrete, plastic, plaster and steel. Our *post mortem* revealed a mutated amalgam of all of these inert materials within her own tissue. By our definitions, she couldn't possibly have been alive."

"So she died?"

"She was terminated. We had no choice."

"You *killed* her?"

"You had to be there, Cardiff. Believe me, we had no choice."

"Some of them return with minimum or no mutation at all," Gilbert mumbled from his seat. "We have two in captivity. They talk of having seen 'The Other Side'."

"The Other Side?" asked Cardiff, eyes still fixed on Rohmer.

"Mental derangement," returned Rohmer. "Brain decomposition. Hallucination caused by trauma. We'll dispose of them eventually, just like the others."

"You *kill* people who return?"

"We dispose of them, Cardiff. That's all."

"Fog lamps," said Jimmy. "Spotlamps. Leather upholstery. Bench seats, front and rear."

"They talk of Heaven and Hell," mumbled Gilbert. "The ones who come back who aren't mutated to the point of monstrosity say that they've seen it. In that netherworld state, while they've been in that state of absorption."

178

"A three-speed car with a column change. Ocelot seat covers. Top of the range. A really tasty car."

"Do you believe in Heaven and Hell?" mumbled Gilbert.

"Will you all *shut the hell up*!" shouted Jimmy, turning from the window. The lethargy and enervation were gone. "How much longer do I have to listen to all of this crap? It's like I've been dragged out of the pub and into a bloody video nasty. Look! If it's dangerous to be here, let's just get the hell *out* of it . . . !"

Thunder boomed in the sky.

The windowpanes of the reception rattled.

And then the strip lights overhead flickered . . . and went out.

The reception area was plunged into a blue-black relief. Distant streetlamps blurred by rain cast eerie blue light into the lobby; great criss-cross squares of it. The strip lights flickered again, providing the faintest luminescence. Gilbert uttered a strangled cry and leapt to his feet with shadow reflections of crawling rain on his spectrally white face. Frye recoiled from the window.

"Shit!" Cardiff fumbled to where he'd seen a light switch, began to reach for it . . . and then stopped. "Was that a strike? A Darkfall strike?"

"No," said Rohmer in the spectral gloom. "Too early."

"The hell with that," replied Cardiff. "Gimme a pair of gloves."

"There are Operative gloves in Frye's case."

"Give them to me."

Frye moved in the darkness to his case, flipped it open and rummaged inside. He flinched when Jimmy took hold of his arm. "Me, too." Frye fumbled again and came out with two pairs of skintight brown gloves of some man-made material. While Jimmy pulled on a pair, Cardiff strode over, took a further pair from Frye and returned to the light switch.

"Unnecessary," said Rohmer calmly.

"The hell with you," replied Cardiff, pulling on the gloves.

179

He flicked the light switch. It made no difference. The strip lights were dead. Reaching over the reception desk, he lifted the telephone receiver. But there was no crackling static – there was nothing at all.

"*All* the power is dead."

"Oh no . . . oh no . . . no, no, no."

Cardiff looked back over to the reception windows at Frye's silhouette. He was not reacting to this latest development, but to something that was going on outside.

Somewhere beyond, on the forecourt perhaps, orange flame seemed to splutter and flare in the darkness.

"Something's happening out there," said Frye, pressing closer to the glass. "I can hardly see, but something is thrashing around by the car. Something is burning and thrashing and . . . oh, no, no, no."

Jimmy pushed Frye to one side to get a better view. Rohmer was already moving to join them as Cardiff replaced the telephone receiver and pushed away from the reception desk. Gilbert backed into Cardiff. He pushed him out of the way.

Something out there was making a noise.

It was a sound of screaming, muffled by the storm. But screaming nevertheless. A sound of hideous pain and anger . . . and surely not a sound that could be made by anything human.

And now there was the loud crashing retort of what could only be a pistol shot, joined immediately by the rattling, roaring sound of thunder in the sky.

"Duvall!" said Rohmer.

"So the bastard *does* have a gun," said Jimmy.

"What the hell is going on out there?" Cardiff shoved Frye aside to peer out into the darkness. Something was burning out there, not in the car wreck . . . but beside it. The storm, the wind, the rain and the continually fogged glass from Cardiff's breath was obscuring the view.

And then something hit the reception doors with tremendous force. Gilbert screamed, a high-pitched squeal of fear, as the reception doors burst open and a dark flapping shape

180

hurtled through on to the floor. Gusts of rain and snow flurried through the opened door as the shape scrabbled on the floor.

Jimmy and Cardiff both saw Rohmer reach into the inside of his overcoat. In one fluid movement, he had drawn what both men could see, even in the darkness, was an automatic pistol. He levelled it, straight and calm, at the shape that was thrashing on the tiles of the reception floor.

"No, Rohmer! It's me!" said the shape, resolving itself into Duvall.

Scrabbling to his feet again, he hurled himself back through the throat of the storm, seized the reception door and savagely slammed it shut.

"Duvall, what the hell . . . ?" began Rohmer, lowering his gun.

Gasping for breath, soaked and dishevelled, Duvall backed away from the doors. He still held his own automatic in his left hand, and he was raising it towards the door as he backed off.

"I've . . . never . . . never seen one like . . ."

"What happened?" shouted Cardiff. "Where's Pearce?"

"We . . . we doused it with paraffin in the car . . . Not easy in the storm . . . we . . . set it . . . alight . . ."

"Where's Pearce?"

"The bloody thing just came alive . . . tore out of the car at us . . . Christ, it was . . . it was . . . it nearly got me, Rohmer."

Cardiff turned back to the window and wiped the fog of his breath from the glass. He leaned close to it and peered out into the night, trying to see what was out there . . .

Just as Pearce's wild and screaming face slammed against the glass on the other side, less than an inch from Cardiff's own.

Cardiff recoiled in shock.

The others pulled away from the window into the centre of reception, watching in horror as Pearce continued to scream in panic at them. He drummed on the window with

181

the flat of white, spectral hands – eyes turned to his left, in the direction of the glass doors, and filled with a fear and horror that paralysed Cardiff.

"Let me in! Let me in! *LET ME IN!*"

Pearce was staring wildly at Cardiff now, hair plastered by rain to his head. There was mud on his face. He glanced back to the doors again in terror. But whatever had been there must be gone, because now he was whirling in alarm, looking around him. He turned frantically back to the window. Behind him, lightning flared, turning him into a stark silhouette against the windows; flooding the reception with white light.

But no one, it seemed, was able to move.

Pearce began to move along the outside of those windows now, hand by hand on the glass, staring inside; as if he was walking on a ledge out there, fourteen storeys high, casting wild and terror-stricken looks from side to side.

"Help me . . . for God's sake help me . . . it's out here . . . God, *Cardiff!*"

And Cardiff remembered the screaming from the walls and the floor and the ceiling; remembered the familiar voice that had screamed his name. At that instant, his paralysis vanished and he moved quickly towards the glass doors.

"Get away from that door!" snapped Rohmer, and Cardiff half-turned to see that the automatic was now levelled at him.

"We've got to let him in!"

"Another step towards that door . . ."

"And what, you bastard? You'll kill me?"

"No . . . but a bullet in the leg won't be pleasant for you."

"You . . ."

And Pearce was screaming again, but this time not in fear.

Cardiff whirled back to see that Pearce's face was squashed up close to the glass, still thirty feet from the reception doors; face contorted, mouth wide and agonised.

There was an engulfing, indeterminate shadow behind and over him . . . something huge. Steam or fog seemed to be wreathed around that massive shadow. Rain hissed all around it . . . and now Pearce was screaming in agony and distress.

Frye was saying "My God, my God, my God . . ." over and over again.

And Pearce was being somehow lifted from his feet, still squashed against the glass, hands and feet drumming in a frenzy against the windows. The monstrous shadow was lifting him.

Then blood began to splatter on the glass from Pearce's open mouth.

"Oh God, oh God, oh God . . ." Frye clutched his hands to his mouth.

The splattering of blood became a dark and arterial gushing.

Duvall lunged forward and fired at the shadow. The roaring detonation filled the reception area like a miniature lightning strike, stabbing pain into everyone's ears. A fist-sized hole was punched in the glass two feet to the left of Pearce's screaming, crimson face.

Something inhuman screeched and bellowed in the storm, and Pearce was swept away from the glass by the shadow, out of sight and into the night — leaving a bloody smear. Pearce's screams were borne away on the wind.

Duvall moved forward to fire again, but Rohmer held his arm — pulling him back.

Lightning flashed outside again.

There was no shadow, but the drifting tatters of smoke from something that had been burning were still swirling in the wind and rain.

"Move back," said Rohmer. "Away from the windows."

Thunder growled in the sky again, and they were all backing away slowly and carefully. Another growling seemed to be coming from outside, and the sound of something breathing heavily. Something large. Or was it only the storm?

Prowling, scuffling, moving around out there somewhere . . .

There was another crash of thunder. The darkened lobby was again lit up in stark, nightmarish black-and-white. Jimmy scanned the dripping windows, waiting for something hideous to crash through those vulnerable glass panes in an explosive maelstrom of glass and storm-driven wind and rain.

Rain hissing on scabrous flesh that was not flesh, dousing the flame, runnelling in scarred troughs . . .

In dreadful anticipation, Cardiff waited, aware of Rohmer and Duvall scanning the windows with their weapons.

Blind, deaf, but able to smell; able to find them by the food smell, even in this raging, wind-swept, rain-driven night . . .

The wind lashed at the frontage, rattling those panes . . . and Gilbert was whimpering again.

Feeding angrily and briefly on what it had taken. Discarding the remnants on the pavement, in the rain. Feeling the strength returning, the hate returning . . .

They waited.

The thunder seemed to shake the foundations of the building. Lightning flickered; jagged fractures in the sky – making shadows leap and leer, in stark black and white.

They waited.

Something scraped against one of the windows.

And then Frye began to scream, the sound of it paralysing everyone with fright again. Frye was screaming over and over now in alarm and desperation.

"Frye!" hissed Rohmer. "Snap out of it!"

"For God's sake." Cardiff moved through the shadows to where Frye was crouched against the wall, next to the reception desk. "Don't snap! That thing will hear . . ." Cardiff reached out to grab Frye and shake him back to his senses.

Jimmy grabbed at Cardiff's arm and pulled him away. "What the hell . . . ?"

Cardiff saw the look of glazed horror on Frye's face, heard him mumbling: "Oh no, no, no, no . . ." And then he saw the same look of horror on Jimmy's face as he pulled him roughly back.

"Don't touch him," said Jimmy in a voice almost too quiet to hear.

Frye was turning slowly in horror to look behind him, at the reception wall.

And now they could all see what was happening.

Frye's left hand had vanished into the wall to the wrist. He looked at it as his forearm began to slide inwards after it; the wall perfectly seamless, with no sign of irruption, no disturbance to its surface. Frye staggered – and then tugged backwards, trying to drag his hand out of the wall.

"No, no, no . . ."

He flung out his other hand towards them in a desperate plea, and Cardiff moved to take it.

"No," said Rohmer. "It's a Darkfall strike. We can't do anything to help him."

"Oh *Christ*!" screamed Frye, his upper arm sliding inexorably and impossibly into the wall. He staggered again, his knee connecting with the wall – and sticking there. The knee itself began to slide into the dark, smooth pastel paper on the wall; smoothly and neatly. "You said it was too early, Rohmer!" screamed Frye again. "Too early . . . too . . . I wasn't wearing . . ." Frye's voice broke up into sobs and his other slashing arm connected with the wall and stuck there. "Please! *Someone* HELP ME!"

"For God's sake, Rohmer!" pleaded Cardiff. "There must be *something* we can do."

"Please, Rohmer! PLEASE!" Frye's shoulder had vanished into the wall, as had his leg and his hip. His other arm was in the wall to the elbow. He strove to keep his face from that wall as it inexorably pulled him closer. His screams broke into hysterical laughter.

"I'm the tar baby . . ." he gibbered.

And then Duvall stood forward, placed the barrel of the

automatic on the back of Frye's head . . . and blew his brains out.

Jimmy and Cardiff recoiled, but Rohmer remained calmly where he was, as the impact flung Frye's sundered head forward, his shattered face smacking into the wall . . . and rapidly becoming absorbed there. The bloodied stain on the darkened wall around that head vanished quickly, blood and tissue absorbed like ink into blotting paper; leaving no trace. Frye's quivering body slumped and then, turning slightly as he was sucked into the wall as if into some vertical view of a bizarre quicksand, he was quickly absorbed — the wall closing around him; unmarked and to their eyes, as solid and impenetrable as ever.

Gilbert was still sobbing.

Only Frye's left calf and foot remained protruding from the bottom of the wall, shuddering slightly as it was drawn in. Thunder resounded again — and they all felt a sudden change in pressure. Cardiff's ears popped.

Only the foot protruded from the wall now. It juddered again, twisted . . . and fell from the wall on to the tiled floor; severed clean at the ankle as if with a butcher's knife.

Mesmerised, they stared at it. A ludicrous but hideous spectacle. Rohmer was the first to break the shocked silence.

"The effect of the strike has worn off. Now you know how the severed hand got there, Cardiff."

"The poor bastard," said Jimmy.

"The effect is escalating even more quickly here than ever before. Keep your gloves on. No skin contact."

"We must get out," said Cardiff.

"Past that thing outside?"

"Is it still there?" burbled Gilbert.

Duvall crept nearer to the glass frontage. There were no monstrous sounds out there in the storm. The hideous blood smear on the window was a running crimson blur in the rain. But there was no way of telling whether the thing was still outside.

"Christ," muttered Duvall. "If you'd *seen* it. I'm surprised it wasn't attracted by the screaming."

Jimmy was still looking in horror at the wall where Frye had disappeared. "What the hell do we do now?"

"Underground," said Cardiff. "Like Gilbert said earlier. That's the only place we can be safe. We can lock ourselves in the basement, away from that bloody thing outside — and until this Darkfall storm blows over."

"Amazing how quickly you adapt, Cardiff," said Rohmer. "Might find a job for you after all."

"Go to Hell. We could have saved Pearce."

"No, we couldn't," said Duvall. "That thing was behind me. It was at the reception doors. Its taking Pearce probably saved our lives. Otherwise it would have been in here."

"You're the ones with the guns, pal. Are you saying that thing can't be stopped with a bullet . . . ?"

"You irritate me, Cardiff," said Duvall. "Why don't you go outside and try to talk it to death?"

"Underground," said Jimmy. "Like the man said. Let's get the hell in the basement and bar the door."

"We'll need my equipment," said Gilbert weakly. "The acoustic effects of continued strikes could deafen us. My equipment can be set at a frequency to emit sound waves that will obviate that effect. We need . . ."

"Get it," said Rohmer.

Gilbert retrieved the portable equipment which Frye had been using and led the way gingerly to the corridor, asking weakly: "Which door? Where?" Cardiff pushed past, and now they were all heading down that corridor past the two elevators on their left; still looking back to the reception doors lest that monstrous shadow should suddenly reappear.

"We should warn people," said Cardiff as they moved.

"How do we do that if the telephones are out?" asked Rohmer.

Gilbert had reached the door marked "Basement". He began to reach for the handle with a gloved hand and then pulled nervously back, remembering what had happened to Frye. Thunder growled, and Gilbert looked around with nervous, pleading eyes.

"No . . ." said Cardiff. "I'm not going down there. Take Devlin down with you, but I'm going back."

"Back out *there*?" said Jimmy. "Past that . . . thing?"

"It's prowling around outside. Anyone passing by on the road or the walkway is in danger."

"There'll be no one outside in this bloody storm," said Jimmy.

"You're either brave or stupid," said Rohmer. "I can't work out which."

"I'm neither," replied Cardiff. "I'm a policeman, that's all. It's my job. The thing is . . . what the hell are *you*, Rohmer?"

They exchanged a long, hard look.

And then Cardiff turned, heading back for the reception. The windows flared again in nightmarish black and white as lightning split the night once more; the explosion of thunder rattling those panes simultaneously.

What am I doing? thought Cardiff as he walked. *Am I really just doing my job?*

"You're cracked," said Jimmy behind him. "Come back and don't be a bloody idiot."

No, you're not so altruistic, said a small voice inside Cardiff. *It's that thing outside, isn't it? That thing that can't possibly exist. You think it has the face of the man behind the wheel, don't you? The face that was hidden from you. You think that thing out there has the answers. It's Death . . . and you want to ask it face to face. Ask it . . .*

Gilbert cried out; a hoarse, guttural grunt of fear and surprise. The others were cursing in alarm. And Cardiff turned back to look.

They were shrinking back from the basement door.

And something was happening to that door; something that he couldn't make out, because it was screened by their bodies.

No . . . not the basement door. But the wall beside the door. There was movement there; movement and light, as if someone was shining a torch beam on it, swinging it wildly from side to side. There were somehow moving shadows on that wall; crawling, shifting shadows.

"What is it?" Cardiff called out.

Gilbert turned to stare in Cardiff's direction as if contemplating another mad dash for the reception doors and then remembered the thing that lay beyond them. Rohmer, Duvall and Devlin were all pulling away from that wall, step by step. Cardiff moved to join them . . . and at last he could see what the others were seeing. There was a spreading stain of movement on the wall; a shifting undulating wave of shadow and light which made absolutely no sense at all. Cardiff spun back to look at the windows to see if that bizarre shifting and swirling of shadows was somehow caused by a lightning flash through the glass panes. But apart from the grumbling in the sky and the hissing of rain, there was no lightning; no reason why this peculiar shadow show should be taking place.

There was something else now; something that hadn't been immediately apparent to Cardiff, but had been seen by the others straightaway and which was causing them to back away from the wall.

There was other movement on that bare plaster wall; movement other than those strange, creeping, shifting shadows. There was a sparkling, fizzling white light in there, too . . . and Cardiff walked forward to look as the others recoiled. That streaked, spluttering light was also crawling on the wall, amidst the shadows. It was mesmerising. The wall looked like a dark and mysterious fresco over which black, swirling thunderclouds were roiling; and within the thunderclouds, the occasional jagged crackle of lightning; an arterial stab of fractured light, like a lightning strike.

And then the wall bulged outwards.

Cardiff froze in his tracks, and now the others were right beside him; all staring back at this impossible sight.

The bulge was taking place about midway in the plaster wall. The dull grey plaster was now completely alive with the shadows and the crawling light, and that wall had somehow become like grey leather or rubber at its centre, where the bulge was taking place. There was a noise now. It was the noise of something stretching and straining under enormous, impossible pressure; as if the very fabric of that wall must suddenly explode inwards, enveloping them in a deadly blast of shattered brick and concrete. Impossibly, there were no cracks in the wall, no tears or fractures. The grinding, stretching sounds were rising to a pitch and behind it all, another low-register noise. Almost inaudible at first, but rising in volume, making their eardrums vibrate.

"Now what?" said Jimmy in amazement. "What the hell is *this*?"

Incredibly, Jimmy could see that Rohmer had something akin to a smile on his face. "Amazing," he said quietly. "Amazing. I never thought I'd . . ."

"The place is falling apart . . ." began Cardiff, as Gilbert blundered into him again, not knowing where to go.

"No, not falling apart," said Rohmer, raising his voice over the groaning, cracking, straining noise as it now became so loud that surely it must burst apart like a bomb, killing them all in the process.

"Get back . . ." *behind the reception desk*, Cardiff started to say, to get some kind of cover before the thing blew apart. But then the noise became so unbearable, he was forced, along with the others, to clap his hands over his ears. The agony of that sound in his head was the same as he and Pearce had experienced in the basement. Jimmy had dropped to his knees and was hugging his head, when the noise suddenly snapped out of existence.

Reeling, Cardiff saw Rohmer standing stock still, hands fastened to his ears in an almost business-like fashion, still staring straight ahead at the wall. Duvall was leaning against one wall, bent double and gagging for breath. Now realising that his gloved hand was touching a wall, he snatched it quickly away in alarm. Gilbert had joined Jimmy on his knees, clutching at his head and shaking it madly, even though the noise had ceased.

But Cardiff's attention was drawn back to the wall. The crawling light and shadow had gone. There was no incredible bulging at the centre; no cracks, no jagged patches where plaster might have fallen under the strain. The wall was as it had always been . . . but at the centre was a black smear, like the blackened smear that might be left by some kind of fire; as if a blowlamp had been held there. The stain was perhaps three feet in ragged circumference and Rohmer took a step towards it as the others began to recover.

"Re . . ." began Gilbert, and his voice dried. He swallowed hard. Cardiff could see that Rohmer was looking back at Gilbert, almost hopefully. "It's a . . . Returner."

And then something was coughed out of that blackened spot with a sound like liquid choking; coughed out from a hole where there was no hole, with such force that the jumbled shape landed with a slap on the corridor floor, five feet from the wall.

"Jesus Christ . . ." said Jimmy.

And then lightning flashed outside again, and now they could all see what it was that had been ejected, impossibly, from that plaster wall and into the corridor.

It was a girl.

She was about seventeen years old, with long dark hair in disarray around her face. She was wearing a white blouse with frills at the cuffs, and a plain black miniskirt. A jade-green pendant on a chain was hanging around her neck. She was obviously in distress, raising herself on all fours, snatching the hair from her face as she looked back in terror at the plaster wall from which she had just come. She began to crawl hastily away from that wall, head turned back over her shoulder to look at it, apparently unaware of their presence. The blackened spot in the centre of the wall had vanished.

"Stay where you are!"

191

The girl cried out in alarm at the sound of Rohmer's shout, swinging back to see them at last. Her hands flew to her face and she stopped, huddled in the centre of the corridor. She began to weep, burying her face in her hands.

"Please . . ." she sobbed. "Please help me."

Rohmer stepped forward purposefully, reaching inside his coat again as he did so.

"Please . . . please . . ."

"Sometimes they come back," said Rohmer, and now he had drawn the automatic and raised it. The girl could see what he was doing, but lowered her head again, sobbing.

"It's just a girl!" shouted Cardiff. "You can't!"

"Stay out of it, Cardiff. You saw that thing outside. You saw what happened to Pearce."

"It's a Returner," mumbled Gilbert. "My God, it's . . ."

The girl's distress was doing something to Cardiff. It was making him feel emotions that he didn't want to have again. The sound of that distraught weeping brought that June afternoon back to him in a stabbing flash of inner pain. In that split-second, he saw the car speeding towards him, heard Lisa's scream, saw Jamie leaving his arms in slow motion. That weeping was *his* weeping; the grief that had overwhelmed him for so long. The horrors of the night had somehow resulted in this bizarre inner focusing.

"She's just a *girl*!" he shouted again.

And saw Rohmer levelling the automatic directly at the girl's head.

Cardiff was not going to allow it. Rohmer was not going to turn a gun on him again, and he was not going to allow this to happen. He lunged forwards, hit Rohmer hard with his shoulder in a rugby charge and grabbed his gun arm. Rohmer was surprisingly strong, but the impetus of Cardiff's lunge spun him away from the girl. They collided with the corridor wall, Cardiff still hanging on to Rohmer's wrist. The girl cried out, shrinking away from their struggling figures. Rohmer tried to hit Cardiff in the face with his other free fist, but Cardiff was expecting it. He kept his head down so that the knuckles grazed over his head. He slammed Rohmer back against the wall again hard, and felt the breath go out of him.

"Cardiff!"

He looked back from their struggle to see that Duvall had stepped forward. He had drawn his own weapon, and the automatic was levelled at him. They stopped struggling.

"Let him go and stand back."

"You can't do this!" snapped Cardiff, feeling Rohmer trying to break his grip now with a hand that felt like a vice. "You can't!" Cardiff heard Duvall chamber the gun with a ratcheting *click!* "So you're going to shoot me if I don't let go, right? Where's the fair play in that, then, Duvall? Learn this trick at Eton?"

"Harrow, actually," said Duvall grimly.

"Duvall . . . ?" said Jimmy in a quiet voice, sidling up to the man in a curious, almost apologetic way. His head still down, fingers tracing on his brow as if still in pain from the noise they had just heard. Duvall turned to look at him. "I think it's best . . ."

And then Jimmy straightened, stepped quickly forward and grabbed Duvall's arm . . . headbutting him with a loud *smack!* Duvall's hands flew to his face as he collapsed to the tiled floor with a thick grunt. Jimmy had the gun in his hands now, and levelled it with a cool and grim purpose at Rohmer.

Cardiff clung to Rohmer's gun hand.

"Alright," said Jimmy. "Drop the gun on the floor, Rohmer."

"Put the bloody thing down, Devlin," hissed Rohmer. "You don't know how to use it."

Jimmy adjusted the gun so that he was holding it with both hands.

"It's easy. Seen it done on the telly lots of times. Now throw it down."

They were all in a frozen tableau. Jimmy with the gun on Rohmer, as Cardiff held him against the corridor wall. Gilbert somewhere behind, keeping out of the way, trembling with fear. Duvall, semi-conscious and moaning on

193

the floor. And the girl, this distraught seventeen-year-old girl from nowhere, still sobbing and watching this insane drama playing out before her eyes. And outside, the omnipresent hissing of the rain; like the very breath of the watchful storm.

"Better drop it," said Cardiff at last as thunder boomed in the sky and the reception glass lit up again with the flash. "That could be another Darkfall strike, couldn't it? Sure that there aren't any tears in your coat, Rohmer? Sure you don't have any flesh contact with this wall?"

Hissing angrily through clenched teeth, Rohmer's fingers opened. Cardiff quickly took the gun and stood away from him, towards Jimmy. Rohmer staggered away from the wall, eyes blazing with fury, hand massaging his wrist.

"Nice trick, Jimmy," said Cardiff as he drew level with him. "You learn *that* one at Eton?"

"Local pub, actually," replied Jimmy. "After closing time."

EIGHT

Outside, in the rain, it turned what had once been its head up to look at the storm. Rain swilled and foamed in its open mouth as it looked at the churning black clouds and the eruptions of fractured lightning. It knew somehow that it belonged there, not here, and when thunder boomed in the sky it heard that thunder in its newly transmogrified body. It felt the thunder although its hearing faculties had been destroyed by the absorption process. It cried out in response; a bellowing gargle of pain and hate and recognition. Rainwater and petrol gushed from the corners of its mouth. The wind whipped the rags of burned and sundered clothes on its greatly enlarged body.

It turned from the storm and from those inside the office block; its need focusing on the ruined corpse that lay on the pavement next to it. The body was lying face up in the rain.

At first only crudely aware of what its new body needed to survive, it had taken the man crudely. Now it knew what its transmogrified form could do; knew instinctively how its own powers of absorption and reconstitution could be used to feed that terrible need.

It scooped the corpse from its crimson resting place on the pavement. A tide of rainwashed blood swept into the gutter. With rain hissing all around it, flowing on its ravaged and transmogrified new flesh of steel and wire and windscreen and rubber, the thing embraced Pearce's bloody corpse; crushing the flesh tightly to its chest; feeling its own new flesh swarming around him, absorbing him, taking him into itself . . . and growing even larger.

195

Even when Pearce's innards had been completely absorbed and digested, the thing's need was still strong. It strode through the black rain to the car wreck in the forecourt, sensing the presence of more food. Stooping to fasten an encrusted claw under the bottom of the car beside the ruined driver's door, it straightened again and heaved with incredible strength. The car rolled over on to its back with a grinding crash, exposing beneath it the bloodied meat of the two policemen who had been supervising the cordon.

It fed.

NINE

Duvall groaned and sat up, holding his forehead. There was no blood since there had been no cut. But his forehead was already swelling blue-white where Jimmy had butted him.

Rohmer took a step towards them, still massaging his hand and then looked back at the girl. Her sobbing had stopped. Hands still held to her mouth, tears glinted in her frightened eyes. "Look, Cardiff," said Rohmer, turning back to them. "Devlin . . . you don't know what you're doing. She may look normal. But none of those who come back are ever really human again. That thing outside . . . that was human once, and look at it."

"Shut up, Rohmer," said Cardiff. "And get over there beside Duvall."

Rohmer moved past them and stood beside his henchman. Cardiff walked over to the girl. Still keeping an eye on the two men, he glanced down at the girl.

"Was he . . ." she said in a trembling voice. "I mean . . . was that man going to *shoot* me?" She seemed on the verge of weeping again, but regained control.

"What's your name?" asked Cardiff.

"Barbara . . ." said the girl. "My name's Barbara Harrison. Can you tell me . . . where I am? And who are you people?"

"Can't you remember anything? You were here . . . in this office block. It's Christmas Eve. You must have been at a party."

"A party . . . ? What are you talking about? I wasn't at any party. Who are you? What's happening to me?" She

197

began to weep again, struggling to rise. Jimmy was beside her now, and took her arm, helping her to stand.

"Don't . . ." hissed Gilbert. "Don't touch . . ."

"Why don't you shut up?" replied Jimmy. "There's nothing wrong with her." She was shorter than Jimmy by a foot; perhaps five foot three, and her long dark hair was cut to fall around her face in an old-fashioned sixties manner. There was plaster dust on her miniskirt and bruises on her legs; apart from that, her dizziness and obvious distress, she looked to be physically all right. Jimmy looked back at the plaster wall incredulously.

"Now listen, Barbara. We need to know what happened to you . . ."

"Ever the policeman, Cardiff," said Rohmer as he helped Duvall to his feet. "Won't you believe anything I tell you?"

"We need to know what happened to you," continued Cardiff. "You were at an office Christmas party, here in this office block: Fernley House. A storm came. And everyone . . ."

"Why do you keep saying that?" said the girl, leaning against Jimmy now. "I told you, I wasn't at a party. Oh, my head hurts so much . . ."

"You weren't at a party? Then tell me, come on . . . what can you remember?"

"We . . . we were driving."

"Driving?"

"John, my brother . . . he'd just got his new car. And he took me out in it for a test drive. Yes, that's it. We were driving . . . driving, and . . ."

"You mean you weren't here in the office block?"

"I told you! We were out driving! The weather began to turn bad, and we drove . . . drove straight into this storm, or something. And John turned to say something to me, something was happening . . . oh God, something was *happening* and John shouted to me, told me to cover my head or something because the road was full of light and a roaring thunder and lightning. I couldn't see. The windscreen was full of horrible light, and I knew we must be crashing

198

because I could see the wheel spinning in John's hand . . ."
The girl staggered against Jimmy's side, near to collapse.

"Come on Cardiff! Let's just get everyone safe, and then you can go out there and do your Lone Ranger impression if you still want to. I won't stop you."

"Alright . . . but uncock that bloody gun before you hurt somebody."

Jimmy carefully lowered it, just as the girl fainted. He swept her up. Cardiff gingerly touched the basement door handle with his gloved hands, still watching the others. When nothing seemed to be happening, he yanked it open.

"Alright, Jimmy. But be careful. We may be protected . . . but she isn't. Watch her hands, face and legs when you pass through there."

Jimmy carefully stepped into the threshold while Cardiff kept the door jammed open with his foot, reaching in to try the lights again. They were still dead.

"Christ, Cardiff. I can't see a bloody thing."

"Gilbert, come here."

The scientist shuffled uneasily, looking back and forth from Cardiff to Rohmer.

"Come *here*, damn it!"

Gilbert shuffled to him.

"There's a wooden plinth screwed into the wall, just on the inside of this door by the light switch. There are torches hanging on it. Go ahead of Devlin and the girl, take one of the torches and lead the way down the stairs into the basement. We'll be safe there, remember? Just like you said."

"Yes, yes," said Gilbert eagerly, stepping gingerly into the darkened doorway while Rohmer and Duvall watched, and Cardiff carefully watched them.

"Now what?" said Rohmer as Gilbert fumbled at the plinth and found a torch. Spirals of light danced on the walls of the basement as he started down. Jimmy followed and was gone.

"Now we all go down there and wait out the storm?"

"You must be joking," said Duvall. Even in the darkness,

Cardiff could see the swelling on his forehead. "Go down there? With that *thing*?"

"Just a girl."

"You're a bloody fool," replied Duvall. "Some of them look normal enough, Cardiff. But we've seen these things up close. They can change. I've seen a grown man torn to pieces."

"Come on, let's go."

"So you're not leaving to warn the others?" said Rohmer. "You're not going to play the policeman after all?"

"So that you can overpower Jimmy, or talk him into giving you a gun back? No, I don't think so."

"That's not a girl!" snapped Rohmer. "It's a monster."

"I'll make a deal. I'll stay with you and hold on to the guns. If she sprouts a second head or grows fangs – *I'll* shoot her. Okay?"

"You're going to be sorry for this," said Rohmer in a quiet, tight voice. Lightning flashed in the reception windows behind them, and it seemed to be a reflection of his own brimming anger.

"Humour me," said Cardiff, waving the gun at them.

When Rohmer and Duvall had stepped down on to the top of the basement landing, Cardiff followed them, carefully letting the door close behind him. Down below, he could see the single torch beam which illuminated Devlin, the girl and Gilbert. Jimmy had laid the girl down on the rough floor. Cardiff took another torch from the wooden plinth as they descended the stairs into the basement, shoving it into his jacket pocket; taking another and switching it on as they descended. In the darkness, he could barely make out the wooden boards that had been nailed into place over the shattered window vents at street level, but even down here they could hear the hissing of rain on the pavements outside and the grumbling of thunder in the sky.

"Gilbert," said Cardiff as they reached the ground level. "Get that machine of yours, or whatever it is, working now. I don't want to have to go through those hellish noises for a third time."

"But I can't see . . ."

Cardiff kept his distance from them, so that the torch beam had a wider angle to illuminate the scene. He took the second torch out of his jacket pocket and tossed it to Jimmy.

"Stick this against the wall over there and turn it on. That'll give us more light to see by. When you've done that, go get all the other torches up there, bring them back and do the same."

Jimmy skipped away up the stairs towards the plinth, just as the girl began to sit up, with Duvall and Rohmer keeping as far away from her as possible. Rohmer's face betrayed no further anger, but Duvall, with his swelling bruise, looked about ready to deal out some serious damage if Cardiff was to drop his guard. The girl sat up again, and began taking in deep breaths. She looked around the basement, and seemed to recognise Cardiff.

"Oh God, it wasn't a dream, was it? I'm still . . . still . . ."

"Alright, Barbara. Take it easy," said Cardiff. "You're safe. We're all safe here, and no one is going to hurt you . . . least of all these gentlemen in the corner."

"Where are we?"

"We're still in the office block. In the basement. It's safe here."

Jimmy returned with arms full of torches, switching each on and positioning them in the brackets of the huge copper boilers, or on the floor so that surreal fans of light were cast against the dirty plaster walls.

"What am I doing in an office block?" asked Barbara. "I was . . ."

"Driving, yes. You told us. Where do you live, Barbara?"

"Number 10, Browning Place . . . in Fernley."

"Fernley, Newcastle?" asked Cardiff.

"Of course, Newcastle. Where else? Where *am* I?"

"You're in Newcastle, don't worry."

201

"Where's John? What have you done with John?"

"We haven't seen John, Barbara. We don't know where he is. You say you live in Browning Place?"

"Yes, I told you. Look, who are you people? Please tell me what's going on. I don't understand."

"You know you're not telling me the truth, Barbara," said Cardiff, shining the torch in her direction now that Jimmy Devlin's torches arrangement was lighting up the basement like the stage of some avant-garde theatre. "No one lives in Browning Place anymore. The last few houses there are derelict and due for demolition. The Council's rehoused everyone who lived in that street."

"I am *not* lying! Who are you people? What have you done with John?"

And then, purely on impulse, Cardiff heard himself ask a crazy question, but a question that was no crazier than the situation he'd found himself in of late, with people who vanished into and out of walls, the hideous death of four people, three of them his own men and a stalking monstrosity from the pages of a horror comic out there somewhere in the night . . . not to mention cars that just fell out of the sky.

"Barbara, what day did you vanish?"

"God . . ." She rubbed her face in a kind of fury now; a fury which she controlled, and through gritted teeth, said: "Saturday. It was Saturday 15th March." And now she could see the puzzlement on everyone's face.

"March?" asked Cardiff.

"Why? What's wrong with that? What month is it now?"

"It's Christmas Eve."

"But it can't be . . ."

"You've been gone nine months."

"Longer than that, I think," said Jimmy Devlin. He was kneeling beside her now, looking into tear-stained eyes that reflected ice-blue in the torch light.

"What do you mean?" asked Rohmer, now taking an interest in the proceedings.

"The thing about nightmares," replied Jimmy, "is that you've got to go with the flow. When everything around you is just plain bloody crazy, you've got to look for the crazy answers."

"What are you talking about, Jimmy?" echoed Cardiff.

"Are those new clothes you're wearing, Barbara?"

"New? Yes, they're brand new, but ..."

"They're fab, aren't they? I like the green jade necklace."

"Please, what are you all talking like this for? It all sounds mad, like ..."

"Like a nightmare," said Jimmy. "Yeah, I know. You say you were out driving with your brother?"

"Yes, yes, yes! Why does everyone keep asking me these stupid questions?!"

"Was it a brand-new Ford Zodiac?"

"Yes. So you *do* know where John is?"

"What year is it, Barbara?" asked Jimmy.

"Tell me what you've done with John? Where is he?"

"What *year*, Barbara?"

"What the hell is the matter with you all?" Barbara's eyes were blazing with anger now, an ice-cold fire reflecting back. "I know what this is. We crashed ... and I've been ill, or I've lost my memory or something. And you all think I'm mad, don't you? You think I'm off my rocker! So you're ... you're bloody well testing me!" Barbara gathered herself, climbing to her feet again, slapping away Jimmy's proffered hand. Tears were brimming in her eyes again. There were dark streaks down her cheeks. Something about that look stabbed into Jimmy's heart, and he didn't know why. Jimmy Devlin, professional cynic — stabbed in the heart by the honesty that flashed in this girl's rebellion against authority. He saw that honesty and within it somehow, a total lack of the cynicism that had marred his own life. He felt the power in that pure anger when she shouted at him:

"Don't *you* know what year it is?"

And then, the nightmare seemed to take further bizarre shape again, when she swallowed down hard on the choking hoarseness in her voice, and she forced herself to control that anger when she spoke again: "It's 1964. Saturday, March 15th, 1964."

The resulting silence disturbed her even more. She looked from face to face in the darkness, faces that seemed to belong to hideous inquisitors, with the torch beams casting harsh angular shadows from below into their upturned faces.

In a quiet, gentle, but troubled voice, Cardiff said, "You've been gone for twenty-six years, Barbara."

"That thing outside . . ." said Duvall.

"It's her brother," said Rohmer. "I don't know how . . . but it's her brother."

"What do you mean . . . *twenty-six years?!*" shouted Barbara in that pure blaze of anger.

"You see now," said Rohmer. "She can't be human, Cardiff. Not after what she's been through. We can't wait down here, wait for her to change into . . . something. You've got to kill her. Kill her now."

"Please," said Barbara, now sounding weary and in shock: "I don't know what's going on. Please don't kill me. Please don't . . ."

"Shut up, Rohmer!" snapped Jimmy. "No one's going to hurt you, Barbara. Don't worry, I won't let anything happen to you."

"Shoot her, Cardiff. Shoot her. I'll clear your actions with Central Office, if that's what you're worried about."

"Shut up! She's as human as you and me."

"When this is over, Cardiff," said Rohmer in a low, threatening voice. "When we're relieved . . . even if she doesn't *turn*, she'll still be taken by our people. They'll examine her . . . and dispose of her. It's standard procedure."

Gilbert finally stood back from the portable machine on the floor. It was emitting a barely audible, low-frequency hum. "That's it," he said. "The effects will be nullified as long as it operates. Do you think . . . Rohmer, do you think the Main Team will relieve us, do you think they'll . . . ?"

"You know the answer to that better than I do," replied Rohmer. "This is a Secondary Darkfall. They'll wait it out and they'll also be keeping Cardiff's people away. So must we. That's always been the intention, so make sure your equipment is blocking *and* recording efficiently." Rohmer squatted down on the floor, resting his arms over his thighs. "May as well get comfortable. I believe you'll be using that gun sooner than you think."

"Maybe I'll just take it from you," said Duvall.

"And maybe you'd like a bullet in the leg," replied Jimmy. "Self-defence, of course."

"Keep your eye on him, Jimmy," said Cardiff.

"Hey, what do you know? I'm on the side of Law and Order," Jimmy chipped.

"You'll be doing time again for this, Devlin," said Duvall. "Just wait and see."

"Yeah," said Jimmy. "Let's."

Cardiff turned back to the girl.

"It's alright, Barbara. It's okay. Believe me . . . nobody's going to hurt you. But you have to answer my questions. Now, you were out driving with your brother and you drove into some kind of storm. Remember? Where was that? Where were you?"

"I'm not sure," she replied. "We were driving on the main road out of Fernley, I think . . ."

"It's important, Barbara. Try to remember."

"This can't be real. It can't be happening to me. It's 1964. It *must* be, it can't be all that time later . . ."

"Where, Barbara? On the main road out of Fernley?"

"Yes . . . yes . . . I remember we passed the pub . . ."

"The Jolly Miller?"

"Yes, that's the pub."

"And you were travelling on that road in March 1964?"

"Yes, yes, yes . . ."

"That's it, then. *That's* what happened."

"What?" said Rohmer. "What happened?"

"This girl and her brother were driving on a stretch of road that doesn't exist anymore. I know my patch well

205

enough. That section of the road, past the pub she's just mentioned, was rerouted fifteen years ago."

"So?"

"So they were driving right through here! That's where the road was. The area has been developed since. This office block we're in didn't exist then. The road just came straight through. They drove into a Darkfall storm. Right on this spot. Remember what you said, Rohmer? Darkfalls occur regularly on or near the same locality. This wasn't the first Darkfall. There was another — on March 15th, 1964. And this girl and her brother drove straight into it."

"Yes, I think I understand," said Gilbert. "The site of the office block is a blackspot, as Rohmer told you earlier. There is a theory that certain spots . . . throughout the world . . . develop what is termed a 'vile vortex', where phenomena can occur. The Darkfall storm . . . the vortex it creates . . . is a more localised variation of the same phenomenon. This is not the first or perhaps even the second time a Darkfall may have occurred here. It may have happened on several occasions over hundreds, perhaps thousands of years."

"But I can't ever remember a storm like this one ever having occurred in this area before," said Cardiff.

"There has been an escalation of recorded Darkfalls in the past decade," continued Gilbert. "But it may be the case that . . . oh my God!"

Something was scraping against the boarded-up windows.

They turned to look up at the hastily nailed boards that had replaced the shattered windows. The sound came again; a long, rasping, scratching sound, as if someone out there was dragging something sharp across the wood. It stopped . . . and now there was only the sound of the rain hissing on those boards, and the almost inaudible hum of Gilbert's machine.

Jimmy pulled the girl away with him, moving back from the outside wall, and the boards; four feet above them at ground level.

"It might just be . . ." began Gilbert again.

And then something slammed hard against one of the boards. Nails screeched and popped, and the board juddered away at the bottom as something outside slammed against the wood. The basement was filled with the hoarse and ragged sound of monstrous breathing. Rainwater began to gush into the basement from around the fractured board.

As one, they shrank away from the far wall, watching rainwater trickling through the cracks in the boards and spattering on the basement floor. That rainwater began to splash over the lenses of two of the torches that Jimmy had placed on the floor, creating a dancing and hellish kaleidoscope of light in the basement.

"What is it?" asked the girl in a weary voice. "What's . . . ?"

"Quiet!" hissed Cardiff.

The wind gusted outside and rattled the loosened boards. Rainwater flurried and troughed through the cracks.

"It's a dream," said Barbara. "That's what it is. Just a bad dream . . ."

"Will you be *quiet!*" Jimmy pushed her further back, as they all continued to watch the boarded windows with breath held tight. In the centre of the room, Gilbert's machine continued to emit its low, barely audible hum.

Thunder and lightning cracked and roared outside like some electric avalanche — and following immediately upon it came the enraged roaring of Something from Hell. A hideously powerful blow on one of the boards sent it splintered and whirling into the basement. Rain and wind gusted through the gap as the dimly glistening form of some horrifying, ravaged *shape* lashed out from the pavement above and beyond them. Another board exploded screeching inwards. The thing's bellowing was drowned by a further thunder crack as Rohmer yelled . . .

"*Get out! Get out and don't touch the walls!*"

. . . and he shoved a petrified Gilbert ahead of him towards the stairs. The question of who had ownership of guns was now forgotten as Gilbert blundered to the basement stairs, closely followed by Rohmer and Duvall. Cardiff pushed Jimmy and the girl called Barbara after them, turning back to look at the ragged aperture through which the storm was venting its fury. Lightning flashed again as the monstrous shape outside seemed to launch itself head first and downwards in a mad and frenzied lunge at the aperture. Another board shattered apart and fell inwards in shards. And in that flare and roar of lightning, Cardiff saw a hideous face straining to look directly at him as huge and ravaged claws that had once been hands thrashed inwards on the brick face of the basement, seeking purchase.

That face was not the blank face that Cardiff had expected.

It was much, much worse.

It was the same burned face that he had seen behind the wheel of that exploded car in the office-block forecourt. It was the same hideously charred and blackened visage, with its one burst eye still cloying within its ravaged socket like an egg yolk. But this face was bigger; swollen and bigger still than the horror in the car.

And this face was hideously alive.

Its one rolling, swollen eye was fixed on Cardiff even as the thing thrashed with blackened, elongated and monstrously deadly arms at the brickwork, trying to heave itself through the aperture and into the basement. Rainwater gushed around that "face" as it opened jaws that yawned with the ferocious, rasping hatred of some monstrous insect. The dirty water surged with its spume of saliva, and when it roared again it roared with the fury of the storm. Cardiff knew that it *wanted* them.

Faced with this monstrous apparition, Cardiff did not freeze in his tracks even as the others clattered up the basement stairs towards the ground floor. Instead, he stepped towards the thing as the others retreated.

"Cardiff!" shouted Jimmy from somewhere behind him. "What the bloody hell are you doing?"

Cardiff stood his ground and saw in one split-second the faces of Lisa and Jamie – and the man without a face who had mown them down. He saw the hideous face of the huge thrashing thing before him, superimposed on that blank mask, and knew that it was the face he had been looking for since the death of his wife and son.

He had been looking for the Face of Death.

Now, he had found it. He could walk right up and ask it the question that burned within him. Face to face, he could ask it: *Why?*

But this hellish, monstrous Face of Death was also the face of an Abominable Idiot. And Cardiff knew at last that even if he could ask the question, it could never provide him with an answer.

"Cardiff . . . Come on!" yelled Jimmy again.

"You're *nothing* . . ." Cardiff said to the thing.

He raised the Browning automatic as if he was at target practice, levelled the sight at the thing's one remaining monstrous yellow eye – and pulled the trigger.

The sound of the shot was drowned by the deafening screech and roar of the thing as its eye blew apart in a shattering viscous whirl of fluid and tissue. Claws braced on the wall beneath it, the thing strained upwards, rolling its dripping head in agony – and something that had been lying tight beneath it on the pavement slid from under its ravaged body and into the basement. Soaked and tattered, crimson and black, it flopped arm-over-leg to the floor like some discarded overcoat or the eviscerated pelt of some large animal, with only the head intact.

And when Cardiff looked at the upside-down dead eyes of that head as they reflected in the torchlight, when he saw the teeth set in a clenched and hideous grin . . . he recognised the face immediately.

It was Pearce.

He had been skinned.

The thing bellowed and lowered its head again, rain-water-spume-blood-oil running from its jaws. And even though its last eye was gone, Cardiff knew instinctively that it could still *see* him. The horror of Pearce's fate and the appalling impossibility of this thing wedged in the windowframe stung Cardiff into action again. He swung the gun up again, fired wildly at that thrashing form and turned back to the staircase. All except Jimmy seemed to have reached the corridor above. He was standing on the landing at the top, face white. As Cardiff scrambled up the stairs he saw Jimmy raise and fire his own gun at the thing. He had never held a gun before, had certainly never fired one. The recoil was unexpected and he staggered backwards as Cardiff reached him, not knowing whether he had hit it or not.

The screeching and thrashing was behind him now as they bundled out into the corridor, and Cardiff turned to slam the door shut.

As he turned back to the eerie blue-blackness of the strip lights in the corridor, Cardiff heard a thick grunt and the slap of someone falling heavily to the tiled floor. He whirled from the door, heart still pumping madly from his encounter in the basement.

Duvall had hit Jimmy in the stomach. He was crouched on the floor, gagging. Hugging his torso with one hand, his other gloved hand was braced on the floor in the knowledge of what had happened to Frye. Duvall was holding the gun now as he looked down at him, breathing heavily. There was an unmistakable smile of satisfaction on his face, even in the dark, as he fingered the swollen bruise on his forehead. Now, Rohmer stepped towards Cardiff holding out his hands and smiling.

"Give me back the gun," he said tightly.

Down in the basement, something roared. But Cardiff could not tell whether it was the storm . . . or the thing jammed in the window aperture, free at last.

"You stupid bastard," said Cardiff. "You don't give up, do you?"

"Give me the gun or Duvall will shoot the girl."

Duvall raised the gun slowly towards her.

"He'll shoot her whether I give you it or not," replied

210

Cardiff. "So I think I'll just keep the gun. When he shoots her, you get a bullet as well."

Barbara was standing apart from them again, fists held tight at her lap. She was biting her lip and looking at the ceiling, as if willing herself awake. Gilbert was fidgeting with his gloves again, looking at the basement door as Jimmy rolled to his knees and tried to keep from retching.

"That thing down there," said Gilbert urgently. "Look, Rohmer, it doesn't matter. Let's get away from here now while we can. While it's in the basement."

Rohmer stared hard at Cardiff. Duvall waited.

Lightning flashed at the reception windows, as if a power line had snapped and trailed its cables over the window. Thunder detonated like an underground bomb.

"The door isn't locked," said Cardiff. "And even if it was, my guess is that our Addams Family friend could just take it off its hinges without trying."

"Alright . . . alright . . ." Rohmer grabbed Gilbert by the arm with a curiously disappointed look on his face, pushing the smaller man ahead of him. Then, to Duvall: "We're leaving."

"The girl?" said Duvall, perplexed. "Are you saying we leave the girl?"

"Yes."

"Is that an order?"

"We're leaving, damn it!"

Duvall lowered his aim.

"There's a side entrance there," said Cardiff, pointing to the door opposite. "There's a corridor leading to a service exit and back staircase."

Gilbert needed no prompting. He moved quickly to the door as Cardiff hauled Jimmy to his feet, keeping his own gun discreetly aimed in Duvall's direction. Jimmy was able to stand unassisted now as Cardiff turned back to the girl.

"Barbara?"

She was still looking at the ceiling: "Things like that just don't exist," she said to herself. "This is a nightmare and I've got to wake up."

"Barbara, move it!" snapped Cardiff. "We're getting out of this nightmare." With sick fear in his stomach, Cardiff took her arm and guided her towards the side door. At any second, that monstrous thing could come bursting through into the corridor from behind.

Gilbert pulled open the side-entrance door, stepped inside . . . and then recoiled. His face was white. Furious with Gilbert's panic, Rohmer pushed past him and yanked the door wide.

Someone was in the corridor.

Rohmer was frozen in the doorframe now, staring into the darkness, and Cardiff could hear a familiar voice whispering in the shadows.

"I came in here . . . I know I came in here . . . I'm sure this is the place . . . I know I came in here . . ."

"What . . . who is it?" Still trying to keep an eye on Cardiff, Duvall joined Rohmer and looked into the corridor.

Thunder crashed . . . and the sound of it seemed to fill the whispered voice with dread.

"God, God . . . I'm sure I came in here! I did! I must have! I can't get out. I CAN'T GET OUT!"

"Jesus Christ . . ." said Duvall.

And now they could all see what was in the corridor.

Something was trying to pull itself *out* of the corridor wall. A human figure was somehow trapped in the plasterwork of that wall at the waist, twisting and scrabbling and thrashing to be free. Sensing their presence on the threshold of the door, it twisted its head up towards them with a ferocious snarl.

Even though the figure was wreathed in shadow, they could see that it was hideously deformed. The eyes were yellow slits blazing in the darkness; the head swollen and contorted. Saliva flew in a spray from hideously enlarged and slack lips. But it was still, despite the deformation, a face that Cardiff recognised.

"Farley Peters . . ." Cardiff felt his stomach lurch again. "The stupid fool tried to sneak in here and got . . ."

212

"CAN'T! GET! OUT!" screeched the thing that Peters had become — and tried to lunge towards them. It remained stuck fast and it screeched again, waving shredded arms as Duvall slammed the door shut and blocked out the hideous spectacle.

"It's another Returner, Rohmer," stuttered Gilbert. "It's stuck, but we can't get past it . . ."

"The main entrance," said Duvall tightly.

Rohmer and Duvall strode away down the corridor with Gilbert close behind.

Jimmy was recovered now and Cardiff followed, still holding Barbara, who continued to shake her head — wanting to awake.

And now what? thought Cardiff desperately. *Into the cars, that's what. You have the panda. The keys are in your pocket. They have their own car. We all head off into the bloody storm, and then this whole horror comic gets sorted out when we're back in the real world.* But then that other manic voice was saying to him: *But are you sure that the real world exists anymore? Are you sure that there's anything left out there beyond the Darkfall? Maybe this Storm to end all Storms has killed everyone else out there? And even if it hasn't, maybe Rohmer can see to it that you'll spend the rest of your life behind bars along with Jimmy Devlin? And maybe . . . ?*

Lightning whip-cracked across the reception windows again — and in the brief instant that the windows were illuminated by the flash, they all saw the monstrous shape beyond. They froze on the spot at the sight of that hideous snapshot; at the sight of the grotesque, massive *shape* in the act of bearing down upon those windows; charging headlong in an insane frenzy towards them. Darkness blotted out the shape again.

And in the next instant, the glass reception doors exploded inwards.

The storm erupted with all its force into the reception area in a whirling, roaring maelstrom of disintegrating glass shards and a wild, bellowing fury of nightmarish,

213

mutated flesh and flailing claws. Cardiff saw Rohmer, Duvall and Gilbert recoil towards him as the hideous black-glistening thing thrashed amidst the collapsing detritus of its entry. Glass exploded and shattered all around it as the storm wind and rain blasted down the corridor at them. At once, he could see that it was the same monstrous night-mare that had attacked them in the basement. While they had been delayed by Duvall's attack on Devlin, the thing had withdrawn from the basement window and lurched through the storm to the front of the building.

In a nightmare-blur of frenzied activity, Cardiff saw Duvall lunging back through the storm in their direction, a shower of sparkling glass on his shoulders; saw Rohmer seize Gilbert by the collar of his jacket and whirl him away bodily from the monstrous, thrashing shape and drag him backwards, hair and coat whipping madly in the hellwind. And in the instant of time available to him, he thought of the only place of possible escape from this nightmare. Not the basement from which they'd come, with its shattered windows giving further access to this horror . . . not the service/access corridor with its hideous wall-bound parody of Farley Peters . . . but the door next to the basement door marked: "Stairs".

Again, in a frenzied blur of storm-driven wind, ice-cold rain, glass and splintered wood, Cardiff was suddenly at that door now, tearing it open with one gloved hand while he pushed Jimmy and the girl through into the darkness. Duvall collided with him in the rush, nearly flinging him to the corridor floor, but Cardiff clung to the door knob and swung himself back again as Rohmer and Gilbert hurtled past him.

And Cardiff looked back to see the thing standing there amidst the destruction. No longer flailing with hideously encrusted, burnt and sinewed arms; no longer bellowing in fury with the steel trap jaws of some gigantic insect or machine. But standing in the blast of the storm and looking at him even though its ravaged eye sockets contained no eyes. The thing was hunched, but even so, Cardiff could see that it was at least nine feet tall and somehow impossibly larger than the burnt corpse he had first seen behind the wheel of that car. He thought of Pearce, swept away and eviscerated; lying down there in the basement like some horrifying animal-skin rug. And then the thing stepped out of the ruins of broken glass, plaster and wood . . . and in his direction.

In the next instant, Cardiff was in the stairwell and had slammed the door shut behind him.

The sounds of the storm were muffled in the blue-blackness. But the sounds of gasping breath rasped and echoed as Cardiff turned to see that Jimmy and Barbara were still standing in the stairwell. Rohmer, Duvall and Gilbert had started up the stairs, and the sounds of their clattering flight echoed back.

"What are you waiting for?" hissed Cardiff, tearing the tie loose from his collar, realising that he still had the automatic in his other hand but had been unable to use it again. "Go on! Get up those stairs!"

"What *is* it?" asked Barbara breathlessly. In the darkness, Cardiff could not see her lips moving, and almost shouted back at her: *It's your brother! That's what the hell it is!* But instead he grabbed her arm and shoved her ahead. Turning back to look at the door, he could see no manual locking mechanism – only a circular brass inset that seemed to need a special key. Cursing, Cardiff fumbled at the mechanism but could find no locking-catch.

Something smashed hard against the door from the other side. The entire frame shuddered, and Cardiff stumbled back. The door was solid but unlocked. Would that thing out there still know how to simply turn a handle? The door cracked and shuddered again; the sound of the impact terrifying, loud and threatening in the stairwell. Cardiff turned, heart pounding and grabbed the handrail, hauling himself up the stairs.

Above him, Jimmy had stopped on the first landing and was looking back. Cardiff waved him on, too breathless to speak. From below, there was the sound of a third impact.

And up ahead again, from the first-floor landing, Cardiff could hear a muffled and urgent exchange of dialogue. The voices belonged to Rohmer and Jimmy Devlin, but he couldn't hear what they were arguing about as he hauled himself around the staircase rail, paused for gasping breath and looked back down into the stairwell.

A black and vicious claw burst through the woodwork of the door with an explosive crash that echoed up and down the staircase like thunder. The voices above stopped arguing, as Cardiff slid down the rail, exhausted and gasping for breath. He sat on the top step, raised the automatic with both hands and aimed it at the arm that was writhing in the aperture below.

"It's coming . . ." he said, without looking up.

He squeezed the trigger and the echo of the shot blasted all around the stairwell.

Duvall was suddenly standing on the step above him, pushing him out of the way and stepping down past him. Bracing one hand on the stair-rail, he began to squeeze shot after shot down into the stairwell. Amidst the crashing echoes and detonating white flashes Cardiff heard Jimmy shouting: "It does no good, Duvall. Can't you see that? Cardiff shot it in the face, and it didn't stop."

Rohmer remained silent, watching as Duvall descended the stairs still firing. Cardiff heard Jimmy curse; a wordless expression of anger and fear . . . then footsteps on the stairs again as Jimmy hurried off. Was he running for it at last? Still sucking in lungfulls of air and wincing at the detonating roar of Duvall's automatic pistol, Cardiff began to haul himself to his feet again by one arm, his gun hand hanging limp. There was a presence at his side now and he saw in surprise that it was Barbara. Cheeks smeared by tears and mascara, she was helping him to stand and all he could think was *How can she still have mascara after where she's been?* And then, from down below, an enraged roaring swelled up to fill the staircase. The staircase walls seemed to vibrate with the sound of it.

And over the sounds of Duvall's pistol shots, a deafening

punctuation to the sounds of the beast and the storm, Cardiff could hear Duvall spitting out words between each shot as he descended. Crazily, he was enraged.

"Can't *burn* you! Can't *shoot* you! Can't . . . !"

The doors on the landing behind Cardiff juddered open with a loud clatter. Gilbert had been standing next to them and almost fell down the stairs in his efforts to get away from those doors as something shouldered them open. Panic subsided when he saw that it was Jimmy. He was wrestling with something on the other side of that landing door, pushing open the door with one foot and shouting: "Come on, then! Give me a hand!" Now they could see that Jimmy was tugging a large metal filing cabinet with him, dragged from one of the side offices on the first floor. They stood watching him as he tried to manoeuvre the five foot cabinet through on to the landing with them. Its drawers kept sliding open and shut as he heaved at it; the juddering clatter joining with the other sounds of cacophony in the stairwell. "Well, don't just stand there and bloody watch me. Help me!" And then Rohmer grabbed at the door at last as Jimmy began to heave it through.

Below, the stairwell door split down its length under the frenzied and monstrous assault. The top hinge flew apart and the door began to judder inwards. Duvall cursed aloud, fired one last shot directly into the door and whatever lay beyond it, heard the resounding roar of anger and rage . . . and then retreated hastily back up the stairs towards them. Rohmer had hold of the filing cabinet with Jimmy now, and Cardiff and Barbara moved quickly aside as Duvall reached the landing again, looking vacantly at the wrestling match with the cabinet.

"Move!" shouted Jimmy, and he and Rohmer pushed the filing cabinet to the top of the landing . . . just as the nightmarishly black and writhing shape of the thing below burst through the sundered door. Rain and wind gusted in around it. Cardiff saw its hideously burnt and decomposed head turn to look up the stairwell at them, just as Jimmy and Rohmer heaved the filing cabinet over.

Crashing and echoing, the filing cabinet toppled end-over-end down the stairs as the thing heaved itself through the door aperture.

The cabinet slammed full against the shape, pinning it down and jamming sideways at the bottom of the stairwell. Cardiff saw its wildly thrashing and monstrous arms, beating and tearing at the dented grey metal of the cabinet.

"Swallow that!" shouted Jimmy.

"A way out?" snapped Duvall at Cardiff. "You know the building, there must be a way out . . ."

"Back staircase," said Cardiff, breath returned at last. "Through the offices on the first floor."

"Then what are we waiting for?" said Jimmy as thunder roared again, and the thing below gave an answering bellow of fury.

Cardiff led the way into the corridor on the first floor. The main office door to their right was emblazoned with the logo: Stasis Computers, and it was open. This, no doubt, was where Jimmy had found the filing cabinet. Cardiff pushed through into the offices. It was open plan, divided by hessian screens at chest-height. A main thoroughfare had been created through the centre of that office with the screens. On the left was what he imagined must be a typing pool, on the right more desks containing tidy ranks of computers for administrative personnel and computer operators. There were plate-glass windows on three sides of the office . . . and what Cardiff saw through those windows brought him to a halt. The others pushed on past him in the doorway, but they too stopped when they saw what was revealed on the other side of the windows.

The office block was in the middle of a hellish whirlwind.

From left to right, a spinning maelstrom of snow and rain was sweeping around the block like a tornado. The effect was dizzying. The voice of the storm was louder up there; a wailing lament of storm-wind against the buffeted glass. Overhead, the strip lights gave out a ghastly flickering blue and the shadows of the storm on that huge expanse

218

of glass created a psychedelic swirl of speckled light in the office which added to the vertigo.

"Darkfall," said Rohmer in a tone of voice approaching real awe, and Cardiff looked at him hard again. He had changed somehow since this nightmare had really descended and impossible things had started to happen. In spite of the immediacy of their terror and danger, he was somehow more self-absorbed.

"What do you all take me for?" shouted Jimmy. "A furniture remover?"

Cardiff turned to see that Jimmy was manhandling another cabinet from behind one of the hessian screens and towards the door. Duvall joined him and began to shove hard, until the cabinet had juddered close up to the office door. "Don't get any skin contact with this, Duvall," said Jimmy through gritted teeth. "You don't want to end up filed in there forever, do you?" Duvall gave him a flinty stare.

Jimmy was changed in Cardiff's eyes, too. But he didn't have time to speculate now as he strode across the office with the others following, down the "corridor" between the screens and towards the double-doors directly ahead which would give access to the secondary staircase.

"How do we get down if the bottom door is locked?" asked Gilbert as they moved.

"We'll have to jump from the first floor," said Cardiff.

"Jump?"

"There's a raised embankment behind the office block. The contractors have been clearing earth back there for landscaping. It won't be far from the first-floor windows to the mound. It's only ten feet or so down, if we pick the right window."

From somewhere below came a great rending and echoing squeal of torn metal. It sounded as if the thing downstairs had finally torn the cabinet out of its way.

And then another Darkfall bolt hit the building.

The thunderclap was deafening. Their hands flew to their ears in unison and they staggered under the immensity of the reverberating impact. The floor beneath them vibrated, and they reeled. Ahead of them, a great crack appeared from ceiling to floor in the wall where the double-doors were set. Somewhere, party glasses slid from a table and shattered on the floor and one of the computer consoles fell from the end of its desk with splintering impact. The glittering green Christmas decorations which had been Sellotaped to the ceiling and walls swayed crazily as if the whole office block was tilting. Plaster dust puffed downwards from the ceiling.

Something was happening at the windows.

At first, it seemed as if the windows had all cracked under the impact of the strike. There was a jagged network of white fractures in the glass of all of them. But those cracks were somehow alive and moving with a pulsing and fractured blue-white light as they looked. Those jagged fractures spread like hissing, living root-fibres on the juddering panes, filling the office with light.

"Lightning!" exclaimed Gilbert.

And they watched the living cloud of electricity which surrounded them flickering and dancing with fingers of thin white crepuscular power; they watched the spidery web of frosted white fire greedily dancing and exploring the windows.

The second impact came, like the slamming of a huge underground steel door ... and just like the sound that Cardiff remembered from the basement. Their hands flew to their ears again, pain stabbing into eardrums.

Oh Christ, not this! Cardiff whirled to Gilbert. "The sound! It'll kill us!"

"No ... no ..." Gilbert winced through gritted teeth. "Not above ground. The acoustic effect will transfer underground."

The detonation faded away to a muted roar.

"See? See?" said Gilbert as if eager to please.

Cardiff shook his head, rubbing at his ears. He looked up to see that Barbara was leaning against one of the hessian

220

screens. He lunged forward and plucked her hand away from the screen.

"Don't touch anything. Don't . . ."

And then he turned back to Gilbert.

"That *was* a Darkfall strike, wasn't it?"

"Yes, so we mustn't . . ."

"Touch anything?"

Gilbert saw what he meant immediately. Barbara had been in flesh contact with the screen, but had not been absorbed. He shook his head.

"She's immune. She's a Returner. So she's immune from that effect now. She's been through that process once, and it seems that she'll stay immune to further absorption. We've had experience of this before."

Duvall was at the double-doors leading to the secondary staircase. He pulled one of the doors open. Somehow, lashing wind and rain was gusting through that opened door . . . and Duvall was slamming it shut hard again, turning back to Cardiff and snapping: "You stupid bastard! You've got us trapped in here!"

"What the hell are you talking about?" snapped Cardiff in return, and pushed past him to the double-doors. Jimmy was at his side now, and they both looked through the glazed front of the doors. Immediately, they could see what had happened.

The Darkfall strike had destroyed the second staircase.

Somewhere above, lightning had impacted on the building and an upper section of the staircase had collapsed in upon itself. A great avalanche of steel and concrete had crashed downwards into the shaft which had been the stairwell; gathering bulk, weight and destructive momentum from floor to floor as it collapsed. Beyond the double-doors lay only a compacted cave-in of concrete slabs and twisted metal, with not enough space for even a small dog to squeeze through. Storm water was running amidst the compacted mangle of that destruction.

"We're trapped up here!" snapped Duvall again.

Beyond the windows, the electrical web of lightning had

now vanished. The swirling rain and snow whirled continually against the buffeted glass.

"Alright ... alright ..." said Duvall, complacently now, as if he could sort out their problems rationally. "It's time to stop pissing about. And the first thing we do, is get rid of *that!*" He raised his gun, pointed it directly at Barbara and, before they could react ... pulled the trigger.

The hammer fell on an empty chamber.

Duvall had used his last shell on the thing downstairs without realising.

"You dirty ..." And Jimmy had grabbed up a nearby typist's chair from behind the screen and raised it with both hands like some huge club, ready to smash it across Duvall's face. Recovering from his surprise, Duvall was ready to throw himself at Jimmy.

"Leave it!" shouted Cardiff, raising his own gun in their direction. "Both of you! We've more to worry about."

"Well, just keep an eye on *it*," said Duvall, without taking his eyes off Jimmy, and meaning Barbara. "When it 'turns', you just be ready with that gun." Jimmy lowered the chair to the floor as Duvall fingered the dark bruise on his forehead. "And when we're out of this, Devlin, you and I have something to settle."

Jimmy laughed, a sound without humour. "You sound just like a policeman."

"Quiet!" hissed Gilbert. His face was a mask of alarm and he was looking back to the office door and the cabinet which was pushed up against it. "I heard it. I'm sure I heard it ..."

The whirlwind raged at the window ... but although they strained to listen, they could hear nothing from the corridor beyond.

"More furniture against the door," whispered Gilbert. "We have to pile more against the door. Stop it from getting in ..."

"No," said Cardiff, noting with rising anger that Rohmer was just standing and watching him with that smile on his face again. "Don't make *any* noise that might attract it."

Jimmy skipped back towards the door and the filing cabinet.

"Jimmy . . ." began Cardiff in alarm and warning. Jimmy waved a hand back at him to be silent, and then he had reached the office door, crouching down low. Carefully, he straightened and looked out through the fluted glass in the upper part of the door. Crouching again, he moved to the other side of the cabinet and repeated the same manoeuvre, craning his head to look out. Then, keeping low, he skipped back to them again.

"No sign of it. No sounds. Maybe it didn't follow us up here."

Thunder shuddered the building again, this time like the sounds of a faraway avalanche. The rumbling resolved into the hissing of rain and the howling of the wind. The hissing of the rain was beginning to sound like whispered voices now; like a multitude of whispering voices in the darkness.

"Maybe it's dead," said Gilbert. "That's happened before, Rohmer. Sometimes they just sicken and die. Like the one you spent so much time talking to. You remember that thing, don't you, Rohmer?"

"Oh yes," said Rohmer, again with that mysterious look on his face. "I remember."

The hissing of the rain was somehow louder, somehow more different in tone . . . and somehow much more like the whispering of a multitude of voices than before. Cardiff turned back to Rohmer, and remembered again that feeling he was sure they'd shared when they'd first encountered each other. He remembered that strong question-mark of recognition: *Is it you?* Perhaps now was the right time to ask Rohmer just what the hell he really was, just what the hell was really going on . . . ?

And then the hissing, whispering of the rain seemed to fill the office . . . and from that whispering, came a voice.

"*Cardifffff . . .*"

It was a whispered voice that spoke his name.

"Oh my God," said Gilbert, looking around.

"*Cardiff, for the love of God, get me out of here. Pleasssse . . .*"

Other whispered voices joined the plea. But this time, the voices were not in the distress of agony that had been heard in the reception area. This time the voices were mournful, rather than agonised. They were afraid and they were lost. Hundreds of voices whispered from the walls, the ceiling and the floors. They were the voices of lost souls, all taking their lead from the one voice that had spoken Cardiff's name. And that same voice continued to beg for his help.

"*Don't leave me here, Cardiff. I don't know what's happening. But I can't bear it. Please, for God's sake . . .*"

"Evans," said Cardiff in an awed voice, as the whispering multitudes took up his name as a kind of saviour's anthem. Those voices sounded like some dreadful surf breaking on a lost and faraway shore.

"I remember them," said Barbara. "From another dream. I think I was somehow with them once. Oh, God. Please help them if you can, Mr Cardiff."

"I can't help them," said Cardiff. "I wish to God I could. But I can't. All we can do now is help ourselves."

Evans' lone voice drifted away, sinking beneath that whispering sea of voices. Those voices merged with the hissing of the rain again . . . and were silent.

"So what do we do?" asked Jimmy, looking back at the cabinet where it was wedged tight at the office door.

"We keep quiet and wait," said Cardiff. "Keep out of sight . . . and wait."

PART THREE

THE DARKFALL

"I beheld Satan as lightning fall from heaven"

St Luke, 10:18

ONE

A great weariness had suddenly settled upon it.

The great thunder which had propelled it towards their hiding-place below ground had somehow ebbed. They had fought back, and it had felt the sting of their fight which had only served to make its hunger and hideous needs greater. The small pain which had been inflicted upon it had only served somehow to make it stronger. It had smelt their flight, trying to escape from their hiding-place and into the night. Consumed by that monstrous need, it had entered their hiding-place at last.

Possessed by that hunger, it had still sensed that there was something different about the female. It knew that she had not been there before, and that she had somehow appeared amongst them from nowhere. It knew that she was different. There was something of kinship about her that registered on a purely instinctive level, and in a way that the thing could not interpret.

It shook away these confusing feelings about the female. They had escaped from it again, but not for long.

It had freed itself from the stairwell and could smell them, not far above it and within easy reach. It had begun to ascend the stairs . . . and then the weariness had overcome it. Even the power of the storm, with which it shared a kinship also, could not assuage the hunger. A vital part of the thing seemed to be ebbing away. And as it slumped to the stairs, it realised at last that the girl was also somehow connected with the storm. The images in its head were confusing and seemed to hasten the dying feeling inside. It gave in to the weariness.

227

Somewhere beyond, the thing that had been Farley Peters — still locked in the corridor wall — gibbered and scrabbled with monstrous hunger. The thing turned wearily to listen, swamped by inertia and the need to sleep.

TWO

". . . sleep," said Barbara. "Maybe it's gone to sleep."

They were crouching and sitting behind the hessian screens in the typing-pool. Everyone was making sure that they were not in flesh contact with any of the furniture, walls or floor. But Barbara was sitting on the carpeted floor, both hands braced before her.

"What?" asked Cardiff.

"I don't know. I just thought maybe that it . . ." She ran a hand through her hair and then took the jade necklace in her hand and began to rub her fingers over it, as if it was a magic charm that could somehow protect her. She shook her head. "It was nothing. Nothing at all."

"*Could* she know what it's thinking?" asked Rohmer. "We've had telepathic contacts before in sympathetic Returners."

"Perhaps," replied Gilbert. "They're brother and sister. They've both been through the same transmogrification."

"Wait . . ." said Barbara. "What are you saying?"

"That thing downstairs," said Duvall tightly. "It's your brother."

Barbara raised her hands to her temples and began to massage. When she spoke again, it was in a quiet, sensible voice: "I know this is a dream. I know I can come through it. But just like dreams, some parts are crazy. They don't make sense. So I'll squeeze those parts out . . . squeeze them out until all of this is over." She looked up again when Jimmy put a hand on her shoulder.

"That's the way to do it," he said. "Don't worry, it'll soon be over."

"I think I know what happened to the girl and her brother," said Gilbert. "I've been thinking about how the constituent parts of the two people and the car could be transmogrified and reassembled – if Cardiff's surmise is correct, that is."

"And?" said Rohmer.

"It's just a theory, of course."

"Spit it out."

"They drove into a Darkfall storm in the middle of a road. I believe that there was a lightning strike on the car. The Darkfall energy could have been attracted by the car battery. As a result, the inert and living organisms were disassembled and scattered into the ether. Those atoms were randomly distributed in the environment. Now that another Darkfall has occurred, that energy has resulted in random reassembly."

"The car battery?" said Jimmy.

"Yes, it's the simplest form of a voltaic cell: a plate of copper and a plate of zinc immersed in a dilute solution of sulphuric acid. A current flows from the copper to the zinc when wires are connected between the plates. The difference in the electrical properties of the metals provides the force that drives such a current."

"Yeah," said Jimmy dryly, still looking at the office door. "Like I said . . . a car battery."

"The energy generated within a Darkfall would be attracted to that kind of interaction, no matter how small. This *must* have happened. Thunderclouds are already highly charged with electricity. And an ordinary lightning flash is simply the breaking down of the insulating properties of air which discharges a momentary electric current to those clouds. A Darkfall strike is . . . how shall I say it? . . . a much more powerful, more *voracious* kind of strike. It affects the properties of animate and inanimate material, resulting in fusion. Such a strike would be immediately attracted to the operation of the car battery. The same thing would have happened in the Bermuda triangle disappearances, don't you see? In those cases where not only people, but the actual aeroplanes, boats or ships themselves actually disappeared from the face of the earth. They were . . . disassembled. And then disappeared in the ether."

"My head's hurting," said Jimmy. "Too many words, man. Too many words."

Thunder boomed again. Pain stabbed into their ears, and this time they kept their hands there until the secondary cracking of thunder had come and gone. The windowpanes rattled furiously, and spidery fingers of crepitating electricity twitched and danced over the glass once more; again creating the illusion that the entire office block was somehow enmeshed in some monstrous spider's web. Swirling snowclouds and rain strengthened the illusion that there was no outside world anymore, and that they had all been transported to some frozen Hell.

In silence, they watched the office door and the cabinet.

The snow and the rain and the flickering of spidery lightning made bizarre, dancing shadows.

Rohmer, who had become so silent, looked at the storm-driven snow and the living electricity which buffeted the window nearest to him. He looked out into the Darkfall.

And he remembered.

THREE

It was the first time that Rohmer's Unit had managed to keep a Returner in captivity for analysis and experimentation. Rohmer did not count Eleanor Parkins from the Fernley House incident. She had been destroyed before they could get her out of the police cell. The other Units, he knew, had only had one apiece. And even though the same scientists were involved in that experimentation, Rohmer could not resist a kind of immature pride in the fact that his unit had more than the others.

The first Returner had been non-vocal. Not surprising in that it no longer possessed vocal cords. X-ray analysis had revealed a complex throat-tract of asbestos fibre, a gullet composed mainly of industrial plastic and a stomach cavity with a basis of fibrillated copper. And yet somehow the thing was still able to consume and digest the normal fats and proteins, converting them to energy, in a complex manner which they had never really been able to explain. Examination had also revealed several hooded eyes in the head, torso and arms; all connected by a massive circuitry of unexplainable nerves and sinew which, although with no brain to relay messages still *saw* them, still swivelled and watched them move about the room as they examined it. Those eyes were made of coloured glass. And just how the hybrid could function without a discernible brain also remained a mystery. The thing had died, and for its death they could also find no reason . . . no more than they could find a reason for how it was able to live in the first place.

The second Returner had killed two men, and had also

232

been destroyed in the process before full analysis could commence.

But the third had been different.

Because the third had been one of their own.

A Darkfall storm had descended on a factory in Leeds four years earlier. It could have been worse; since the first strike had occurred at 9.30 p.m. after the main factory work-hours, and only a skeleton-crew shift had been in operation at that time. Twenty-three people had vanished from the face of the earth. And a team had been sent in as normal for initial investigation, only to retreat almost immediately when their equipment had registered the fact that this was a Secondary Darkfall.

But Charles Bissell did not return from the factory. An associate of Gilbert, he had insisted on moving in with the team, even though his presence was not necessary, for first-hand examination. And when the roster was called on evacuation, he was missing.

They had waited for the Darkfall to blow itself out, which it did in spectacular fashion. One entire section of the factory had collapsed before the storm had finally dissipated. The team had moved back in again, carefully sifting and analysing.

Bissell's body had been found lying on a pile of rubbish, face down.

But he had not survived the Darkfall. He had been absorbed in some fashion ... and then Returned. And when the first person to find him had turned him over, presuming him dead, he had bitten a chunk out of that person's thigh. The finder had almost died, and Bissell had been restrained and returned to the Unit for full examination. The missing twenty-three persons had remained missing ... so far. But there were life readings in the walls, floors and turbine-generators within the factory itself.

Bissell's own molecular composition, including the clothes he had been wearing, had proved just as chaotic as expected. They assumed that he had been absorbed by machinery of some kind; since his own individual chromosomatic make-up was principally metallic.

Strait-jacketed to restrain his flailing and deadly limbs, Bissell had been returned to the Institute for examination and analysis. Although still recognisably human in shape, and with a skin covering of normal human skin, X-ray analysis had revealed a new and scientifically impossible internal network of industrial steel and plastics. A complex combination of aluminium, steel and copper had replaced his skeletal structure, making him too heavy to stand alone, lest his skin should rip open under the strain. A specially constructed harness had been devised for him in one of the clinically white rooms where analysis was conducted. Externally, Bissell appeared normal, with little sign of metamorphosis – except for his eyes. They had no irises and were a glinting, ebony black.

Importantly for the Unit, Bissell was a "talker".

Three tapes of recordings existed, supervised by Gilbert. And Rohmer remembered those conversations almost by heart.

Bissell sat in his chair/harness, grinning. He was pumped full of sedation, but none of it seemed to work and Gilbert had decided against more in case he died. A bib had been tied around Bissell's neck to collect the raw, liquid plaster which oozed from his mouth where it congealed and hardened. The assistant putting that bib on him had foolishly come too close. Bissell had bitten him with teeth composed of white aluminium. He had chewed, swallowed and licked his lips while the man was taken away, screaming.

Eventually, Gilbert had switched on the tape and asked, "Do you feel like talking, Bissell?"

The thing that had once been Bissell laughed again, raw plaster splattering on the tiled floor.

"Ever stood under an overhead power cable? Ever felt the electrical field? Listened to its hum?" His voice had a hollow echo to it, as if there was nothing inside him. "Ever felt the hairs on your skin stand up?"

"Yes."

234

"Aha . . . aha . . ." And then, in agonised pain: "Christ, Gilbert! Do something to help me . . . do something to . . . Did you know that crops don't grow so well next to pylons and power cables? Did you know that? Farms crossed by electricity cables have more calves still-born or deformed than those which don't. That's . . . that's because chromosomes are affected by electric and magnetic fields. That's why . . . why . . ." Bissell chuckled hideously, ". . . I Yam What I Yam." He chuckled again, this time like the Popeye cartoon character. Far from being funny or ludicrous, the sound was deeply chilling.

"And what are you?" asked Gilbert. "Can you tell me that, Bissell?"

Bissell looked hard at him with unblinking black hatred, then with pain. The overhead strip lights glinted in the blackness of his eyes.

"I've . . . opened up. I can see behind the surface of matter. Almost a different realm. I don't see you, Gilbert. I see . . . I see your shape and your vibration. I can sense your emotional state. You're afraid of me. And you have a good right to be . . . because . . ."

"Because?"

"You're not a person to me anymore. There is no such thing as a 'person'. When I look at you I see . . . I can only see . . ."

"What can you see?"

"You're food, Gilbert. Just . . . food." Bissell howled then, like some kind of demented animal. When he spoke again, it was as if he was fighting with something within; fighting to retain control of his humanity. "The body has a defence mechanism to protect it from invasion by foreign substances. Darkfall gives the inert material an 'animate' characteristic; it makes it react in the same way to a human absorption. Because this time . . . this time . . . it's not a virus, or a pollen, or a transplanted organ . . . it's human material. The inert material engulfs the foreign substance in contact with it. Then its own 'white cells' surround it. Try to eat it. Remove it. But they can't. Do you see,

235

Gilbert? Do you see? It's like the specific immune defence response in human bodies. The invading substance is not eliminated . . . but altered. By the building's defence mechanism, just like antibodies." Bissell began to laugh again, his voice choking on the liquid plaster. "I'm an antibody. I'm full of antibodies. Isn't that funny, Gilbert? Antibody? Do you get it? Do you . . . OH, MY GOD, HELP ME, GILBERT!"

Something inside Bissell seemed to crack and splinter, and even though there was no longer any recognisably human tissue, nerves or organs beneath that covering of skin, Gilbert knew that the scientist was in a mortal distress of agony. He winced, waiting for that skin to split. But it didn't happen and Bissell's cries choked away. The scientist sagged in his "harness".

"Bissell? Can you hear me? Can you . . ."

"Feed me, Gilbert. Give me what I want. Give me something to eat."

"We've tried that, Bissell. We've tried to find the right combination of fluid proteins and . . ."

"Fuck that! Try something raw. You know what I want. Don't you? Come over here and . . . and . . . oh God, Gilbert. Don't come near me. There are . . ." Bissell fought against his own inner horror, biting down with aluminium teeth on a tongue of industrial rubber. He still felt human pain, and it made him retch. The purely animal function of retching brought him back again. ". . . there are four forces operating in the . . . in the universe, Gilbert. You know that. Gravity, the nuclear force inside the nuclei of atoms, strong and weak . . . and electromagnetism. Can you tell me what an electric charge really is? No, of course you can't. None of us can. Science can never deal with any questions about the essence of things. Isn't . . . isn't that true? Even though we believe we're so . . . so . . . bloody CLEVER! God . . . God . . . Death isn't defined by the absence of a heartbeat. It's defined by the absence of electrical activity in the brain."

"What are you trying to say?"

"Did you know that life began on earth when lightning struck the sea? Did you know that?"

"What . . . ?"

"Electricity, Gilbert. That's what this is all about. The nature of electricity. We think we've harnessed it. We think we understand it. But we haven't . . . and we don't. It's a fundamental property of nature, and we've reaped the advantages of its light side . . ." Bissell laughed again; an abominable liquid croaking. "But there is a dark side. And the Darkfall is the manifestation of that dark side. There's more to Darkfall than science can explain. It's bad now. But it's going to get worse. Much worse. Because . . ."

And then Bissell had looked directly at Rohmer with those hellish, black eyes . . . and he had smiled.

"Mr Rohmer? Why is your heart racing? What is exciting you so much?"

God, can it read my mind? thought Rohmer. Can it really see what I'm . . . ?

"Yes, of course I can," continued Bissell. "And I'm not going to talk to you anymore, Gilbert. I have to eat. And you won't let me. So if I can't eat, I won't talk." Bissell's eyes never left Rohmer as he spoke, and Rohmer knew what the thing meant when it said it wouldn't talk to Gilbert anymore. But Rohmer had to know the answer to the questions that had fascinated and intrigued him for so long; the questions that bore down on him with ever-increasing force during the drug-induced hallucinatory periods that were now so frequent in his life. Now he knew that the Darkfall effect did have the answer to those questions and that Bissell could give him those answers. So while Gilbert tried to entice Bissell to talk further, and Bissell kept silent, still watching him across the room, Rohmer saw the promise in those night-black eyes . . . and he began to lay his own plans.

FOUR

". . . sick," said Gilbert, in a hushed voice. The wind and the rain, and the hollow reverberation of the storm brought Rohmer back from his reverie. Gilbert was talking to the others in a quiet and urgent voice; his whispers like the quiet and urgent washing of the rain on those shuddering windows. Rohmer focused on the present again. Gilbert, with the edge of terror still in his voice, was talking to keep himself sane; and the others were listening to try and make sense of the nightmare in which they found themselves.

They were fools.

Only Rohmer knew the real truth.

"What do you mean?" whispered Cardiff, and Rohmer felt the cold chill of withdrawal gnawing at his soul. He looked at them with contempt, fumbled in his pocket and found the pill. Turning back to the storm-rinsed windows and the dangerous electrical crackle of Darkfall lightning on the glass, he popped the pill and watched the water running down the glass in ever-increasing and mysterious rivulets.

"This building is sick," continued Gilbert. "Surely you've heard of sick building syndrome?" He laughed. It was a fragile and unconvincing sound. "But it's true. There was a German doctor, back in the 1950s. His name was Hubert Palm. And he propounded evidence that a great many of the ailments we have in modern society have to do with the way we construct our buildings. Buildings are our 'third skin'. Modern construction technology, synthetic compounds and materials we use in constructing the buildings we live in or work in . . . and the suffusion by those structures of electricity . . . create electrostress, or 'electrical diseases'."

"You talk as if this building was *alive* or something," said Cardiff.

"It is," replied Gilbert. "But only in the sense that a tree is alive. Not sentient . . . just living. And the effects we've seen are caused when a Darkfall strike is absorbed by a building. There is a massive intake of electricity. And it's electricity and our real lack of understanding of what it actually is that . . ."

The pill took effect, and Rohmer tuned out again and into the storm. As Gilbert's words faded, he was back at the Unit again, listening to the thing which had once been Dr Bissell as it said . . .

FIVE

"I knew you would come."

"Yes . . ."

"Did you bring me what I need?"

"Yes, I have it here."

"And it's still alive?"

"Yes."

"Then give it to me."

"Not before we talk."

"No! Give it to me now . . . or . . ." Bissell chuckled, and then whined, mimicking a spoiled child. The sound was hideous. ". . . or I won't talk."

Rohmer controlled the squirming of it in his hands, held it still, feeling its heart race in the presence of the thing. Did it know?

"Of course it knows," said Bissell, reading his mind again. "Now, give it to me."

"The strait-jacket stays on."

More of that hideous laughter: "Ohhh . . . you don't trust me."

"That's right."

Rohmer looked down at it, felt his gorge rise.

"You want the real answers, don't you?"

"Yes . . ."

"Then do it!"

Much later, when it was finished and after Rohmer had left the cell to be sick, the thing's head had sagged forward on to its chest. Was it dead? No, it couldn't be dead! Not after . . .

"You're very clever," said Bissell, looking up at him again. "The way you contrived to be alone with me, despite the supervision and monitoring."

Bissell seemed so much calmer, now that he had fed. There were no spasms of grinding agony.

"You think you're different, don't you, Rohmer? You've always felt that way. Ever since you raped and killed that cadet in military school . . . just to show yourself that you could do it. Weren't sick then, were you?"

Rohmer broke out into an immediate, drenching sweat. The thing felt his discomfort and laughed again.

"Yes, I know you, Rohmer. I see the real you. And I see what you really want. And what you want is . . ."

"To see as you do. I want to . . ."

"Be more than human. You envy me, Rohmer. Do you envy my agony?"

"I fed you."

"You want me to be your mentor, Rohmer? You want me to be your gateway to another world? You want your perceptions heightened . . . and you want to shirk off all notions of human morality. Isn't that right?"

"When you were talking to Gilbert. You said there was 'more' to the Darkfall than science could explain . . ."

The thing laughed once more.

"Talk to me, damn you!"

"Alright, alright . . . I'll tell you what you really want to know . . ."

SIX

"Come on, Rohmer? Are you just going to sit there and stare out of the bloody window?"

Rohmer was back in the present again. Duvall was shaking him by the sleeve, bringing him back.

"So what do you want me to do?"

"Well . . . are we just going to sit here waiting . . . or what?"

"You're welcome to go downstairs and see if that thing's still about," said Jimmy.

"It's dying," said Barbara. It was clear that this knowledge was distressing her. "I can feel it."

"So we'll take *Mister* Cardiff's advice," said Rohmer. "We'll sit tight and wait for the storm to blow itself out."

"We could break one of those windows," continued Duvall. "It can only be about thirty feet or so to the ground. Higher than from the back staircase like Cardiff said. But as there's no bloody staircase left, it's still our best option."

"I'm not sure anymore," said Gilbert. "That Darkfall lightning out there on the windows, that electricity."

"Well?" snapped Duvall, a little too loudly; and enough to make him look nervously back in the direction of the office door.

"If we break the glass, we might draw the energy to ourselves."

"Great. You mean we'll be struck by lightning?"

"Not your day, is it, Duvall?" said Jimmy, and Duvall glared hard at him again with a look that spoke again of reckonings to come after the nightmare was over. Jimmy

242

returned the look, and then turned to Barbara. She was shuddering.

"Nineteen sixty-four was a great year for music," he said. She looked up at him. "Seriously, I mean it. Some of my favourite music came from 1964."

Barbara swallowed hard, trying to shrug off the feelings which were so distressing her. "The Beatles are my favourite . . ."

"Yeah, The Beatles. Now there's a group. Let's see, 1964. They were just starting out. Had their first hit in 1963 with . . . 'I Wanna Hold Your Hand'. Great stuff. And just think, Barbara, you've got all of their other songs to catch up on."

"My friend Angela and I argue about John Lennon and Paul McCartney. She likes Paul best. I like John. Is he still . . . still writing songs?"

"Well, John was . . . he was . . . Yeah. Yeah, that's right. Still writing songs. Still as good as ever. Let's see, 1964. Cilla Black. What about her?"

" 'You're My World'. That's a lovely song."

"Still going strong, Cilla. Wife and mother now. Does game shows and things. Just think, all that music to catch up on . . ."

"I wonder if my folks are still . . ."

"Look, Barbara. Everything's going to be fine. I promise you. Once we get out of here. I'll help you to find them."

"It's going to be okay," said Cardiff.

Thunder cracked again, stabbing at their ears. The spider-web lightning twitched and surged at the windows, as if hunting for some small crack in the glass through which it could get to them.

Duvall turned back to Rohmer in disgust.

"So we wait?"

Rohmer did not answer. He was watching the storm again . . . and remembering.

"Electricity," said Gilbert again, and all except Rohmer turned to listen to him again, because there was nothing else any of them could do. "Invisible, silent. We generate

243

it at will, turn it on or off by flicking a switch. If we didn't have it, we couldn't live. Everything would stop. Our society would be plunged into darkness. Offices, factories, industry, communications, transport . . . all of it grinding to a halt. We depend upon it completely . . . and our dependence makes us so vulnerable to its dark side. We really know so very little about it."

"Shut up, Gilbert!" hissed Duvall.

"Let him talk," said Cardiff.

Gilbert continued, as if he hadn't even heard the interruption. "The earth is a massively complicated network of patterns of electrical energy with that magnetic field made even more complex by the minerals, water, rocks . . . and mankind's own addition of man-made structures. And that electrical energy also affects human beings. It affects us physically, emotionally, mentally . . ."

And spiritually, thought Rohmer, again tuning back in to Gilbert's words.

"Inside of us all," continued Gilbert, "there are extraordinarily complex and subtle electric fields, permeating every tissue, every bone, every muscle, every cell. And our own electrical fields interact with the electrical fields in the environment . . ."

Gilbert's eyes seemed glazed, and Jimmy looked at Cardiff in a way that seemed to say: *We've got to shut him up, Cardiff. He's cracking up or something. He thinks he's back at college, giving a lecture.* Cardiff quietened Jimmy with a gesture that meant: *Let him talk. We might learn something.*

". . . These fields in humans were discovered back in the 1940s and 1950s. Not only humans, of course, but also plants, animals, trees . . . even raw protoplasm. They're called L-Fields: bioelectric and electrodynamic fields of life. And it's the interaction of these electrical fields with the Darkfall electricity that causes these . . . things to happen."

You're a fool, Gilbert, thought Rohmer, still listening, but watching the storm. *All of this knowledge, and you still haven't discovered the real truth behind it at all.*

"The Darkfall electricity ... that Dark Energy ... is drawn to electrical fields. Somehow there is a fusion of new, raw Dark Energy. We're none of us safe. Think about it! Everywhere you look ... cables, wires, pylons. It's all around us. Radio, television, radar ... all manner of electromagnetic transmissions in the air. How long before Darkfall starts to spread further afield? At present, we've identified the recurrence of 'vile vortices' where Darkfall happens with a certain regularity. Like here! But how long before it starts to ..." Gilbert stopped, shuddering. He wiped a trembling hand across his face, and took several deep breaths to calm himself down.

So near, Gilbert. And so far. Perhaps I will have the chance to be your Teacher. Perhaps I'll be able to show you the Real Truth.

"It's dead," said Barbara. "I can feel it."

"Can she know that, Gilbert?" asked Duvall urgently.

"Yes, it's possible. If she does have that telepathic link. We've known something like it before."

"Are you sure?" Duvall asked the girl.

"I could feel ... I could feel it before. Now I can't feel anything at all. It just died away ... now it's gone."

"Rohmer?"

Rohmer turned back from the window to look at Duvall.

"Come on, Rohmer. If that thing really is dead, I think we should take the chance."

"That Darkfall lightning on the windows ..." began Gilbert.

"We don't know for sure that it'll strike," said Duvall. "If that thing's dead, isn't it worth taking the risk to get away from here?"

"It was always the intention that we stay through the Darkfall and monitor the activity," said Rohmer.

"To hell with that!" snapped Duvall. "After everything that's happened, we can't stay here."

"Rohmer," said Cardiff quietly. "You don't want to leave, do you?"

Rohmer smiled his infuriating smile.

"I bet you don't have official clearances," continued Cardiff. "Something about this entire operation never rang true for me from the start. Bringing your own people in here, your own scientists . . . and not telling them, not briefing them. There was something else going on in your mind, wasn't there? Something that has nothing to do with your Darkfall Units. Isn't that right?"

"We can't leave," replied Rohmer. "You heard Gilbert. The lightning . . ."

"I think he's right," said Duvall, standing. "You've been acting bloody peculiar for months now."

"We're staying," said Rohmer. "That's an order."

"What do you say?" said Duvall, turning to Cardiff, looking for a new leader.

Cardiff looked at Jimmy and Barbara.

"Whatever you say," said Jimmy in response to Cardiff's unspoken question. "I suppose we're with you."

"We'll risk it," said Cardiff. "It's better than staying here, making a mistake, and getting sucked into the wall. But you have to decide for yourself, Duvall. I have no jurisdiction over you." But Duvall was already on his feet and heading for the office door. All except Rohmer and Gilbert climbed carefully to their feet. Another thunderclap exploded above, ringing their ears. The secondary blast was louder still. Gilbert reacted to the shock of it; reacted to the shuddering he felt in the floor, and to the fact that the others were moving away now, towards Duvall and the blocked office door. He looked back to Rohmer, still looking out of the window.

"Rohmer. What's wrong with you? Why don't you . . . ?"

"You're a scientist, Gilbert," replied Rohmer. "But you're blind."

"What is the point in staying here? My equipment is in the basement, people are dead and . . ."

"There are so many things you don't know. Things you need to learn. Things I could teach you."

"I'm going with them." Gilbert waited for some response

from Rohmer. There was none. Lightning seemed to reflect from the windows in his eyes, and to Gilbert it seemed as if Rohmer was possessed of some inner, terrifying power. He scrambled to his feet to join the others.

Duvall was carefully pulling the cabinet aside from the door when Jimmy reached him and began to help. Duvall stopped momentarily when Barbara and Cardiff drew level.

"You're sure it's dead," he said flatly.

"I told you. I could feel its presence, and now I can't. It was dying."

"Come on," said Jimmy, and began to tug at the cabinet again. Duvall rejoined his efforts and the edge of the cabinet caught against one of the floor tiles making a long, keening screech. They paused. Thunder rolled and grumbled beyond, and the eerie blue glow from the overhead strip lights flickered momentarily. And now the cabinet was pushed aside.

Duvall licked his lips, looked at Cardiff . . . and pulled open the door.

There was nothing in the corridor beyond.

Duvall could see the two elevator doors, and directly opposite to him, the door marked: "Stairs", through which they had dashed. It had swung back on its spring-loading, and was closed again. Duvall looked back at Cardiff.

"Give me the gun."

Gilbert joined them now. Cardiff looked at him, nodded, and then turned back to Duvall. "No offence," he said. "But I don't trust you around guns." He slipped past Duvall and into the corridor.

Cardiff paused at the stairwell door. They couldn't see his face, so he raised his eyes heavenward, gritted his teeth, and gave a small prayer.

Then he slowly began to open the staircase door.

SEVEN

Cardiff slowly pushed at the door, widening the thin jet-black wedge. Lightning flickered, and that blackness beyond the door was momentarily lit up. Shadows danced and jumped. Cardiff licked his lips, heart hammering. He could feel the storm wind and rain gusting down the ground-floor corridor and into the stairwell. Was that thing behind the door somewhere, waiting? Gigantic, monstrous and powerful; waiting on the stairs for him to open the door wide, so that it could seize him, drag him away and do to him what it had done to Pearce?

Something inhuman bellowed and roared in the stairwell.

Cardiff froze in fear.

But the stabbing pain in his eardrums was almost welcome, as the roaring subsided to a grumbling, faraway avalanche and he realised that it was only the sound of the storm.

Body slick with sweat, despite the chill that had descended on the office block, Cardiff pushed the door open further, keeping the gun well in front of him.

"I can see it . . ." he whispered to the others.

It was down below, lying on the stairs. And Cardiff could see what had happened. The filing cabinet was dented and torn, shoved to one side at the foot of the stairs, and the thing had crawled out from beneath it, trying to crawl up the stairs after them. Its monstrous supine silhouette was clearly visible on the stairs. And in death, the thing had shrunk to the size that Cardiff remembered from when it was first discovered in the wrecked car.

Cardiff moved out on to the landing, still keeping the gun well in front of him, and ready to use it if the thing should show any signs of stirring. He paused, turning back to Barbara and the others as they moved tentatively out on to the landing to join him.

"Barbara, are you sure about this?"

"Honestly, Mr Cardiff. I could *feel* it before. But now there's nothing. I can't hear it inside anymore."

Cardiff looked back down the stairs again. "We've got to be sure."

He began a slow and careful descent, stopping only once to turn back and whisper over the grumbling of the Darkfall: "Keep that door open . . . in case I have to come back quickly. And stay well back."

Another careful step.

Jesus Christ, let it be dead.

Another step. Thunder rumbled and echoed in the stairwell.

I don't want to . . . die? Is that what you were thinking? After all this time, when you didn't care whether you lived or died? Are you saying you want to live, Cardiff?

Another step. Lightning flickered in the ragged aperture where the ground-floor staircase door had been. The shadows around the thing undulated, giving it the appearance of life. Cardiff hesitated. There was no more movement. Now he could see that it was lying face down.

Are you saying this bloody nightmare has changed you? Given you a taste for life? Well, Cardiff . . . I'll go to hell.

"Probably," Cardiff mouthed, naked fear making him tremble as he reached the step above the thing.

It *had* shrunk, back to something that approximated the size of a human being. But he recognised the abominably shredded and mutated head, and the bloodstained and distorted arms that ended in claws which could never have been human. The thing was wearing clothing still; shreds of fabric still clung to it and were somehow interwoven with the grey and leprous flesh.

Cardiff nudged at that swollen head with his shoe. With

249

horror, he felt it *give*. But the thing did not move. He braced his hand on the staircase rail at his left and looked around him into the shadows. The stairwell itself was twenty feet or so below. He took a deep breath, wedged his shoe under that head and began to heave the thing over on to its front, bracing his hand against the railing. It was a difficult job. The thing seemed glued to the staircase. Cardiff braced his gloved gun-hand against the wall on his right. Now, with both hands braced, he slid his foot further under the thing's head and upper shoulder . . . and heaved again.

It slid messily over and Cardiff stood quickly back, gun at the ready.

But the thing was dead.

He waited . . . and then stepped down to look closer.

The monstrously distorted face was somehow different, and Cardiff edged around to look still closer at it.

Two yellow and glazed eyes flickered open.

Cardiff shrank back against the staircase. But now he could see that the thing was hardly a threat. It had been split open from neck to crotch. Indeterminate grey and fibrous innards pulsated in the darkness. Those hellish cataract-eyes blinked and Cardiff thought: *Eyes? How can it have eyes? I shot out its only eye . . .*

And then the thing spoke.

"For God's sake, Cardiff," it croaked. *"Help me . . ."*

It weakly raised one ravaged and shredded arm towards him. And, at last, Cardiff could see that the mutated horror on the stairs was not the thing from the wrecked car, not the thing that had been Barbara's brother from 1964.

It was Farley Peters, the journalist.

Moreover, it was the thing that Farley Peters had become. The thing which had been imprisoned in the corridor walls and which had gibbered and clutched at them with insane and monstrous hunger.

Farley Peters — no longer imprisoned. No longer in that wall. And with his body gutted and ready for . . .

"For Christ's sake, get away from there, Cardiff!"

shouted Jimmy from the landing, the voices of Duvall and Barbara joining in frantic chorus. Cardiff spun from Peters to look at them. They were waving frantically, and Cardiff was now aware with sudden terror of the massively looming shadow from the stairwell, on the other side of the stair-rail. And all he could do now was to turn in horror as that bellowing, roaring *shape* lunged with an encrusted claw through the metal stair-rails, which bent and squealed.

Talons closed through the lapels of his jacket, his shirt and his flesh.

A roaring, dripping maw yawned with monstrous hunger.

It dragged Cardiff to it, through the bending metal of the stair-rail.

EIGHT

"You bitch!" yelled Duvall.

He lashed out hard at Barbara with the back of his hand. The blow caught her on the cheek and she fell against Gilbert. They both staggered back out into the corridor. Before Jimmy could react, Duvall had brought his hand around again and hit him squarely on the jaw. Jimmy went down, grabbing at the stair-rail for support. The staircase was filled with the sounds of bellowing, screaming and thrashing shadows as Duvall burst back through the door after Barbara. She was leaning against the corridor wall, stunned. Gilbert looked on helplessly. The door snapped shut behind Duvall as he came, muffling the hideous sounds from below.

"You knew! Didn't you?"

Duvall seized her by the hair, dragging her away from the wall.

"No, don't . . ." said Gilbert ineffectually.

"You knew that thing wasn't dead," continued Duvall. "You wanted to trick us into believing that it *was*!" And Duvall emphasised his rage in that last word with another blow to Barbara's face. The shock and force of it sent her reeling back against the wall once more. Panicking again, Gilbert yanked open the door to the office from which they'd just come and slipped inside. Barbara tried to follow, but Duvall slammed the door against her and she cried out in pain as he pulled it open again, grabbed her arm and threw her into the office. Barbara's foot skidded and she fell to the floor in the "corridor" between the hessian screens. "I knew it all along. Knew it!" snapped Duvall

... and leaned down to take the monster by the throat and throttle the life out of it.

In the next instant, Jimmy had shoulder-charged him from behind.

Both men hurtled on over the top of Barbara in a tangle of limbs, crashing to the office floor. Jimmy was still on top, still conscious of not wanting any flesh contact with the floor. He aimed a blow at the back of Duvall's head. Duvall felt it coming and twisted. Jimmy's fist skimmed his cheek. Duvall lashed backwards, but Jimmy had leapt to his feet, colliding with one of the hessian screens. It toppled over to the floor with a flat *whap!* and Jimmy backed off into the centre of the office as Duvall scrambled to his feet at last. Gilbert had scurried back to Rohmer and Jimmy could see that Rohmer was still sitting on the desk near the back double-doors where they had left him. Whether he was still staring out of the window at the storm or watching them made no difference. Because Duvall had risen to his feet and was looking hard at Jimmy, nodding his head.

"Right," he said, almost too quietly to be heard. "Right, Devlin. You've been lucky, very lucky. That's twice. But let's just see what your streetwise, closing-time training can do."

And Jimmy knew that this time he was in serious trouble.

Lightning was flickering at the windows, casting those crazy shadows beneath the dim electric-blue of the strip lights as Duvall advanced towards him. Behind Duvall, Jimmy could see that Barbara was pulling herself to her feet. He looked around him for some sort of weapon, backing off as Duvall walked slowly towards him. Now that slow stroll was picking up speed and grim purpose as Jimmy grabbed at a wire "In" tray full of papers. He scooped it up from the desk and threw it into Duvall's face. But Duvall smacked it dismissively aside and jabbed two steel-hard fingers at the base of Jimmy's throat with a cold and precise disdain. The pain was excruciating, and choking. Instantly, it seemed, he couldn't breathe and as his hands flew to his throat, Duvall swung up his right arm so that the point of his elbow hit Jimmy squarely in the face. Blood jetted from his nostrils and Jimmy went backwards over a desk, taking a computer console with him. Its glass screen shattered on the floor, and Jimmy struggled to rise. But now Duvall had the time, the training, the balance and the strength to deliver a kick to Jimmy's midriff; a controlled kick that had all of Duvall's force behind it, from the hip. Air whooshed from Jimmy's lungs and he somersaulted again, slamming hard against another desk and sliding to the floor.

There was a grim smile on Duvall's face as he advanced.

Jimmy saw him coming through blurred vision and wished that he could get to his feet, but he couldn't move. There was a curious connection now in his mind between the time that Sergeant Barry Lawrence had knocked him silly in the pub and this new blurring of his mind. *It's all a dream*, Barbara had said to him. And now he knew what this was all about. He was in a dream. It was *his* dream. *His* nightmare. When he woke up, he'd be lying on the floor of the boozer, and Sergeant Lawrence would be lifting him to his feet, dragging him outside to the panda car. None of this nightmare stuff had happened. How *could* it have happened? As this dream-man called Duvall advanced towards him in slow motion, Jimmy's dream-brain raced, providing answers with utter certainty. Cardiff was still one of the bastards who had put him away, not someone who had been duped by a fellow officer with false evidence, certainly not someone he had come to respect. And the dream-woman called Barbara from 1964? She wasn't real either. How could she be? Just a fantasy based around Pamela, based around her old songs. And representing someone he had wanted Pamela to be.

The dream-man called Duvall seized Jimmy around the neck in a way which was surely too painful to be a dream and yanked him to his feet, throwing him on to a desk. When the pain lanced into his back, the shock of it made him cry out loud . . . and he knew that he hadn't been dreaming. Duvall was still holding him by the throat.

"A lesson to be learned here, Devlin," he said through gritted teeth as he raised his other hand in front of Jimmy's face. Those two steel-hard fingers would blind him. "Just call it the advantages of a public school education . . ."

Jimmy could not fight back. He resorted to his only hopeless defence . . . and screwed his eyes shut.

Something cracked and shuddered.

I'm blind! Am I blind? he screamed in his mind.

But no . . . he was able to open his eyes. And he could see.

He could see that *Duvall's* eyes were screwed shut in pain as he loomed over him. He could feel Duvall's grip on his throat relaxing, could see Duvall's poised hand lowering. And he watched as Duvall staggered away from him, his weight gone. Behind him, as he staggered from view, Jimmy saw Barbara standing with the neck of a broken whisky bottle in her hand, seized from one of the Christmas party tables. She had smashed it over Duvall's head from behind. And now Jimmy had taken her hand as she hauled him back from the desk and . . .

. . . and she pulled Jimmy to his feet. Her face was hurting badly where Duvall had hit her, and she could hardly believe that a dream could be so realistic. Except that now, she realised, this could not possibly be a dream. But also not reality. Certainly not reality as she knew it. Now she knew what was *right*. She knew who to trust and who not to trust. And she had dragged herself to her feet again and watched as the man called Duvall had sadistically begun to kill the boy who had protected her. The other man had also tried to protect her. But the other man — Mr Cardiff — was dead. The nightmare thing, the thing they had said was her brother (but she *knew* that this was impossible) had killed him on the staircase. The monster called Duvall wanted her dead. And when the only remaining one within this living real-nightmare-dream who felt real to her was threatened, she had to act.

She had taken that whisky bottle from a nearby table and brought it down with as much strength as she could muster on Duvall's head. He had staggered away, head soaked in whisky and shoulders glittering with a new dandruff of broken glass as Barbara pulled Jimmy Devlin back from the desk and . . .

. . . Duvall lunged back again, in an utter and consuming rage. Uncontrolled and dazed, he seized the rim of the desk and heaved with a burst of anger. Barbara screamed and dragged Jimmy away as the desk flipped over to the floor with a crash. Jimmy was a heavy weight in her hands. He slumped to the floor and she tried to drag him clear.

But that burst of uncontrolled anger had assuaged the pain in Duvall's head and neck, had given him back that cool and grim purpose. Barbara looked up as she dragged Jimmy to one side, and saw Duvall stoop to pick up the broken neck of the whisky bottle that she had dropped. The Darkfall lightning scratched and flickered with its spider legs at the nearby window . . . and Duvall kicked savagely at Barbara's head, spinning her away from Jimmy. That new and *unfair* pain gave her a new savage thirst for proper revenge. Stunned but ineffectual, she yelled in righteous rage and tried to pull herself to her feet, wanting nothing else but to throw herself at Duvall as . . .

. . . Duvall took Jimmy by the throat again, and drew back his other hand with the broken bottle.

Darkfall thunder exploded in the office block.

Duvall was jerked away from Jimmy, spinning on his heels so that he was facing the office door again. There was a look of stupid surprise on his face, and Barbara followed his gaze, uncomprehending.

Cardiff was standing at the office door, gun raised in Duvall's direction.

And Barbara looked back at Duvall to see the slowly spreading dark stain between his shoulder blades. Sobbing, she seized Jimmy roughly again and began to drag him away, towards the office door. Duvall watched her, still with that stupid expression on his face. He staggered, as if drunk, and watched as Cardiff stepped forwards, still holding the gun before him. Cardiff was clutching at his shirtfront with the other hand. There was blood on his hand and shredded shirt.

And then it seemed that Duvall understood at last that he had been shot. Screaming like an animal, he raised the broken glass in his hand and charged drunkenly towards Cardiff.

Cardiff pulled the trigger again, and there was another thunderclap in the office.

The impact of the bullet hurled Duvall backwards, passing clean through his chest and puncturing the window behind him. He reeled, but kept his feet. The broken whisky-bottle neck fell to the carpet and he clutched at his chest, as if in imitation of Cardiff. His face screwed up in agony, and from behind him there was a hiss of escaping air through the bullet hole in the window.

Cracks spread from the bullet hole across the window, like frozen lightning.

And then the window exploded outwards behind Duvall into the Darkfall. Screaming, Duvall was sucked backwards out of the window in a cloud of broken glass and was instantly gone.

Hell erupted into the office block. The storm wind of the Darkfall blasted through the shattered window with a howling roar; rain and snow gushed into the office. Thin, blue-white tentacles of fire stabbed from ceiling to floor, from desk to hessian screen. The living, crackling lightning stabbed at the overhead strip lights and the office was suddenly filled with a hail of exploding, flying glass. A glass partition in the typing-pool imploded with a shattering roar. Spider legs of electricity hissed and danced over the computer terminals. One by one, the glass screens exploded.

"*Come on!*" yelled Cardiff, and seized one of Jimmy's arms, dragging him to his feet. Barbara dragged at the other arm, and they staggered to the office door as the Darkfall lightning continued to destroy the interior of the office. They literally fell against the door. It swung open

257

and they staggered into the corridor, away from that scene of Hell in the office.

But for Barbara, the nightmare was not over. Because now Cardiff was hauling them through the staircase door and back on to the first-floor landing. And the sounds of Hell were still there. From somewhere below, in the stairwell where Barbara knew that Cardiff must have died, were the nightmare sounds of bellowing and screeching and thrashing shadows.

"*Come on!*" yelled Cardiff again, dragging them both up the next flight of stairs.

"What's happening?" shouted Barbara, still clinging to a dazed Jimmy. "You're dead. You must be dead. What's . . . ?"

From below came the agonised and hideous sounds of someone being torn apart.

"No time," snapped Cardiff grimly. He clutched at his chest again, and now Barbara could see that the shirt was shredded and that blood was running freely from deep gashes in Cardiff's chest. "If we want to live . . . we climb!"

They began to ascend the staircase, holding Jimmy between them.

NINE

Gilbert had watched the violence in the office, frozen in fear and unable to prevent any of it. When Cardiff had come back from the dead, he had shrunk away back down the hessian-screen corridor towards Rohmer. And when Cardiff had shot Duvall, he had turned in helpless horror to where Rohmer sat, hands spread wide in appeal.

But Rohmer just sat and watched, his face a blank mask.

And then Cardiff had shot Duvall again, the window had blown out taking Duvall with it . . . and the nightmare of Darkfall had been admitted to the office. Crying out in terror, Gilbert had watched the snaking electric-blue lightning as it invaded the office, spreading destruction. He had covered his face from flying glass and watched the two men and the Returner escape through the office doors. And when the lightning had forked inwards through the window and shattered the typing-pool window, Gilbert had turned back to Rohmer in helpless appeal. Rohmer was still sitting on the edge of the desk, his hair and coat whipping in the hellish stormwinds which had been admitted. Only now he was smiling as he looked around him at the chaos.

Furious now in his terror and at Rohmer's unconcern, Gilbert had struck out at him.

Rohmer seized his wrist and with apparent ease, twisted. Gilbert sank to his knees in pain, beating at Rohmer's vice-clamp grip. Now on his knees on the office floor, with Rohmer sitting above him smiling into the storm, Gilbert had begun to weep. Glass exploded all around them. Lightning jabbed and sparked against the walls. And when

Gilbert looked up at him again through blurred vision, he could see that Rohmer was talking, although he could hear no words.

"Don't worry," Rohmer was saying. "Don't worry. We're in the presence. We won't be harmed."

Gilbert shrieked when the strip light directly above them exploded, and sparks rained down on their heads.

TEN

Jimmy had pulled himself together again when they reached the third landing. He pulled away from them both long enough to wipe blood from his face and to lean on the stair-rail, sucking in deep breaths. His throat still felt constricted after Duvall's blow. Down below, in the darkness of the stairwell, the bellowing and thrashing had ceased. But something down there was breathing, and the susurrant echoes of that breathing drifted up to them.

"Come on, Jimmy," hissed Cardiff. "We can't wait. We've got to climb."

At last, it was registering with Jimmy that Cardiff was not dead, not torn to pieces by the thing down there.

"What . . . ?" he began, and Cardiff impatiently shook his head.

"Never mind that now. Just *climb*!"

Down below, they could hear the sounds of the thing shambling on the staircase. It was coming up after them again.

"*Climb!*" hissed Cardiff again, and they started up the stairs once more.

And as they climbed, Cardiff replayed the nightmare down below.

The thing had him.

It was dragging him towards it through the stair-rails, its claws fastened in his flesh. And Cardiff knew, truly, that he didn't want to die after all. He had twisted in that grip, tried to bring the gun round to bear on that monstrous maw. But his arm was twisted, and now he could feel the thing's putrid breath in his face. Down below on the

261

staircase, the thing that had been Farley Peters was trying to crawl up the steps towards him. It was making a mewling sound.

And Cardiff knew, as the thing pulled him sharply back against the metal stair-rails with an echoing clatter, that the thing had double-backed to the sounds from the service corridor, had torn the still-imprisoned Farley Peters from the wall. It had dragged him back to the stairwell, had gutted and fed from him to regain its strength.

Bellowing, the thing was trying to reach over the stair-rail with its other encrusted, decomposing claw. It snatched at Cardiff and he tried to twist away from it, pain like fire stabbing into his chest where the thing had him gripped with the other claw.

Peters was at his legs now, holding in his own transformed innards with one hand, and clutching at Cardiff's leg with the other. Cardiff could feel hot breath on his leg, and knew that the Peters thing wanted to bite him.

The thing beyond the stair-rail slashed downwards at Cardiff again and caught his sleeve. It began to lift him over the stair-rail.

And then Peters sank his own hideously transformed jaws into the thing's arm as it lifted Cardiff.

The Shape bellowed and twisted, with Peters' mouth still firmly clamped on its monstrous arm. Something with the consistency of cement began to splatter from Peters' ripped torso, but still he clung on to it in the renewed savagery of his hunger. The thing dropped Cardiff back on to the steps, and now the grip was gone from his chest.

Cardiff threw himself backwards against the staircase wall, as the thing from the stairwell lunged backwards into the darkness, taking the flapping and gutted body of Peters with it, still fastened to its arm. Cardiff fired blindly into the roaring, shrieking mass as he began to scramble back up the stairs.

Breath sobbing in his throat, hand clutched to the deep slashes in his bleeding chest, Cardiff saw the monstrous shadow of the thing smashing Peters' rapidly liquefying

body against the stairwell wall, as if it was beating a carpet.
He had turned then, and scrabbled upwards to the door.

And now they were climbing fast, and Barbara was saying: "Oh God, I can feel it again! It *tricked* me! It knew that I could sense it, just as it can sense me."

They reached the next landing and swung themselves around it, clambering up the next set of stairs.

"It laid a trap for us, Mr Cardiff. It deliberately switched off its mind to me, to make me think that it had died."

Cardiff looked over the stair-rail, and saw a monstrous shadow reach the first-floor landing. The shadow was turning on that landing, moving up the next set of stairs after them. Down below, whatever was left of Farley Peters was smeared on the wall.

"How many floors?" gasped Jimmy.

"Fourteen," said Cardiff through gritted teeth as they continued to climb.

"Christ. And then what?"

"Just climb, Jimmy. It's coming."

ELEVEN

Gilbert screwed his eyes shut, waiting for the other windows to explode out into the Darkfall, dragging both Rohmer and himself into those hellish, spinning whirlwinds. Rohmer was still talking to himself, still keeping that vice-clamp grip on Gilbert's wrist. But that pain was the least of his worries.

Another strip light exploded in the roaring maelstrom, showering them with glass. But Rohmer continued talking, undisturbed.

Gales of snow and rainwater drenched them, but still Rohmer laughed softly to himself.

Gilbert waited for the lightning strike that would finally find them, and began to babble a hopeless prayer.

And then the crackling explosions and shattering of glass ceased. The wind and the rain and the snow still howled and blasted through the ragged aperture where the window had blown out, but the electricity and lightning seemed to have gone. Gilbert kept his eyes screwed shut, waiting for it to return.

When it did not, he opened his eyes again, looking up through squinted vision at Rohmer, sitting above him and silent at last. And with a smile on his face to show how enormously pleased he was. Gilbert looked around, the rain and the wind freezing his face, whipping at his hair. The lightning *had* vanished, even though the storm still continued to ravage the office interior. He tried to pull free of Rohmer's grasp, but could not.

Rohmer looked down at him, smiled, and began to talk

again; continuing the one-sided conversation that Gilbert had been unable to hear so far.

"'All the unmeasured ether flames with light.' Alexander Pope's words, Gilbert. Extending from the moon to the ends of the universe, the fabric of the stars. And the key to interweaving realms and planes of being: will, spirit, the soul . . . the divine."

Rohmer looked to the storm blasting through the blown-out window.

"Fire, air, water and earth. And electricity in the ether, Rohmer. The energiser that interpenetrates the physical world and shows us the higher aspects of reality . . ."

"Rohmer!" Gilbert cried into the storm wind. "What the hell is the *matter* with you? We can't stay here and . . ."

"He wouldn't speak to you, Gilbert," continued Rohmer, still staring at the shattered window as if willing the lightning to return. "But Bissell spoke to me. He gave me the answers."

"Bissell? But what . . . ?"

"You were too blinkered to see. Too narrow-minded not to suspect."

"For God's sake, Rohmer!"

"The Darkfall is more than a physical manifestation," continued Rohmer. There was somehow a smell of sulphur in the air now and Rohmer's eyes seemed to be glittering in triumph. He took a pill from his pocket, and popped it into his mouth. He smiled.

"It's a spiritual manifestation!"

The smile was gone again, and Rohmer glowered down at Gilbert. Now the scientist had final confirmation that Rohmer – the hard, forceful, determined and organised Rohmer – had lost his mind.

"Listen to me, Gilbert. As a scientist, you and your kind have been completely unaware of what your tampering with the physical world, with electricity, has done. It's always been a Dark Force, and you've only succeeded in harnessing a minuscule aspect of it. Without realising it, your nuclear scientists are black alchemists. Once, it was the quest to transmute lead into gold. Now, it's transmitting uranium into even denser matter — lead and plutonium. Substances not found in nature. Transmogrified substance!"

"Rohmer. Please. You're not making any sense. We've got to . . ."

"I've got to make you understand. The first atomic bomb. Where was it exploded?"

"Rohmer, please . . ."

Rohmer twisted Gilbert's wrist hard, making him cry out in pain.

"God, Rohmer!"

"Where?"

"Alamagordo!"

"That's right. And do you know what happened then? No? Let me enlighten you. The planet Saturn crossed the heavens at exactly the point that Pluto had been discovered. Did you know that? Pluto . . . the God of Hades. Did you know that the planet Saturn is associated with lead? And the hydrogen bomb. Where was . . . ?"

"Rohmer, let me go!"

"*Where?*"

"Bikini!"

"That's right. And on the instant that it happened, Uranus — the electrical disruptor — crossed the same point in the sky. A new force was created and released on earth, just when those planets, when those vast disruptors were aligned. The real force that is electricity has a name, Gilbert. What we think of in simple terms as electricity is related to the creative forces in the universe in ways that we cannot imagine. The Chinese think it's 'Chi'. But its real name . . . is Ahriman. The ancients called it the God of the Underworld. Intelligent, objective, calculating, cold. The polar opposite of the Devil . . . but nevertheless, the Devil."

Lightning flickered outside in the storm once more, drawing Rohmer's attention.

"Don't get me wrong, Gilbert. Not the Devil we know.

Not an entity. But a force. And a force that isn't remotely interested in us as people ... as individuals. It's one of the principal forces at the core of the universe, perhaps not the main force, but something that can give us immediate enlightenment if we ..."

Rohmer laughed with wild enthusiasm.

"... flick the right switch!"

His laughter died away, and he continued: "I've been privileged to learn, Gilbert. I knew that Bissell had the answers that I really wanted. And when I gave him what he wanted, he gave me what I wanted. Gilbert, Gilbert. You and your kind have got it all wrong. All wrong! The universe is a spiritual construction, not solely a physical construction. And do you know why the Darkfall effect is truly happening? Truly?" Rohmer twisted hard again at Gilbert's wrist, eliciting another cry of pain. "It's the pettiness, the frustrations, the greed, the evils that men do – big and small. It's cruelty, murder and rape. It's child abuse, paedophilia. Genocide. Torture. War. All of it eating away at the spiritual fabric of existence for thousands upon thousands of years. Now that fabric of our existence is coming apart under the psychic emissions of a billion, billion spiritual 'cancers'. Now, the force that is truly Ahriman – the Darkfall – can break through with increasing frequency until everything – *everything* – ceases to exist as we know it."

Gilbert was silent now, staring hard at Rohmer. The man was mad – but there was finally a bizarre logic to what he was saying.

Beyond the windows, the night exploded.

For an instant, the plate glass all around them flared blue-white, the building shook as the pain of a Darkfall strike stabbed into their ears again. For Gilbert, it was agony ... but for Rohmer, the sound produced ecstasy. He jumped to his feet, still holding on to Gilbert's wrist, as a second strike hit the building. Cracks zig-zagged from floor to ceiling, chunks of plaster fell in spattering clouds from the walls and three more windows exploded inwards.

267

Minute shards of glass slashed across Rohmer's ecstatic face. Thin threads of blood glittered on his forehead and cheeks.

"Vitalism!" shouted Rohmer into the storm, taking a step towards one of the exploded windows, still holding Gilbert's wrist and dragging him off balance as he moved. "The Great Chain of Being! Even Plato was closer to the truth than you and yours, Gilbert. Don't you see? The earth itself is *alive*. Everything lives! Even the inert, if it's infused with Darkfall. But we're special, Gilbert. Very, very special. Because as humans, only *we* are instinctively aware of the spiritual essence of the universe. Only *we* look for self-transcendence."

Lightning flared and flickered beyond the shattered windows and Rohmer took another step forwards, as if he wanted to join it. Gilbert was dragged with him, and twisted to rise as Rohmer wiped streaks of blood from his face. Rohmer turned and looked down at him.

"Self-transcendence, Gilbert. Transmogrification. All those Returners. They were all more like animals than human, weren't they? All except Bissell. He was a real scientist, questing after truth. The Darkfall absorption in that Leeds factory didn't turn him completely insane like the others. That's because he wasn't as terrified, wasn't as ignorant as the others. The absorption destroyed their minds, but not Bissell. He gave the clue, Gilbert. The clue!"

Rohmer swung downwards, seized Gilbert and dragged him to his feet, holding him as close as a lovers' embrace. Gilbert struggled, but could not break free.

"I killed somebody once, Gilbert. I killed him for no more reason than I wanted to do it. What comes from me is as much to do with the Darkfall erosion as anything. But that doesn't mean to say that I can't be absolved of that. It doesn't mean that I can't be transmogrified beyond the human to another plane to find the Real *Me*!"

Gilbert twisted again, taking Rohmer off balance. They fell against the desk that he had been previously sitting on. It scraped to one side as they slid to the carpeted floor.

Rohmer still held Gilbert tight as he thrashed to be free. Rohmer began to make shushing noises as if Gilbert was a child who needed to be restrained for sleep.

"Bissell told me what he should have done when his hands began to be absorbed in the floor. He should have stayed calm, he shouldn't have panicked. He was sure that the fear and the terror of the absorption was the reason for loss of mind and humanity. Can you imagine, Gilbert? What if someone could undergo that absorption with a cool . . . dare I say it? . . . scientific rationale. Wouldn't that truly be self-transcendence on Return? Isn't that More than Human? Being able to see other planes, other realities. And to Return, free of the shackles of human physical embodiment. Free of human morality. Able to be the Real *You*!"

"Rohmer! Let me up . . ." Gilbert thrashed on the floor beneath Rohmer's weight. Rohmer seized him by the throat to restrain him, as if Gilbert's physical resistance was also some kind of intellectual resistance to what he was saying; as if that grip could force Gilbert to see sense.

"All it needs is a lack of fear. When it happens, accept it with cool scientific appraisal. Don't fight it, embrace it. Allow the Darkfall to absorb you, allow it to transmogrify you. When you Return, you'll be . . . you'll be . . ." Rohmer was bursting with the ecstasy of the prospect, ". . . be . . ."

Darkfall exploded in the skies. The building cracked and shuddered again. Pain stabbed in their ears, plaster dust swirled and was swallowed by the gusting storm winds and blasting rain.

"See! See!" shouted Rohmer into the storm, rain and blood running from his face and dripping from his chin. "It's beckoning." He gripped Gilbert's chin and forced it up so that he could see the blue-white flickering of Darkfall lightning beyond the broken windows. "Remember what Bissell said, even to you!"

"Let me up," sobbed Gilbert. "For the love of God, let me up!"

"Go first," said Rohmer, staring intently into Gilbert's eyes. "Now that I've told you the truth, you don't need to fear. You're a good man of science. You must want what I want. To know."

"You said that this was a Primary Darkfall, not a Secondary . . ."

Rohmer released his grip around Gilbert's neck, grasping his face instead so that his jaw clamped shut and further speech was impossible.

"Go first," said Rohmer. "Without fear."

He began to push Gilbert's face towards the carpeted floor.

Gilbert tried to scream, but his mouth was clamped shut by Rohmer's grip and only a ululating, muffled howl vibrated from his throat.

"Without fear, you idiot!" screamed Rohmer. "You're a scientist!"

Gilbert sobbed with a horrifying and muffled terror.

"Without fear!" screamed Rohmer again . . . and pressed Gilbert's face down hard on to the carpet.

Gilbert's forehead sank into the pile with a *crimping* sound like a footstep in fresh snow. He began to sob uncontrollably. Rohmer snatched his hand quickly away from Gilbert's mouth, staggering back to his feet and watching in awe as Gilbert was able to scream at last: a naked shriek of terror. He began to beat at his head with his gloved hands as his face began to sink into the floor.

"Stop it, you bloody fool!" shouted Rohmer. "Don't fight it!"

Gilbert tried to squirm away, pulling his mouth into a distorted rictus. Spittle sprayed from his mouth . . . and now, with one last deeply horrible squawk, his face was dragged completely into the floor. His body began to thrash wildly. Rohmer stood back, screaming obscenities at him.

One of Gilbert's gloves flew off, and the next time his hand hit the floor it stuck and began to sink into the carpet pile. Thunder crashed and boomed outside. Darkfall electricity crackled and danced on the rims of the shattered windows.

Gilbert's squirming body vanished into the carpet like quicksand.

Screaming in fury, Rohmer lunged to the spot where he had vanished, stamping his feet as if dancing on Gilbert's grave.

"Without fear, you bloody weakling! I said without fear! Don't you want to be . . ."

The Darkfall exploded in the skies beyond the windows. Jagged blue lightning stabbed through one of the ragged gaps and found the only thing in the office block that was moving. A piercing bolt of blue fire hit Rohmer between the shoulder blades, flinging him across the office in a shower of sparks. He collided with a hessian screen, and sprawled on the carpet.

". . . changed?" he gasped.

His back was hideously burned and smouldering, the long black coat split up its length to the collar. Rohmer rose to his knees, lifting first one hand and then the other in front of his face to see if the material of his gloves was broken. "Not yet, not yet. I'm not ready." The gloves were unbroken.

He rose unsteadily and turned back to the shattered windows, breath coming in sobs. His teeth were blackened, his hair singed. Smoke rose around him.

He smiled.

"Thank you . . . thank you . . ."

He turned and tottered towards the office doors.

TWELVE

They reached Floor 9 on the staircase when the Darkfall strike shook the building. A massive crack zig-zagged like lightning through the plaster of the opposite wall as the sounds of thunder roared in the stairwell. Great chunks of plaster fell from that wall, crashing and exploding in clouds of dust to the ground floor, nine storeys below. That dust was billowing and choking them as they struggled to ascend. The second strike was even more fierce. The stairs juddered beneath their feet, the stair-rail vibrating visibly and emitting an echoing *whanng!*

Jimmy tottered back two steps, reached for the wall to steady himself, and then saw the blood on his gloved hand. He snatched it back hastily and then looked up to where Cardiff and Barbara were hanging on to each other under the storm's onslaught, coughing and choking in the shower of plaster. Jimmy looked at his bloodied hand and then back to Cardiff, and to Cardiff's bloodied shirt front.

"Come on!" choked Cardiff. "It's coming . . ."

"The blood, Cardiff! The blood!"

From somewhere below came an enraged crashing and bellowing.

"What the hell's the matter with you, Jimmy? We've got to . . ."

"No, wait," snapped Jimmy. "Flesh contact with the wall — that's what they said. That's why we're wearing these gloves. But what about the blood?"

"What . . . ?"

"There's blood on my hands, blood on your clothes. Is that 'tissue'? Is that flesh contact? Shit, Cardiff . . . what happens if we *touch* anything when we have blood on our hands and clothes?"

"Christ," said Cardiff through gritted teeth.

A monstrous shadow lurched on the stairs two floors below.

Cardiff looked at the blood on his hand, where he had been clutching his chest.

The shadow below screamed and howled.

"Come on," said Cardiff. "Move!"

The thing staggered on the stairs as a slab of plaster from above exploded on its shoulders, shrouding it in a cloud of dust. It lashed out at its non-existent attacker, groping through the plaster-dust with encrusted, mutated talons. Finding nothing, it lashed at the walls and screamed in fury.

The Food Smell was still above it, and those pangs which had been temporarily assuaged by what it had found in the wall below, were now growing ever-sharper once more. Above the roaring and cracking of the storm, it could still hear their voices, still smell their presence. It lunged to the stair-rail in the blue-blackness, straining to "see" where they were. More plaster chunks exploded in the thing's face and it staggered back again, lashing out.

Barbara! Baaaarbaaraaa! I need you . . . need . . .

It lunged up the stairs again, after them.

Barbara stepped down to Jimmy, her white face frozen in fear, and seized his arm.

"Oh God, let's go! I can *hear* it. It's calling to me in my mind, and it's *horrible!*"

And now they were climbing again as the building grumbled and shook. Below, something exploded with an echoing crash. It seemed as if the entire structure of the office block must surely collapse in a grinding, tearing, disintegrating avalanche of rubble. Cardiff staggered and almost fell back against Barbara. Jimmy grabbed him and shoved, and they were climbing hard; breath catching tight in the choking dust-air. Above them, something gave way with a long, rending metallic screech. An indeterminate mass of concrete and steel plunged down the centre of the stairwell, exploding like a bomb on the ground floor below.

Another piercing roar, and the stabbing pain of a Dark-fall strike. Jimmy fell headlong forwards, throwing out his hands instinctively to check his fall.

"Jimmy! No!" shouted Cardiff, whirling to see what was happening.

But he was too late.

Jimmy sprawled, his hands now braced solidly on the steps in front of him. He looked up directly into Cardiff's eyes, gritted his teeth, and waited for his hands to sink into the concrete.

"I know it wasn't you that set me up, Cardiff. It was Pearce."

The Secondary strike stabbed pain again, the detonation reverberating long and loud.

"Look after Barbara . . ."

"Jimmy!" shouted Barbara. "Look . . . look. It's alright."

Jimmy's hands were not sinking into the concrete.

With a sob of relief, he pushed himself away from the step and back to his feet again. Cardiff seized him with a bizarre feeling of savage relief as Jimmy gazed at his blood-ied hands.

"Thought I was going into the concrete, Cardiff. I really did."

"Really would be a hardened criminal then, wouldn't you?"

Barbara was shaking her head now, the jade pendant dancing around her neck. The thing was speaking to her again, and the sensation was deeply horrifying. "Please, please. Let's just get *away* from here."

They climbed.

THIRTEEN

Rohmer staggered like a sleepwalker through the second-floor door leading out into the stairwell. He waved weakly at the plaster dust which billowed at him, did not flinch when a tangle of wire, metal and concrete shattered to pieces against the far wall and dropped into the tangled wreckage on the ground floor below. The landing shook beneath his feet as he tottered to the staircase and looked up. He could see nothing above him, but knew that they were up there.

"Brother . . ." he said, and then the dust caught in his throat and he retched. Coughing blood and phlegm, he raised his voice and shouted up the staircase into the sounds of the storm and the destruction. "Brother! Wait for me, brother!"

Smouldering, he began slowly to climb.

FOURTEEN

The clouds of dust swirled and parted as it leaned out over the stair-rail, looking up. And now, two flights higher up on the other side of the staircase shaft . . . it could "see" her, also leaning over the banister and looking down. It "saw" the look of horror on her face, felt that peculiar flooding of complicated emotion within, and then the all-consuming hunger. It called to her over the raging of the storm: "Baaaarbbbaaraa!"

"Oh God, Mr Cardiff!"

Barbara jerked back from the stair-rail as they continued their ragged ascent.

"It's just below us . . . and it *saw* me!"

"Don't . . . don't . . ." There was a band of tight steel around Cardiff's chest. His breath was catching in ragged wheezes. ". . . don't stop . . . keep moving!"

It hauled itself up the steps after them, urged on by the hunger. It could sense the food/thing called Barbara's terror. It could feel her strength ebbing away.

A whirling chunk of concrete hurtled from above, bouncing on the stair-rail beside it with an echoing clang! *A jagged shard imbedded in the thing's chest, making it stagger.*

Pain.

Hate and rage and hunger bellowed from its insectile jaws in a spray of spume as it tore the concrete chunk from its body and discarded it on to the stairs. Up above and opposite through the swirling, billowing clouds, it could see the food/thing that the others called Jimmy, standing at the rail. He had flung that concrete chunk at it, and was

276

shrinking back now as it lunged furiously at the stair-rail roaring its lust and its hate at him across the gap, before . . .

"Brother . . ."

. . . turning back to the stairs, taking another three steps upwards and feeling that gnawing pain of hunger inside. The wall at its left cracked and split. Rain and wind began to spit through that crack, but the thing's attention was focused on the Food above as it . . .

". . . brother . . ."

. . . continued to climb, clutching at the stair-rail and heaving its monstrous bulk upwards. Saliva and spume dripped to the stairs beneath it in mucous puddles and . . .

"Wait for me, brother!"

. . . it turned at last, looking back down the way it had come for the source of that voice. Without eyes, it scanned the billowing clouds of plaster and concrete, the tangled rain of rubble and collapsing masonry . . . and at last it saw the blurred form that was climbing the stairs to meet it. It recognised the Food Smell of this one, knew from its "link" with the food/thing called Barbara that this was the one they called Rohmer.

It looked up to where Jimmy Devlin had been standing. He was gone with the others, still climbing to get away. And then it looked back at the slowly ascending form of Rohmer, calling to it as he came. There was something about Rohmer's voice, something about the way that he called to it.

It turned, feeling the hunger gnawing at the mutated contortion which was its gut, and began to descend towards him.

A cloud of choking plaster dust enveloped Rohmer on the stairs. White powder settled on his blackened face, making him look like some ghastly clown in smeared make-up. Coughing, he waved at the dust, dimly aware that his back was hideously burned, but the pain was somehow muted. He could smell his burnt flesh, could feel how the fabric of his long black coat had been fused into his charred flesh. He knew that by rights he should be dead or dying, but the drugs inside him and the knowledge that he had been *touched* by that wonderful power from the skies, obliterated it all. He felt a strange kinship with the thing somewhere above him on the stairs, and he called . . .

"Brother . . . ?"

. . . again, as he waved at the all-enveloping grey cloud. It thinned, and now he could see something moving above and beyond him. A monstrous shambling shadow was moving down the stairs through that dust cloud. The staircase shuddered and groaned, and Rohmer put out a gloved hand to steady himself on the quivering banister. More rubble and tangled metal fell past him and down into the stairwell. The dust cloud spiralled in a vortex over the stairs and was sucked away into the staircase shaft.

The thing stood at the landing on the tenth floor, weaving from side to side and looking down to where Rohmer stood on the ninth.

He held his arms wide and smiled: "Brother!"

Spume, saliva and blood dripped from John's misshapen head as the thing he had become started slowly to lumber down the stairs.

"We can't leave him," said Cardiff, looking back over the rail on the twelfth floor at what was happening below. He started back down.

Jimmy caught him by the sleeve.

"Cardiff, are you bloody crazy? Leave the bastard!"

"I can't leave him to that . . . that . . ."

"*Why NOT?* For God's sake, come on and let's get out of here. We don't owe him anything after everything we've been through. The man is insane."

Cardiff pulled away from Jimmy's grasp. "Do you think I *want* to go down there for Christ's sake? I just can't let . . ."

"This is a hell of a time for Lone Ranger tactics . . ." began Jimmy.

But Cardiff had already started down the stairs. Thunder roared and another crack appeared through the plaster wall beside them. The staircase juddered again and Jimmy heard the metal staples and stanchions holding the staircase to the wall begin to split and crack. Barbara looked at him helplessly as he pushed on past her and staggered down the staircase after Cardiff.

"Brother?" said Rohmer, arms still held wide as the thing came on. A rasping, dreadfully sibilant sound was coming from the chaotic, nightmare jigsaw that was its face and jaws. Its arms were no longer weaving at its side . . . they were raised. The deformed talons on the end of those dreadfully shredded and mangled arms were grasping through the air towards him. There was no sign of kinship on that dreadful visage, no sign of recognition . . . and Rohmer suddenly began to feel that strange elation leaking away from him. He took a faltering step back as it took another step down towards him. Four more of those steps and it would be on the landing. Was it . . . could it *really* . . . be grinning at him with a face that was not a face?

"Brother . . . ?"

"Get away from it, you bloody fool!" Cardiff had appeared on the tenth-floor landing above and behind the thing. The thing seemed to falter momentarily at the sound of his voice, half turning that huge and dreadful head in his direction . . . and then turning back to Rohmer again as it took another shambling step down. From somewhere behind Rohmer on the ninth floor came the sounds of an avalanche of shattering glass.

"Is it you?" Rohmer asked the thing. "Is it you?"

And Cardiff was looking at Rohmer now with stunned surprise as he fumbled with the gun in his jacket and Jimmy Devlin was suddenly at his side.

Rohmer shrank back against the wall on the ninth-floor landing, a wall that was suddenly covered in spreading black patches. The thing took another step down . . . and then Jimmy yelled: "WATCH OUT, CARDIFF!"

This time, the thing was turning slowly to look back up at them. Cardiff had raised the gun in the thing's direction, but Jimmy had pulled him back, and now Rohmer could see the undulating, spreading black patches on the wall all around them both on the tenth-floor landing. He could see the web-like crackling traces of energy in those spreading black patches, could see now that the wall was *bulging* in several places around them as they backed off. The staircase shaft was filled with the continuous avalanche sound of thunder now, and Rohmer cried out in alarm when he felt something in the wall at his back suddenly press outwards against him. He jerked away from the wall . . . and saw it bulge towards him as if it were made of canvas and something alive on the other side was trying to push through with both hands. He could see finger-like indentations.

The thing on the stairs turned back to him.

On the tenth-floor landing, Cardiff and Jimmy Devlin backed away from the three living faces which jabbered and contorted from the bulging black stains on the wall. A hand emerged from the plaster-work beneath one of those faces, groping blindly for them. That hand and arm were the colour and consistency of the plaster from which they had emerged. Another hand appeared, fingers groping and clutching. Jimmy looked around in alarm. There were spreading stains and sections of bulging brickwork all over the staircase.

"Oh Christ, they're *all* coming back . . ." said Jimmy in a strangled voice as he backed away up the stairs. Cardiff was waving the gun back and forth at the emerging nightmare.

And then the thing on the stairs finally decided between the Food on offer . . . and whirled with the savagery of its dreadful hunger, shrieking with a roaring bellow that sounded like several hideous demons at once. It lunged up the staircase after Cardiff and Jimmy. Cardiff saw it coming, spun away from the things that were emerging from the staircase wall and fired at it. The shot blew part of the thing's "face" away, but did not halt its monstrous advance. Cardiff saw those mutated talons groping through the dust-choked air, knew that he had somehow escaped this thing once before . . . but that he could not hope to get away from it again. A thought came to him unbidden as it reached the tenth-floor landing, this ravaged, monstrous nightmare with its dreadful hunger and its billowing shroud of plaster dust: *"Is it you?"*

Suddenly too weak to lift his gun, knowing that it would do no good anyway, Cardiff saw it come. He hoped that the first Horror of its embrace would take him away quickly, hoped that while it fed the other two could get away . . .

Something exploded by his shoulder; something that gushed white foam and hissed even more angrily than the thing which was bearing down on him. Cardiff was suddenly soaked by the gushing, white flurrying of that "something" and staggered to the banister as someone pushed past him in a welter of foam and spray.

It was Barbara. And she was striding past him, holding the fire extinguisher that she had torn from the wall on the landing above. Keeping the nozzle trained directly on the thing, she strode across the landing towards it. A shroud of white liquid splattered over the thing's head, coating it. Grim-faced, teeth set, she quickly flashed the nozzle from side to side so that the entire upper half of the thing's head and torso were covered in the stuff. And Barbara yelled at the thing as she advanced: *"Get! Out! Of! My! Head!"*

She could hear it now. Not the bellowing and screaming that the thing made as it raised mutated claws to its face, but the other sounds that it was making in her head.

No, Barbaaaraa! Food, that's all!! Just Want Eat and . . .

Barbara knew that the thing had no eyes to be blinded, but she knew from the sounds that it was making in her head that the foam and the spray were nevertheless "blinding" it in some way as it staggered back, waving its claws.

The velocity of the spray from the jet began to falter.

"Ohhh, please . . ."

And then the thing backed into the wall where the nightmare shapes were emerging. One of the disembodied arms

281

from the wall clutched at the thing's sodden torso, seizing a concreted fist full of the thing's ravaged substance. Another arm was groping at its head. It snapped foam-filled jaws at the second arm, severing it and spitting it to the floor. But another arm had appeared on the other side of the thing, grabbing its shoulders. Shrieking, the thing staggered in pools of white foam, clutching blindly. Beside it, the wall bulged and *coughed!* Something indeterminate, man-shaped, but horribly misshapen and grey was spat from the wall and into the pool of froth at the thing's thrashing feet. It writhed, grasped ... and sank its face into one of the thing's legs.

The fire extinguisher made a sound like water going down a plughole ... and then dried up. Yelling in fear and anger and grief, Barbara swung the extinguisher underarm with all her might. The red cylinder whirled through the air and struck the thing full in the face. It tottered, and the extinguisher bounced clanging down the stairs towards Rohmer, still cowering on the ninth floor from the hands that were emerging from the wall down there. The thing tore itself free from the wall as Barbara ran back to the stairs. Jimmy seized her as she joined them, and they all scrambled hastily away up the juddering staircase. At the next landing, they looked back.

The thing was thrashing on the landing. Now, they could see that three hideous and mutated forms were clinging to it. The grey shape still clung to the thing's leg, still worrying its head into its "flesh". In the frenzied blur, it seemed that the thing had more than two arms. On the thing's shoulders, a tentacled brown mass with a recognisably human face clung to it; like some hideous leech. The thing lashed backwards with its talons, trying to dislodge the thing, but it clung fast. And now they could see that fastened to the thing's chest was another, more human figure than the others, this one impossibly wearing a dark business suit and clinging to that monstrous breast like some kind of adult baby trying to be suckled. The combined shrieking of the thing and the nightmare shapes that clung to it sounded as if there was wholesale slaughter taking place in a Zoo in Hell. The staircase shuddered again as thunder roared. Other arms and faces were appearing in the walls down there, clutching and beckoning like something from Dante's inferno.

The thing bellowed and lunged sideways at the stair-rail. It shattered.

For one second, the thing lifted his head to where Barbara stood on the eleventh floor with the others. It raised one claw towards her.

"Oh God, John. *I'M SORRY!*" sobbed Barbara, hands flying to her mouth in grief and distress. And in that one instant when brother and sister really did recognise each other at last, the stair-rail disintegrated with a rending, metallic screech. The thing twisted for balance, claws flailing. The Returners which were still fastened to it gibbered and ranted and squealed.

And then the thing fell from the landing and into the staircase shaft.

"JOHNNNYYY!" screamed Barbara.

The shrieking and gibbering were lost somewhere below in the explosive crashing and roaring of the Darkfall Storm and the destruction it was causing.

Rohmer was staggering up the stairs towards them. Dark and hellishly swollen shapes were falling out of the walls behind him, squirming in darkness on the landings and staircase. The wall on the tenth-floor landing was suddenly a hellish tapestry of contorted and silently screaming grey faces, some human . . . others like nothing on earth.

"Wait . . . wait . . ." breathed Rohmer, staggering past those faces. The others saw his hideous burns, the tatters of his clothing, his singed hair and white face. His teeth and fingernails were black. He started up the stairs towards them. Struggling against nausea, Cardiff clambered down, seized his arm and dragged him up the staircase, dimly aware that the staircase below was alive with writhing, squirming, *climbing* shadows.

The thing that had been Barbara's brother was gone.

283

But the Hordes of Hell were after them now.

Rohmer understood at last as the others dragged him up the stairs. The thing that had fallen into the staircase was just like all the others. All the others, except Bissell. He had sensed no kinship in that monstrous thing's visage, because it had lost its mind in the Absorption by succumbing to fear; the way that Gilbert had succumbed to the fear. It was an Inferior Returner. That fact reinforced his beliefs as Cardiff and Devlin dragged at his sleeves, pulling him upwards. They reached another landing and started up a new staircase.

Something exploded far below, and Rohmer heard Devlin exclaim in a grim voice.

Glancing over the vibrating banister rail, Rohmer could see that the staircase up to the sixth floor had been wrenched from its supports in the stairway shaft and had collapsed in a roaring cloud of rubble and concrete dust. On the remaining flights of stairs below them, he could see squirming, thrashing grey-black forms crawling and tottering up through the swirling concrete dust. Something with burning yellow eyes was looking up at him. When their eyes met, it gave vent to a loud and ululating howl, like some monstrous wolf. The other things on the stairs joined in: a hellish chorus of shrieking and ranting and gibbering. It was Feeding Time for that Zoo from Hell.

The stairs beneath Rohmer's feet juddered violently again, and now he was being dragged to the top of the flight. Even the girl was hanging on to him, the girl who had Returned . . . but Rohmer did not shrink from her now, he only smiled a ghastly smile and saw her horrified reaction to that smile as they climbed.

"What . . . do . . . we do . . ." gasped Jimmy as they moved. "When . . . we . . . get to the top?"

Cardiff's breathing was a rusty wheezing: "Christ knows."

And now they were on the top-floor landing. Above them was one more flight of stairs leading to an Exit door marked: "Roof".

"If He has a helicopter up there waiting for us, then I'm a Believer," said Jimmy. He clambered ahead up the remaining flight of stairs to the Exit door, expecting a lever-bar that he could depress and push. But there was not. It was a functional wood and steel door . . . with a functional lock. He grabbed the door handle and twisted.

The door was locked.

Jimmy wiped the blood from his face, checked his gloves and then hit the door with his shoulder. Hard. He had hoped that the force of his impact would burst the door wide open. But it did not . . . and pain seared his shoulder and the side of his neck.

"Shit!"

He stumbled back from the solid door. Behind them, down the staircase, they could hear the Hordes of Hell shrieking and gibbering and scrabbling up the office block staircase after them.

"Let me . . ." began Cardiff.

"No!" Angrily, Jimmy stood back, braced himself on the alcove walls with either hand and kicked out at the lock. Once, twice, three times . . . and the door juddered, giving a crack of light along its length. Anger fuelled now by small success, Jimmy kept on kicking.

The girl looked back over her shoulder and saw contorted, writhing shadows on the landing below them. Something shrieked, and the echoes bounced all around them.

"For God's sake, quick, Jimmy!"

And this time, Jimmy lunged at the door again with his shoulder as he had done first, all his weight behind it. The lock shattered and the door swung open. Jimmy fell outside, carried by his own impetus, sprawling on a flecked grey surface. The alcove was suddenly lit by mad, dancing, chasing light. A chiaroscuro of white and blue and green. Shadows leaped and crawled. Behind Cardiff and Barbara, darker and more hideous shadows pounded and scrabbled through orange light towards them.

Cardiff pushed Barbara through ahead of him and then

285

followed her. Even as he swung that door back hard to slam it into place, the inevitable horror of their situation flashed through his mind: *Jimmy's smashed the door lock. How the hell do we lock it and keep those things on the other side?*

Cardiff tried not to panic; saw the heavy-duty hasp swinging on the door, the lock lying on the white-gravelled surface of the office-block roof. Strange shadows were chasing over the surface, as if some gigantic light bulb was up there, swinging around, making their shadows leap and dance. What the hell could they . . . ?

And suddenly, there was a monstrous, gibbering shadow in the alcove stairwell, reaching for them. Standing forward, Cardiff pulled the automatic out of his inner pocket, aimed and fired.

The gun bucked in his hand. The sound was heavy and somehow flat, any possibility of echo swallowed by the peculiar atmosphere and crazy light patterns on the top of the office-block roof. The shadow screamed and clutched the dark, liquid mess that had been its face, staggering backwards. More than anything else right now, Cardiff did not want to see that face, before or after the bullet hit it.

Probably an improvement, some hopelessly casual and inappropriately calm voice said inside him, as the thing thrashed wildly back in a liquid blunder, falling back down the stairs and into its fellows, causing a momentary confusion. Hopelessly, Cardiff flung himself at the door and swung it shut, knowing that there wasn't a hope in hell of keeping it locked against them. He leaned heavily against it.

"Look out, Cardiff!"

Jimmy was at his side again now, and Cardiff could see that he had torn what looked like a TV aerial from its mounting on the roof and was holding it like some bizarre kind of devil's tripod. Suddenly, he knew what Jimmy intended . . . and flung the broken hasp back against its housing, holding it there tight. Jimmy jabbed downwards with the haft of the aerial, thrusting it through the hasp in place of the lock and leaning down on that hasp with all his strength and weight. The aerial haft juddered into place.

They both started back from the door, eyes fixed on it.

And then became aware of Rohmer, somewhere behind them, saying: "Look ... Look ..."

They turned. Barbara was kneeling, on the rooftop, not far away, looking up into the sky. And Rohmer was walking in a small circle, hands at his sides, also looking up as mad shadows and light chased all around them.

At last, they both looked. And couldn't believe what was happening in the raging sky above them. Clouds of colour swirled and blossomed and chased and eddied, in a vast, silent whirlpool around the office block. Standing on the rooftop, they were in a "calm" eye of some strange and awesome hurricane. And all around and above them, the myriad colours of a supernatural rainbow bathed them in the flowing reds and greens and blues and yellows of some spectacular, cosmic storm. They were somehow centrestage in some bizarre planetarium. Awestruck, they watched that firestorm of light and cloud in a domed funnel all around.

"The Darkfall . . ." said Rohmer in a voice that was too quiet to hear. "We're in the middle of the Darkfall. I never thought it could be . . ."

Suddenly, the sky above them exploded.

A thermal, swamping blue-white light turned the air and the surrounding canopy of electrical chaos into a hissing negative print. For an instant, their four gigantic shadows leaped across the gravelled roof of the office block as they flinched from that explosion. The hissing negative images dissolved away again, and now they could see another chasing crack of electric blue splitting the whirling chaos of the Darkfall storm; a crepuscular shattering of that dome by another ferocious blue-lightning bolt. Jagged blue-white lightning cracked across that massive chaotic canopy in a roaring avalanche of sound. Another hissing negative black-white swamped them, momentarily negating the whirling St Elmo's fire all around. For one incredible second, as a third Darkfall crack of thunder rent the air, it seemed to Cardiff that their very presence on the roof had caused the sky to erupt like that. He turned to the others, saw their look of new horror and then jerked his head skywards again as a further massive blue-white fracture of the sky appeared . . . and that fracture suddenly erupted from the canopy with sizzling deadliness towards them.

Cardiff tried to shout a warning, but Jimmy had already thrown himself bodily at Barbara and they both fell heavily to the shale – an instant before the thunderbolt hit the roof. The Darkfall bolt had been drawn by the partially glassed canopy which covered the elevator housing. Cardiff covered his head with his hands as the canopy exploded with a detonating roar in a firestorm of sparks, concrete and whirling glass. The rooftop juddered beneath them and chunks of plaster and concrete whirled into the sky. Jimmy lay on top of Barbara, covering her head with his hands and waiting for the chunk of concrete which would end it all for them. A part of him felt that it might be the best way. But now the roaring detonation was over; the fireball of sparks had returned to the sky, and the debris had scattered over the roof without damage to them. Jimmy rolled over and saw Cardiff scrabbling towards them on hands and knees, checking his clothing for tears.

"Are you alright?"

"Yeah, we're okay."

"It's the Darkfall, Mr Cardiff," said Barbara. "All around us. We're at the top, at the peak of its power. I can sense it."

"Where the hell is Rohmer?" asked Cardiff.

"Dead, I hope," said Jimmy.

"Don't say that, Jimmy," returned Barbara.

Twenty-five feet away, Rohmer was already climbing to his feet, looking in awe at the thirty-foot ragged hole that had appeared in the top of the office-block roof. The canopy and concrete ceiling over the elevator shaft had been blown apart and smoke was drifting up through the aperture.

"We can't stay on the roof," coughed Barbara, still winded from Jimmy's rugby tackle. "It's too dangerous. Just by moving around, we're drawing it to us. I can sense it." She sat upright at last, pulling a hand through her tousled hair. Jimmy suddenly felt her stiffen.

"What is it? What's wrong?"

"Something else . . ." she said in a small voice. "Something else is happening."

Cardiff and Jimmy scanned the rooftop, looking back to the Exit door, expecting to see it broken down or smashed open and the horde of monstrosities pouring out over the roof towards them. But the door was still holding, the aerial quivering in its hasp like the antennae of some strange insect.

"There," said Barbara quietly, and pointed to the ragged aperture where the Darkfall bolt had hit. Another section of steel-ribbed concrete fell inwards under its own weight, and they heard its crashing disintegration as it fell into the office-block interior. But something else was happening over there.

Blue light was flickering, wisping and dancing along the rim of that aperture, like sparks of dying neon. Threads of that neon were now quickly racing along the rim of the office block, along the contours and outline of the aerial-mast structures on the roof; a will-o'-the-wisp electric blue identical to the power which was surging over their heads. Power from the Darkfall bolt had been poured into the building again, and the residue of that power was sparking and dancing across the roof now in a gridwork pattern of blue force. The neon sputtered and flashed and dashed fizzling around the outline of the Exit door. Within, something squealed and the pounding on the door stopped.

The power skittered and danced around them, but did not touch them. And now it seemed that the power of that explosion had done something to the raging, flashing walls of force all around the office block. The blue electricity force along the rim of the office block was sending small, wavering bursts like miniature thunderbolts, back into the walls of force from which it had come. Mad spiderwebs of blue leapt back greedily into heretofore-invisible blue veins in the air, which seemed to have been marbled into the very essence of the force barrier. The power of the Darkfall was pulsing and throbbing in those blue-white skeins; varicose fractures of power pulsing and swelling all around them. And now they could see that the roof of the office block was surging with that residual power. The building itself seemed to have acquired veins and arteries in a crisscross network clearly visible in the fabric of the building. There was no heat from that throbbing, pulsating power despite the brilliance of the Darkfall energy.

But now the things behind the Exit door were active again. The rooftop door juddered once more and this time something on the other side screamed in rage and frustration and began to tear strips of wood from the door with mutated talons and teeth. It was a bestial, terrifying sound; a bellow of insane rage. Jimmy turned away from the door and the pulsating throbbing blue on all sides.

Barbara was gone.

Jimmy jumped to his feet.

She was walking towards the ragged gap in the roof where the bolt had hit. Her shadow spread gigantically behind her and for an instant, it seemed that huge, black wings had sprouted from her shoulders. But it was only shadow writhing in that blue light, and now Jimmy was shouting . . .

"No!"

. . . and running towards her, when he saw that she had raised one hand and was reaching forwards in wonder to touch a sizzling blue line of power as it danced and pulsed on the rim of the aperture like a fallen power cable.

"Barbara!" shouted Jimmy. "Don't touch it!"

"I can feel it, Jimmy." She turned her head to look back at him, but her hand was still reaching for that power line. "I've been lost in there somehow. Joyriding with my brother. But it let me go. Maybe I can find out something to help us. Maybe I can . . ."

290

"Don't *touch* it!"

Barbara touched the spluttering blue neon.

"No, Barbara!"

Thunder crashed in the sky as Barbara was enveloped in a brilliant white light. Her hair flew around her head and shoulders as if in a raging wind. The jade pendant around her neck danced wildly, glittering like a piece of frozen fire on a chain. She seized that pendant with her free hand as Jimmy staggered backwards, shielding his eyes from the brilliance of the glowing power which surrounded her. Her face was incredibly beautiful.

"It doesn't want me," said Barbara in a voice that echoed as if she was standing in the middle of some huge cathedral, not on an office block under this raging Hell Storm. *"Whatever it is, it doesn't want me."*

"Of course it doesn't want you!" shouted Rohmer, staggering towards her. "It's rejected you before, why should it want you now?"

Jimmy seized Rohmer by the lapels.

"What the hell do you mean? What do you *know*, Rohmer? WHAT?"

Rohmer laughed, not resisting Jimmy's grip, even though he stood taller than him. "I tried to tell Gilbert that the Darkfall is spiritual in essence, not physical. But the stupid fool wouldn't listen. He couldn't . . ."

"What the hell are you talking about?" Jimmy shook him by the lapels.

"Look," said Rohmer. "Look at her . . ."

Cardiff was beside them both now, and they turned to look at her, Jimmy still retaining his grip. Barbara was still in the centre of that glowing light, her eyes screwed shut as if concentrating hard.

"She's trying to help you. But it won't matter. She was rejected once, untouched by the Truth. And you're both going to die soon."

Jimmy shook Rohmer again, smelling the nauseating stench of burnt flesh.

"Black Alchemy, not Science!" shouted Rohmer, snatching himself out of Jimmy's grip. "Can't you see what she's wearing? The jade pendant?" Rohmer spread his hands wide as if the answer was obvious, then laughed at their stupidity. "Jade! *JADE!* Don't you know anything? Jade was the stone the mystics wore to protect them from electricity and the force that is contained within it. Don't you see? She was Absorbed and Returned, just like her brother. But the jade protected her from the Effect."

"You mean she's . . . normal?" asked Jimmy, turning back to her with a strange expression on his face.

"Normal?" laughed Rohmer. "Just what do you consider to be normal? What do you consider . . . ?"

Barbara's eyes flew open.

"I can see, Jimmy!" she shouted. *"I can see!"*

She spread her hands wide as thunder racked the skies again. A fizzling blue crepitation of electricity was dancing around the edges of the glow that surrounded her.

"Down not Up! Down not Up! Down not . . ."

The glowing aura expanded, the light now suddenly too brilliant for the eye. Jimmy, Cardiff and Rohmer covered their faces as it reached its supernaturally brilliant peak, the very air alive and crackling with its power. Thunder crashed overhead again in the swirling chaos of the Darkfall storm.

And now the light was gone, and Jimmy looked back through blurred vision to see Barbara suddenly slump over into collapse. He ran to her as the rooftop juddered beneath them again.

Don't be dead, Barbara. Please don't be dead . . .

He held her close, turning her face to him.

She opened her eyes.

"Thank God . . ." said Jimmy.

Her eyes reflected the roiling, sparkling blue of the ice/firestorm thundering in the sky above them. They were the most beautiful eyes he had ever seen. She turned those eyes to him. And somehow there was another aura around them both now; a shimmering blue aura. Jimmy looked around him in wonder. They were *glowing* . . . and when he looked back across the rooftop he could see that Cardiff was also somehow surrounded by his own shimmering blue aura, like St Elmo's fire. He was looking at his hands and then around him, with a mixture of disbelief, concern and awe on his face.

Rohmer too had been affected. But his aura was different. He was swathed in a red glow of light . . . and something about the difference of that light revolted Jimmy.

He turned back to Barbara. She was smiling at him now and he felt as if his heart was going to burst. He wanted to say something to her, *anything* that could express the way he was feeling about her now . . . but her expression showed him that no words were necessary. No response was required. The great blue aura bound them together.

But the sound of a juddering *crack* was somehow cutting through their heightened emotions; an ugly, immediate and threatening sound that went against everything that had just been shown them. It had come from the rooftop Exit door. Even as they looked, something had smashed a hole through the woodwork of that door . . . and a black, squirming, taloned arm was tearing feverishly at the splintered aperture, trying to make it larger. Another sharp cracking of splintering wood, and a jagged shard was pulled inwards. Now, that hideous black arm was scrabbling through the widened hole – reaching for the quivering aerial mast which had been jammed into the hasp. And they were aware now of the shuddering office block beneath them, collapsing piece by piece beneath the savagery of the Darkfall.

They watched as Cardiff, glowing blue, clambered to his feet, moving backwards in their direction. Rohmer was still standing, arms apart, glowing red, and staring at the sky.

The sight of that scrabbling arm was quickly dispelling the overwhelming surge of emotions they were experiencing as Cardiff joined them.

"There must be something . . . *something!*" said Jimmy, looking around for some kind of way out, knowing that it was hopeless in any event. That hideous horde of monstrosities would be bursting through the door at any moment. Nothing could save them. Cardiff checked his gun again, hoping somehow that there would be more shells in there than before. There were not. Jimmy helped Barbara to stand. She was trying to speak, trying to tell him something; but unable to find her voice yet as he pulled her with him towards the others.

They backed off — watching the rapidly disintegrating Exit door.

They had reached the edge of the building, only a foot-high mini-parapet between them and the swirling black-blue chaos of the shimmering Darkfall. Jimmy looked over the edge . . . and could see no bottom. It was as if the office block vanished forever downwards into its surrounding ice-storm.

The gnarled claw of whatever lay beyond the door had found the aerial and was yanking it free. Cardiff followed Jimmy's gaze into the bottomless chasm. Then they were exchanging glances — and both knew what the only options available to them would be.

There were two.

They would rather jump into that Darkfall nothingness than stay on the roof and be torn apart by the monstrosities behind the door. Or Cardiff could use the shells in that gun for another purpose.

"Down . . ." Barbara struggled to speak. "Down . . . not Up . . ."

"Rohmer!" exclaimed Jimmy. And the other two looked quickly around to see that Rohmer, his shimmering red aura now subdued and somehow *mottled*, was walking towards the door. "Rohmer! What the hell are you . . . ?"

"I know what I'm doing." Rohmer's voice echoed back to them across the roof as he strode purposefully to the door. He grabbed the aerial from the grasp of the thing on the other side . . . and began to wrest it free, not only from the thing's grasp but also — deliberately — out of the hasp itself.

"You bloody fool!" Cardiff started forward. But was

brought to a halt when Rohmer yanked the aerial clear and the Exit door flew open with a crash.

Something large, black and contorted, yet still somehow indeterminable, collapsed out of the doorway and on to the rooftop at Rohmer's feet. Its immense and gnarled arm was still fastened in the shattered door. Cardiff saw the thing's eyes; yellow and feral; saw a glimpse of ragged teeth. And behind it, a jumbled mass of contorted and heaving bodies – even now ready to burst out on to the roof in a hideous mutated nightmare. But in that instant, Rohmer had stepped forward into the doorway; his mottled-red aura filling the doorframe and blotting out from their vision the nightmare shapes beyond. And the screaming, howling, gibbering things were now somehow quietened as Rohmer took another step forward, *over* the thing that was lying at his feet. The effect was instantaneous. The thing beneath him jerked hissing away back into the doorway, dragging its gnarled arm clear of the shattered door and away, as if in alarm or pain. Beyond the red haze in which Rohmer was now so clearly silhouetted, the invisible things beyond the haze were retreating from Rohmer and his strange aura.

"What's happening, Cardiff?" asked Jimmy.

"I don't . . . don't know. Yes . . . yes, dammit. They're *afraid* of him."

"No, it won't last. It can't last. They can sense its Darkfall power, but it's wearing off. They'll tear him to pieces." Even as Jimmy spoke, their own blue aura faded to nothingness.

Rohmer was back in the stairwell now, beyond the Exit door. His red aura was fading as he moved slowly and purposefully within. They saw the aura begin to diminish as Rohmer reached the first flight of stairs inside and began to descend, the hideous shapes still retreating before him. They could see his hand on the rail and now they could hear that Rohmer was talking to them, although they could not hear the words above the juddering and roaring of the disintegrating staircases. The red aura vanished. Rohmer had moved down out of sight . . . and the stairwell was filled once more with the mad fluttering light and shadow from the reflected Darkfall.

"What's he doing? What's he saying?" said Jimmy.

"Never mind why or how," replied Cardiff. "Let's just get back to that door and fix it so they can't come back."

"And then what? We can't stay up here forever. They'll get through that door eventually after they've killed Rohmer. There's no way we can stop them . . ." Jimmy's last words had fallen on deaf ears. Cardiff was running back to the Exit door. They followed. Barbara was still trying to speak, but she was too weak.

Jimmy stepped aside and retrieved the bent aerial, holding it like a spear. It was a small comfort to have this as his only weapon, but it was a comfort none the less. Cardiff kicked the door wide open, holding his gun in front of him just in case there was something still inside there. But apart from the leaping contorted shadows, the doorwell at the top of the stairs was empty. Jimmy and Barbara joined him, just as Cardiff stepped into that stairwell and uttered a curse of revulsion. The floor was slick with a viscous slime; no doubt from the things that had attacked them. Beyond the stairwell, they could see below, the faint red tinge of Rohmer's aura again. He was somewhere below them on the shuddering stairs and now they could hear his words as he descended, echoing back up the stairs to them, even above the sounds of destruction and the hideous slithering and rustling sounds of the things that still continued to retreat down the stairs from him.

"It's alright . . . alright . . . I've come . . . I'm here . . ."

"What on earth is he *doing*?" said Cardiff. He crept stealthily to the banister rail. Jimmy followed, still holding the aerial haft like a weapon. Down below, as the aura faded, they could make out shadows on the walls below; hideous, undulating shadows.

"I'll take you back . . ." continued Rohmer. ". . . I've seen what's there . . . I know where you've come from . . . I know what's happened . . . I know your pain . . ."

Cardiff reached the rail and looked over and down. Concrete dust was swirling and billowing in the throat of the staircase shaft. Something exploded far below.

Rohmer was three flights below, standing on the stairs with his hands held out like some strange preacher delivering a sermon in Hades. His aura was flickering and fading. Soon it would be gone. And now Cardiff could see the monstrous forms which filled the staircase below Rohmer.

"My God . . ."

The shapes on the stairs were truly from some monstrous nightmare; so much so that Cardiff's mind rejected the images that were trying to register there. If the thing that had been Barbara's brother was from Hell, then this horde must surely come from some even lower substrata of Hades. Only impressions were registering with Cardiff, as if too long a contemplation of what lay down there would send him mad.

Black and grey.

Tentacled and taloned.

Eyes and teeth.

Somewhere amidst that horde was another man in a business suit, somewhat akin to the thing that had been clinging to Barbara's brother when the monstrosities had fallen into the staircase shaft. Standing, still and silent, like Best Man at some Hideous Wedding . . . except that this man had no face. No face at all, just a circular cavity in the front of his head, where the face should be; a cavity that was fringed with coiling worm-like extremities.

Something like a centipede with a human face was fumbling at the wall, trying to climb.

Something naked, with skin patterned like wallpaper and with long flowing black hair, hung over the banister looking down into the swirling plaster and concrete-dust clouds.

Something like a machine; with twisting, undulating

297

coils of electrical circuitry which buzzed and snapped. Compacted glass and valves; crumbling white asbestos powder. Squatting like some monstrous inside-out machine, leaking oil and slime . . . but somehow alive.

And just below Rohmer, sitting on the steps and staring up with an expression of reverence and wonder on its hideously recognisable face . . . was Gilbert.

He was naked, but his skin was somehow the colour and the texture of the carpet on the second floor; a mottled green and black. There were cigarette burns on that "skin", where party revellers had dropped their cigarettes on to the carpet and stubbed them out. Gilbert's chubby pink face was somehow *stretched* . . . as if the moulding of his new face had gone wrong, and his face had melted in the Oven. The jaw hung long and low to his chest. Drool curled from his monstrous upper jaw and lip. His arms, monkey-like, were crossed on his chest. His spectacles, one lens broken, had been completely imprinted into his monstrous face, giving him a racoon-like mask.

"I know your pain . . . I've come to heal you . . ." Rohmer began to laugh; a hideous, gleeful sound that echoed and bounced in the stairwells.

"He's flipped his fucking lid," said Jimmy.

"Don't you know . . . don't you know?" laughed Rohmer again, berating the horrors with a sweep of his hand. "I've come . . . come to lead you."

"Maybe we can sneak down," said Jimmy. "Maybe we can sneak down to the next landing. Find a place to hide. To hole-up until this storm's over."

"No . . . no . . ." Barbara was twisting her head from side to side in negation of Jimmy's last suggestion, but still could not find her voice properly. "Down . . . down . . ."

"Look!" hissed Cardiff.

Rohmer was taking his gloves off, finger by finger, in a grand theatrical manner as if he was going to perform some neat magical effect.

"I'll show you . . ." continued Rohmer. "I'll show you . . . I can do it . . . I can go . . . *and come back!*"

And now Rohmer was holding up his hands before the monstrosities like a miracle healer. "Wait! Just wait!"

Rohmer turned from them and faced the outside wall, hands still held out in front of him.

"He's not . . . he can't . . ." began Jimmy.

Rohmer stepped forward and thrust his hands flat against the walls.

"No!" exclaimed Barbara involuntarily, and her cry echoed down the stairs.

Dozens of hideous and mutated eyes turned in their direction.

Rohmer began to scream as his hands began to sink into the wall. The things turned to look at him again as Rohmer thrashed at the wall, suppressing his agony now as they watched. But this time, Rohmer was looking back up the stairwell to where Cardiff, Jimmy and Barbara stood horrified in the shadows. With a mixture of mad delight and pain on his face, Rohmer threw back his head and howled: *"It's easy! Easy. You just don't have to resist, that's all!"* Rohmer's hands had vanished cleanly into the wall, and now they could see with horror that Rohmer was actually pushing himself into that wall. His forearms vanished, sliding easily into the plasterwork without leaving a mark; just as if he had been pushing them into mud.

"Transcendence, Cardiff!" howled Rohmer again. *"To know the truth! To live forever! To fly!"* Rohmer screamed again, this time in real pain as his elbows vanished into the flat white surface without trace. The wall was nearing Rohmer's face. He twisted back to the things on the staircase below him, which watched silently. *"Wait for me! I know your pain! I know it . . . know it . . . know it . . ."*

And then with a scream of defiance and elation, Rohmer thrust his face forwards and headbutted the wall. Instantly, his face was sucked into the plasterwork. Barbara turned away from the sight and clutched at the rail in sick horror as Rohmer's head was engulfed. His juddering, spasming body was sucked greedily into the wall . . . and even as it was happening, they could see that Rohmer was still forcefully *pushing* himself into the wall. His feet beat a savage, echoing tattoo on the steps as his torso slid from view. Spasming and kicking, his legs followed. His feet slid into the living tissue of the wall and now it was as if Rohmer had never been there at all.

The things on the staircase were silent, still watching the wall.

"We've got to get away," hissed Cardiff. "We've got to . . ."

Dozens of feral eyes were beginning to turn back in their direction. They knew that they were there.

". . . fasten this bloody door."

The thing with Gilbert's stretched face turned away from the wall and began to clamber up the steps, eyes fixed on them.

They fled from the landing back towards the Exit door.

"Why . . . ?" said Barbara in distress, still fighting for her voice.

"Because he's mad," said Cardiff flatly as he dragged her back towards the Exit door.

"*Mad?*" said something from the darkness of the stairwell shadows.

"Christ!" Jimmy recoiled back against the rail.

A face was forming on the wall beside the Exit door. A contorted, twisted, mutated, hideous face was pushing out from the fabric of the scarred plasterwork of the wall like a living death-mask. It began to laugh; a horrifying gargle of sound that mixed pleasure and hideous pain as the eyes on that wall-face opened and Cardiff saw the black pits of Hell reflected in there.

It was Rohmer's face.

But it had been hideously transmuted with something that had been behind the plaster of the wall when Rohmer had been Absorbed. Rohmer had intermingled with the steel and concrete and plaster and brick of the office block wall. But he had taken most of his new physiognomy and structure from the living thing that had been crawling in the wall when he entered.

300

It was a spider.

And now the spider that was Rohmer was coming back. Hands began to push out from the wall; hideously gnarled fingertips like the roots of trees were breaking the surface of the plasterwork ... and now the wall itself was bulging slightly as the dark mass of Rohmer's new body began to push itself out from the wall.

"For God's sake!" shouted Jimmy. "Put a fucking bullet in it before ..."

The thing that had once been Rohmer lunged out from the wall, still imprisoned at the waist but now with its arms free and thrashing out towards them. Jimmy yanked Barbara away from him as it tried to seize her. Horrifying spider-eyes glittered insanely in the darkness. They staggered back against the rail as the thing hissed and writhed and struggled to be free from the wall faster than the process would allow. They were trapped at the rail.

"*Transcendence, Cardiff!*" hissed the thing again. On the next lunge it must be free.

"Your choice, Rohmer," said Cardiff grimly ... and raised the revolver. A hand of tree-roots and frost and ice and cracking plaster erupted from that wall in a shower of plaster dust, encircling Cardiff's wrist. The face in the wall began to laugh. Jimmy lunged forward, holding the aerial like a spear. He stabbed it directly into Rohmer's swarming, ever-changing visage and the Rohmer-thing shrieked as the aerial embedded there; one of its spider-eyes popping in a gelatinous mass. Gnarled and mutated claws scrabbled at the quivering aerial ... and Cardiff yanked his hand from the grip of the thing. Jimmy pulled Barbara away from its thrashing embrace and out on to the rooftop again. The Rohmer-thing slashed out with a claw and Cardiff was hurled aside as it continued to shriek and scrabble at the protruding aerial. Cardiff collapsed in the doorway, and Jimmy lunged back, grabbed him by the coat lapel and dragged him back on to the roof. Barbara joined him, grabbing Cardiff's arm and hauling until they were free of the doorway and back on the rooftop. Rohmer's thrashing

301

form was now almost free of the wall completely. His shrieks were now joined by a chorus of other insane sounds as the mutations below rushed and scrabbled up the staircase once more. One of its thrashing arms connected with the Exit door, slamming it open. With a final bellow of rage, the thing that had been Rohmer was at last free from the wall and thrashing in the stairwell; its hideous form doubled-over and tearing at the aerial.

Jimmy and Barbara kept on dragging Cardiff until they were in the centre of the rooftop, next to the still-smoking crater-hole where the Darkfall bolt had split the roof. Smoke drifted upwards into the great raging canopy of St Elmo's fire above and around them. They helped him to his feet, watching in fear as Rohmer finally managed to pull the aerial from his "face". He stepped into the door-frame, aerial dangling from one claw, ooze dripping to the shale on the ground. Even from where they stood they could see the ragged hole in the middle of his hideous face. But something was happening there as it stood watching them with its one good eye. There was movement taking place on that face; shapes were arranging and rearranging there like clay.

"Transcendence," said the Rohmer-thing again, tossing the aerial disparagingly to one side with a brittle clatter. And now the thing's face was complete again; the ragged hole smoothed over; a new, yellow and feral eye staring at them.

"Did you feel it, then?" Cardiff heard himself ask. "Did you find your Other Side?"

The thing advanced one step. Behind it, they could hear the other monstrosities drawing near.

"There's nothing," the thing seemed to gargle at them. "Nothing. Only a new *Me!*"

"How did he do it?" asked Jimmy. "How did he come back?"

Still with its gaze fixed on them, the Rohmer-thing reached out with one claw and seized the Exit door. With what seemed effortless ease, it wrenched the door from its

302

hinges with two sharp movements. It discarded the door to the shale roof.

"No *way to hide, children. Not from me.*"

FIFTEEN

He could feel the newness of his transcendence; could feel how he had been changed. His flesh was now more than flesh. As he stood, watching them cower before him on the roof, he could feel the vibrancy, the exhilaration, the power of the Darkfall surging through him. It was part of him, just as he was part of it.

Rohmer's Absorption had constituted the most hideous agony he had ever known. But his faith in what lay ahead had sustained him; had contained his agony. Within that plaster wall, within the concrete and the steel and the wiring lay the agony of his salvation. He had become one with the bricks and mortar, had allowed his flesh to dissolve and melt into the very fabric of the building and with the spider. The others, he knew, had fought that inevitable process; had been horrified and anguished by the Absorption. And in their resistance to the Darkfall, to the process, to the Absorption — they had lost their minds. They had lost that necessary essence of self as their physical and spiritual mind had been absorbed and changed.

Not Rohmer.

He knew now that he was more than human; knew that his flesh was not human flesh — it was now a complex structure of organic and inorganic materials. His very molecules were fused with the essence of concrete and bitumen and steel and plaster and plastic and paper and insect.

He was Liberated.

Liberated not only from his body (which he could now reform and reshape at will) — but also from anything which had constituted human morality.

304

*He was not human anymore. Therefore, human moral-
ities would no longer apply to him. He was Primal. And
that within him which he had suppressed, that within him
which had poisoned him with guilt need no longer do so.
The Darkfall had suffused him with a new Power and he
would use that power for further transcendence. Within
him, he could feel the ever-changing flow and melding of
flesh and blood and concrete and liquid plastic; all of it
finding its right place, its right reaction, its right purpose
in this new Body he had been given. He remained still for
a while, savouring the bliss and the agony of his transcendence at last.*

*"Reborn," he said aloud with a gargled voice. Raw,
liquid cement spilled from his mouth and flowed like oat-
meal down his chest. His chest heaved and sucked like the
thorax of some hideous insect; legacy of the insect life
which had been absorbed and transmogrified within him
as he had been drawn into the office-block wall. The ribs
of his chest flexed, stretched and opened outwards like
the clutching legs of some upright and monstrous spider,
pushing and kneading that spilled cement back into his
body as if spinning an internal web. The ribs squirmed, in
perfect symmetry, back to the body again and were still.*

"Reborn."

*He liked the word. For that was truly what had hap-
pened to him. Every Messiah must be reborn. Only a Messiah could understand the potential of this new Flesh.*

*He watched the three before him on the shaking office-
block roof. He could sense that they were cowering, waiting for his next move.*

He despised them for what they were.

He despised them for their humanity.

*They would die. And the fuel of their death would feed
him. He had never tasted blood, had never eaten raw
human meat, but now . . .*

*And then he heard the shuddering sounds of something
huge collapsing in the stairwell; heard and felt the grumbling, crashing roar of masonry and steel. There was a*

screaming intermingled within that great roaring. He turned back to the Exit as a cloud of dust spewed forth and engulfed him. The screaming was fading now, swallowed by the great avalanche sounds ... but he had recognised the agony and the fear in that screaming, which had not issued from human throats.

He looked back to the three on the roof from his engulfing dust cloud, then back into the darkness of the stairwell.

The three could wait.

He was needed by his Own.

SIXTEEN

"He can't be killed," said Barbara in a quiet voice, as the Rohmer-thing vanished through the dust cloud and into the guttering shadows of the stairwell. Overhead, another shattering crack of Darkfall energy caused the whirling ice-storm barrier to pulse with blue force. They flinched and waited. There was no further bolt from the sky — just the continuous grumbling and shuddering of the storm and the ever-swirling colours of its nightmare rainbow.

When the dust cloud swirled away, Rohmer had vanished from sight — and now, somehow, this acted as a trigger for Jimmy. A dark and violent rage swelled inside him. Pulling away from Barbara, he strode across the rooftop towards the shattered Exit door.

"Rohmer!" shouted Jimmy. "Come back here, you bastard!"

Barbara tugged hard, trying to stop him. "What are you *doing*, Jimmy? Stop it! Stop . . ." Her voice had returned.

Jimmy was reacting to the fear and the unknown and the terror in a purely instinctive way. The sickness of fear in his stomach, the continuing attacks on their very existence, the horrifying uncertainty of whether they would ever get out of this nightmare alive — all had converted within him to desperate rage.

"Come out of there, Rohmer! Come out of there and I'll . . ."

Cardiff was at Barbara's side now, grabbing at Jimmy's other arm. Jimmy pulled free of both. They were standing at the ragged lip of the blasted crater and Jimmy stooped, grabbed a chunk of concrete and hurled it at the Exit door.

The concrete exploded on the lintel in a spray of dust. But there was no movement from within.

"Come out and get it, Rohmer! Come out and . . ."

Cardiff and Barbara had grabbed him now. His breath was coming in heavy sobs, but he no longer resisted them as they stood there beneath the raging Darkfall.

"Don't snap, Jimmy!" said Cardiff fiercely. "Don't snap now. We need you."

Jimmy took a deep breath and looked down into the ragged aperture which had been blasted by the Darkfall bolt. A hole had been punched through the roof and through the reinforced concrete platform ten feet below on which the elevator gearbox, winch and motors were housed.

And Barbara was shaking his arm now, as he stared down into that ragged shaft.

"Down, Jimmy. Not Up. That's what I felt."

Cardiff was looking hard at the Exit door for signs of Rohmer and the others. "God knows what he's . . ."

"Listen to me, Mr Cardiff!" said Barbara. "We haven't got much time. The Darkfall isn't going to subside, it's not going to blow itself out. There's nowhere we can hide. Because this building will *collapse*. It's going to happen. The Darkfall storm is going to tear it apart. And the only chance for us is to go *Down*!"

Jimmy's rage had subsided. He turned back to Barbara as she continued: "Believe me, I know what I'm saying. There's never been a Darkfall as powerful as this one. We have to get down and take refuge below ground. Anything living above ground will be . . . oh, what's the word? They'll be . . . *dissipated*. It's like they were telling us before, when we were in the basement and John . . ." Barbara swallowed hard. "John tried to get in and kill us. They told us that if we'd waited out the storm below ground, then we would be safe from the Darkfall effects. We've got to get down again, get below ground to avoid the dissipation. And this building will collapse, believe me."

"Even if we get down there," said Cardiff, glancing back

down through the ragged aperture. "What makes you think being in the basement will save us? This office block is fourteen storeys high. Have you any idea how much concrete and steel that represents? If the building collapses straight down on top of itself we'd have to be a quarter of a mile underground not to be squashed flat."

"Maybe it won't collapse straight down," said Barbara. "Maybe the storm will blow it outwards, or sideways or away altogether or . . ."

"That's a lot of maybes," said Cardiff grimly.

"It's our only chance!" shouted Barbara.

Jimmy continued to stare down into the shaft. Overhead light from the Darkfall cast great chasing shadows in the chasm; the rumbling sound of its power echoing in the seemingly bottomless depths. It was like a mineshaft into Hell.

"Down," he said at last, and his eyes seemed glazed as he stared down into the flickering shaft. "Yes . . . we've got to go down again."

Cardiff peered into the pit. "It's a nice idea, Barbara. But it's just not possible. We can't reach the elevator cable from here. There's no way to reach it . . ."

"Don't need to climb down the cable," said Jimmy quietly, his voice almost drowned by the rumbling of the storm. "That hole has blasted straight through the roof and the concrete platform underneath, hasn't it?" He ducked down to the rim of the ragged hole and peered sideways and down. "Yeah, I thought so."

The sky detonated again overhead. Jimmy did not flinch. Cardiff dropped to his knees, looking anxiously back to the Exit door for signs of Rohmer. He had vanished. He gripped an exposed girder in the roof and, leaning over, followed Jimmy's gaze.

"Look, it's not possible . . ."

"I think it *is* possible, Cardiff."

"How the hell can you . . . ?"

"I've burgled two office blocks through the elevator shaft. I think I know my way around."

Jimmy swung around so that his feet were dangling over the edge of the chasm. Barbara rushed forward, hand held out to him.

"Jimmy! Be . . ."

Jimmy braced his hands on the lip and shoved, launching himself into the shaft.

Cardiff cried out too, grabbing for him as he slipped into the darkness in a fine spray of rubble and dust, expecting to see him whirling away down into the darkness in a contorted jumble. Amazingly, Jimmy had grabbed a dangling wire from the ruined fabric of the roof and used it to steady himself as he landed on the solid edge of the shattered concrete platform ten feet below. He hopped away from the ragged edge, dragging hard at the wire to make sure that it was still fastened tight as he wrapped it around his gloved wrist and forearm. Wiping dust from his bloodied face, he looked back up at them . . . and grinned.

"God, Jimmy!" exclaimed Cardiff.

"Easy," said Jimmy, holding out his hand to Barbara. "Now, come on. And just be careful not to tear any of your clothing."

Barbara glanced nervously down into the pit.

"Take my other hand," said Cardiff. She grabbed it, looked hard at him, and then stepped out over the rim. Cardiff lowered her, her feet scrabbling first on the ragged concrete of the roof and then into space . . . as Jimmy leaned out over the edge of the winch platform and grabbed her free hand.

Barbara saw the chasm yawn beneath her . . . and suddenly she was standing next to Jimmy. Gasping, she stood back from the rim and into comparative shadowed safety.

"Okay, Cardiff . . ." began Jimmy, but Cardiff was already lowering himself gingerly over the ragged edge. Jimmy watched as he carefully lowered himself all the way down until he was hanging by his fingertips. His suit was crumpled and stained, his hair wild, and Jimmy had a powerful image of the man as he'd first seen him on arrival at this hellish office block: calm, neat and with carefully

310

parted hair. The twat who had put him away on a false charge. Even though he knew now that it was Pearce who had been responsible for the trumped-up charges on other jobs, Cardiff was still a copper, after all. The kind of man he hated, almost instinctively. A *copper*, for crying out loud. And after everything that had happened to Jimmy, maybe he should just let this slightly overweight Detective Inspector dangle on the edge for a bit, let him suddenly thrash around, trying to get purchase, begging for help. Let first one hand, and then the other fall away from the rim of that ragged ledge on the roof. Let him twist his head back, eyes wild, screaming for help ... as his other hand finally lost its grip under the overweight of too many police-club-luncheon-dinners, and he fell twisting and sobbing into the shaft.

But apart from the stark physical contrast of his now dishevelled appearance, there was something incredibly *different* about Cardiff in Jimmy's eyes as Cardiff twisted one hand away from the roof and flung it out towards him.

Jimmy leaned out, still braced by the wire around his left arm and wrist ... and grabbed Cardiff's arm. Cardiff's eyes were glazed in a naked anxiety about the drop below him, even though he steadfastly refused to look down into it. Jimmy heaved, and Cardiff swung across to the concrete platform with him, feet scrabbling on the edge ... and then they were safe. Jimmy unwrapped his arm as Cardiff stood back from the edge.

"You're a gutsy old bastard," said Jimmy. He smiled at him. He couldn't help it.

"I'd like to keep my guts intact, if that's okay," returned Cardiff, dusting himself off.

Jimmy hurried on past him, checking the concrete platform beneath his feet as he moved, feeling the shuddering vibration of collapse somewhere below. Barbara and Cardiff followed him tentatively into the darkness towards the dark jumble of machinery ahead.

"How many lifts are there in the building, Cardiff?"

"Two ..."

"Yeah, yeah . . . I see. Look, we're standing on the concrete platform that houses the gearboxes and motors for the elevators. They weigh about a ton each, so that platform's reinforced with steel bars. Back there, where we climbed down . . . there's just a sheer drop between floors all the way to the basement. Nothing to hang on to, nothing to climb down."

"Thanks for not telling me that before, Jimmy."

"It's a pleasure. Now look . . . look . . ."

They had reached the first of two sheave gearboxes and motors, housed in four-foot-high, three-foot-wide, semi-cylindrical steel containers. Jimmy quickly squeezed past the first, standing between them. Cardiff could see a corded cable, only four inches thick and consisting of six separate half-inch, oil-based strands, descending from the gearbox and vanishing through a cylindrical hole in the platform. Something seemed to explode close by and the platform vibrated again.

"That came from the staircase," said Jimmy tightly. "We walked over the top of it back there."

"It sounds like Hell," said Cardiff.

"It is," rejoined Barbara. And now Jimmy was stooping down low between the gearboxes, hunting for something. He found it, standing quickly again and yanking open a service trapdoor.

"That's it!" exclaimed Jimmy. "Come on . . ."

Barbara and Cardiff squeezed past the first gearbox and motor. Jimmy was already stooping down and staring into the shaft below. The flickering blue light of Darkfall was dancing upon his face as he looked. Cardiff joined him, staring down into the shaft.

The elevator cable from the gearbox dropped away from the concrete platform, swaying precariously before vanishing into the blackness of the chasm below. Darkfall light was somehow flickering down below in the shaft, giving an eerie blue incandescence to the sheer concrete walls. The sounds of the Darkfall storm echoed back as if there was some underground sea down there somewhere in the dark-

312

ness, its pitch-black surf booming hollow on concrete shores. The platform shuddered again and a chunk of concrete suddenly fell whirling into the pit, rebounding from the shaft wall in a spray of disintegration before vanishing into the dark. Seconds later, there was a hollow, echoing crash as it hit the roof of the elevator.

"Alright, Jimmy. You're in charge. How do we climb down?"

Jimmy pointed. "Okay, we're looking down into one of the two elevator shafts. It's not too wide. Maybe twelve feet square. Same as the width of the elevator cab. Now, just down and opposite to us . . . can you see, Barbara?"

"Yes."

"Just down and opposite by another twenty feet or so is a recess. That's an alcove for the elevator doors on the fourteenth floor. There are fifteen alcoves all the way down to the basement, floor by floor. But we can't open them . . . and even if we could, I don't suppose we would want to, knowing what's on the staircases. Right . . . on the shaft wall at our left down there . . . see that? That's the counterweight, that heavy square bugger of metal. It's at the thirteenth floor so that means the elevator is down on the ground floor, and it's going to stay there. If the electricity's out, and the counterweight's up here, it means we're not going to get squished by an elevator that decides it's coming up. The elevator cab is heavier than the counterweight. Laws of gravity, see?"

"Should have been an engineer, Jimmy . . . not a burglar."

"Alright, no jokes. We haven't got time. I'm telling you this because we're going to start down in a second, and I want you to know the layout."

"I'm feeling dizzy . . ." said Barbara, and Jimmy looked up to see her recoiling from the trapdoor, steadying herself with a hand on the gearbox-motor.

"It's okay, Barbara. Okay. You don't have to look. Just listen. See the counterweight guides. See, Cardiff? They're two parallel steel runners set into the wall, all the way

313

down. But they're no good for us, nothing to hang on to. On the *other* walls, though . . . either side . . . are the steel runner-guides that the elevator fits into on its way up and down. They've got . . . whatchacallit?"

"Indentations," said Cardiff. "I can see them."

"That's the word. Just like . . ."

"Rungs in a ladder."

"You catch on fast, Cardiff. You'd make a great office burglar."

"If we get out of this you might have a partner."

Darkfall thunder or the sounds of a further collapse in the building shook the platform to such an extent that they reeled against each other and made grim nonsense of their jokes. Barbara clutched at the steel housing.

"Alright . . . alright . . ." she said. "So it's the steel runners for the elevator cab."

"All the way down," said Jimmy, not trying to react to the further chunks of concrete that fell into the shaft in plumes of dust and rubble. "Easy-peezy-lemon-squeezy . . ."

"Whaaat . . . ?" said Barbara, in a weary and humoured tone that belied the hypertension and the fear and the horror that threatened to enervate them all in the face of this ghastly nightmare.

"North-of-England Geordie-talk, circa 1991, Barbara. When we get out of here, I'll teach you all about it."

"Jimmy?"

"Yes?"

"You get to buy me all the records I've missed since 1964. Right?"

"Better believe it."

"Pardon?"

"That means . . . cool. I can dig it."

"That's old-fashioned talk, Jimmy," replied Barbara. "But I know what you mean. Thanks."

"Any records he can't buy you," said Cardiff, "I'll give you. I was young once myself, you know."

And now Jimmy had flipped the trapdoor hatch all the way back with a flat *slap!*

"Okay," he said.

He was trying to smile again, but with the blood-smears from his Duvall-busted nostrils and the concrete dust on his face, it just wouldn't work.

He persevered with the smile when he spoke again.

"Let's go . . ."

SEVENTEEN

Rohmer slid into the flickering shadows of the stairwell and stood for a moment with what had been his hand on the stair-rail. The rail was juddering violently.

He could no longer hear the screams, but there were other sounds now, almost lost in the all-enveloping roar of the rumbling avalanche below. They were like the sounds from some bizarre aviary; a high-pitched chirruping and squealing and rustling. There were the sounds of other animals, too: the sounds of heavy ragged breathing, squawking and chattering.

He strode through the slime at the top of the stairwell to the head of the quivering stairs and looked downwards into the guttering shadows and the rising clouds of dust.

All but two flights of stairs – from Floor 12 to 14 – had buckled away from the wall structure and collapsed into the staircase shaft, taking with them most of Rohmer's Reborn. That had been the sounds of the great rumbling explosion and the screams.

With no remorse for the death of his Reborn, Rohmer leaned further forward, concrete oozing from his jaws . . . and saw the survivors.

There were still six or seven Returners on the remaining staircase, hanging on the banister railings. One of them, the thing that looked like a centipede with a human face, was crawling up the wall.

Rohmer walked down to meet them, and when he turned on the fourteenth-floor landing, he opened what had been his arms wide in greeting.

316

"Reborn!"

They turned as one to look up at him.

Gilbert was still there, crouching on the staircase with his stretched face and his monkey-claws.

Something in rags and with two heads kneaded its crackling steel fingers like some kind of worry-bead combination. One of its faces was grinning insanely, the other identical face had a look of sorrow.

Other indeterminate shapes undulated in the darkness.

And Rohmer knew instinctively that they had heard and seen his struggle with the Old Flesh and were in awe of him. But there was little of real kinship there as they shifted uneasily before him. The Transcendence had destroyed every vestige of reason in those New Brains. Only hate and rage and hunger . . . and now fear, remained. But there was still, Rohmer could sense, a vestige of something that wanted to make sense of this new condition. And it was that sense that kept them instinctively waiting and watching; waiting for Rohmer to tell them what to do.

"I'm not human anymore," said Rohmer, the Messiah. "And neither are you. We're all . . . New."

The staircase on which the things crouched juddered violently, and they swarmed up to him, stopping just below the fourteenth floor to gaze up at Rohmer, like some ragged Horde from Hell.

"I'll give you back your Minds. Because we can create our own rules now. We can do what we want without limit. I'll lead you."

The things on the staircase could not understand what he was saying. But there was a kinship now, an understanding of the emotion behind Rohmer's words. They began to howl. And that unearthly noise echoed up and down the rumbling, roaring stairwell.

"I will lead you. Because I am your New Saviour . . ."

Rohmer laughed: a horrifying, rasping bass sound . . . and the things on the staircase tried to laugh with him.

Grinning through cement-encrusted fangs, Rohmer

317

turned his attention back to the Exit door aperture on the roof — and to what was still out there on the roof.

"Follow," he said.

EIGHTEEN

Jimmy sat on the edge of the trapdoor aperture, legs dangling. Bracing his hands on either side of the aperture frame, he pressed up with all of his weight on his hands and suspended himself directly over the drop . . . and then lowered himself, quickly compensating for the change in balance by snatching one hand across to join the other.

Now he was hanging from the trapdoor aperture by his fingertips, with a fourteen-storey drop below him.

Jimmy swung once towards the elevator cable and grabbed it with one hand. Letting go of the trapdoor rim, he seized the cable with his other hand and clung to it. Now he was in the centre of the shaft, and the sway factor wasn't as bad as he'd thought once it had his weight on it. Maybe twelve inches. Jimmy entwined his legs and feet around the cable and stretched out with one hand to the far wall, grabbing one of the metal tracks for the elevator cab.

Christ, don't let my gloves tear.

He let go of the cable and clung to the rail, screwing his eyes shut against the sweat and blood that was running down his face.

"Jimmy, are you okay?" called Cardiff.

"Yeah . . ." He climbed up the rail and waited.

Barbara was taking deep breaths.

"There's no other way," said Cardiff. "Just don't . . ."

"Yes, I know. Just don't look down."

An unholy howling sound was issuing from somewhere

319

above; ghosts of that echo swirled and eddied within the guttering elevator shaft.

"Rohmer will be back with those things shortly," said Cardiff. "And then it'll be too late anyway . . ." Barbara stepped forward, and Cardiff took off his belt as they'd discussed. He wrapped it around her waist, fastening the buckle tight and knotting the loose end around his gloved fist. "It's a dream, Barbara. Remember? That's what you kept telling us. It's only a dream. Keep thinking it."

She watched Cardiff finish knotting the belt in his fist and took his other hand as she stepped towards the trapdoor aperture. Cardiff waited for her to sit down on the edge, but she had paused and he looked back to her to see that she was studying him intently. There was a tear-gleam in her eyes.

"I'm glad I dreamed you two."

There was a strange, aching lump in Cardiff's throat when he spoke again.

"Come on, love. Let's go."

Without a further word, Barbara sat quietly on the trapdoor ledge. Cardiff lay flat on the concrete platform as she lowered herself through, jaw set. Now she was hanging by her fingertips, her long black hair whipping. Bracing one hand on the gearbox housing, Cardiff stretched to keep his exposed face and neck from contact with the concrete platform . . . and then clutched tight on the belt, taking her entire weight on his other arm.

"Alright, Barbara. Let go!"

Barbara's fingertips left the trapdoor aperture, and Cardiff felt the agony of stretching muscles in his arm as she swayed over the shaft.

Hurry up, Jimmy! yelled Cardiff in his mind, teeth gritted. *Hurry up, before I . . .*

Below, Jimmy had grabbed Barbara with one hand and pulled her over to the metal rails.

"Okay! Let go, Cardiff!"

Cardiff rolled back from the aperture as Jimmy began to unfasten Cardiff's belt from her waist. He lay there, resting on one elbow, sucking in breath. A feeling of dreadful enervation was beginning to creep over him.

God, I don't know if I can do this. We've come so far . . . but I just don't know if I've got the strength left.

There were cramping pains in his chest again. He could feel the open wounds in his chest searing and throbbing. The trauma and the fear and the immense physical effort seemed as if they must catch up with him at last. What if he let them go on without him?

So you've found reasons for living again, a voice seemed to whisper to him. *And now you just want to throw it all away again? Is that what Lisa and Jamie would have wanted, Cardiff?*

The sounds of Beasts echoed from somewhere above again.

"Cardiff!" shouted Jimmy, his voice echoing in the elevator shaft. "Come on!"

They need me.

Cardiff swung his legs over the edge of the aperture and lowered himself down again.

Barbara had climbed down so that she was almost opposite to the fourteenth-floor elevator-doors aperture, to give Jimmy and Cardiff more room. "That's it . . . that's it . . ." he heard Jimmy say. "Just like before, Cardiff. Just like before. Easy . . . easy . . ."

Pain like liquid fire was stabbing in the arm which had lowered Barbara.

Christ, this is it! I'm going to fall!

His burning arm jerked free from the aperture, and he groped blindly for Jimmy, spinning helplessly in mid-air. The fingers of his other arm slid from the ledge.

And Jimmy had him now as he fell, hanging on tight as Cardiff slammed hard against the metal rails with an echoing, metallic crash. Jimmy clung tight as Cardiff thrashed at the rail, grabbing for purchase. At last, his feet had found one of the "rungs", and he hugged the rail tight as Jimmy climbed down to Barbara.

321

"Right . . . right . . ." said Jimmy. "We've done it. The rest is easy . . ."

"Lemon-squeezy," said Barbara in a breathless, frightened voice.

"You said it, Barbara. Now, look. I'm going to climb past you. I'll go first, then you and Cardiff . . . Cardiff?"

"Yes . . . yes . . ." gasped Cardiff, heart hammering. "I'm okay."

"Cardiff follows last. Remember what I said? Just like a ladder. See the rungs? Okay, then . . ."

Jimmy clambered nimbly past Barbara and then paused when he was just below her, looking up.

"We'll all take a step together, so that there isn't a gap between us and no one gets in trouble. Right? Here we go, then . . . Step!"

They began to climb down.

NINETEEN

Rohmer exploded on to the roof under the whirling pyro-technics of the Darkfall storm. He was Pack Leader, and the others were close behind him; a howling ravening nightmare infused with the bloodlust that they had scented from their Messiah.

Rohmer strode ahead, scanning the rooftop for signs of them.

The others shrank back, awed by the cloud-shattering fury of the Darkfall storm and sensing its part in their new Birth.

Rohmer was unafraid of the sky. It was part of him. And as he scanned the rooftop and found that his prey had gone, the bloodlust inside him swelled and threatened to swamp his Reason. The insectile instinct he had inherited with his new body was struggling for superiority. He fought it, howled in frustration and finally reached the gaping hole in the roof down which they had climbed. He could smell their presence somewhere below. Behind him, the others were overcoming their awe of the Darkfall and the crackling blue lightning that cracked and shivered around the office block. Soon, their bloodlust would return and they would join him in the hunt. But he was the Leader, and as such he was entitled to First Kill.

He thrust his horribly insectile face into the ragged gap, mandibles working, but could see nothing. He smelled the girl now, and wondered with the Spider part of his mind rising in lustful anticipation: what would happen if I impregnated her? What would she give birth to? Could that be the New Beginning?

323

Rohmer leapt into the crevasse, grabbing at the wiring which hung from the interior of the roof. Swinging his bulk down, he landed with the agility, ferocity and hunting instincts of a Wolf Spider.

Still, he could not see them in the darkness. But their smell was strong and he slid through the shadows towards the sheave gearboxes and motors of the elevators as the first of his Minions reached the hole in the roof and began to scrabble after him.

The smell was emanating from the trapdoor between the steel housings, and Rohmer emitted a hissing sound of pleasure.

Another explosion racked the building and the concrete platform shifted beneath his taloned feet. He felt something crack and give way. Behind him, one of the Newborn scrabbled for purchase on the ragged edge of the concrete platform, missed its footing, and plunged screaming into the abyss.

Unconcerned, the Rohmer-thing moved towards the trapdoor.

TWENTY

"Step!" shouted Jimmy, and they all moved downwards again. "Step!"

The sound of a gigantic explosion somewhere boomed and echoed in the shaft. They felt its vibration in the metal rail and clung tight. Above them, the concrete platform cracked and shifted.

"Shit!" exclaimed Jimmy, looking up.

Plumes of dust began to fall from it, enveloping them.

The elevator cable was swaying in the centre of the shaft.

Cardiff remembered Jimmy's words: *The gearboxes and motors for the elevators. They weigh about a ton each, so this platform's reinforced with steel bars.* If that concrete platform collapsed into the shaft . . . ?

Suddenly, there was something moving in the trapdoor aperture.

They had all seen it at once.

"Come on! Move!" shouted Jimmy. "Step! Step!"

The monstrous, swarming spider-face that was Rohmer hissed down at them.

"Step! Step! Step!"

TWENTY-ONE

Rohmer saw them desperately trying to escape. His blood-lust had given him a roaring of the blood which he could actually feel.

He judged the width of the aperture and knew that he could not follow them. Liquid concrete slavered from his jaw, dripping into the pit.

The centipede-thing with the human face was swarming towards the trapdoor hatch. It was thin enough to get through and could climb down the smooth concrete wall of the shaft. Ravening, it tried to squeeze past Rohmer and through the gap. Rohmer hissed angrily and lashed out with a taloned foot. The centipede-thing was kicked away across the concrete platform. It curled into a tight, obscene ball of legs and chitinous armour as Rohmer slammed the trapdoor shut.

There was another way to get them.

There was still a staircase leading down to the twelfth floor: each staircase giving access to the interior landings . . . and to the elevator doors which led into the shaft.

Rohmer slashed his way back through his Minions towards the hole in the roof. The Others milled in confusion . . . and then followed their Master.

TWENTY-TWO

"Step!" shouted Jimmy, and missed his own footing.

He clung to the metal rail as his feet kicked in space.

"Shit!"

He found the rung and righted himself again.

They had passed the elevator doors on the fourteenth floor and were nearing the thirteenth.

What the hell is that Rohmer-thing doing up there? thought Jimmy. The concrete platform shuddered and cracked again. A shower of fine grit fell on them. *That's it! The bastard's trying to bring that platform down on us somehow.*

Barbara had breathed in some of the concrete dust and began to cough.

"You alright?" said Jimmy, wiping dust and grime from his face and eyes.

"Yes, yes . . . was that . . . ?"

"Yes," said Cardiff. "It was Rohmer. Just keep going."

Jimmy was directly opposite the elevator doors on the thirteenth floor now. He glanced briefly at it as he descended . . . and heard the first scrabbling sounds on the other side. His stomach tightened in a spasm of fear. Now he knew what Rohmer was doing.

"*Christ! Come on . . .*"

The elevator doors began to rattle and vibrate.

"What is it?" shouted Cardiff.

"They've followed us down the staircase! They're trying to open the elevator doors."

"Oh, God . . ." said Barbara. Jimmy was below those doors now, and she was opposite to them. There was a

327

crack down the centre of those double-doors; only a half-inch, but now they could hear the gibbering and the ranting and the squealing of the horde on the other side. Those hellish sounds were invading the shaft, echoing up and down nightmarishly. Barbara could see the flurrying activity of claws and talons in the small gap, trying to get purchase, wriggling and gouging between the double-doors. Now those monstrous things were throwing themselves at the door in a gibbering, howling fury.

"Take it easy, take it easy," said Jimmy. "Just concentrate on climbing down . . ."

At last, Barbara had climbed past those doors.

Cardiff was directly opposite now, dangerously close. Something larger than the other nightmare shapes had pushed itself past them to the double-doors . . . and Cardiff could see steel talons in the crack between them, trying to force the doors open. He could hear the sounds of that thing's monstrous breathing, and knew that it was Rohmer. Behind it, the others still howled and squealed in voices that were a bestial combination of the human and the inhuman. Horror swamped Cardiff. The nightmare, lustful sounds were striking some terrifying chord inside him. Were these the kind of sounds a deer or an antelope might hear just before and during the time it was brought down by a pride of lions? Cardiff was soaked in sweat. Any kind of death would be better than *that* kind of death.

But now he was past those juddering, banging metal doors.

"*Step!*" shouted Jimmy again, looking up. They were moving too slowly. Jimmy wiped one hand hard on the right rail, and looked at his glove. The rail was greased. If he slid down, would the glove tear?

A screeching sound began to issue from the doors above, echoing like a banshee's scream in the shaft. The doors were being pulled apart.

Jimmy decided, gripped the rails, and kicked his feet off the rung. He slid ten feet before jamming his feet into a rung again, frantically checking his gloves. They were untorn.

"Faster, Barbara! Faster! Come on! Step! Step! Step!"

Barbara hurried down, face set. Cardiff was well clear of the doors at last, still looking up to the recess as he descended and the banshee wail suddenly became an echoing, juddering crash. The sounds of Rohmer's horde burst into the shaft now; a horrifying caterwauling and howling and gibbering.

Rohmer's monstrous face appeared over the edge, looking down, claws braced in the aperture. The spider-legs that had been his ribs flexed outwards from his torso in rage, grasping at the air. Other horrifying visages swarmed around him, writhing and undulating and howling down after them. Rohmer snarled in anger ... and then something leapt past Rohmer into the elevator shaft and hit the far concrete wall with a wet and scrabbling *slap!*

Cardiff saw the bristling, indiscernible ball stick against that wall. Appendages were twisting and curling around it, like some huge sea anemone.

Rohmer roared at the thing in rage.

And then it uncurled on the wall, still sticking there, but somehow uncoiling itself into a long, thin and monstrously undulating shape, six feet long, and now hanging vertically on the shaft wall. Cardiff could see as he scrabbled downwards that at the bottom of that hideous shape was a large matted object, the size of a human head. That object was emitting a gibbering, buzzing sound now, as Rohmer roared at it again.

The object twisted ... and looked down at Cardiff.

It was the centipede thing, and its hideous parody of a human face grinned as it swarmed down the shaft wall towards him. Poison was dripping from obscene and gnashing teeth as it came, buzzing and howling.

Face drained of colour, hand trembling, Cardiff hooked his left arm around the metal rail and fumbled in his inside pocket with his right hand.

The Rohmer-thing bellowed again, and the others joined

in with him as the centipede thing fixed its eyes on Cardiff's face. Its hideous multiple legs swarmed in undulating waves of motion as it lunged for him. The gun was suddenly in Cardiff's hand, pointed up at the thing, and its hideous head was only inches from the gun barrel when Cardiff pulled the trigger. The detonation echoed long and loud, like thunder, and the thing's head was suddenly an obscene stain of squashed insect on the shaft wall.

It dropped past Cardiff, writhing, and vanished into the darkness below. Jimmy and Barbara recoiled in terror and disgust as it passed them.

And up above, the Rohmer-thing was laughing. It was a hideous parody of a sound. His monstrous visage withdrew from the aperture, and the others followed him once more.

The concrete platform above juddered and cracked. A shower of grit and dust swept downwards into the shaft.

"Come on!" Cardiff shouted into Jimmy and Barbara's upturned faces.

On the staircase beyond, they could hear the frenzied whooping, echoing cries of the horde's descent. They were heading for the next set of double-doors on the twelfth floor.

We're never going to make it, thought Jimmy desperately. *We'll never make it to the bottom. They'll just keep at it until they get us.* And then: *No! No . . . that staircase only goes so far. It fell apart at the bottom. We've got to keep going. We can do it . . . we can do it . . .*

"Step, Barbara!" he shouted up to her.

He had reached the double-doors at the twelfth. Rohmer and his monstrous Legion were scrabbling at it already. He could see a blur of hideous motion through the thin gap and hurried on down past it.

"Step! Come on. Step and . . ."

The double-doors crashed open with a sound of thunder.

Barbara was directly opposite on the metal rail. Her own scream was drowned by the hideous and exultant screaming of the Horde as a multitude of grabbing, clawing, mutated arms burst through the gap towards her.

330

"Barbara!" yelled Jimmy, arm outstretched to her as she recoiled from them . . . and fell from the metal rail into the shaft.

"Nooooooo!!!"

Barbara twisted in the air past him. Jimmy grabbed for her . . . and missed.

"Barbara, nooooo!!!"

Her wildly flailing arms and legs connected with the elevator cable. She twisted awkwardly, and now Jimmy was sobbing like a child as Barbara had her arms around the cable and was spinning in mid-air, her fall arrested. Unhesitatingly, Jimmy flung himself off the metal rail after her, caught the elevator cable and whirled down around it, legs kicking.

And now Jimmy had her by the fragile collar of her blouse, now her shoulder, now her arm. She clutched for him as he wrapped both legs around the cable and grabbed her outstretched hand. They were spinning wildly on the cable . . . but he had her.

Above them, the things in the door recess renewed their shrieking chorus, and Jimmy threw back his own head and howled at them: a wordless yell of defiant fury. He slithered further down the cable and now Barbara was wrapped around him as they spun together on the cable. She was shaking in terror, her eyes screwed shut. Jimmy snapped off his yell, and crushed her head to his breast. "It's okay . . . okay . . . I've got you . . . I've got you . . ."

Cardiff had seen it all from above the double-doors. There was a large gap between them now. He was on the rail above the door aperture, they were well below it, on the cable. Rohmer was roaring into the shaft again, down at Jimmy and Barbara.

Above, the concrete platform cracked and shifted with a grinding judder that shook the walls of the elevator shaft. More clouds of dust plumed downwards.

"Go, Jimmy!" yelled Cardiff. "Go!"

And now Rohmer was turning his monstrous face up to look at where Cardiff was clinging.

Jimmy shifted position again, and was able to halt the uncontrolled swaying. "Barbara . . . ?" He was almost too breathless to speak. "Are . . . are you okay? Can you hear me?" Barbara nodded her head against his chest. "Listen, we have to move quickly. Cling tight to me. Not the cable. Can you hear me?" Barbara nodded again and Jimmy began trying to pry her other hand from the cable. She clung tight. "Trust me, Barbara. Trust me. Take hold of me . . ."

Barbara let go and clutched tight around Jimmy's torso.

Christ, he thought, as he took her weight. *Let me be able to do this.*

Jimmy began to slide precariously down the elevator cable.

"That's it!" shouted Cardiff. "Go . . ."

Rohmer was climbing out into the elevator shaft, gripping the guide rails and looking down at them. He reached for the elevator cable.

"No you bloody DON'T!" yelled Cardiff. He lowered the gun and fired.

Thunder detonated in the shaft again, and the bullet blasted a hole in Rohmer's shoulder, spinning him away from the cable. Rohmer roared up at Cardiff . . . and then steadied himself again, looking back down to where Jimmy and Barbara were descending.

"Come on, you bastard!" yelled Cardiff again. "Come up here after me, if you can!"

Rohmer reached for the cable again, intent on following them down.

Cardiff fired again.

Part of Rohmer's face blew away in a hissing spray. He screeched up at Cardiff again, his face beginning instantly to re-form once more.

Cardiff pulled the trigger again . . . and the gun emitted a brittle *click!* It was empty. Cursing, Cardiff threw the gun down at Rohmer and it smacked harmlessly against the spasming, twitching spider-legs in his torso. Rohmer was about to turn his attention downwards again, when a

332

fierce and mysteriously instinctive rage flooded Cardiff.

"Is it you?" shouted Cardiff. "That's what you wanted to know, wasn't it, Rohmer?"

Rohmer snapped his head up, the true part of his personality rebelling against the hideous and mounting escalation of spider-bloodlust which was becoming dominant.

"Is it YOU? Remember, Rohmer? Remember? Well . . . it IS me, you fucking bastard. Hear that? IT'S ME!"

Howling, Rohmer swung into the shaft, seized the metal guide rails with his mutated talons . . . and began to climb up after Cardiff.

Already, the horde in the recess were swarming back up the stairs to the floor above . . . and to where the double-doors were already wrenched open.

TWENTY-THREE

Rohmer watched the man above him climb, and the part of him that was not Spider screamed over and over in his mind: "It IS him! It IS him! It IS him!" as he climbed up after Cardiff.

Now Rohmer was aware that the others were scrabbling up the staircase again, towards the opened doors on the floor above. From there, they could take Cardiff. But he could not allow that to happen. Because now that he knew that Cardiff was the one, only Rohmer would take him: only Cardiff knew the answers to the Ultimate Mystery. When Cardiff was consumed, Rohmer would have those answers.

Rohmer howled and roared as he climbed, reaching out with his monstrous voice to the emotions of the Horde as he had first done with the Surviving Returners at the top of the staircase. They continued their ascent. He howled again, long and loud, echoing and reverberating in the shaft . . . and this time the Horde was milling in confusion on the staircase. They ranted and gibbered and wept . . . but they no longer climbed the staircase.

They would attend upon the Desires of their Master.

Rohmer laughed his hideous laugh . . . and continued to climb.

TWENTY-FOUR

Jimmy continued to slide down into the fractured blue-blackness of the shaft. Barbara's weight around him was a hideous strain, but they were moving down fast ... perhaps too fast. The details of what was happening above were lost in darkness as they descended. Now, Jimmy was aware that Barbara was weeping against him. "Mr Cardiff. Oh, Mr Cardiff."

They were falling too fast. He was sure of it.

"Oh God, Jimmy. It's too late. Too late ..."

Jimmy gripped tight, trying to slow them down, afraid that his gloves would rip, keeping his face back from the cable to avoid any skin contact.

"The Darkfall is going to destroy the building, Jimmy."

"We might ... might ... get away ..."

"I can feel it coming, Jimmy. *I can feel it.*"

Jimmy tangled his leg on the cable again to act as a brake, praying that his trousers wouldn't tear.

TWENTY-FIVE

Cardiff looked back down at Rohmer. Although he could not understand why the things on the staircase had stopped, he sensed that the Rohmer-thing had some kind of control over them.

Jimmy and Barbara had vanished into the darkness and Cardiff prayed that they would make it. He knew now that his own position was completely hopeless. He had climbed past the double-door aperture on the thirteenth floor. At the top of the shaft, he could never reach the trapdoor in the concrete platform. Even if he did, where could he hide from Rohmer? His only other recourse was the double-doors on the fourteenth floor . . . and the prospect of being torn apart on the staircase by Rohmer's horde.

And everything above ground will be dissipated, Barbara had said.

Maybe the finality of that, the finality of "dissipation", was the most hideous of all.

"Climb, you bastard! Climb!" Cardiff snapped at himself.

His only comfort lay in the possibility that the building might collapse before they could get to him.

Lungs aching, chest burning, Cardiff continued to climb.

TWENTY-SIX

Rohmer's mutated claws were hindering his attempts to climb.

Cardiff had almost reached the fourteenth floor, and the thing that had been Rohmer did not want him to fall before it got to him. The answers were to be found in the sweet Tasting of Cardiff's blood and meat.

Angrily, Rohmer growled at the steel claws that gripped the rails. Deep inside, the insect essence of Rohmer wanted to climb, knew that it should be able to climb just as it was able to see and hear and breathe through the ventricles in its sides and waist . . . but its inability was filling Rohmer with rage.

A chunk of concrete exploded on Rohmer's shoulder, knocking one claw away from the railing.

He roared in fury at his awkwardness, climbed again to the double-door recess on the thirteenth floor and clambered into it. Looking up, he could see that Cardiff was no more than twenty feet above.

Rohmer would take him from the door recess on the fourteenth floor.

TWENTY-SEVEN

"There!" shouted Jimmy. "There it is!"

Barbara finally looked as they slid down the elevator cable, to see the battered and dented roof of the elevator car. Chunks of concrete had impacted on the roof, twisting it out of proportion. Crumbled chunks of it lay on top and were jammed around the sides. The cab itself was tilted at an angle.

"We've made it, Barbara! We're *down!*"

Jimmy gripped tight on the cable, rashly heedless now of the prospect of torn gloves.

They jerked to a dangling halt, four feet from the battered metal roof.

Jimmy tried to disentangle Barbara from him. But she was still clinging tight.

"Come on, Barbara. Let go."

"I can't . . . I'm sorry, Jimmy . . . I just can't . . . let go."

"Yes, you can. Lemon-squeezy, remember?"

And now Jimmy was able to lower Barbara away from him, down towards the roof. She let go, dropping with a hollow clang on all fours. Jimmy swung down to her, his legs weak. He collapsed to his knees beside her, breathing heavily. Their arms were around each other now, and their kiss was savagely passionate and relieved. They parted, and now Jimmy was swatting the chunks of rubble away from the roof, searching for the service hatch.

"It's happening, Jimmy," said Barbara quietly and desperately. "Here it comes . . ."

TWENTY-EIGHT

Cardiff saw the Rohmer-thing clamber into the thirteenth-floor recess, and vanish from sight.

Instantly, he knew what was going to happen. He looked up at the recess on the fourteenth floor, then at the trapdoor in the concrete platform. That platform was now a crazy-paving of cracks. Concrete dust was falling continually in billowing, choking clouds.

Heavy, monstrous breathing on the staircase.

The gibbering, piping and squealing of the things below.

The thunderous avalanche of Darkfall thunder above.

The Darkfall will destroy the building, Barbara had said. *The building will collapse.*

Dissipation.

Below, the possibility that Jimmy and Barbara had made it somehow to the basement.

The elevator cable swayed in the centre of the shaft.

A yawning chasm of darkness below.

The blank face of the car driver who had killed his wife and child. The blank face that stood for the idiotic Face of Meaningless Death at the hands of meaningless men, monsters and idiots.

Cardiff did not even consider the feasibility of the idea when it sprang into his mind. It simply came. In a desperate, flooding rush . . . it came.

"Lisa!"

Cardiff let go the metal rails and flung himself at the elevator cable, catching it with both hands. It shuddered violently. Cardiff swung around it.

Gripping tight, he dropped like a stone.

339

TWENTY-NINE

Cardiff's mind reeled, the yawning black chasm spinning up to meet him as he fell. Somewhere above, he had a fleeting image of the Rohmer-thing thrusting its head into the elevator shaft and screaming in rage, and now the elevator cable was shredding his gloves as he dropped.

Below, he could see a tangle of mutated arms and claws grasping back through the aperture for him as he fell, saw a crazily tilted view of the thing that had been Gilbert; its monstrously elongated face and jaw snapping at him.

He lashed out as he spun down the cable, felt his heel connect with that face, heard the strangled scream . . .

. . . and dropped past them into the shaft.

Howling and shrieking.

His own terrified voice, or the sound of the things above?

He must be dead.

Dead and dropping into the Pit of Hell.

The fabric of his gloves was completely shorn away now. The cable was biting into his flesh and shredding his hands. But the contact of his flesh with the inert material of the cable was so brief at any one point that it could not "meld", could not hold and absorb him as he fell.

The shaft spun up to meet him.

He could not breathe.

Something was burning . . . was it his hands?

Were his hands on fire?

Screaming again.
The Pit.
Was
It
Bottomless . . . ?

THIRTY

Jimmy jammed the twisted iron bar he had found on the roof into the hatch and leaned on it with all of his weight. The hatch groaned, creaked and then burst open. Jimmy threw the iron bar into the cab . . . and then felt the elevator cable vibrating on the roof. Barbara grabbed his arm, crying out loud, and Jimmy jerked his head up expecting to see a ton of concrete on its way down into the shaft.

A figure was hurtling down the cable towards them.

A whirling, kicking, spinning figure that looked like . . .

THIRTY-ONE

Cardiff saw the blurred outline of figures down below, of the square compartment on which they were kneeling, and knew that he was dropping too fast; knew that the speed of his fall would kill them all when he hit.

The figures whirled from his vision again and gritting his teeth, Cardiff gripped as tight as he could, straddling his legs around the cable.

The cable tore through his hands, through the flesh, and to the bone. The material of his trousers singed and burned.

"Chhhriissssttt!"

Jimmy and Barbara cowered back against the roof of the elevator, expecting the impact . . . and Cardiff jerked to a halt six feet above them, his legs entwined in the cable, his hands jerked away from the cable itself. Barbara leaped to her feet and grabbed for him.

"Mr Cardiff, Mr Cardiff! Your hands . . . oh God, *your hands*!"

Jimmy was at her side now, reaching up and pulling Cardiff free from the cable. Were his legs broken?

"Don't . . . don't . . ." said Barbara, voice catching, ". . . don't let his hands touch anything."

They lowered him to the cab roof. His eyes were glazed, and he was mumbling as if in a fever. Jimmy checked his legs. The fabric of his trousers wasn't torn, and it didn't seem as if anything was broken. But his hands were raw pieces of bloodied meat.

"Christ, Cardiff. You're a *hell* of a bloke."

Above them, the sounds of howling had stopped. But the sounds of Darkfall thunder, and the juddering, cracking sounds of the disintegrating concrete platform filled the throat of the shaft.

"Barbara, you go first, down into the elevator. That platform's going to . . ."

He stopped.

The elevator cable was vibrating again.

Something else was coming down.

"Rohmer," said Jimmy through gritted teeth.

Barbara dropped quickly through the hatch and into the elevator cab. Jimmy grabbed Cardiff's legs and heaved them over the side of the hatch. "Sorry, mate. No time. Tuck those hands under your armpits."

Cardiff weakly did as he was told and Jimmy seized him by the collar of his jacket, swinging his dead weight down into the hatch as if he was a sack of potatoes.

Barbara grabbed his legs . . . and Jimmy let go. Cardiff sprawled to the cab floor, and Barbara quickly grabbed for him, making sure that his face and hands were clear of the floor.

The vibration of the cable was intensifying.

Jimmy grabbed the hatch cover, looked up once, and then dropped into the elevator cab, clashing the hatch cover behind him. He landed badly, and felt pain stabbing into the calf of his left leg. Wincing, he stepped over Barbara and Cardiff on the floor and flung himself at the double-doors. He tried to drag them apart, but they would not open. Anxiously scanning the darkened interior of the cab, Jimmy saw the twisted iron bar that he had thrown down earlier, seized it and lunged back to the elevator doors again. Jamming the iron into the crack between the double-doors like a crowbar, he tried to lever the doors open.

The doors opened two inches. Rain and wind gusted through the gap from the ground-floor reception area . . . and then the doors jammed solidly.

"Shit!"

"What is it, Jimmy?" Barbara was cradling Cardiff's head in her lap, keeping his hands away from the floor.

"The elevator's jammed between floors. Between the

344

ground floor and the basement. Must have been the concrete dropping on it from above."

Jimmy stepped back to look, the iron bar dangling from one hand.

"There's only three feet or so of the elevator below the ground level."

"Get down here with us Jimmy," hissed Barbara. "On the floor."

"What?"

"It's coming, Jimmy. The Darkfall power is reaching its peak, just like I said. We have to be *below* ground level! The building . . ."

"If it comes down while we're trapped in here, we've had it. We have to be right in the basement at least if we . . ."

And then something landed on the roof of the elevator with a jarring thud that made Jimmy stagger to keep his feet. The cab had dropped two or three inches only under the impact. More concrete or . . . ?

The elevator hatch was flung back with a loud crash.

A cloud of cement dust gushed into the cab, choking them.

Nothing else moved up there.

"Jimmy, Jimmy! Get down! *It's HERE!*"

Waving the dust from his face, Jimmy stepped forward with the iron bar held like a weapon.

Yes, it was a chunk of concrete, that was all.

"JIIMMMYY!"

Jimmy stepped gingerly forwards again, carefully craning his head to look up through the aperture.

And then a monstrous human-insect face thrust through the aperture, liquid cement dribbling from encrusted jaws. Jimmy recoiled, and Rohmer screamed in rage at them. The Rohmer-thing began to clamber face-first through the gap. Jimmy lashed at that monstrous face with the iron bar, felt it connect with the thing's mandibles. Rohmer screeched, and now one of its claws was through the hatch, slashing out for Jimmy, steel talons grasping and clutching.

345

Jimmy dodged, lashing out again, the iron bar hitting that claw, metal on metal, with a ringing clatter. Barbara cowered down, shielding Cardiff's face, as Jimmy lunged at Rohmer again jabbing the iron bar like a spear. It sank into Rohmer's Spider face, and he thrashed backwards withdrawing his arm and head, dragging the bar out of Jimmy's hands. On the roof of the elevator, Rohmer tore the bar away and flung it into the darkness of the shaft.

Jimmy stood defiantly below, hopeless but waiting.

Rohmer gathered himself in rage, stared down into the hatch, and howled in fury. He lunged down towards the hatch once more. This time he would take them all.

A half-ton of concrete fell into the shaft from the collapsing platform above.

One second later, the Darkfall erupted with all its ferocity on the office block.

THIRTY-TWO

The gathering energies of the Darkfall around and above Fernley House office block had reached their peak. Focused in inexplicable ways on what had been happening inside the building and the emotional energies which were expended there, the multiple energies coalesced into a blue surging fireball which flooded into the howling ice-storm whirlwind raging around Fernley House. Instantly, it completely engulfed the building.

The fireball exploded, unleashing all of its energy in a multiple lightning strike into the brickwork.

Blue Darkfall electricity exploded into the offices, into the corridors, into the very fabric of the building; vaporising anything that might be "alive".

And Fernley House blew apart as if it had been hit by a bomb.

All of the windows in the Polytechnic across the motorway imploded with a shattering roar.

The nearest buildings on the outskirts of the city centre shuddered, some suffering structural damage.

Rescue vehicles from central, regional and local police headquarters, which formed the cordon on the outskirts of the Darkfall were tipped over on their sides in the blast.

Seismic readings for the area were unparalleled.

And then the storm was gone. Instantly and completely, the whirlwinds and the sky-shattering lightning were no more.

Only a light snow fell, almost vertically, from an untroubled and windless sky.

This time, the snow was staying, giving the streets and the roofs and the motorways a white sheen.

THIRTY-THREE

Darkness.

Complete and utter darkness.

But there were no more sounds of thunder; no more sounds of a rumbling avalanche, or the screeching, gibbering sounds of things from nightmare. Only the quiet dribbling hiss of water somewhere, and a creeping, dank, winter chill.

"Are we dead?" asked Barbara, and felt Cardiff move in her arms.

"No," said Jimmy from somewhere else in the pitch darkness. "I don't think so."

"The way I'm hurting," said Cardiff, "I would say not."

"Where are you, Barbara?"

"Over here, Jimmy. Follow my voice."

She heard movement, and at last felt his touch on her arm.

"Are you alright?"

"Yes, I think so," replied Barbara. "I can't . . . can't really tell. There was a noise, and I can't remember what happened."

Jimmy reached out in the dark and felt cold metal.

"We're still in the elevator cab. The roof's been squashed down above us." He reached up and tapped on metal again, a mere three feet from his head. "One side of the cab's been stoved in over there. There's huge chunks of concrete and rubble pushing in, like there was an avalanche or something. God . . . I think . . . I think we've survived it. There's no more thunder, no more Darkfall." And then Jimmy's memory flooded back. "Rohmer!"

"He's dead," said Cardiff. "I think the concrete platform caved in on top of the elevator. It killed Rohmer and drove us right down into the basement. You were right, Barbara. We were slammed underground and it saved us. But it was a stroke of luck we were trapped in here and couldn't get out."

"Why?"

"The elevator is reinforced. It probably saved us from being crushed. If we'd been in the basement I don't think we would have survived."

"Will we survive, Mr Cardiff? Are we buried alive?"

"I don't know, Barbara. I just don't know . . ." Cardiff winced at the savage pain in his ruined hands. Barbara shifted her position in the darkness and began to tear strips from her skirt, fumbling for Cardiff's hands in the utter blackness and then binding them.

"The Darkfall *has* gone, hasn't it, Barbara?" asked Jimmy.

"Yes, it's gone. I can't feel . . . anything . . . anymore."

"Then there must be people out there waiting for the storm to blow out, like Gilbert said. If we sit it out, they're bound to come and rescue us."

Silence now, and Jimmy's words seemed to hang emptily in the darkness.

"Do you think it'll come back?" he said again at last.

"Yes," said Barbara. "It'll come back. Unless we change."

"What?"

"I don't really know. It's just a feeling I got when I was . . . was *touching* it. The Darkfall's more than Rohmer and Gilbert said. There's much, much more to it than that. I don't know if I can really explain it properly. But there's more to it than the scientific stuff they were talking about."

"Electricity," said Cardiff. "The Darkfall is the Dark Side of Electricity. That's what they said."

"Yes, I know," replied Barbara as she finished binding Cardiff's hands. "But there's still more to it than that. The Darkfall has something to do with *us* . . . with people.

What they are, and what they do. The worse they are, the more cruel they are, the more hateful they are . . . makes the perfect conditions for Darkfall to happen. Oh, I don't know. My head hurts and . . ."

"Listen!" hissed Jimmy.

Silence. Just the dribbling of water somewhere.

"I can't hear anything," said Cardiff.

"No, listen. I can hear . . ."

And now they could all hear it. A movement in the rubble somewhere above; a scraping on the metal wall of the elevator; a shifting now of the rubble where it had ruptured the elevator wall.

"They've found us," said Cardiff in a quiet and weary voice. "Thank God. They've found us."

"In here!" shouted Jimmy, crawling towards the source of the noise. "We're in here!"

The shifting and scuffling of rubble was louder now, more energetic, as their rescuers drew near. Jimmy laughed out loud when he heard the sounds of exerted breathing from somewhere behind the rubble. He began to tear at the concrete and the plaster himself.

"Barbara?" he called in joy over his shoulder as he worked.

"Yes?"

"Seems like I'm going to have to get a full-time, respectable job if I'm going to be able to afford all those records you want."

Barbara laughed. To Jimmy, it was one of the most beautiful sounds he had ever heard. He pulled away another chunk of rubble.

And Rohmer's monstrous, shrieking face burst through the gap, jaws champing.

"Oh my GOD!" Jimmy hurled himself backwards away from the Horror, scrabbling back to the others as the Rohmer-thing thrashed and scrabbled in the rubble to get at them. Its head was surrounded by the same hideous red aura that they had seen on the roof. Blood-soaked and horribly crushed, the thing was in a frenzy of hate and lust as it screeched and roared at them. The cab was lit vividly red by the hideous aura emanating from it. The same collapsing concrete which had driven them underground had also smashed Rohmer underground with them.

"When will it end?" screamed Barbara. "When will it END?!"

Rohmer's hideous eyes fixed on Cardiff as its claws lashed at the rubble and it slid further into the cab.

"ISSSSSS ITTTTTT YOUUUUUU?" hissed Rohmer, and Cardiff knew that, finally, it was the time for answers.

Ignoring the savagery of the pain in his hands, Cardiff scrabbled to legs that threatened to collapse under him, and grabbed a chunk of concrete from nearby. He lunged forward past Barbara and Jimmy as Rohmer groped inwards with his steel-claw hands.

Cardiff slammed the concrete chunk directly into Rohmer's face, and was instantly splattered with a nauseous ichor. Rohmer thrashed, screeching, and Cardiff felt a claw slice into his leg as he raised the concrete and struck again, this time with hate and sudden realisation.

Is it you?

He had been looking for Death. And he had instinctively perceived Rohmer to be the agent of his demise. Rohmer . . . his executioner.

Cardiff slammed the concrete down hard again.

Is it you?

And Rohmer had been looking for that Answer, too. Looking for a transcendence from the self-disgust he had felt, looking for that same Death . . . even though his madness had driven him to look for that Answer in the Absorption of Darkfall. Rohmer had also instinctively perceived that maybe Cardiff was His Own Executioner.

"Iss it you, Brottther . . . ?" hissed Rohmer.

Cardiff screamed in rage as he smashed the concrete down hard again. "I'm no kin of yours! I'm no Brother to You!"

Rohmer slumped to the floor of the cab, claws still

thrashing, head hideously pulped and incapable of reforming.

"I'm going to live, Rohmer! I'm going to LIVE!" Cardiff slammed the concrete down hard on the Rohmer-thing's head again, and tottered away from it, collapsing. "To live . . . to live . . ."

Barbara and Jimmy were dragging him away to the far corner of the cab as he looked back at Rohmer. His shattered body was spasming and twitching, the claws scraping feebly on the metal floor of the elevator.

"We were both mad," said Cardiff weakly, but purged. "Looking down the barrel of some sort of bloody gun. But I'm not going to die, Rohmer. I'm not . . ."

The Rohmer-thing raised its shattered head, and looked directly at him with its one remaining, hideous eye.

"Itttt . . . *wassss* . . . yoouuuu . . ." hissed Rohmer.

Sibilant breath rattled from the Rohmer-thing. The red aura surrounding it faded. It spasmed once more.

And died.

They wept.

THIRTY-FOUR

Darkness again.

And in the renewed, utter blackness of what they knew must now be their grave, the cold of winter had descended to find them. It crept through the rubble, ice-cold water trickling and pooling around where they lay. It soaked their clothes and numbed their flesh. The sound of that trickling water was preternaturally loud, like the dirge of water in forgotten caves.

They had huddled together in the darkness to share their warmth and at first they'd talked and shared as only those who've been through Hell can. And even when the cold and the exhaustion and the horror of their ordeal had taken away further words, no words were really necessary to vocalise their special Bond.

The bitter cold had also taken the pain away from Cardiff's hands, and he was glad of that. But he knew that when the cold which enshrouded their bodies began to dissipate, and the false warm-glow began ... then this was the onset of hypothermia. The lowering of their body temperatures would lead to a drowse, presaging a sleep which would lead to the sleep of death.

Was that the kind of death he had been destined for after all?

Death ... It's had so many chances. On the day when the faceless man took Lisa and Jamie away, but he didn't take me. And the thing that had been Barbara's brother. It had its chance to take me then. And Rohmer. But perhaps more importantly – the elevator shaft. I gave it the

354

best chance of all, but it refused to take me up, just as it refused to take up its option on all the others.

Ice-cold water.

The frozen chill of Death on his face.

The feel of Barbara's loving embrace.

Jimmy, at his side in the darkness, with one hand on his shoulder.

I'm to be denied the death I was looking for. A violent, bloody death where I could scream at the meaninglessness of it while I was going, just as I screamed my denial at Rohmer. I wanted to die because I'd lost them both. And because I'd lost them, everybody else's loss made it worse. But I don't want to die now because being dead doesn't help, doesn't make sense of their being taken away. I can help others with their loss, try to even up the scores for them . . . because I'm good at what I do. Crazy . . . it's taken this nightmare to show me . . . now . . . the death we'll share . . . will just be a slow drowse . . . into the last sleep . . .

Somewhere in the darkness, something moved.

Cardiff felt Barbara's body shudder in fright. She clung to him, shivering. He heard Jimmy seizing a piece of rock with numb fingers, felt him shifting to protect them both.

Rohmer?

No . . . he (or it) was dead. The sound was coming from the other side of the pulverised elevator . . . and now there was more movement. A sly shifting of rubble.

Cardiff pulled Barbara closer to him as Jimmy pushed himself towards the sound, trying to raise the rock.

Rescuers? Or another of Rohmer's nightmare horde, trapped in the rubble and hunting for food?

The sly shifting became a frenzied and frantic scrabbling. Something was tearing at the pulverised metal of the elevator cab above their heads. The squealing sounds of rending, tearing metal filled the small space in which they were huddled. Light spilled into the grave. Rain began to fall on their bodies. From above, the sounds of tortured and desperate breathing. Jimmy collapsed over their legs

355

exhausted, dropping the rock. Barbara sobbed, and stroked his head.

Cardiff held them both, staring defiantly up at the cab roof.

No tears, no prayers.

Rescue or Death.

Heaven, Hell or Darkfall.

At least we're together.

And then a voice from somewhere above said: "Hey . . . there *is* someone alive down here."

Snow began to drift down into their upturned faces, and Cardiff could feel Jimmy beginning to laugh.

"Know what day it is today, Cardiff?"

His laughter had a good, clean, beautifully honest sound.

Cardiff began to laugh too, feeling it rising and swelling inside him. Barbara was laughing with them both now as they looked up at the hole being torn in the elevator cab roof. That laughter was not far removed from tears, but reinforced that special Bond within.

"Yes, Jimmy. And it's a hell of a way to spend Christmas."

"Thence we came forth to see the stars again."

Dante

356

EPILOGUE

It began gradually, as it always did, bringing with it a myriad of symptoms to those living below. Headaches, nausea, neck pain, migraine, disorientation and a draining of energy. Parents became irritable, blaming Christmas and all its paraphernalia for their loss of temper with the kids, never dreaming that its onset always brought such symptoms, not realising that sixty per cent of the population suffer at least one or more of these symptoms as a prelude to a thunderstorm.

Dogs scratched at doors and were let outside to do their business, where they vomited – another symptom of an oncoming storm. Cats fussed, could not settle, and would not be stroked. Cattle that had not yet been led to shelter lay down and would not move until coaxed.

Between pylons, the overhead power cables carrying five hundred kilovolts reacted to its gathering. The electrical field around them began to swell, causing temporary power surges and blackouts throughout the region. Dozens of people living within close proximity to these pylons felt a prickling of anxiety, and discovered with only mild curiosity that the hairs on their arms were standing up, another not unusual phenomenon.

It gathered and moved over the city. Already, its thunderclouds were charged with electricity as it passed. When the insulating properties of the air broke down, the clouds would be discharged with a momentary electric current ... and the first lightning flash would occur. The chances of a lightning strike on a house or person are four per cent of one in twenty-five.

But this storm was different.

The rain was harsher now and growing more intense by the minute. The Storm had ceased to move. It had found its nucleus, and would stay while it continued to build strength. The roiling clouds darkened from grey to black, and the first grumblings of thunder resounded within them.

It had begun again.

In Kiev, Sydney, Rome and San Francisco . . . a Storm was coming.